THE
Wife Test

THE
Wife Test

BETINA KRAHN

BERKLEY BOOKS, NEW YORK

THE WIFE TEST

A Berkley Book / published by arrangement with
the author

For information address: The Berkley Publishing Group,
a division of Penguin Group (USA) Inc.,
375 Hudson Street, New York, New York 10014.

ISBN: 0-7394-3536-1

BERKLEY®
Berkley Books are published by The Berkley Publishing Group,
a division of Penguin Group (USA) Inc.,
375 Hudson Street, New York, New York 10014.
BERKLEY and the "B" design
are trademarks belonging to Penguin Group (USA) Inc.

PRINTED IN THE UNITED STATES OF AMERICA

Prologue

"I AM SORRY TO BE THE BEARER OF bad tidings, Your Grace, but it seems that the delegation bearing your ransom has arrived and the sum is . . . short."

"Short?"

"Not enough, Your Grace." The Earl of Norwich winced at the sight of a nobleman of such stature, even a French one, caught in such a circumstance. Of all of the duties that followed a major victory like the battle at Crecy, this was to him the most disagreeable: ransoming nobles back to their homes and families. It was in such trials that a nobleman learned his true worth to his family and the value of his alliances.

"How can it not be enough?" The Duke of Avalon looked as if he might choke on his tongue. "You accursed English!" He strode angrily away and then back, running his hands down his face. "Edward has bled me dry—paupered my lands and tenants—all but beggared my relations with his demands. There is nothing left to give him!"

"Surely there is something more, Your Grace."

There was the crux of the matter. King Edward, feeling

both the flush of victory and the press of finances, was determined to wrest a bit more gain from his newly conquered French subjects.

"There is nothing, I tell you," Avalon declared hotly. "Not another sou's worth of value to be scraped from my holdings."

"Truly? No more horses . . . oxen . . . flocks . . . furnishings . . . ironwork? No more of that marvelous wine your lands—"

"*No more*, I tell you. Edward has taken my coin and plate . . . my horses, cattle and sheep . . . plundered the squeezings of my grapes . . . stripped the tapestries from my walls and the furs from my beds! He's even emptied my falconry . . . taken my prize hawks!" Avalon threw himself onto a nearby bench, his burly frame braced against pain stirred afresh by this recitation of his losses.

Norwich studied the embattled duke and experienced a guilty tinge of relief that it was the French undergoing these humiliations and not his countrymen. Drawing a hard breath, he settled on the bench beside his prisoner.

"Then perhaps your forests—"

"I've hardly a bush left for a bird to nest in."

"How about craftsmen? Smiths, coopers, or goldsmiths . . . or shoemakers . . . Edward is exceedingly fond of a fine pair of boots." He looked over to see Avalon shaking his head and felt some of the duke's despondency creeping into his mood. "Or *cooks*. God knows Edward's kitchens could stand improvement. His table is widely considered an embarrassment."

"If I were to go home to my lands this moment," Avalon said bitterly, "I would do well to eat bread and curds prepared by my own hand. My people have been picked clean and my brother is seeing the bare bottoms of *his* coffers as well. My son will inherit naught but bare land!"

Norwich sighed again, crossed his arms, and propped his chin in his hand.

"A pity you don't have a few nubile young daughters. In time-honored tradition, you could have them *marry* you out of your ransom debt."

There was a moment's silence as Avalon absorbed that worldly sentiment. His eyes began to flit back and forth and his body slowly tensed.

"But I do have daughters." He strained to keep his face impassive and his rising hope in check. "A veritable covey of daughters. Lovely young things . . . accomplished, modest, bidable girls . . . who will make true *brides of virtue.*"

"You have daughters?" Norwich sat up straight and stared at Avalon in bewilderment. "Your lineage is well known. Why have we not heard of them?"

"They've been secreted away at a convent not far from Rouen. To be honest, they are . . . well . . . not born of my wife. But their legal status as my issue can be remedied with the stroke of a pen." His gaze focused intently on some unseen tableau. "The funds I donated when they entered the convent could serve as dowries . . ."

"Saint Juniper's Wounds!" Norwich bounded up, his countenance ruddy with relief. "Why didn't you say something before? King Edward is scrambling for a way to compensate his nobles. Brides! Good God—*a duke's daughters*—he'll be ecstatic!"

Avalon shoved to his feet, looking as if the weight of the world were sliding from his shoulders.

"If you would be so good as to send in my aide-de-camp, Norwich, I can send to the convent to make arrangements straightaway."

The English earl was at the door when he turned back for a moment.

"How many daughters did you say you have?"

"Ahh . . . four or five, I suppose . . ."

"You *suppose?*"

Avalon quickly recouped.

"Four—I have four eligible daughters." He drew up to his full height. "And you tell that bastard Edward he's got to give me back my birds if he wants to improve his mongrel English bloodlines with *my* daughters!"

Chapter One

"DEAREST HEAVEN. HE'S GONE MAD."
The abbess sat down with an undignified thud.

"Who, Reverend Mother?" Elderly Sister Archibald asked, squinting and bending to steal a peek at the parchment drooping in the abbess's hand.

"The Duke of Avalon. He says he has officially 'recognized' his daughters and commands that they be prepared to travel to London to be 'wedded by King Edward to his valiant nobles.' And I'm to provide them a dowry from the donation he made when each entered the convent."

"His daughters?" Venerable Sister Archibald frowned and settled on the edge of a chair across the polished table. "But 'e hasn't any daughters."

"He hasn't made any fatherly 'donations,' either." The Abbess stared in deepening outrage at the letter, which was signed in the duke's own unmistakable hand. "Another little detail that seems to have slipped his mind."

"Defeat and captivity 'ave been known to do odd things to a man," Archibald ventured.

The abbess responded with a snort. "Avalon has the constitution of a wild boar and the tenacity of a bear-baiting dog. It would take more than a few English battle blows to make him forget the number and sex of his offspring."

Battle blows. The abbess sat bolt upright and pored over the letter again, reading between the lines on the parchment and adding in the fact that the missive was delivered by a contingent of English knights and men-at-arms, who even now were waiting for a response in the nearby village. They had said the duke was being held for ransom after the defeat of the French forces at Crecy.

"It can only be"—she shoved to her feet, her gaze darting back and forth as she put the pieces together—"the old fox is having trouble raising his ransom and intends to pass off our charges as his daughters to help him pay." The idea, given form in words, weathered all of the tests of plausibility she could put to it. "How dare he even think of using our maidens in such a deception?"

But she knew how. The duke had long provided protection for the renowned Convent of the Brides of Virtue. Even through the perilous days just past when the fighting was at its fiercest, he had sent a contingent of soldiers to secure their gates. Those men, combined with the convent's stout walls, had kept them from being overrun in the fighting and then protected them from the bands of soldiers pillaging the countryside after the fighting ceased.

And it was well known that the worldly duke didn't believe in waiting for Heaven to reward his good deeds. He insisted on payment from more earthly and immediate sources.

"Not only does he demand we send him four dutiful and accomplished daughters . . . he expects us to furnish them with dowries. Four dowries! We'll be no better off than the Convent of the Claires . . . the *Poor* Claires!"

Roundly furious now, the abbess began to pace the polished stone floors of the richly paneled and draped audience chamber, clasping and unclasping her hands. Her black veil and robes billowed ominously with each abrupt turn.

"How dare he behave as if the maidens in our care line his purse like coins . . . to be spent at his discretion?"

"It's an outrage, it is." Sister Archibald's eyes narrowed. "Our girls may be poor an' orphaned, but they're noble-born, every one. They're meant for proper, noble husbands, not *Englishmen*."

The abbess turned and leveled a gaze on her best friend and confidant.

"English nobles are no different from any others, Archie . . . except perhaps a bit more preoccupied with stealing one another's property." She gave a hiss of disdain. "Avalon must be taking lessons from them."

No different from any other noblemen. She stopped short, suddenly seeing the duke's demand in a different light. He wanted to marry their charges off to noblemen . . . which, when she thought about it, was exactly what she and the rest of the good sisters had in mind for them.

The maidens placed in the care of the Order of the Brides of Virtue were nobility's lesser daughters . . . orphaned by illness or conflict, declared surplus in a house filled with girl children, or fallen victim to mismanaged and failing fortunes. What they lacked in family and property, they were groomed to more than make up for in character and capability. Wives obtained from the Convent of the Brides of Virtue were widely considered to be pious, pleasing, well mannered, diligent, and learned in household arts and management . . . considered worthy keepers of the keys in houses great and small.

What did it matter, the abbess asked herself, if those houses belonged to the conquering English?

What did matter—*and mattered a great deal*—was the fact that the convent and the order were expected to supply each with a dowry worthy of a duke's donation. Instead of adding to the convent's treasury—bridegrooms were required to make generous donations—these marriages would all but deplete it! There had to be a way to comply without beggaring the convent.

Sister Archibald watched all-too-familiar lights stealing into her friend's expression and folded her arms emphatically.

"Tell me yer not thinkin' of sendin' them to him."

"What choice do I have? Sooner or later he'll be freed, and he's not the sort to forgive a refusal to help him in his hour of need. All I can do is try to reduce the damage done to the convent's coffers." The abbess turned her attention to the door and consideration of what lay beyond it. "We have that wonderful wine the Earl of Whitmore sent as a part of his tithe. . . ."

"Ye'd turn our lambs out into th' world bearin' th' unearned shame of bastardy?"

"According to the letter, the maidens will be sent to the King of England himself, who will marry them to his nobles. That and the duke's considerable renown will go a long way toward countering any stigma they might face." The abbess's eyes began to dart back and forth over some mental balance sheet. "I suppose we could scrape together a few bolts of cloth. Baron Beaufort sent some fine woven goods not long ago. . . ."

"But the maids . . . how will ye know they're matched proper?"

"I'll send someone—one of the sisters—to see they are dealt with fairly." The abbess produced her keys and opened a large carved cabinet sitting to one side of the hearth. She glowered at the ironbound chest stored in the bottom of it. "I suppose there's no getting around it. We shall have to send *some* coin. . . ."

"It's decided, then?" Archibald sagged in disbelief. "As simple as that?" It was some time before the elder sister spoke again, and when she did, there was sadness in her voice.

"Who will ye send, Reverend Mother?"

CHLOE OF GUIBRAY BIT HER LIP AS SHE arched her aching neck, then quickly reapplied her ear to the edge of the tapestry-draped niche. Every word had etched itself into her mind. Taken all together, they made staggering news. Four maidens from the convent would be transformed into daughters of the Duke of Avalon and sent to the English king to be wedded to his nobles. The process by which this change of parentage would occur was a little fuzzy to her just now, but the abbess and Sister Archibald seemed to think it possible.

Imagine—her mind swam with possibilities—being claimed as a daughter by the great Duke of Avalon. She had heard of his splendid castle, his many knights, his fine lands and horses and vineyards. He was a rich and powerful lord. And he was claiming four young women from the convent as his daughters and sponsoring them in marriage.

Sister Archibald's final question stopped her breath.

Who would they send?

"Alaina, of course. And Helen. Probably Lisette de Mornay." The abbess paused. "I shall have to think about it. Perhaps Claire de Lyon or Margarete of Cologne."

"There is another, Reverend Mother, who would be perfect," Archibald said haltingly, suggesting either deliberateness or trepidation.

"Who?"

"Chloe."

The sound of her own name on the elder sister's lips made Chloe's heart begin to race. Just as suddenly the abbess's answer stopped it.

"Out of the question."

"She'd be right as rain for it," beloved old Archibald insisted.

"Don't be absurd, Archie."

"Well, she's got no father of 'er own," the elder nun continued.

"Precisely. We know nothing about her parentage. We cannot sponsor a girl as a noble bride without knowing she was born of noble blood."

"She *could* be of noble blood. She is clean of limb and delicate of face. She's quick of wit an' winnin' of way . . . as much as any of the maids ye just named. Why not let the duke claim 'er?"

"The duke counts on the brides we send being suitable in every aspect . . . *noble* daughters, of proper birth. God knows who fathered Chloe . . . on what sort of unfortunate creature . . . under what inauspicious stars. All there was on the bit of parchment tucked in the basket with her was the name 'Gilbert.' "

"Don't ye mean Guibray?"

Archibald sounded as puzzled as Chloe suddenly felt. There was a brief pause in which the abbess sighed heavily.

"I read that scrap of parchment myself. It was Gilbert. An *English* name. No doubt some English churl set upon some poor, innocent French lass and—" She paused a moment. "It became Guibray after some of the sisters misunderstood the name and thought it to be the French town. The old abbess and I didn't see any reason to correct them. She may as well be from Guibray."

"But ye've said she's not for takin' vows," Archibald persisted.

"She has a permanent place here as my clerk."

"But surely ye know, she hopes to marry someday and have babes—"

"And paupers have hopes of being kings!" There was a stark silence after the abbess's outburst, and her next words came taut and filled with strain. "I've spent years training her to read and write and cipher. Chloe is useful to me here, and it is *here* she will stay. Is that clear Sister Archibald?"

The elder sister's reply was slow in coming and laced with resignation.

"Yes, Reverend Mother."

Chloe peeled herself away from the niche and shimmied out of the narrow space between the wall and the great wooden cupboard where the convent's surplus linens and fabric were stored. Reeling, she wobbled down the passage and out onto the colonnaded cloister that lay at the heart of the great stone convent.

The sun was out, the sky was robin's egg blue, and the wisteria that wrapped the stone columns was showing pale green leaves. A damp, earthy scent of spring renewal mingled with the warmth of the chatter of girls hurrying along the colonnade and sitting in the courtyard working on their stitchery. The fair Alaina, the regal Helen, and the bewitching Lisette sat together in the sunshine, plying busy fingers over birch hoops as they exchanged confidences and shared dreams of futures that, unknown to them, were already in motion around them.

Chloe of Guibray stood in the shadow of the colonnade, watching, just as she would soon stand at the convent gates and watch until the cart bearing them toward the English court was out of sight. Chloe, the abbess had just declared, was not destined to take such a journey. She would have to wave and wish the lucky brides "godspeed," then return to her parchments and ink-stained fingers and to the drone of prayers and the bells marking the hours of the endless days. Chloe of Guibray was fated by the shameful circumstance of her birth to be caught in a vow-less nether region of femininity . . . considered neither pious enough for holy vows nor pedigreed enough for marriage vows.

The realization was devastating.

She had always known that the questions associated with her origins set her apart somewhat from the covey of maidens tended by the sisters. But if her murky parentage had sometimes occasioned whispers and dubious looks, her strong personal qualities had earned her special opportunities . . . an education in Latin and letters; access to the convent's precious books—even Holy Scriptures; and permission to be present whenever the abbess and her assistants met to entertain visitors or to make decisions. She had always believed that the extra training was meant to compensate for her lack of a pedigree and diligently applied herself to the learning.

Her knees now buckled and she stumbled against a cool stone column. All of that study and extra work . . . they hadn't been grooming her for a marriage, they had been sharpening her wits and skills to make her into something useful for the convent. A tool. Destined to give full and faithful service. A tool. Nothing more.

It didn't seem to matter to the abbess that a marriage

into a real family, even one of modest means, was the abiding dream of her heart.

Her early years at the convent, listening to girls speak of the homes and people they had been torn from, had bred in her a yearning for the deep and lasting connection of "family." She had no memories or stories of her own, so she privately created some for herself, piecing them together from details of the families and homes she had heard described. But as time went by her curiosity about her origins outgrew that girlish pacification of her longings. Unable to satisfy her need to uncover that most fundamental of secrets—her parentage—she became driven to discover other secrets instead . . . any and all other secrets.

In time, nothing in the convent escaped her . . . not the special ingredient the kitchen sisters put in their prized hot-cross buns at Easter, where the stableman slept when he went into the village, how many chickens the pot boy filched to take to his uncle, the various rivalries among the girls, the wine that old Sister Galletea sneaked to her chamber each night, nor the resentment the abbess felt toward Father Phillipe, who came each day to say their masses and hear their confessions. There wasn't a secret in or about the convent that she hadn't searched out and claimed as her own. And always she had justified her passion for secrets by keeping the tantalizing tidbits to herself and by Father Phillipe's assurance in the confessional that learning another's secret, even by subterfuge, was not an officially recognized sin.

But when you listen at corners and window ledges and door latches, she told herself as she made her way from column to column along the cloister walk, sooner or later you're going to hear something you wish you hadn't. Whether eavesdropping was an official sin or not, she was being punished for it. To hear herself assigned a dismal fate and to be unable to utter the slightest protest . . .

When she reached the small upstairs chamber she shared with one of the novices of the order, the misery she had been struggling to contain overwhelmed her. She collapsed on her straw-filled pallet and let the tears and sobs come until she seemed to run out of salt and her breath came in convulsive gasps. Hearing voices approaching her door, she sat up, wiped her face, and righted her garments to make herself presentable. But the voices passed by and she was left sinking again into despair, staring at the rush-strewn floor through bleary prisms.

There would be no husband, no children, and no home except the one she had always known. The longing for family sharpened to an ache in her chest that made it difficult to breathe. How could the abbess be so cruel? Just because she didn't bear the name of a noble—

Gilbert. The second shock of that purloined conversation struck her anew. She wasn't from the city of Guibray as she had always believed, at least not anymore than she was from any other place. It had been an English name, Gilbert, that had accompanied her in the basket that bore her into the sisters' care. Her heart beat faster as the full impact of it descended on her. This was the first real clue she had ever had to her true identity. Her spirits began to rise.

Had her father been an Englishman, as the abbess said? Or was it her mother who had borne that name? The truth of it could only be found in England . . . land of woolly sheep and greedy kings and victorious armies . . . and *Gilberts* . . . some of whom might belong to her.

England. Suddenly it sounded like the Promised Land. She had to go, to search for her beginnings and learn the secrets of her past. She would never have a future unless she did. What did it matter who was sent to London, as long as they were suitable for matrimony? The duke was claiming daughters that weren't his own; he could scarcely object to being claimed as her father until she could discover hers.

Sister Archibald was right; she was perfect for the duke's ransom. The abbess was just too stubborn—or selfish—to see it. Resolve straightened her spine and filled her heart with fresh hope. She had to take matters into her own hands, had to find a way to include herself in that bridal delegation.

Her gaze darted around the small chamber, and she slowly began to smile.

Becoming the duke's fifth daughter shouldn't be so hard for someone who, of late, had become the abbess's reading eyes and writing hand.

Chapter Two

THE CRUDE WOODEN DOOR OF THE loft over the tavern banged open, and the opening filled with a huge, black-clad form with burning eyes and white-knuckled fists. On the sour straw pallets that filled the chamber there was a flurry of curses and bare body parts as men-at-arms scrambled to untangle themselves from their partners in illicit pleasure.

"Worthless sons of curs—on your feet!" Sir Hugh of Sennet ducked through the doorway and charged inside, grabbing first one groggy soldier and then another, yanking them to their feet and shoving them toward the door, where his lieutenant waited. "I ordered you to stay *on* duty, *at* the ready, and *out* of the cursed taverns!" He ripped a tunic from beneath a fleshy pair of buttocks— eliciting a feminine squeal of protest—thrust it into its owner's fumbling hands, then planted a boot in the wretch's backside. The fellow shot out the door, glanced off the knight waiting outside, and went careening down the steps to join his comrades.

When the chamber was cleared of men, Hugh of Sennet ducked back outside, stomped down the steps, and stood with his fists jammed onto his waist, glaring at the soldiers struggling to don their garments. His sniff of indignation quickly turned to a wince.

"They smell like piss pots. Get them cleaned up," he ordered their sergeant, "and ready to travel at a moment's notice." Then he addressed the men themselves. "If I have to pull any of you out of a tavern again before we reach London, I'll personally deal each of you a hundred lashes! Is that clear?"

The prodigals turned a bit pale beneath their sun-weathered skin, nodded, and stumbled off toward the nearby stream under a tirade from their sergeant.

"A hundred?" Sir Graham of Ledding, Hugh's second in command, lifted an eyebrow. The number had grown all morning. This was the fourth tavern he had cleaned out, and from the tightness of Hugh's broad shoulders and big fists, it appeared he was on the verge of mayhem.

"Should have been *two* hundred. This is the last tavern?"

"I believe so." Graham looked around the small but bustling village. "Amazing that there should be so many taverns in so small a berg."

"Every hut and hovel becomes a tavern when there are soldiers nearby," Hugh said with disgust, striking off for their camp at the edge of the village.

"This waiting is hard on the men." Graham fell in beside him and watched him peel his fists open and stretch his cramped fingers.

"Three bloody long days," Hugh said, lengthening his stride and setting his heels down harder as irritation overtook him again. "What the devil is taking them so long?"

Graham shrugged. "They're women."

"They're not women, they're *nuns*. And what's so hard about packing up a few maids and shipping them off?"

"They're not just maids, they're *brides*. And brides travel with *stuff*."

Hugh stopped in the rutted path and glowered down at him.

"And you would know this because . . . ?"

"I was wedded once."

"What?" Hugh frowned and searched Graham's broad, pleasant face.

"It's true. I was wedded early on . . . at seventeen . . . to an heiress who was all of thirteen. She came with enough stuff to fill Windsor Castle."

"But you're not married now. What happened to her?"

"She died in a fever that swept through the shire." The knight's face took on an odd, wistful cast. "She was a sweet thing. Cheerful. Bidable. Pleasant."

"So it was you who got the *one*," Hugh said, continuing on.

Graham sighed and followed.

"Women aren't so bad."

"Yes, they are. They're a plague upon mankind. Fickle, flighty, irrational, undisciplined, faithless . . . carnality embodied . . . smoldering heaps of ensnaring desire . . ."

"Sweet Jehoshaphat, have you been translating Saint Augustine again?" It was Graham's turn to look disgusted. "I wish the king would keep you out of that monastery library."

"And I wish he'd let me *stay* there. Instead he sends me charging off at the head of a column of randy, home-starved soldiers to haul back a clutch of nubile, marriageable young temptresses—"

"Who have been raised in a nunnery," Graham inserted.

"Where all of their true urges and inclinations have been suppressed."

Graham brightened visibly. "You think so? You think they'll be ripe and eager for the plucking?" He grinned. "God, I hope so! If any of them have red hair, I want to be first in line!"

"Not you, too." Hugh gave his friend a shove, but had to work to avoid a smile. "I'll have enough trouble with the rest of these drooling idiots."

"Not drooling. Just anxious to be home." Graham canted a look at him as they reached the tents. "Aren't you the least bit curious about these maidens?"

Hugh paused in the midst of settling on a folding bench

in front of his tent and looked up with a faintly wicked smile.

"Have you ever *seen* the Duke of Avalon?"

"No."

"Well, I have. And if these females are any of *his* seed, they'll be nothing to look at, believe me."

Graham seemed a bit deflated. "Still . . . even plain as burlap, a woman who is willing can be worth a lot to a man who is wanting."

If that was meant to be reassuring, it missed the mark by a mile.

"In any case," the goodly Graham continued with a shrug, "it's a measure of the king's trust in you that he would send you on such a mission."

Hugh thought about that for a moment, remembering the twinkle in Edward's eye and the snickering in the great hall when he was charged with the responsibility of retrieving the Duke of Avalon's daughters from a French convent. Edward trusted him? Edward was *taunting* him. His jaw flexed in annoyance. Sending him on such an errand and assigning him a force of intemperate, ignoble wretches who had been away from home for so long they'd forgotten every bit of Christian behavior they'd ever . . . and after all of the loyalty and service he had rendered . . .

A thatch-headed fellow running toward them caught Hugh's eye, and he straightened, drawing Graham to attention as well. The fellow called out his name and when Hugh beckoned with a wave, he lumbered up and stood heaving for breath before gasping out a message.

"She wants ye." More wheezing and panting. "Th' abbess."

CHLOE STOOD IN THE COLONNADE ACROSS from the inner gate with her heart beating in her throat, watching the abbess welcome the English king's men to the convent. They were huge and plated with armor and, as they passed, they smelled of horse and leather mingled with a peculiar vinegary tang that piqued both her interest and anxiety. Drawn by the unknown and compelled by her desire to find a way to join the maids leaving for England, she followed the abbess and the Englishmen and slipped inside the paneled audience chamber behind them.

The abbess seated herself in her ornate chair and motioned the knights to take the chairs across the large center table from her. They removed their helms, tucked them under their arms, and sat down heavily. Their expressions, as Chloe moved around the wall to better observe them, were utterly grim.

"I have sent for you so that we may agree on the time of your departure and so that you will know our requirements for the maids' conveyance," the abbess declared. "You will be escorting our maidens to London and marriage, for which they must take dower goods. We require three wagons for the baggage—large hay wagons will suffice—and drivers who can be—"

"Three wagons?" The tall, dark knight's voice rumbled forth like the Almighty's must have from Sinai. "For *baggage*?"

"Along with drivers who can be trusted," the abbess finished her thought and adamantly continued. "And of course, we shall need someone to help load them. Then there is the matter of transporting the maids themselves. We shall require two smallish or one good-sized cart."

"Out of the question," the tall knight declared, meeting the abbess's gaze full on . . . a potentially disastrous bit of bravado. "Tell me how many females will be traveling with us, and I will secure them mounts."

"Our maids are unfamiliar with horses," the abbess declared tautly. "As I said, Sir Hugh, carts are required."

"And we must supply *drivers*," the shorter, fairer knight echoed, catching Sir Hugh's gaze and leading it directly to Chloe, who stood several paces away, watching with widened eyes.

She felt the commanding knight's attention fall on her like a touch, then travel boldly over her, lingering on her hair, her face, and her breasts. She watched his mouth draw into a grim line and blushed furiously.

He bridled at her modest reaction and turned a dark look on the abbess.

"Perhaps I should see the rest of these maids I am to escort."

"Their looks are not important." The abbess folded her hands on the table and narrowed her eyes.

"Not to you, perhaps," Sir Hugh declared irritably. "But if my men are to be in close contact with them for the duration of the journey, I may have to take precautions to ensure their safety." This time something in his intense gaze communicated his full intent to the abbess, who frowned.

"Chloe"—the abbess motioned her forward—"go and find Alaina, Helen, Lisette, or Margarete."

Chloe's mind was racing, so as she hurried along the colonnade and through the courtyard she nearly bowled over Alaina and Lisette as she rounded the corner toward the maids' dormitory. They flushed and sputtered excuses as they righted themselves, and Chloe realized they had been lurking at a corner, peering toward the doors of the main hall.

"The abbess sent me for you. Come with me." Chloe seized them by the hands and dragged them toward the hall.

"Have you seen them up close?" Alaina asked anxiously.

"What are they like?" Lisette demanded, halting and pulling on Chloe to make her stop as well. She turned to face them and, seeing their anxiety, responded with all of the poise she could muster.

"They're just our escorts," she declared, "but they're large and powerful and, unless I miss my guess, not especially happy to have such duty."

It was only when they reached the audience chamber and she opened the door that she realized she had said "our escorts" . . . included herself in the group . . . and that the others had by all appearances accepted it. She smiled weakly. There were advantages in being known throughout the convent as the abbess's able and trustworthy clerk.

When she ushered them into the audience chamber, the men turned to watch them approach, and the silence that fell was almost deafening. The abbess beckoned them forward, and Chloe pulled the others to the side of the table, where they squeezed her hands and nudged closer to her, making it all but impossible for her to withdraw. The abiguity of her presence between them made her heart beat faster, but no one questioned her being there.

Sir Hugh rose with his scowl deepening and a muscle in his very square jaw flexing. He glared pointedly at his comrade, whose huge eyes and gaping mouth communicated something akin to delight, then turned to examine the trio with mounting horror.

"These are the maids I am supposed to escort *all the way to London?*" He seemed to choke on those last words. "The Duke of Avalon's daughters?"

"Of course," the abbess said, rising, her face paling so that it blended seamlessly with her wimple. "Why? Is something amiss?"

"I cannot take them like this." The tall knight continued to stare in horror at them, then forcibly shook off the effects of his shock. "They will have to be . . . disguised . . . their faces hidden, their shapes disguised."

"Disguised? Whatever for? You have men to protect them, do you not?"

"It is my men that—see here, the men I lead are not my own. They crossed the channel with Edward, fought heroically, and have held these lands for months without relief." Seeing that his words missed their mark, he dropped his gauntlet-clad fists onto the table with a thud and leaned over them with eyes glittering. "They are far from home, starved for comfort, and not to be trifled with. Do I make myself clear enough, Reverend Mother?"

Apparently so. The abbess looked downright skewered by his words. She turned to look at the girls on either side of Chloe, evaluating them in a new light. After a moment she turned back to the knight, scowled, and nodded.

"For their own safety, then," she said irritably. "But

just how do you suggest I disguise both their faces and forms? Put bags over their heads and wrap them in horse blankets?"

Three pairs of eyes now turned on Chloe and the others; one registering motherly dismay, one monastic horror, and the third, bold male appreciation.

"H-how about habits, Reverend Mother?" Chloe spoke up impulsively. "Wimples and veils on bowed heads obscure faces." When no silencing scowl descended, she hurried on. "And they have plenty of room for stuffing. In truth, no one looks twice at a group of plump, prayerful sisters on pilgrimage."

Habits. Her heart seemed to beat in her throat as she waited for their response to her flash of duplicitous inspiration. Habits, she had just realized, could be made to hide identities from more than just homesick soldiers.

The abbess looked to the formidable Sir Hugh, who pulled back across the table, glowering, but gave a nod of approval. She turned to Chloe with a grim smile of approbation.

"Habits, it is. I shall leave it up to you and Sister Archibald to find some old habits and fashion whatever will be needed."

TWO MORNINGS LATER, AS A PALE SILVER sun began to pierce the mist of the damp spring dawn, the main courtyard of the convent filled on one side with armed soldiers on horseback and on the other with nuns and maidens clustered in skittish little knots that tightened whenever an oath or a burst of laughter issued from the soldiers. Between the two factions stood three overloaded hay wagons and a large mule cart meant to carry the maids themselves. On the seat of each conveyance sat a driver handpicked by Sir Hugh himself . . . mostly grizzled veterans who waited with undisguised resentment at having to abandon a perfectly good saddle for such duty.

Inside the inner gate the abbess was giving the maids last-minute admonitions and Mother Archibald last-minute advice, all while demanding to know where Chloe was with the packet of legitimation and marriage documents. Then one of the young girls rushed to her side with a leather folio bearing the seal of the convent, and the abbess relaxed a bit.

"Godspeed." She kissed each of the maids on both cheeks and sent them out to the cart. Then she embraced Mother Archibald. There were tears in her eyes when she released her closest friend.

"Please, dear Archie, reconsider. It won't be an easy journey, and I couldn't bear it if something should happen to you. Let me send Sister Rosemary or Mary Montpellier—"

"No, Reverend Mother." Archibald seized the abbess's hands and squeezed them. "I must go. They'll need a seasoned head to see to their good and make sure they're dealt with proper. Even if I stayed, I would not sleep a wink until I knew our sweet lambs were safe an' well-wedded."

The abbess straightened her spine and inserted her hands into her voluminous sleeves. Her expression was so grave as to be almost suffering.

"Then go with God, Archie. May He work His good and generous will through you." The abbess turned quickly and stepped out into the court to speak with the knights into whose hands she was placing four of her precious maidens and her beloved friend.

Sister Archibald sighed as she watched the abbess take up the heavy mantle of office again, and wiped away a tear. In truth she dreaded the journey and what lay at the end of it. Halfway through a deep breath, she was startled by a tug at her elbow. It was one of the youngest girls at the convent.

"Ye mus' come, Sister. It's Chloe—she needs ye bad."

"Where is she?" Without an instant's hesitation Archibald lurched into motion and followed the child toward the novices' chambers.

But the girl was running on ahead, leaving the venerable Archibald no choice but to trail along behind. The child took her through several turns to the stairs that led down to the cellars. Archibald slowed and paused to glance back over her shoulder, wavering. They expected her, were waiting for her. But then she thought of Chloe— dear, bright, and loving Chloe—and feared that the departure of the others was causing her great distress. Still burdened by her conviction that Chloe should have been included in the duke's adoptions, she had to answer the girl's cry for help.

A lighted lamp sat on the landing of the steps, and the child picked it up and waited for Archibald to catch up before taking her deeper into the cellars. When they reached the cold cellar, the girl handed her the lamp and raced back up the corridor. Scowling, Sister Archibald pushed open the door.

It took a moment for her to spot Chloe, who stood on the far side of the cellar beside a chair that looked suspiciously like one from the abbess's own solar. Beside her, planks laid across upturned casks formed a makeshift table that was spread with linen, bread, cheese, fruit, and a flagon of wine. It took yet another moment for Archibald to realize why she had difficulty spotting Chloe. The girl was wearing a wimple and a veil. *A habit.*

"Bless you for coming, Sister Archie!" Chloe seemed vastly relieved as she hurried toward her friend and mentor with outstretched arms.

"What's this about, child?" Archibald peeled Chloe from her shoulders and thrust her back to look into her anxious eyes. "What's wrong? I'm due to leave any moment—"

"I know, Sister Archie." She seized the nun's hands and pulled her toward the chair. "I must beg your forgiveness for what I am about to do. I know the abbess thinks me unworthy to be a bride, but I know in my bones that she is wrong."

"Oh?" Archibald's eyes flew wide. "Oh, *no*, child."

"I have to go to London with the others."

"No, no, *no*, child!"

"I promise I'll do my best—I'll make the convent

proud. I've explained it all in this letter." She stuffed a folded parchment into Archibald's hands and pushed her gently but firmly back toward the chair. "I'm taking your place."

"But ye cannot!" Archie tried to resist. "I have to go myself—to see our girls matched and mated proper—"

"I know, I know—I'll take care of them for you, I promise." Chloe was near tears as she gently pushed the elderly nun onto the chair. "I give you my sacred vow that I will see each of them well-wedded before I finish my quest."

"Quest?" Archibald was now both alarmed and confused. "What nonsense is this, child?" She tried to rise. "Ye must let me go."

But Chloe refused to move or to allow Archibald to leave the chair.

"I heard the abbess tell you I am came from the English *Gilberts*, not the town of Guibray." Tears sprang to her eyes. "Don't you see? I have to go to London and discover my real parents. Unless I do, I can never have a family of my own. And as much as I feel a duty to the convent, I cannot help believing I have a duty to learn the truth about my birth. Please. Sister Archie"—her voice cracked—"please understand and don't hate me."

Her tear-filled eyes met Archibald's, and in that moment the depths and longing of her heart lay open and exposed, vulnerable. It was a plea for help as much as for forgiveness.

Compassion rose in the elder nun's heart. The tension in her rotund form melted, and she reached up to cradle Chloe's damp cheek in her hand.

"I could never hate you, child." Her age-faded eyes filled with tears. "Go. And may all Heaven be with ye."

Chloe gave a small sob and pressed her forehead against Archibald's. A moment later she backed away and swiped at her tears with her palms.

"I promise you, I'll take good care of your girls. They'll have the best husbands England can offer." She backed toward the heavy ironbound door. "I've brought you some things to eat and there are blankets and some extra oil for the lamp. The kitchen sisters come often to get things from the cellars, and if you call out after a while, someone will find you." She paused, said, "Goodbye, Sister Archie," then darted out and slammed the heavy door.

Archibald heard the bolt being thrown, crossed herself, and bowed her head. When her fervent prayers were finished, she issued a great sigh, reassured to leave it in the Almighty's hands. Then she leaned forward to inspect the repast Chloe had provided.

There were the special sweet grapes they got from the Champagne region. That pungent cheese with the blue veins and yellow rind . . . her very favorite. She felt the crusty loaf of bread and realized it was still slightly warm. Creamy butter, too. Then her gaze caught on a footstool to the side, beneath the stack of blankets and furs, and she smiled ruefully. That Chloe. She had thought of everything.

The remaining conflict in her heart began to still.

Their lambs were in good hands.

She broke off a piece of bread and lay a slab of the cheese on it, sniffing the pungent aroma. Then she poured a cup of wine and sat down to savor the tastes. After a few moments she dragged the footstool over, propped her feet on it, and pulled two blankets from the pile to tuck around her.

The Reverend Mother was going to be furious. If experience was any guide, she would storm and rail and order penitent rations for the entire convent as a lesson in the wages of disobedience. Archibald reached for a bunch of the plump, sugary grapes and popped them in her mouth one at a time. No doubt the abbess would send someone after the bridal party to haul Chloe back to some grave and horrible punishment. Unless . . . unless the bridal delegation was already too far away. . . .

She was warming up nicely in the blankets. She wiggled her feet and took another sip from the rich wine in her cup. She really ought to call out . . . get rescued . . . warn the abbess what was afoot. . . .

"Help," she said softly. Then she sipped again and leaned her head back with a mischievous bit of a smile. "Help me. I'm locked in the cellar with the convent's best wine and cheese. . . ."

Chapter Three

HUGH OF SENNET HELD HIS BREATH as the last habit-clad figure emerged from the inner gate and hurried toward where he stood waiting at the back of the cart. At last. He hoped the fact that the old nun was late didn't mean she would cause delays on the journey. He had enough to worry about.

Extending gauntlet-clad hands, he averted his eyes and gave the old sister what should have been a boost up into the cart. But she proved lighter than he expected, and there was a muffled cry and then a thud. When he looked, she was sprawled on the floor of the cart with her habit bunched up around her knees, baring much of her legs. He grabbed a handful of habit and yanked it down over the exposed flesh, mumbled something of an apology, and abandoned her to the assistance of the maids in the cart.

He wheeled and looked up to find Graham's eyes the size of goose eggs. Clearly *he* had seen it, and there were half a dozen other men staring fixedly at the cart and its occupants, trying to decide if they'd seen what they thought they had. With an audible groan, Hugh headed for his mount and climbed aboard, giving the order to move out before his rear even touched the saddle.

The creak of wooden wheels, the clank of armor, and the thud of hooves mingled with calls of "Godspeed" from the sisters and maidens huddled on the far side of the yard. It should have been a relief to be under way, but deep in his gut Hugh had a feeling that something was not right. And as the first miles rolled by, his intuition proved correct.

The trouble, he realized with no small horror, began with himself. All he could think about was those bare legs. Long . . . smooth . . . shapely . . . he scowled as he examined the image branded into his mind's eye. He couldn't believe that those were the knees of a old nun who had spent a lifetime on them in prayer and penitence. But, as anyone at Edward's court would gleefully confirm, he was scarcely an expert on women's legs. Or any other female part, for that matter. How would he know what an old woman's knees should look like?

Not that he had *looked*, really. He had merely glimpsed. *Seen*. And "seeing" was not the same as "looking." As the old brothers from the monastery had often said: one couldn't help seeing, but, with God's help, one could keep himself from looking. *Looking* involved intent. And it was often the beginning of a chain of actions that, left unchecked, would carry a man straight to Perdition.

A burst of girlish laughter interrupted his high-minded thoughts. He looked back and spotted Graham wending his way back to the maidens' cart. Reining sharply around, he went charging toward the cart himself. As he reached Graham's side, he followed his friend's gaze to a bevy of wimple-wrapped faces turned their way. Clear young faces . . . cream-smooth and sun-blushed . . . set with big, vivid eyes and rosy lips upturned in smiles . . .

God in Heaven.

"Graham!" he barked out, startling his friend. "Take the lead!"

As his second in command pivoted his horse and rode to the front of the column, Hugh realized that the men assigned to ride behind the cart were staring at the maids and listening intently. It was eager, girlish talk from lilting young voices. His stomach began to knot. He had been so concerned about disguising their appearance that it hadn't occurred to him that their *voices* could give them away!

"Silence!" he ordered, turning his mount to ride alongside the cart. "You must be quiet." Their smiles and chatter evaporated. He looked through the group for the elderly sister, trying to recall her name. He didn't see her and scowled. Wasn't she the one he had "tossed" into the cart? "From now on, you will speak only to each other and only in whispers."

"Why?" one of the maids, who looked oddly familiar, demanded.

"Because it is necessary"—then he added, more for his own conscience than for them—"for your safety. Where is the sister who accompanies you?" He craned his neck to see past them. "I would speak with her."

"She was taken ill at the last moment and could not come," the familiar one declared, rolling up onto her knees on the bench built into the side of the cart and gripping the top edge. "She asked me to see to the others. Whatever you would have said to her, you may say to me."

It took a moment to register.

"Do you mean to say"—he forced himself to remain calm and lowered his voice—"that there is no nun amongst you?"

"There is not," the appointed one declared. "Are we in some kind of danger? I was given to understand that the countryside was quiet." He felt his gaze drawn to hers and frantically forced it to the top of her head instead. Was she the one he had tossed arse-over-elbows into the cart?

"Blessit, yes, you're in danger. And you will be until you're wedded in London. From now on . . . you're not to gawk at the countryside or my men . . . you're to talk only to each other . . . and never above a whisper."

"A whisper?" She indicated what she thought of his edict by flagrantly violating it. "We are not criminals or madwomen," she said succinctly, "to be forbidden that most normal and natural of human intercourse."

He felt color draining from his face.

Natural . . . intercourse.

"You have your orders, Sist—" But she wasn't a sister. "Just who the devil are you, anyway?"

"Chloe of Guibray."

"Very well then, *Sister Chloe.* Keep your group together, their heads down, and their voices low." He glanced down at her face, and his gaze dropped inexplicably lower. Was it her legs that had been burned into his— A muscle near his eye twitched, and he jerked his head irritably. "I wouldn't want to have to haul the lot of you to London trussed up like gooses for roasting."

He jerked his reins sharply and shot off toward the head of the column, leaving Chloe staring after him in disbelief. Her cheeks caught fire and her eyes burned as if he'd thrown sand in them . . . which, after a fashion, he had.

"Chloe?" The others crowded around, and she turned to find herself facing four alarm-filled faces. "What's happened?" Helen spoke for them all. "Did we do something wrong?"

Chloe had no more idea than they did about what they might have done to deserve such a ban on their behavior. But she did have the vivid memory of the high-handed knight taking one look at her and demanding that the abbess put bags over all their heads. Her face flamed. It seemed he hated the sound of women's voices as much as he hated the sight of women's faces.

Wretched man.

"We've behaved with nothing but maidenly virtue," she declared, to bolster her own confidence as much as theirs. "We will continue to do so, and Sir Hugh can save his blessed 'goose-trussing' for someone else."

"Being ordered to speak only in whispers is a grave punishment," rosy-faced Margarete said, clearly unsettled. "We must have offended someone with our thoughtless chatter."

"My chatter is not thoughtless," Alaina said imperially.

"Nor is mine." Helen copied the stubborn tilt of her friend's chin.

"*They* don't seem to mind us talking." Sultry Lisette de Mornay had turned to smile boldly at the soldiers riding behind them.

Chloe followed Lisette's gaze and saw the nods and smiles that answered her overture. They certainly didn't mind. But something made Chloe remember that Sister Archibald seemed to think that Sir Hugh took his duty to safeguard them quite seriously. Perhaps he had a reason beyond his own personal distaste.

"I will speak with Sir Hugh when we stop for a rest and find out why he believes we're in such danger."

Talk in the cart gradually returned to normal, except for volume, and centered on the rest of the journey and what lay ahead for them in London.

"They say it is nothing like Paris," Alaina said grimly. "It rains all of the time. I imagine the streets are always foul with mud."

"Surely not," Margarete said, frowning. "It's the king's own city . . . surely there will be some fine roads and grand houses. There is a bishop in London, is there not? That means a great church, perhaps even a cathedral."

"They ship wool to other cities on the Continent," Helen contributed a voice of reason. "So there must be a good bit of trading and some fine markets."

Lisette, who sat nearest the driver, turned impulsively and tapped the fellow on the shoulder. When he grunted and glanced her way, she smiled sweetly. "Have you been to London, Mattias?"

How she knew his name, Chloe could only guess. Lisette had a way of learning such things. Chloe made a mental note to observe more closely Lisette's methods of gathering information.

"I 'ave," the burly driver said, sitting a bit straighter.

"*Ooooh!* Would you tell us what it's like?"

"Wel-ll . . ."

"Oh, *please*," Lisette entreated in her most musical and compelling tones.

A moment later she was rewarded by a nod, and she eagerly beckoned everyone else forward in the cart to hear.

"There's lots of folk there," Mattias said, rubbing his bristled chin. "Some god-fearin', an' some wicked an' shameless rascals. There's houses stacked up like sheaves in a hayrick . . . set so close they lean out over the streets. An' food—why there's everythin' to eat ye can think of. Stout ale on ever corner. Soft bread an' pasties . . . meat pies, sweet cakes, an' honey wafers . . . capons big as heifers . . . sows the size of oxen . . ."

"And markets and shops? Are there good shoemakers?" Margarete asked.

"And silk merchants and goldsmiths and furriers?" Alaina demanded.

Mattias nodded. "Plenty of them . . . an' more."

"Have you seen the king's castle?" Chloe asked.

"Windsor? That ain't in London. But I been there. We camped just outside the bailey an' walls, once."

"What's it like?" Chloe held her breath, hungry for images to feed her imagination.

"There's a great round keep in th' middle . . . sits up on a hill . . . wi' good arrow slits and plenty o' high walls around. Ye can see the country for miles around. . . ."

HUGH LOOKED BACK TO FIND THAT THE cart and the wagons had fallen well behind the front of the escort party. As he rode back to see what was the matter, he found the maidens clustered at the front of the cart, beaming with interest as old Mattias rattled on about something. The driver had all but abandoned the reins, and the two mules were virtually ambling along at will. And if that weren't bad enough, the men who were supposed to be maintaining a rear guard for the column had ridden up nearer the cart and were watching with great interest as the young "nuns" conversed with old Mattias.

"Dammit." He flinched at his profane lapse. He'd have more than usual to confess when he got back to the priest at Windsor. "Mattias!" He drew his horse up with a jerk. "What the devil do you think you are doing?"

"Sarr!" The driver snapped to attention and tightened his grip on the reins, giving the mules a crack on the rumps to get them moving. "Drivin', sarr."

"The devil you are." Hugh reddened, chagrined to realize that the old soldier wasn't too old to appreciate that bevy of fetching smiles and sparkling eyes. He groaned silently. There probably wasn't a man in all of Christendom old enough for that. "Stop the cart and get down."

"But, sarr—"

"Down!" He shifted in his saddle and called to the driver of the first baggage wagon: "You there—Withers! Come and replace him." Then he turned to Chloe and the others. "And you"—he lowered his voice—"I told you to keep your heads down and not to talk to any of my men."

The one called Chloe surged to the front of the group and stood up to equal his height as he sat glowering from horseback.

"We've done nothing wrong, sir." She moved to the edge of the cart. "Mattias"—she nodded toward the old soldier's retreating back—"was graciously answering a few questions for us about London and the king's palace."

"Which has nothing to do with his orders to drive the cart and keep his eyes and ears to himself." He glowered at the soldier approaching the cart. "You understand this duty, Withers? You drive and keep strictly to yourself." The fellow glanced briefly at the "nuns," nodded, then climbed onto the seat board and took up the reins.

"We are not a contagion, Sir Hugh," the appointed one declared.

He wheeled his mount and headed for the front of the column, muttering.

"I wouldn't bet on that."

But he had bet on it, he realized as he looked over his shoulder at least fifty times during the next hour. And once again he had lost. Their second driver had quickly been infected with the same plague of garrulousness and affability, and now the cart was veering off the road, heading for the edge of a broad forest.

"What the devil?" He charged back to order the driver to keep to the road and again found himself facing a hot-eyed Chloe of Guibray.

"We *asked* him to pull the cart over." She stood braced at the front of the cart. "We must stop long enough to see to our personal needs."

"Absolutely not." He spotted the wagons and mounted riders following them and furiously waved the wayward wagons back onto the road. "We'll stop only when we reach a village where we can get feed and water for the horses."

"But we *must* stop."

"We will stop when I say we stop, and not before!" he roared. Then she folded her arms and lowered her voice so that he had to concentrate to hear her.

"Unless you have some way of convincing our nether parts to cease their natural function, Sir Hugh, I suggest you allow Withers to continue with us toward the trees." There came a whimper of distress from the group behind her. "And quickly."

She had him, Hugh realized. There was a chuckle off to his left, and when he looked over, Graham was a few feet away leaning on the pommel of his saddle, trying not to grin.

"All right, dammit!" He flung a finger at the nearby woods. "Take the cart over there!" As the heavy wooden wheels groaned and labored toward the trees, he glowered at Chloe. "You'd better be quick about it. We have a long way to go to reach the coast, and the ship is *waiting*."

Chloe and the others jumped down from the cart without assistance and scurried into the trees. Hugh jerked his gaze away and spotted several of his men dismounting.

"Back on your mounts!" he bellowed. "*We're* not stopping here!" Their dark looks and grudging compliance caused him to climb down from his horse and plant himself squarely between his men and the maiden-infested forest.

Saints Abundant, he hated this duty . . . protecting a clutch of headstrong maidens from both themselves and his own comfort-starved men. What could the abbess be thinking, sending them off without an older, wiser head to act as chaperone and disciplinarian? He should have headed straight back to the convent the minute he learned the old sister wasn't among them.

He glanced longingly north and west, in the direction of the ship that was waiting for them. It was still a hard day's ride to the coast . . . a day's sailing across the Channel and a day up the Thames. Three more days—four if the winds and tides didn't favor them—before he would be rid of the lot of—

He spotted Graham dismounting and heading for him with clenched fists, and he drew a long-suffering breath.

"A bit harsh on them, weren't you?" Graham spoke in compressed tones, looking off into the trees so that his annoyance wouldn't carry to the men.

"They survived the battle at Crecy. They'll survive this."

"I meant the maids. They're not prisoners, you know."

Hugh leveled a hard look on him.

"I have a charge from the king to get these females back to London safely." He jerked his head toward the men scanning the edge of the woods for stray glimpses of his charges. "Can you imagine what would happen if our little 'sisters' decided to try out their new womanly wiles on this wolf pack? We'd have to run the poor bastards through to keep them from ravishing the chits."

He drew Graham's gaze with his to where a couple of soldiers had edged their mounts near Mattias's wagon to talk with him. He could just imagine what the old veteran was telling them about the little nuns with the big eyes and soft lips and musical voices—

A scream tore through both the air and Hugh's preoccupation in the same instant, and all he could think was that *it couldn't be*. His men were all there in front of him, all accounted for—

A second scream, from a different voice, jolted him to

action. Ripping his sword from its scabbard, he shouted at Graham to "Come with me!" and plunged through the underbrush, into the trees. Graham hesitated only long enough to signal several soldiers at the front of the column to follow, and the men had their weapons drawn before their feet even touched the ground.

As Hugh charged through the trees, slashing at low-hanging branches and ducking snags and broken limbs, he prayed that he was overreacting. Let it be just a rat or snake or wild pig . . . something that had startled them. But a sudden chorus of screeching terror caused every muscle in his body to tighten to battle readiness. No wintered pig ever caused such caterwauling.

When he finally burst into the small clearing, there it was—his worst nightmare come to life. His charges had stumbled onto what appeared to be a band of brigands lurking in the forest. Two of the maids were already captive in the thieves' arms, kicking and thrashing furiously as they were being dragged toward the trees, and the rest were fighting desperately to keep from being taken.

"Release them!" he bellowed as he charged across the clearing. At the sound of his voice, the maidens' cries intensified, and two of the men broke away from them to meet him with blades drawn.

The clang of metal on metal unleashed battle-honed responses, and instantly he was fully engaged and bearing down on his ragged opponents. He hacked and slashed and thrust, his blue-edged steel glancing off their blades, his practiced military footwork matched by surprisingly adroit movements. His senses sharpened to anticipate every arc and angle of their blade work. Their counters and slashes had an unexpected crispness and precision that required him to focus entirely on the fight. He was scarcely aware of Graham and some of their men arriving to join the battle. The brigands fought savagely at first, but then, finding themselves outnumbered, abandoned their prizes and withdrew with a cry that any soldier who had fought Frenchmen in recent months knew full well: "Fall back!"

The cry distracted his remaining opponent just enough for him to find an opening in the wretch's shoulder. The bandit fell with a thud, and Hugh staggered but managed to remain upright, bracing on his thighs to gulp air.

The sudden stillness was just as disorienting as the sudden violence had been. As his breathing returned to normal, he sheathed his blade and turned back to check his men and see to his charges. There had been no casualties on their side, and the maidens were still here. As his men watched anxiously, he helped the young women to their feet and handed them off to Graham. Four . . . only four?

He knew instantly which one was missing. The bold and presumptuous one . . . the brazen and audacious chit who always . . . He spotted a lump of faded black in the tall grass not far away.

Chloe of Guibray lay in a crumpled heap. He dropped to his knees, rolled her over, and gathered her unwieldy but thankfully not-dead weight into his arms. The bastards had struck her; she had a red mark on one cheek, just below a lush crescent of dark lashes.

"Sister . . ." He gave her uninjured cheek an awkward pat. "Chloe of Guibray." Alarmed, he gave her a gentle shake. "Can you hear me? Open your eyes."

His heart began to beat again as her eyes fluttered open. She blinked and licked her lips as if to speak, but no words came out. Her arm flopped uncooperatively as she tried to reach up to touch her injured cheek.

A wail went up from one of the others, and immediately he was assailed by hysterical females talking and weeping all at once. They bore down on him and Chloe with outstretched arms, reaching for and demanding reassurance of each other.

"Stop—you're going to make me drop—"

He felt a brief, disorienting tilt and then a jarring thud that was accompanied by squeals. He was suddenly on his back at the bottom of a jumble of limbs and veils and straw-stuffed habits. He froze with a protest trapped in his throat as the scent of women—ripe, lilac-and-linen scented femininity—engulfed him. They were pressed

against every living inch of his overheated body and
showed no inclination toward vacating that volatile territory.

"For g-godssake!" he finally sputtered, pushing at
something alarmingly small, round, and pillowy. "Get
up—get off me!"

Graham's ruddy face appeared above him, and the
maidens were lifted from him in short order. He pushed
up to a sitting position and found a limp, familiar form
still draped across his lower body. The injured Sister
Chloe came to life, struggled up onto her arms, and raised
her head. This time her eyes focused and looked up to
meet his. They were big and blue . . . astoundingly clear . . .
as open and unsullied as an April morning. He experienced a strange sinking sensation . . . as if he were being
drawn into a pool of warm, soothing water. . . .

After what seemed an eternity, she seemed to realize
where she was and scrambled off him, landing on her rear
with a thump.

"Chloe!"

"Ohhh, look at you!"

"Are you all right?"

The other maids crowded around to pull her to her feet,
right her veil, and smooth her habit. She collected herself
with a deep breath, then brushed aside their concern to
confront him. The change in her caught him a bit off
guard.

"Who were those men?" she demanded.

"B-brigands and thieves," he answered, struggling to
recover his own self-possession. "Exactly the sort of danger I've been warning you about."

It was a lie, out and out. He had been so concerned
about his own men's wayward impulses that he hadn't
even considered someone else might try to assault them.
Lying *and* ineptness in his duty. *More* to confess when
he got back to the—

"Uncommonly good fighters, for common thieves,"
Graham mused, breaking into his thoughts.

The observation jarred together several impressions in

Hugh's mind, and he strode over to where the injured thief lay. He scrutinized the man's ragged garments and then stooped to brush back a torn flap on his shirt. Beneath it was an expanse of mail. Scowling, he picked up the man's weapon and then examined his hands. Such calluses came only from wielding a blade, and often. He sensed Graham's presence beside him and pointed to the exposed armor and the man's hands. As he rose, he examined the sword, then handed it to Graham.

"Not your ordinary brigand," he observed.

"No indeed."

"He's not dead. . . ." For the first time in several days he had a rational thought. "We'll take him along and question him when he wakes."

They turned and there stood Chloe of Guibray, with her face pale and her brow knitted into a frown.

"What do you mean, 'not an ordinary brigand'?"

The sound of men crashing through the trees all around set the maids screaming and running for him. Hugh and Graham drew their swords, and their men rushed to help them form a shield around the women.

The rest of the escort party burst from the trees, their blades drawn and their battle-honed bodies primed for action. It took a moment for the two groups to realize that they were in fact on the same side.

"What the devil are you doing here?" Sir Hugh demanded of his men.

"Tho't ye might need help, sarr," Withers declared, lowering both his sword and his chin.

"Be the li'l Sisters safe?" old Mattias asked, moving toward their huddle but halting in his tracks at Hugh's fierce expression.

"Safe enough. Now, get your worthless hides back to the wagons!" He motioned the rest of the company to join them. "All of you!" Then he turned to the rattled maidens. "You, too. These woods are not safe, and we still have many miles to go before we reach the coast."

He should have known better. Whatever made him

think they would climb blithely back aboard their cart and continue on as if nothing had happened?

"Absolutely not." Chloe stepped forward, her determination growing as the others crowded together behind her. "My sisters have survived an ugly shock. They need rest and nourishment, not more jostling in that awful cart."

"You can rest along the way."

"We will do no such thing." She straightened her shoulders and glanced up at the lowering sun. "We must make camp and continue on tomorrow."

"Camp?" For a moment that was the only word he was capable of saying. Frustration choked off all others.

"That might not be a bad idea, Hugh," Graham mused, looking at the one called Margarete, who stood nearby, as pale as her wimple and starting to sway.

"Not you, too." He glowered, then caught the concern in his lieutenant's face and turned just in time to see little Margarete hit the ground.

A LONE FIGURE WATCHED FROM HIGH IN the canopy of trees as the wagons and cart left the road and the drivers pulled them into a circle. He quietly shifted branches and then squinted to make out the fact that the women were hovering in concern over one of their number. The soldiers hurried to fashion a makeshift tent for them from the felts used to cover the goods in the wagons, while the tall, black-clad knight sent a detail of men into the trees. He held his breath as they neared his perch—but only to gather firewood.

Camp. The watcher smiled. They were making camp for the evening.

As twilight fell and fire bloomed in the middle of the circle, the observer climbed down to join the shadows on the forest floor and slipped from tree to tree, pausing, listening for signs of detection. But there were none. The arrogant English hadn't pursued the "bandits," and, now that they were camped, hadn't even posted sentries. If only Edward's men had been so careless at Crecy!

Keeping to the edge of the trees, he made his way toward a wrecked stone cottage at the far edge of the woods
and a horse that had been left for him. Soon he was riding,
charting his course by moonlight toward the ordained ren-
dezvous.

After some time in the saddle, he approached a set of
ancient ruins, slowed, and whistled into the silence. Men
materialized from among the scattered stones to greet him,
and soon he was ushered to the center of the ruin. There,
a number of small fires lighted a military camp in which
some men wore rags and others wore armor.

"It's about time." A short, stocky man in elegant velvets rose from the center of the camp and glared at the
arrival. "What news have you?"

"They made camp, *seigneur*. I waited to be sure. The
women . . . one was injured or overcome, and they would
go no further."

"And the man they took prisoner?" the lord demanded.

"Has not yet come to his senses. They have posted no
sentries."

"So they do not yet know . . ." The nobleman scowled
and paced away, then back, rubbing his hands together,
thinking. "There is still time to prevent the little tarts from
reaching the coast and boarding a boat bound for London." He turned a fierce look on the captain of his guards.
"If you cannot steal them away, then you must at least
render them unfit for matrimony. Do you understand what
I am saying, Valoir?"

"*Oui, seigneur*." The knight Valoir's face twisted into
a smirk. "I understand."

The lord took a deep breath and looked to the east,
scanning the moonlit ridge of the horizon, calculating
their best odds of success.

"Dawn would be the best time to catch them unawares."

Chapter Four

THEIR CAMP THAT EVENING WAS A modest victory, as victories go, but a significant one in Chloe's eyes. She had gone toe-to-toe with the arrogant knight and, in the end, gotten what she wanted. It meant that even if she could not control what happened to them, she could at least influence it. More important, it put a seal on her leadership for the other maids, who had been badly shaken by the attack. Their first experiences in the world outside the cloister walls were proving to be somewhat harrowing.

"I had no idea what was happening. I didn't see or hear anything before they grabbed me," Helen said as they huddled together inside the makeshift tent.

"Nor did I." Alaina pushed up her sleeve and inspected her wrist with blooming indignation. "I think the wretches may have *bruised* me."

"I'll never go in the woods again," Margarete said fervently, glancing over her shoulder in the direction of the trees. "No matter how badly I have to *go*."

"It does no good to dwell on it," Chloe said, putting her arm around Margarete and reaching over to squeeze Helen's hand. "There are guards ringing the wagons ...

we're safe now. Let's talk about something else."

"*Oui*, something else, please." Lisette said, glancing at the slice of golden firelight coming through the tent opening. "Did you see how he fought? Our knight protector." She gave a low whistle. "*Mon Dieu*, what a swordsman!"

"Lisette, your language," Chloe said, unconsciously mimicking Sister Archibald and achieving the same dismal result: Lisette's smile contained not a trace of repentance.

"Then let us talk of his long, muscular legs and broad shoulders." There was a giggle of response. "And his hands . . . such big, powerful ones . . ."

"He is so very strong." Helen put in with an admiring roll of her eyes. "Did you see how easily he lifted Chloe?"

"And so awfully tall," Margarete put in, not quite catching the spirit of the others' comments. "It hurts my neck to have to look up at him."

"It is not his size or power that draws *my* eye," Alaina pronounced her judgment. "Have you not noticed the way he moves? Long, sure strides . . . as if with each step he measures the world for conquest."

"And those eyes." Lisette's gaze drifted to some internal vision. "So dark and searing. They glow like hot coals at the center. I swear—"

"Don't swear," Chloe said by reflex, even as she was plunged by Lisette's words into a steamy swirl of memory.

"Sometimes I can feel his gaze all the way through my habit and gown . . . reaching inside my skin." Lisette shivered eloquently, and the others giggled.

Searing eyes. Long, powerful legs. Big body. Once again Chloe felt the plank-hard frame of the unyielding Sir Hugh beneath her. She had found herself lying facedown across his lap, and when she pushed up on her arms and looked around, her gaze had sunk straight into his.

Rich, russet-and-sable eyes shaded by thick lashes filled her vision. They did seem to burn like glowing coals. Her attention gravitated inexplicably down his face to his straight, slightly arched nose and then to his broad, boldly curved lips . . . sleek, like fine velvet. Looking at them made her own lips feel strangely naked and sensitive. His square jaw and corded neck were sun-bronzed, and she noticed that his damp hair curled slightly as it escaped the bottom edge of his helmet . . . soft hair, like fine-spun silk that sent a tickle of curiosity through her fingers.

That meeting of eyes had lasted only a moment, but it was long enough to awaken every one of her senses. And its effects lingered strangely; even now her heart was beating faster.

"Chloe?" Margarete said, rousing her from those unsettling thoughts.

"Yes? What?"

"Are you well? You look flushed."

"Fine . . . I-I feel fine." She straightened and touched her hot cheek and blushed even hotter. "But it is warm in here. I think I'll get some air."

As she ducked out, she heard Alaina say something but didn't catch it.

"Tell Sir Hugh we must have some straw to make pallets. I simply cannot sleep on bare ground."

Inserting her hands in her sleeves, Chloe paused for a moment to take in the cool air and survey the camp. Across the central fire, she spotted Sir Hugh and Sir Graham leaning over the injured bandit. Thinking she might be of some help in tending the man's wounds, she hurried over. But as she approached, she realized they weren't treating him, they were threatening him.

"How did you know?" Sir Hugh was demanding. "Who told you about them?" He grabbed the front of the man's shirt and gave him a shake that elicited only a moan. "Tell me and we'll bind your wounds and carry you to the nearest town. Keep silent and we'll leave you to bleed and die where you lay."

The possibility of them abandoning the injured man horrified Chloe.

"What are you doing?" she called, hurrying toward them.

"This is none of your concern." Sir Hugh intercepted her, blocking the way to the prisoner. "Go back to your tent."

"I have some training in the healing arts. I can treat the man's wounds and see them properly bound."

"You'll do no such thing," he gritted out. But her narrowed eyes and raised chin must have convinced him that she would not be easily dissuaded. He seized her by the elbow and dragged her out of the man's hearing. "He knew."

"What?"

"He said they were supposed to steal *the maids*. They knew you weren't nuns. I need to know how they learned that and where they were supposed to take you . . . who is behind this attempt at abduction."

"How could he possibly—"

"Now, go back to your tent and keep your nose out of things that don't concern you."

"How can you say this doesn't concern me?" She wrested her arm free. "In fact, I should be the one to question him." She started back to the prisoner, but he caught her and hauled her back to him.

"She may be right." Sir Graham's reasoned words intruded, and they both looked up to find him staring at them, his gaze focused on Sir Hugh's grip on her shoulders. "Sometimes a gentler touch is more effective."

Sir Hugh jerked his hands from her, and with an air of vindication she hurried over to the prisoner. Peeling back the brigand's tattered shirt, she probed gingerly through the damaged mail overlaying the wound.

"I'll need some clean water and cloths." She looked up at Sir Graham. "And I will need my small chest from the cart."

The injured prisoner watched her through slitted eyes that closed altogether when a wave of pain crested over him. She asked his name as she removed his ripped shirt and unbuckled the mail underneath. As the pain subsided, he whispered, "Jean."

"I am sorry if this hurts you, Jean, but the wound must

be cleaned or it will fester." She set about using the cloths and water, then retrieved a packet of dried herbs from her chest and poured some over the wound before binding it tightly. Then she gave the fellow some watered wine and washed his forehead.

"Sir Hugh says you thought the Sisters and I were maidens," she said gently. "Why would you think such a thing, Jean? Did you not see our habits?"

"He said . . . it was . . . disguise," Jean rasped out.

"Who said so?"

"*Le capitaine*."

"You have a captain? You're a soldier?" she asked. "In whose service?"

The fellow closed his eyes and in the middle of shaking his head lost consciousness. She expelled a deep sigh and looked up to find Sir Hugh staring darkly at her.

"That was certainly helpful," he said irritably.

"It was at least Christian," she rejoined. "And I learned he's a soldier and sent by someone to abduct us."

"Which we already knew." When she showed surprise, he gestured to the discarded mail. "They wore armor beneath their rags, used well-made weapons, fought like seasoned soldiers, and at the end were ordered to 'fall back.' "

"This is absurd." She pushed to her feet, frowning, and rolled her sleeves down. "Why would anyone wish to abduct us?" She glanced at the heavily loaded wagons. "Surely they would rather steal our dower goods."

"One would think so," Hugh said tartly. "Any half-wit would prefer something more useful or at least more merchantable. Which raises the question of how they learned you were maids in disguise. Who knew of our plans?"

"All of the Sisters knew we would wear habits. Several donated old garments. But who would they tell? They never see anyone from the outside wor—" She reconsidered that. "Well, there *are* several girls who come from the village each day to help in the kitchens. And the farmers who deliver grain and poultry and vegetables. The needy come to beg food at the kitchen door . . . oh, and tenants come to see the abbess for permission to cut a tree or build a new cottage, or to seek Sister Bernice's healing herbs, or to ask the priest to christen a babe or bless a field for plant—"

"So, in point of fact, the whole bloody shire probably knew!" He seemed to choke momentarily with frustration, then forced himself to calm. "Wonderful. Excellent. Now that the *how* of it is no longer a mystery, we can move on to the *why*." He gave her a scorching look that started with her feet and worked upward to her reddening face. "Why in the infernal blazes would anyone want to steal the likes of you?"

She jerked back with a half-stifled gasp, then whirled and strode back to the tent, missing Sir Graham's comment.

"Do you have even the faintest notion of how big a jackass you are?"

Chloe paused outside their makeshift quarters, her heart pounding and her bruised face throbbing. She forced herself to breathe deeply for a moment. As her inner turmoil subsided, she heard the others inside talking and dreaded the prospect of facing them just now. Shoving her hands up her sleeves, she began to walk the encampment. The men's stares and occasional nods in her direction reminded her of Sir Hugh's edict of silence, and she found herself looking toward the woods. A bit of silence might be exactly what she needed just now. She wouldn't go far, just into the first few trees.

Old Mattias spotted and stopped her. When she said she needed to visit the bushes, he insisted on escorting her.

"No, no, you musn't trouble yourself. I won't go far. Just into the trees."

The old warrior stood scowling after her uneasily.

The waxing moon provided enough light for navigation, and she relished the soft "shushing" sound made by the tall grass as she waded through it. When she reached the trees, the moon shadows enveloped her in a soothing darkness, and her tense shoulders and knotted stomach began to relax. Twice she paused and looked back toward camp to make certain she could still see the glow from the fires. Her eyes adjusted slowly to the darkness and her hearing was piqued to greater sensitivity. She located a fallen log, tested it for soundness, then sat down to have a stern word with herself.

Why should it bother her so that Sir Hugh found her so . . . What? Troublesome? Annoying? Intolerable?

Her face flushed as the memory of his glare and disdainful words washed over her again. She wasn't imagining it; his reaction was every bit as personal as it was official. What if her future husband reacted to her the same way? What if there were some grave deficit in her character or physical appearance?

Admittedly, she wasn't as fair as the lovely Alaina, or as graceful and dignified as Helen. Few women were. And she hadn't the sultry magic of a Lisette or the sweet, unworldly delicacy of a Margarete. But, truth be told, he seemed to hold them in a measure of contempt as well. Perhaps what she felt as a special hostility toward her was only directed at her because she was the one who spoke up and demanded proper treatment.

An image of the abbess confronting the officious Father Phillipe rose in her mind, and as the abbess's spine straightened, so did Chloe's. There were ways of dealing with critical, arrogant, overbearing males, she reminded herself. And, anyway, it would only be for a few more days, until they reached London. That was where the real test of her leadership would—

A branch cracked in the distance: a loud popping sound that spoke of a sizable limb subjected to substantial force. She came to attention, listening, searching the deep shadows for some clue to its location. Several moments passed before she heard a second snap . . . quieter this time, but closer. She shot to her feet, gathered up the hem of her straw-stuffed habit, and began to move.

Calculating that the sound came from her right, she traveled to her left to avoid whatever caused it. But as she made her way along, she heard the intruder—some*one* not some*thing*, she hoped—changing course and cutting between her and the camp. She moved faster, slapping away twigs and branches that clutched at her garments and held her back. Her only hope of reaching that circle of safety was to be quick and quiet.

But as she fled toward safety, it seemed every step in the rustling undergrowth betrayed her position. When she glanced over her shoulder to look for her pursuer, her foot struck a rock and turned. She stumbled, grabbed her twisted ankle, and hopped up and down, biting her lip to keep silent. As the first rush of pain subsided, she made herself go on, but was reminded by each step that every movement in the darkness was a potential plunge into disaster.

What direction was she going? Was she close enough for someone to hear if she cried out? How would they know it was her? Please—she beseeched angels and archangels and the entire host of heaven—let there be just one of them this time!

Abruptly what had been a slow and stealthy pursuit changed into an all-out chase. A thud and the thrashing of underbrush set her to open flight. She bolted for the dim glow coming through the trees, ignoring the pain in her foot and the slap and sting of the wiry branches. The faint light seemed closer with each desperate heartbeat, but so did that pursuing shape . . . until suddenly it loomed out of the darkness . . . human . . . male . . . bent on intercepting her.

With a cry of fright, she reversed course.

She felt him closing the distance, heard a growl of determination and the crashing of vegetation as he charged after her. Suddenly she was struck from behind and propelled forward . . . into a nearby tree.

The impact winded her. For a moment all she could do was clutch the bark and gasp convulsively. She was consumed by the struggle to breathe, until a huge shudder racked her and her stunned lungs finally expanded. With the battle for breath won, she channeled her energy against the weight pinning her to the tree. Twisting and shoving, she managed to turn and face her attacker, whose hand clamped hard over her mouth. As he drew back to look at her, she found herself staring up into a pair of hot black eyes framed by an angular face and a mane of unruly dark hair.

"You!" he snarled quietly, trying to contain her. "I should have known."

There was no mistaking the owner of that irritable voice, but it was a moment more before she would trust her senses and cease struggling.

"What—"

"Hush!" he whispered, raising his head to examine the darkness around them, evaluating every rustle, sway, and chirp in the now-quiet forest. He was pressed so tightly against her that she could feel the tension coiled in his big frame and the control he exerted over every breath.

"Have you no sense at all?" She felt a contraction tighten his loins and ripple its way up through him. "You were attacked in these woods mere hours ago, and here you are wandering around alone in the dark!"

"And what are *you* doing out here?" She matched his furious whisper, wishing her crazed heart would slow and hoping he couldn't feel the way it was pounding. "Skulking around the woods at night—"

"I was posting a night watch, and Mattias reported that one of the 'Sisters' came out into the trees and hadn't returned."

"So you came charging out here like a lunatic, chased me, and knocked the very living breath out of me?"

"You could have been one of the brigands, back for another try."

"Do I look like an outlaw?" She grabbed the edge of her veil and held it up. "How many brigands do you know who wear a religious habit while stealing and pillaging?"

"I couldn't see your cursed hab—"

"I nearly broke an ankle back there." Her bodily complaints and outrage both grew. "I'm scratched all over . . . my habit is picked and torn and probably filthy . . . and my face . . ." She reached up to feel for additional damage and realized her hand was stinging. "Owww."

"What's wrong?"

"I must have found a patch of briers along the way."

He seized her hand, and when she complained, his touch gentled.

"I don't feel any blood." He slid his fingers over her palm, sending a shiver up her arm. "You'll survive."

"You sound disappointed," she snapped, trying to pull her hand away.

"On the contrary," he said with a sneer that was not quite up to his usual standard. "I can't afford to . . . to have one of you . . . 'matrimonial pearls-of-great-price' . . . damaged while in my care."

Standing there in the dappled moonlight with him pressed emphatically against her body and rubbing slow, deliberate circles on her palm with his thumb, she grew confused. Then she looked up and his shadow-softened features began to brand themselves into her impressionable senses. Lisette's and Alaina's words came back to her. Tall . . . strong . . . courageous . . . dutiful . . . he was the paragon of knightly perfection. Her awareness broadened to include the sensation of his battle-seasoned body molded against hers. The overwhelming warmth and hardness of him were so new and compelling that for a time they distorted her thinking. Handsome . . . intense . . . physically gifted and stirring to watch . . . he was also a prime slice of masculinity. And here he was in the dark with her . . . pressed tightly against her . . . filling her vision . . . breathing his strange, spicy heat into her head and lungs . . .

Why? Out of nowhere came the voice of a little "abbess" inside her. *Why was he still pressed against her? Especially when he'd made it so clear that he found her objectionable?*

Did it matter? She silenced that inner abbess. He was here with her and this bodily contact with him was so pleasurable. Her gaze fastened on his lips, which were parting . . . seemed to be lowering . . .

Shouting and sounds of crashing vegetation erupted all

around them. Galvanized, he drew his sword and whirled into a crouch, ready to defend her.

A dozen men brandishing weapons burst from the trees, led by Mattias and young Withers. Their battle cries died in their throats and their blades lowered as they recognized their commander and spotted Chloe, frozen and wide-eyed, behind him.

"What the devil are you doing out here?" Sir Hugh demanded, straightening and lowering his sword.

Mattias peered pointedly around him to Chloe and seemed a bit uneasy.

"Well, ye didn't come back, so we tho't ye might need some help. Wouldn' want nothin' to happen to the little Sister there."

"As you can see," Hugh snarled, grateful for the darkness that hid his reddening face, "she is perfectly safe."

He, on the other hand, was in great danger. Of forgetting every lesson on lust and licentiousness he'd ever learned. Of succumbing to a temptation he'd never faced before. Of doing something unforgivably stupid.

"Now get back to camp." Frantic to escape their scrutiny, he seized her wrist and pulled her along through the trees, setting a wickedly purposeful pace over logs and around snags. He could almost feel his men's eyes boring into his back, questioning what he was doing with the little Sister out here in the dark. And with damned good reason. If they hadn't interrupted him . . .

He had to do something. If nuns' garb wasn't enough to protect the maids from his men's baser urges, then he'd have to find something that did. They needed a better disguise . . . something truly convincing . . . something that could make even Chloe of Guibray look nothing like a woman.

When they reached the camp he dragged her across the circle, straight to the fire built in the midst of the wagons.

"Sit!"

At first she just stood glaring at him. Then, apparently remembering his strength and his willingness to use it, she tucked her arms with a jerk and sat down on one of logs that had been dragged near the fire.

Chloe watched as he conferred with Sir Graham, who seemed stunned by whatever he was saying and stared uneasily at her across the flames. Then Sir Graham strode off to speak to some of the men and Sir High-and-Mighty came to deliver what she sensed could only be bad news.

"We need your garments." When she just blinked at him, he expanded on it. "Your habits. You'll have to remove them and hand them over."

"What?" She shot to her feet, listing slightly as she tried not to put weight on her injured ankle. He seemed utterly serious. "We'll do no such thing."

"They were meant to provide you protection and security, were they not?" He leaned down to speak slowly and succinctly, as if he were explaining to a child. She was a twitch away from slapping him silly. "Well, after today, they will only provide you protection if *someone else* is wearing them."

That took a moment to register. It annoyed her that she couldn't think of a clever and devastating rebuttal.

"And, pray, who do you think *should* wear them?"

He seemed to sense victory at hand and pointed to a clutch of soldiers being herded their way by a grim Sir Graham.

"Them? *They* will wear our clothes? And what, pray, will *we* wear?"

He turned to young Withers and ordered him to remove his mail and tunic, holding out a hand to receive them. She watched with dawning comprehension as he hooked fingers in the garments' shoulders and held them up to her.

"Ohhh, no."

"Oh, yes." His smile was laced with vengeful glee. "And you've no one to blame but yourself . . . you gave me the idea. 'How many brigands do you know who wear a religious habit?' Sound familiar?"

*   *   *

LATE THAT SAME NIGHT, MILES AWAY, one of the pot boys from the village ambled down the convent's cellar steps to fetch some eggs and soon raced back up the steps with word that someone was trapped in the cellar.

By the time the kitchen Sisters arrived and drew back the rusty bolt, the abbess, who had been making her nightly rounds, was herself flying down the passage. Together they flung open the door and discovered Sister Archibald sitting in a chair the abbess had scoured the convent for that morning . . . wrapped from head to toe in blankets and sipping from a cup of Bordeaux's best libation.

"Archie! Are you all right?" As the chill-shrouded Archibald proclaimed her well-being, the abbess paled. "What in heaven are you doing here?"

"I DID CALL OUT, YE KNOW," ARCHIBALD insisted later as she sat in the abbess's private solar sipping the hot barley water they insisted she drink and regarding that humble brew with a wistful expression. "Again an' again, I called. And ye can only call out so much before yer throat gives out."

The abbess gave her a skeptical look. Her old friend's voice didn't sound the least bit "given out," and the wine-warmed glow of her face didn't make her look especially distressed by her ordeal. The Reverend Mother strode to her writing desk and sat down in her newly returned chair with her jaw hardening. "How could she think she would get away with it? I'll send to the bishop straightaway and ask for an envoy to ride after them. We'll haul her rebellious little carcass back to the convent and—"

"I think ye'd best read this first." Archibald pulled out the letter Chloe had left with her and carried it to the desk. "It may change yer mind."

"I sincerely doubt that."

But as the abbess read Chloe's earnest words, the lines of her face softened. She looked up to find Archibald wearing a wistful, enigmatic little smile that she knew to be both an expression of hope and a canny appeal to the highest and best in a human heart.

"I can't help thinking you had some part in this," she charged.

"Not me," Archibald said emphatically. "Surprised me in the cellar, she did. Locked me right in."

"But you're not the least bit sorry she did, are you?"

"Truth be told? No. I always thought our little Chloe should go." She did her best to catch both her friend's eye and her sympathy. "All the girl wants is some sweet babes of 'er own. Ye know what it's like, Reverend Mother . . . wantin' to hold flesh of yer flesh next to yer heart . . . needin' a place to belong."

The abbess seized a quill and shifted her chair to face the parchment laid out on the desk. In a trice, she had flicked open the ink pot and was stretching back to the length of her arm, tucking her chin and squinting . . . determined to fill that parchment with frothing hot words. After every letter she had to hold the parchment up and farther away to be certain where to put the next one.

"Sulphur and brimstone!" After a frustrating quarter of an hour, she slammed the inked quill down on the parchment, where it made an ugly blotch. "The chit's robbed me of my eyes and hands. I can't even write a letter ordering her brought back!" She pushed back in her chair, stewing in her own incapacity.

"And you!" She turned her frustration on Sister Archibald. "Where is all of that concern for 'our dear lambs' that you plagued me with? Who's going to speak for our maids now and see them properly mated?"

"Chloe." Archibald folded her hands at her ample waist and adopted a beatific expression, sensing things were going her way. "The girl's got pluck and she doesn't miss much—ye said so yerself. Between her an' the Almighty, they'll see our lambs settled right." She moved around the desk to put her hand on the abbess's shoulder. "Let her go, Reverend Mother. Her destiny's not with us. Never has been."

The abbess thought on that. Though her pride and con-science still stung, she heaved a sigh of decision and gave the hand on her shoulder a pat.

"Very well, I shall leave it in the Almighty's lap. Let's hope *He* has more success with her than I did." But she couldn't help one last flare of annoyance. "And I suppose, in Christian charity, we ought to light a few candles for whoever gets saddled with her for a wife."

Chapter Five

"DON'T LIKE THIS, SARR." WITHERS jammed a finger beneath the edge of the wimple constricting the edges of his face and gave it a tug. "It ain't nat'rul."

"I believe that is the point, Withers," Hugh said, studying the five newly appointed "Sisters" as they stood beside the campfire enduring muffled chuckles and taunts from their still-armored comrades. Upon volunteering for a "dangerous and important" mission, the five had been stripped of their arms and garments and every last vestige of masculinity—even whiskers—then were handed the maidens' habits to don. Their sullen faces were now reddened from both the shaving they endured and their embarrassment at being turned into females . . . even temporarily.

"Why d'we 'ave to wear these things at night?" Mattias snatched the black woolen out from his chest, stretching it as far from his skin as possible.

"We don't know when they'll attack," Hugh said with strained patience. "But they didn't get what they came for the first time, and we must assume they will be back. You five will have to be prepared at all times . . . until we're safely aboard the king's ship and under sail."

"It's chokin' me," burly Hiram complained, yanking on his wimple. Stitches popped. "Won't sleep a wink wi' this cursed thing 'round me neck."

"I don't look like no 'Sister,' " the gangly swordsman who went by the name of Fenster growled. He raised the hem of his habit, which was already perilously short, and looked down at his hairy knees and enormous feet. "You ever seen a female wi' feet like this?"

"I can honestly say," Hugh responded, "I have been spared that horror." He turned to Graham, who was working to keep a sober face. "We may as well get them settled in the tent."

"Oughta at least get t' wear me own bags b'neath," Willum the axeman muttered as he fell in behind Sir Graham. "Got a right big draft up me arse."

Some of the goods had been removed from one wagon and placed in the cart to make a protected space for the maids to sleep. There was a singularly awkward moment as the maids were filing out of their tent and the men were lumbering in to take their places. Each contingent glared at the other, then at the garments they had been forced to forfeit. Both sides swallowed their objections and moved grudgingly along.

While Sir Graham went over the plan with the Sister-impostors one more time, Sir Hugh led the maids-in-men's-tights around the wagons, keeping to the shadows so they would be shielded as much as possible from his men's sight. He averted his own eyes as he helped them climb into the wagon and told them to stay put. As they found places to sleep on top of the crates and barrels, they scratched vigorously and complained.

"This is indecent," Alaina declared, tilting her nose up and as far as she could from the tunic she was wearing.

"Ungodly. Un-Christian," Helen gritted out, rubbing the coarse fabric against her itching arms.

"A man is forbidden to wear a woman's garments. It's against the laws of the holy church," Margarete said, staring in horror at the stained and baggy tights she had been assigned. "And to force us to wear men's clothes is *twice* the abdom . . . abiminiom . . . abdominatium. . . ."

"*Abomination* is undoubtedly the word you're looking for," Chloe said, folding her arms irritably. "But I don't think it applies here. The brigands are still at large, they know we're not real nuns, and they have orders to carry us off. I hate to have to agree with Sir Hugh's reasoning, but our good and honorable habits can only protect us now if his men wear them in our stead."

"Perhaps the exchange will offer hidden benefits," Lisette intoned, lifting one tights-clad leg to study in the moonlight. "We'll all be caring for husbands and their garments soon. What better way to learn about men than to spend a bit of time in their tights?"

Chloe stared at her, and then at the others, who apparently hadn't caught her double meaning. She was going to have to keep a closer eye on Lisette.

"I can think of better ways," Helen declared, contorting an arm around her back to scratch. "Watching them in a tournament, for one."

"Dining with them at celebrations and on feast days, for another." Alaina pushed up her sleeves and scratched all the way to her shoulders.

"Walking with them," Margarete added, scratching her lower half.

"Oooh . . . in the dark," Lisette said eagerly, rolling up onto her knees. "Where they can steal kisses that take your breath away."

When Chloe turned to look, Lisette was smiling in a way that seemed somehow prim and mischievous at the same time. Walking in the dark with a man was one of the things specifically forbidden in the Sisters' teachings on virtuous conduct. It was considered an invitation to—

Her breath stopped. She'd just sampled a variety of "walking in the dark." If they hadn't been interrupted . . . the thought staggered her . . . would Sir Hugh have kissed her? If he'd been about to kiss her, he couldn't find her that repugnant or objectionable. And if he didn't find her so objectionable . . .

Her reasoning stood every test of sense and logic she could put to it. Her heart began to beat again. It was suddenly as clear as rainwater: his hostility toward her had more to do with *him* than with *her*.

"Try to get some rest," she told the others. "We have a long day ahead. But with Heaven's help, tomorrow night we'll be aboard ship, out of danger, and back in our own garments."

As she settled amongst the others, on hard wooden crates and barrels beneath itchy woolen blankets, she heard Alaina's determined muttering.

"Not without a bath, I won't."

A PREDAWN MIST SETTLED OVER THE camp, curling white and thick in low areas, covering blankets, shields, and helmets with dew. By the time the sky had begun to gray with first light, the moisture had softened the long grasses around the camp enough to keep them from rustling a warning to the men dozing in groups on the ground around the circle of wagons. Even the two sentries posted in nearby trees had been lulled by the chill and the stillness into a state of reduced awareness. The faint swish of sodden grass and the moisture-muffled snap of small twigs underfoot were all but lost in the heavy morning air. The brigands were halfway through their camp before they were even spotted.

It was the soft, metallic "chink" of mail meeting plate armor that made one of the men sleeping near the wagons raise his head. He saw a man in ragged clothes signaling with an arm movement that repeated that all-too-familiar sound. Then came a muffled but unmistakable cry from the direction of the Sisters' tent, at the same instant someone on the far side of the camp raised an alarm. He was on his feet in the next instant, reaching for his weapon and shouting to his fellows of the attack.

The invaders abandoned all attempts at stealth to slash and rip back the felt covering of the women's tent. They poured inside, grabbed the habit-clad figures, and hoisted them—albeit, with some difficulty—over their armor-clad shoulders. As the men bearing the "maidens" staggered toward the trees, the others formed a tightening phalanx at their rear, fighting off Sir Hugh's contingent while retreating strategically toward the forest. A few of their number fell, but most closed ranks and battled on as their comrades fled with their substantial prizes.

Hidden in one of the baggage wagons, Chloe and the others clutched each other and listened with anxious relief as the sounds of fighting began to die. Desperate to see what was happening, Chloe pried Margarete's fingers from her arms and pushed up to peer over the side of the wagon.

She could make out flashes of metal and feverish motion at the edge of the woods. There was some shouting and the remaining brigands broke off the fight and fled. Instead of giving chase, Sir Graham ordered the rest of his men back to the camp and their horses. Sir Hugh was right behind them, but as he neared camp veered toward the wagons instead of a saddle.

"Stay down, dammit!" he shouted as he spotted her above the wagon's rim. She gave their ruined tent a quick glance, then ducked back down into the wagon and reassured her terrified companions.

"It's Sir Hugh. The brigands wrecked our tent—I think they may have made off with our replacements!"

Moments later they heard the clank of harness chains and the thud of hooves approaching and realized the soldiers were hitching the wagons. A wooden wheel groaned as someone used it to climb up to the plank that formed a driver's seat. Chloe stretched up to see over the cargo and was relieved to find Sir Hugh himself seizing the reins and slapping the horses into motion.

"Where are we going?" she called out, crawling over and around dower goods to the front of the wagon.

"To safety," he called out. "Get your head down."

"But we can't just abandon Mattias and the others!"

She braced herself against the wagon's pitching side and pushed herself up higher to look behind them. The other wagon, the cart, and a string of empty horses were rumbling along in their wake. The sight of Sir Graham and the rest of the men headed into the woods after the brigands reassured her. She walked her hands around to the front and seized the edge of the driver's seat.

"You're not going to help them get Mattias and Withers back?"

"Will you get out of sight?" he ground out. When she didn't move, he was forced to answer. "They were supposed to be taken."

"They were? Why?"

"So they can learn who is behind these attacks."

"But then, why is Sir Graham riding after them?"

"It won't look right if they're not pursued." He sounded as if he spoke through gritted teeth as he smacked the horses' rumps with the reins, trying to get them to move faster. "Now will you bloody well *get down* and *stay down*?"

"Ohhh." It made complete sense. "A Trojan horse, of sorts." He looked over his shoulder with surprise, just as her eyes flew wide. "What will they do when they do learn they don't have marriageable young maidens?"

THE FRENCHMEN CARRIED THEIR CAPTIVES through the forest toward the same deserted cottage their scout had made use of the night before. By the time they reached the waiting horses and flung their burdens facedown across the saddles, their backs were straining and muscles were screaming.

"*Dieu*—they are heavier than I remembered," one of the men snarled, giving his captive's rump a smack. The whine and thrashing that produced delighted him. "Eh? You like that, *ma petite*?" He smacked her again.

"This one—she has had her nose too long in the trough," another of the brigands growled as he stuck his foot in a stirrup and swung up behind the maid he'd carried. His outraged captive managed to deal him a hearty *thwack* on the shin and he yelped. Retaliating, he brought a fist crashing down on the back of her head, and she went limp.

"*N'importe*, Ricard. You will work that roundness from her!" another of the outlaws called with a wicked laugh.

The raiding party kept to the valleys and the fast-disappearing shadows as they raced across the countryside. They flashed grins at each other and fondled their captives' upturned bottoms. The maids' frantic protests only stirred them to bawdier humor and greater anticipation.

Their destination, a rocky outcropping overlooking a bend in the river, was deserted just as they hoped. "*Le seigneur* is not here yet!" one called as they reached the shelter of a cluster of stone crags.

"We work quickly, eh?" Another bashed a proud fist against his chest.

"We must work quickly again," still another suggested as they halted and slid from their mounts, "if we would enjoy the spoils of victory before *le siegneur* arrives!"

The maids were dragged from the horses cringing and trying desperately to hide behind their veils. Out came bottles of wine, and several of the brigands shed their scabbards and began unlacing their tights in preparation for taking their share of the spoils.

"This one is mine!" One seized a maid and hauled her to her feet. She rose . . . and kept rising . . . until she stood almost a head higher than he. "*Bon Dieu*, she is a big one!" His laughter had an edge of bewilderment that was soon replaced by bravado. "There will be plenty of room for Ricard under those skirts, eh?"

With his comrades watching, he hauled the gangly wench against him and was astounded by the strength of her resistance. "Let us see what treasures you are hiding under there, *ma petite!*" Despite her frantic resistance, he managed to yank off her veil. The long, bony face and big nose sticking out of the wimple caused him to recoil briefly.

"Try the other end, Ricard!" one of his fellows yelled.

The harried Ricard grabbed for his prize's habit and wrenched it up to reveal an expanse of scarred and stringy legs. He winced in spite of himself, drawing hoots of derision and mimicked dog howls from his comrades.

"We should have let the English *keep* that one!" came a jeer as the rest of the bandits rushed to lay claim to the other maids and the stony crag filled with sounds of scuffling and thrashing.

Humiliated by his choice and determined to punish his victim for it, Ricard tried to wedge his hand between the wench's long, hairy thighs.

"Open up, *chien*. I will show you what your ugly uncles would not!"

Tall, gangly Fenster had suffered more than his quotient of indignity. He and his fellow impostors were about to be found out. He parted his legs and stood his ground as the wretch rammed a hand straight into the razor-sharp blade he had strapped to the inside of one thigh.

The Frenchman jerked back with a screech, but the others paid no heed, thinking it must be him inflicting the pain. He grabbed his badly sliced hand, gurgling disbelief as Fenster ripped the blade from his leg and straightened to his full height with a snarl of fury.

Nearby Mattias, who had been wrestled to the ground by three rut-maddened brigands, took advantage of their horror when they threw up his habit to reveal stout, bandy legs and an unexpected rack of male tackle.

"Arrrhaaaa!" he roared as he ripped his short sword from its hidden scabbard and came up wild-eyed and ready for blood. "Swive *this*, ye pox-eaten cur!" With a single thrust he dispatched the brigand who had been about to ravish him.

Withers had cleverly torn the seams of his garment to give him quick access to the short knives he wore beneath it. At the first howls of battle, he wrenched his hands free and slid them through those openings for his blades. The wretch pinning him to the ground reared suddenly with a cry that was somewhere between a gurgle and a scream.

By the time the rest of the brigands went for the blades

they had so arrogantly discarded, the five "maidens" were upon them, battling hard for blood and honor. And winning.

Later, after the five had restored their disguises and lay sprawled on the tops of the rocks ringing the stone niche, watching for the lord who had ordered their abduction, Fenster looked over at Mattias with a sober expression.

"Ye know . . . that could'ave been th' little Sisters, instead o' us," he said.

Mattias thought on that for a moment, then yanked his veil forward to better shade his eyes as he scanned the fields below. He scowled, seeing that event and the memories of many that had come before it in a troubling new light.

"Glad I ain't a woman."

THE SUN WAS DIRECTLY OVERHEAD WHEN Sir Graham's men and the valiant sister-impostors came racing on horseback across the fields toward the dowry wagons. Sir Hugh reined the horses and climbed down, standing with his fists propped at his waist while they dismounted. Chloe and the others scrambled to the rear of the wagon, their hearts in their throats, counting habits and looking for wounded.

"The good news is—those brigands won't be trying to abduct the Sisters again," Sir Graham called as he dismounted.

"And the bad?" Hugh scanned the habit-clad men for signs of damage.

"The fighting was done before our mysterious lord arrived."

"What?" Hugh strode over to the disheveled "Sisters," demanding an explanation. "What the devil were you doing, revealing yourselves before their leader got to you? You were under orders to shrink and shriek until you learned who he was."

"We couldn't, Yer Lordship," Fenster muttered, lowering his head.

"Why the hell not?" Hugh roared.

"They was—" Mattias glanced at the maids staring at them from the back of the wagon and lowered his voice. "They was about to 'ave their way wi' us."

Hugh stared at Mattias, then Fenster, Hiram, Willum, and Withers. To a man they hung their heads and hid their reddened faces. He didn't know whether the reaction working its way up through him was anger or laughter. To prevent both, he rubbed his face until he could form a suitable glower.

"Just like the cursed French to wreck both their plan and mine with their unholy eagerness for a bit of ball—" He halted, appalled by what he'd barely left unsaid, then addressed the five again. "At least you spared the Sisters a vile and terrifying experience." He shouted to the rest of the company: "Mount up. We have a ship to meet. England awaits."

Then he turned to the wagon and found the maids climbing down and scurrying for the nearby bushes, revealing themselves to the whole company in their male garments. He looked with horror from his men's avid gazes to the maids fleeing through the grass and underbrush. Whenever he got one thing settled, another ran willy-nilly out of control—it was like trying to herd chickens!

"Where in blazes do you think you're going?" he roared. "Get back in that wagon!"

"We will," Chloe of Guibray responded as she turned her back on him and headed for the bushes herself. "As soon as we've paid our respects to Nature."

As he stood there, telling himself that tearing out his hair would probably save time when he someday entered the monastery and had to have his head shaved in a tonsure, his wayward eyes dropped to the sway of her hips as she strode defiantly away. Sweetly rounded buttocks. Long, shapely legs . . . sinfully visible in a pair of men's tights. Every muscle in his lower half contracted.

"Damned infuriating females." He turned straight into Graham's discerning gaze and flinched, hoping his friend hadn't seen him *looking*. "I should have let the damned Frenchmen take them. Would have saved five poor, unsuspecting Englishmen from a fate worse than death."

"FOOLS!" SOME DISTANCE AWAY ONE VERY irritable French lord was swinging down from his horse to survey the remains of what had once been a group of seasoned fighters. "Idiots! Look at them!"

Every man in the *compte*'s escort was doing just that, and wincing. The evidence was unmistakable: the men in the raiding party had died with their privates exposed . . . anticipating pleasure when, in fact, they were facing death.

"Died with their *pissots* in their hands instead of weapons!" The *compte* stalked among the corpses, toeing one after another with his boot in a gesture of contempt. "And not a sign of the tarts they intended to skewer. You'd think the bastards could have managed to kill at least one!"

"T-there are many tracks. They must have had help, *mon seigneur*," his red-faced captain, Valoir, offered.

"You think so?" He flew at Valoir and seized the top of his breastplate, jerking the taller soldier down to his level. "Twice now you and your men have failed to abduct a handful of bastard females. Mere women. Simple bags of flesh and vice."

"Who are protected by an escort of experienced soldiers," the captain forced each word past the humiliation filling his throat. He was making excuses and his lord hated excuses.

"Your men have experience, too, *n'est-ce pas?*" the *compte* said ominously. "Only their experience has been at *losing* battles." He released Valoir with a shove, and it took a moment for the proud soldier to gain his bearings.

"I will take the full garrison and intercept them at the coast," Valoir declared, starting for his horse.

"Don't be absurd!" the *compte* snarled, stopping him in his tracks. "How far would you get with an armed garrison in English-held territory before the English intercepted you? And even if you made it to the coast . . . after two attacks in two days, they would have to be imbeciles not to be prepared. And they are *not* imbeciles." Reason began to assert itself, and the lord drew a hard breath and began to pace.

"We must give them time to forget, to think they are safe. It may require crossing the Channel, but we can still keep them from marrying and completing Avalon's ransom." Even in the midday sun his smile was chilling. "Failing that, there must be any number of ways to render the dirty little tarts unmarriageable."

Chapter Six

THE WAGON BEARING THE DUKE'S daughters had yet another distractable driver that day before Sir Hugh stormed down off his horse and took up the reins himself. At first he sat like a great, forbidding gargoyle, scowling off toward the west. He refused to stop or slow or speak in more than single syllables until Chloe informed him that Alaina and Margarete were growing faint from the sun. He looked irritably over his shoulder, glimpsed Alaina and Margarete feverishly beginning to loosen and shed garments, and immediately stopped the wagon.

While he herded the maids out of his men's view, Hugh had Graham and the others scour a nearby copse of trees for sizable but supple branches. At his direction they arched the small limbs over the bed of the wagon and covered them with a felt, creating a shade on the sun-facing side.

His reaction to the maids' appreciative squeals and the way they pressed close to squeeze his hands and pulled him down to press his cheek with theirs surprised Chloe. It wasn't hostility or annoyance or even his usual sneer of superiority. He clearly hadn't expected such gratitude and was caught with his guard down. Then he looked up and saw her staring at him, and she could have sworn he reddened as he pulled away and barked orders for them to climb back into the wagon.

As they got under way again, she thought about his expression as he extricated himself from the others' clutches. There was more to him than met the eye. He made quite a display of his dislike for women, but in unguarded moments he showed a far less prickly attitude. He was a puzzle. And if there was anything Chloe couldn't abide, it was an unsolved puzzle.

For one brief, intensely lucid moment she felt herself teetering on the brink of something . . . suspended in time, potent with free will, and caught between choice and possibility . . . then plunged head-over-heels into the irresistible thrall of curiosity.

Of all the men the king might have sent to escort them, why did he have to choose Hugh of Sennet? Surely there were other knights who were equally as capable and far more willing. Then it occurred to her that he might have chosen Sir Hugh precisely because he was unwilling. Any man genuinely appreciative of feminine charms might find five fresh young maids too much of a temptation. But that didn't explain Sir Hugh's aversion to women. What could have caused him to dislike women so that he didn't want to see their faces or even hear their voices? A bad mother? A wicked sister? A pretty but coldhearted maid?

As she studied his broad back, the desire to know became like an unreachable itch. She climbed to the front of the wagon and stood on her knees beside the seat.

"Pardon, Sir Hugh, but can you tell me what will happen when we get to the king's castle? Do you know what is planned for us?"

"No," he declared, frowning.

Did the man ever do anything but scowl?

"Well, you are taking us straight to the king, are you not?" Chloe asked.

"Yes."

"Is Windsor Castle a busy place? Are there always many people there?"

"Yes."

One would have thought she was trying to pull his teeth. She drew a determined breath and changed her tactic. "When nobles come to the castle, where do they stay?"

"In tents. Or chambers."

"Do you know where we will stay?"

"No."

"And are there dinners and feasts in the evenings?"

"Sometimes."

"Great feasts where ladies wear their finest gowns?" Alaina broke in, scurrying forward to hang on to the seat and peer up at him. "And show off their new slippers and headdresses? And musicians compose songs to their beauty?"

He exhaled heavily and after a pause gave Alaina a quick, wary glance.

"There are many fine clothes," he said, again facing the road ahead. "People always wear their best when appearing before the king."

"And dancing?" Margarete joined them, to hang over Alaina's shoulder. "Are there musicians and entertainments in the evenings? Does everyone know how to do Italian steps? Does the king have a fool who makes everyone laugh?"

"Many of the lords and ladies enjoy a bit of dancing. There are often jugglers and mummers . . . sometimes traveling players. Some say the king has a whole host of fools that make him laugh." He leaned slightly in their direction and lowered his voice: "But *he* calls them his 'privy councillors.' "

Chloe stared at him. Was that a jest? As the others nodded eagerly to one another, she bit her lip, watching. He was talking to them. Actually *talking*.

"Is there a chapel or a church with colored glass windows?" Helen had come forward and nestled beside Chloe. "Is that where we will be wedded?"

"I have no idea where the marriages will take place. But there is a chapel . . . served by several priests who hear confession and celebrate masses."

"Never mind the church." Lisette pushed through the others to present her prime concern: "Speak to us of *les hommes*. These husbands we will have . . . who are they?"

"I have no idea."

"Then tell us about your nobles who have no wives," Lisette persisted and the others seconded her request. "Are the *seigneurs* all old and warty, with hairy ears and missing teeth? Or are there some who are young and manly . . . like Sir Graham?"

That caused him to glance down at Lisette. He considered her for a moment—during which she lowered her eyes and produced what Chloe guessed must be the first blush she had managed in years—and he made a sound that might have been either a throat-clearing or a chuckle. As he turned back to his driving, his gaze snagged on Chloe, and for a moment their eyes met. A tic of panic flitted through his expression . . . guilty surprise . . . as if he'd been caught doing something shameful. Like being sociable. Or human.

What the devil was he doing? Hugh chided himself. In spite of his determination to ignore them, he had found himself listening to their chatter for the last several miles. It seemed innocent enough . . . talk of the convent, their anxiety and hopes for the end of the journey, recitations of calendars for planting and for household maintenance to keep their memories sharp, and a recounting of the things and people at the convent that they would miss. It was when they began to speak of their heartfelt gratitude to the men who were abducted in their stead that his resistance had begun to melt. They were young . . . cast out of the only home they'd known into a great and perilous world . . . pawns in a game of thrones that they neither recognized nor understood.

What was the harm in answering a few of their questions . . . as long as he didn't look at them? For, as the monks had so fervently averred, it was *looks* that led to lust . . . and lust to sin . . . and sin to degradation. Unchecked, each step forged a link in a weighty chain that dragged a man down to eternal damnation. As long as he didn't *look* at them, he told himself, he would be all right.

"Unwedded noblemen . . ." He rubbed his chin, thinking. "There is the Earl of Ketchum . . . a somewhat older fellow who never married. He recently inherited from his childless brother and has need of an heir. And my friend Sir Simon, newly made the Earl of Candle, is yet unwedded. He is a valiant knight who has distinguished himself on the field of battle and in the lists at tournaments. . . ."

IT WAS SUNSET WHEN THEY HEARD AND saw seagulls swooping overhead, and smelled the tang of salt in the air. Sir Hugh urged the horses faster and craned his neck for a first glimpse of water and sail. But, when they stopped on a high spot overlooking the sea, he spotted whitecaps, cliffs overlooking a narrow stretch of beach, a modest village with fishing boats lining the shore, and no sails.

"No," he said to himself. "No, no, no!" He dropped the reins and jumped down from the wagon to rush to the brow of the cliff. He stood motionless for a time, paralyzed by the sight of uninterrupted waves as far as the eye could see. "Oh, bloody hell, *no!*"

Chloe watched with rising concern as he paced furiously, uttered several colorful variations on "damnation"—which caused her to put her hands over Margarete's ears—and then dragged Sir Graham out of earshot for what appeared to be a volatile consultation. At length they returned to the wagon to announce that the ship had undoubtedly weighed anchor to outrun some weather and would return soon. They would descend to the beach and camp there for the night, in order to be ready to leave the instant the ship appeared.

"We are not going to the village?" she asked, glancing toward the cottages huddled a half a mile away, at the top of the cliffs.

"No need," Sir Hugh declared, averting his eyes as he climbed back onto the wagon seat.

"Of course there is *need*." She took up that gauntlet, scuttling across the barrels and crates to once again stand on her knees beside the driver's seat. "We're hungry and the hampers the sisters provided are empty."

"We'll eat aboard ship," he responded tersely.

"Which, presumably, will be before we all die of hunger."

"One can only hope." His tone left ambiguous the nature of that hope.

"We have other reasons for wanting to visit the village," she said irritably. "We need certain curatives." That got his attention.

"Someone is ill?" He turned slightly and gave them a furtive glance.

"Bitten, actually."

He showed a satisfying alarm. "Who? Where? By what?"

"All of us. All over." She pulled out the neck of the tunic she wore. "By the disgusting vermin that inhabit these garments along with us."

"Fleas." He gave a snort of dismissal and again slapped the reins.

She rolled up her sleeve and shoved a naked arm in front of him, causing him to jerk to one side to avoid contact with it. But he couldn't avoid seeing that her skin was marred by a dozen small red bites and streaks from scratching.

"We look more like plague victims than noble brides." She watched him glance quickly at her arm, then away. "You need further proof?"

Instantly he was surrounded by a forest of bared arms that were peppered with angry red spots and well-scratched patches.

"Of course, I don't have much experience in such matters," Chloe said, glaring at him through that alarming display. "But I imagine that arriving at the king's castle looking like half-eaten fleas' dinners could damage our value as 'matrimonial pearls-of-great-price.' " When he glanced up, she smiled with a vengeful air. "It *could* appear as if we hadn't been treated well on the journey."

He turned, against his better judgment, and beheld five blotchy, well-scratched faces. Then they began to open their tunics to show him the bites on their slim, elegant throats and the tops of their creamy breasts.

"Damnation." He slammed his eyes shut. "Why didn't you just tell me they were being eaten alive?"

DESPITE ITS LOCATION AND FREQUENT traffic with seagoing vessels, the village was not especially well supplied with fresh water, herbals for nostrums, or clean accommodations. After an exhaustive search, Sir Hugh managed to find a large metal tub and a cottager on the upland side of the village who for a few pence would allow them the use of his hearth. And while Graham was busy locating and retrieving the maids' trunks for them, Hugh was forced to escort Chloe from cottage to cottage in search of some acceptable goose grease, dried spurge, a bit of fresh cowslip, and some ground oats.

From her trunk she produced a mortar and pestle, and while the others began to bathe in the oat water she mixed for them, she worked to concoct a soothing unguent on a small table outside the cottage door, while Hugh paced nearby. He paused periodically to inspect what she was doing.

"Are you certain you know what you're doing?" Hugh demanded.

"I studied herbal remedies with our convent physician."

"*Studied?*"

"Of course."

"Maids in a convent *study*?" He gave a snort of disbelief. Then, snagged by the memory of something she'd said, he began to search and assess her anew. "How do you know about the Trojan horse?"

"I read Homer's great poem. The convent had a goodly number of books. The abbess taught me Latin and English and some Greek and Italian."

"You read?" He nearly strangled on the words.

"All of us do . . . at least church Latin. Though, in truth, some of my sisters have no real interest in it. And unless used, it is a skill quickly forgotten."

"Females who read." He gave a skeptical roll of the eyes, then peered over her shoulder at the grease and herbs turning into a green salve. "Are you sure that stuff won't burn holes in their skin?"

"It's just grease and herbs. But perhaps you should test it." She dipped her finger in the bowl and deposited a glob on the back of his hand.

"Hey!" He jerked back, but she grabbed both of his wrists to keep him from wiping it off. "Let go."

"Give it a moment," she ordered, tightening her grip on him. "Do you feel anything?"

"No!" he declared adamantly.

"You're certain? No burning? No itching?"

"No." He reddened, both embarrassed and relieved.

"The only thing you're in danger of," she said tartly, "is having softer skin."

"I don't want to be any softer." The minute he said it he felt strangely exposed and wished he could unsay it. Clearly, she sensed how revealing a comment it was. After a moment she looked up, searching his face. He refused to meet her gaze.

"Very few of us get to be what we want, Sir Hugh." Her hands gentled on his wrists. "Heaven makes its plans without us."

Whatever Heaven's plans, he told himself vehemently, they could not include the unholy anticipation surging in his veins or this overpowering urge to lose himself in the sky-blue eyes that were tugging at him. And while the Almighty undoubtedly created those rose-petal soft lips and that curvaceous little body, He could never have intended them to send salacious heat boiling up the walls of a man's body the way it was his. Clearly, Heaven wasn't the only agency making plans for the inhabitants of the here-below!

In spite of that inner theological debate, he found himself gravitating closer to her and turning his head to meet her gaze.

Fire-kissed locks were threatening to escape the thick braid lying on her shoulder. His throat tightened. Her throat was so slender and soft . . . skin delicate as lily petals. His jaw clenched. The sun had caused her cheeks to bloom with becoming color—

"Where do you want these?" Sir Graham's voice broke over them and caused them to lurch apart. Chloe bumped into the table, whirled, and looked up to find him holding a small trunk and leading a contingent of men in habits carrying other baggage.

"Here, by the door." She busied herself with settling the trunks and missed the amusement in Sir Graham's face and the anger in Sir Hugh's.

"I'll be seeing to the horses," Hugh declared. "The rest of you get back to the damned beach and get out of those damnable women's weeds!"

With her cheeks aflame, Chloe watched him stride away.

"That is the most profane man I've ever seen," she said irritably.

Sir Graham, who was bending toward a sizable crack in the rough cottage door, snapped upright and looked at her in surprise.

"Hugh? Not hardly." He strolled over, bent to take a sniff at the stuff she was concocting, and then straightened and followed her frown to his friend's back. "The man's as close to a monk as can be found at Edward's court."

That jolted Chloe.

"A monk? His every other word is a condemnation of someone or something to everlasting torment. What order would permit such blasphemy?"

"He isn't always like this." Graham smiled ruefully. "Ordinarily he is the sanest, most rational man I know.

He has the king's full trust and richly deserves it. It's just that . . . he doesn't exactly . . ."

"Want to be here. Escorting us," she said, seeing Sir Hugh's contempt in a new light. "He hates women."

"Oh, no. That is, I don't believe he personally bears women any ill will." Graham extended a hand for hers and led her to a bench by the cottage door. "He has associated with too few actual females to be able to judge. Mostly the ladies of Edward's household—who, admittedly, are not always the highest and best representatives of their sex—and the serving women he must deal with in the ordinary course of days."

"Has he no mother or sisters? No kinswomen?"

Graham raised his eyes overhead as if looking for guidance in answering.

"His mother died early. She bore only the three sons. Hugh was the third, and not required for assuring succession to the title, so he was sent to a monastery to be trained for a life in holy service."

"He was raised in a monastery?" She looked with surprise toward the place where Sir Hugh had disappeared. "It's a wonder he hasn't shaved his head and donned a hair shirt."

"Not for lack of trying." He chuckled. "Growing up, he wanted nothing more than to take vows and spend his life in scholarly bliss among the books and illuminations in the abbey library. I was sent to the abbey for a time and was tutored along with him. He was a quick and able student. But the abbot had other plans. He insisted Hugh be trained additionally in languages and the arts of diplomacy and war . . . made him into a warrior-monk, like the Templars. Then he handed him over to the king . . . a gift, as it were. A very *useful* gift. One that would constantly remind the king of the abbot's loyalty."

"A tool," she said quietly, her mood suddenly sober.

Graham nodded. "He still believes he will one day be dismissed from court to enter the monastery and take vows. But I doubt that will ever happen."

"Why do you say that?"

"His eldest brother was killed five years ago in a border skirmish. His second brother was killed at Crecy. Like it or not, when his father dies, Hugh will succeed him as Earl of Sennett."

The irony of it struck her to the very core. Both she and he had been raised in religious orders. But while she yearned to make a life outside the narrow confines of religious life and vocation, he would gladly reject precious family ties and worldly freedoms to return to them.

"Chloe?" Lisette's voice intruded on her thoughts, and she looked up to find her sister-by-adoption peering at her and Graham from the edge of the partly opened door. "Oh, I did not know you were busy with *le bon monsieur*. I beg you, look inside my trunk for a length of toweling. I would not ask it of you, but"—she glanced with unabashed flirtatiousness at Sir Graham—"I have already taken off all my clothes."

He sprang to his feet as if shot from a bow.

"I have duties." He backed away, his gaze fixed adamantly on the toes of his boots. "If you need assistance, you have but to say the word."

As he fled, Chloe planted her hands on her waist and scowled at the one responsible for his haste. "You must learn to be more modest of eye and speech, Lisette. If you continue to look at men the way you just did Sir Graham, they will most certainly misunderstand."

"Oh"—Lisette glanced after the retreating Graham with a sultry smile—"I doubt that."

HUGH MADE HIS WAY DOWN THE DARK-ened path that hugged the side of the cliff, headed for the fires on the beach below the village. The food and ale that lined his belly had improved his mood. Now, as he paused to survey the camp, he didn't see anything that indicated female presence, and his mood improved still more. He took a deep breath of sea air and strolled down onto the sand.

Two days were gone and, with any luck, only two re-

mained before he discharged his duty and deposited the
five maids in the king's privy chamber. It was heartening
to think of the surprise in store for Edward when he beheld Avalon's surprisingly fair and nubile progeny. It was
less so to think of what would happen to the maids when
they reached Edward's court.

He recalled their artless questions about Windsor.
Their girlish hopes and dreams shone through their carefully edited curiosity. They wanted young and handsome
husbands . . . men of knightly birth, priestly morals, and
princely disposition. And they were bound to be disappointed. Edward would realize instantly what a plum had
fallen into his lap and would undoubtedly give them to
the most advantageously wealthy and militarily capable of
his unmarried nobles. Men like the old Earl of Ketchum . . .
with his fat purse, rickety legs, and fanatical passion for
hunting hounds.

Just imagine Chloe of Guibray with—

No, *don't* imagine.

He shook off thoughts of what their arrival at Edward's
castle would mean and trudged on through the sand.

The driftwood fires cast a golden sphere of security
over the wagons and the men camped on the beach. The
tide was beginning to come in and the gentle rush of
breaking waves provided a rhythmic and restful background for the sounds of their voices. For them, the coming voyage signaled the end of an arduous and uncertain
journey. They had boarded ships bound for France more
than a year and a half ago and in the intervening months
had battled their way across the Aquitaine, then contended
with rogue lords and defiant houses on the border between
French- and English-held territory. Now they were on
their way home. He watched their faces and envied them
their anticipation.

For him, *home* was not a possibility. A small, gray
stone abbey near Oxford was as close to a home as he
had ever known. But it would likely be a long time before
he would see its gates and cloister again, much less take
up a life there. He was bound to Edward for as long as

the king desired his service. And even when the king did release him, there would still be the problem of his inheritance and his old father's dynastic demands.

He settled himself just outside the circle of firelight, on an upturned barrel beside one of the wagons. His thoughts began to drift, and he found himself stroking the back of his hand . . . trying to decide if it felt softer in any way.

Alarmed, he sat upright. He was *not* softer. Not in any damned way. He was a seasoned warrior . . . a soldier in the armies of both his God and his king . . . impervious to the wiles and enticements of the world. Immediately the memory of Chloe of Guibray's face—the details of her hair, her skin, and eyes—rose in his mind's eye to challenge that claim.

An embattled soldier, honesty demanded he admit.

Banishing those images of her took such concentration that he failed to realize, at first, that another object had entered his vision. Pale and rectangular. Bobbing between sea and horizon. Moving steadily closer.

When he succeeded in wrestling Chloe of Guibray back behind the door of the forbidden in his mind, he finally saw it.

A sail.

Chapter Seven

HUGH JUMPED UP AND LOOKED around for Graham. Spotting him across the fire, he called out and pointed toward the sail.

"The ship!"

Suddenly the entire camp was on its feet, looking seaward and cheering.

The ship *Fairwind* followed the tide in to a boisterous welcome. By the time the first longboats reached the beach, Hugh had already organized his men into work details, setting them to transferring cargo from the wagons into the longboats and ultimately into the ship's hold. They worked eagerly, exchanging banter of home, and some even broke into song.

After consulting with the ship's mate on the space available, Hugh positioned himself on the beach to sort the horses they would take and oversee the hazardous process of swimming them out to the ship. He assigned to Graham the task of driving the wagons and cart back up the cliff road, delivering them to the local stableman, and collecting the payment they had negotiated. Against his better judgment, he also charged Graham with collecting the maids and their belongings and hauling them down to the beach.

He was thigh-deep in surf, helping to drag one of the longboats ashore when Graham returned with the cart full of trunks. Behind him in a tightly knit group, came the maids on foot. Hugh waded out of the water toward them and stopped by the fire, momentarily speechless.

They'd been a serious distraction before, but now were nothing short of a temptation. Their gowns were simple and they wore small, plain caps over their unbound hair, but such modest dress only emphasized the extravagance of their natural beauty. One was tall, cool, and delicate, with flaxen hair and skin like alabaster . . . another was short and freckled, with a torrent of vibrant red tresses and pouty-child lips. The third was a sultry, dark-eyed vision with a swirl of black hair and curves that tried the seams of her gown. And the fourth was as elegant and regal as a Greek statue, with eyes like emeralds and skin like polished marble. It was as if they had been purposefully chosen to represent the full range of feminine attractions.

He glanced around and found that every man left on the beach had stopped dead and was staring slack-jawed at them.

Chagrined by his own silence, he motioned Graham to begin loading their trunks into the longboat, and then looked out at the ship they would have to share. By the time they reached London, it was going to seem awfully damned small. He wondered if it would be possible to stow the maids somewhere below deck and out of sight . . . say . . . with the horses. He could just imagine what *she* would say to that.

"Chloe of Guibray," he demanded, turning back to them with a scowl. It was a testament to their powers of distraction that he only now realized she was missing. "Where is she?"

"She told us to come ahead," the one called Alaina answered as she and the others stared in wonder at the longboats and the ship anchored offshore. "That is our ship? We're leaving soon?"

"With the tide," he said irritably. "You just left her there?"

"She said she would be a while yet," the little redhead informed him.

"We don't have a while . . . we're leaving *now*." He rubbed his face vigorously. "Graham! Get these females loaded on the next boat and stay with them." He struck off for that isolated cottage, muttering, "If she makes us miss this tide—"

THE OTHERS WERE GONE AND SHE WAS finally alone. Heaving a sigh of relief, Chloe added another log to the fire, filled two buckets from the rain barrel, and laid out her precious soap and toweling. As much as she loved her new "sisters," she was in dire need of a bit of peace and solitude just now. She stripped her male garments, muttering "good riddance," and stepped into the oat water. Closing her eyes to the state of the gray slurry, she knelt in the tub and began to splash it on her and rub handfuls of it over her skin. When she was well-scrubbed and covered with a thin, oaty paste, she reached for one of the buckets of rainwater and rinsed herself clean. Then she wetted her hair and used her soap on it. She had just finished her hair and stood for a final rinse when a loud voice outside the door caused her to nearly jump out of her skin.

"Open up!"

She gasped and clasped her throat with both hands. Then the door rattled and thumped against the crude latch.

"No! Stop!" She lurched from the tub onto one of the water-soaked wooden planks they'd laid on the dirt floor, just as the aged wood around the latch splintered with a resounding "crack." The door flew open and she was caught halfway between tub and table. A large, dark form surged inside the cottage, and she screamed and dived for her toweling.

She banged into the table—"Owww!"—and then dropped behind it as she frantically wrapped the linen around her. With her heart beating in her throat, she stuck her head up over the edge and found herself facing none other than Sir Hugh. He stood with his head bent to avoid the low roof beams, staring at her.

"What are you doing?" Her voice was thin and shrill. "Get out of here!"

"Y-you were supposed to stay with the others." He sounded a bit reedy himself.

"How dare you break in on me?" She glanced down to make certain she was decently covered, then rose. "Have you no shame?"

"I didn't know you were still . . . the others said . . . I thought you were just . . ." He staggered back, but forgot to duck and smacked the low door frame with a resounding *thunk*. He grabbed his head between his hands and stumbled back outside. "Dammit, dammit, *dammit!*"

"At least have the decency to close the door!"

But the rotten planking now hung askew, attached by only one hinge, and he was staggering around dazed and doubled over. Frantic to cover herself, she seized her shift and managed to pull it over her head. It caught on her damp toweling and wet hair, and she had to wrestle it down over her body.

"The ship is here and we're leaving tonight . . . now," he called out, bracing on his knees. "I came up here to haul you down to the boat."

"And all but ripped the door from its hinges," she said, tugging furiously on the toweling beneath her garment and finally succeeding in removing it.

"You were supposed to be finished." He straightened abruptly and turned his back to the door opening. "And if you had been, I wouldn't have had to—"

"It's not my fault you charged through a latched door like a wounded bear." She wanted desperately to throw something at that broad set of shoulders.

"But it was your fault that I—"

He halted, but her eyes flew wide as his statement finished itself in her mind. . . . *saw her naked.* Then he confirmed it.

"What the devil were you doing standing there without a stitch on?"

She covered her heart with her hand, truly shocked. He made it sound so vile, so . . . intentional.

"I was *bathing*. That's the way it's done, without garments. Or don't you English practice that particular refinement?" She reached for her gown and yanked it over her head. "Your men seem never to have heard of it."

"Oh, we English bathe all right. At the *proper* time. In the *proper* manner."

How dare he suggest that her mode of bathing was in any way *im*proper?

"I had a thousand fleabites to treat. What could possibly be improper about washing myself and dabbing on a bit of—" She paused, glaring at his back, realizing what he meant and dumbfounded by the implication that she had somehow contrived to have him glimpse her as God and Nature made her. She blushed from the core out. Every inch of her body was suddenly red with humiliation . . . which quickly gave way to anger.

Trembling now, she settled her gown over her shift and freed her hair from beneath it. Her fingers felt as thick as sausages when she tried to draw and tie the laces at her sides.

How dare he say such a thing to her? What had she ever done to make him think her wanton or immoral? As she paused, struggling to stay in control, an earlier insight returned. His snarls and insults weren't about her, they were about him. *He* was embarrassed, so he accused *her*.

She wiped off the soles of her feet and stepped into her slippers.

Looking again at his impenetrable back, she recalled what Sir Graham had just said about his monastic ambitions. It was his desire to forsake "the flesh" and all worldly pursuits and pleasures. No doubt the sight of her nakedness was an unwelcome reminder of the "flesh" he intended to forswear.

Then she thought of the austere and unflappable brothers she had seen when they stopped for lodging at the convent while on pilgrimage. A brief, unintended glimpse of nakedness would have proved no trouble for them . . . or for any monk truly committed to a life of purity and contemplation.

The memory of the way Sir Hugh had trapped and held her in the darkened woods came flooding back, causing her to catch her breath. Clearly, Hugh of Sennet was not as monkish as he would like to think. Then it wasn't the sight of her nakedness that infuriated him so, it was his own wayward response to it!

She plopped her cap on her wet, tousled hair, gathered her belongings into her arms, and pushed him aside as she bolted from the cottage. He bristled at the contact and glowered as she halted before him and looked him in the eye.

"What bothers you more, Sir Hugh?" she demanded with stubborn insight. "That you saw me naked or that you *liked it*?"

She could hear him sputtering and storming along the trail behind her as she strode down to the beach. She could see his incendiary glare on her as Mattias helped her into one of the longboats and the sailors rowed her out to the ship. She could feel his need to respond weighting the air around her as he followed her onto the ship's deck and ushered her and the other maids into a hastily constructed corral of trunks and crates lashed to the rear of the main deck.

After ordering them to "sit!" on the trunks and to stay there until told otherwise, he paused near her and lowered his voice.

"*I did not.*"

After an hour of hugging the coast and waiting for a favorable wind, the sails filled and the ship turned westward. The Channel was unusually calm for springtime, and the maids' fears of being washed overboard soon dispersed. When they were permitted to visit the aft railing to answer nature's requirement, she took a circuitous route back to their makeshift berth on the cargo and passed close enough for him to hear her.

"Did, too."

He flinched visibly, and as she climbed the two steps to their makeshift quarters on deck, she could feel his frustration simmering. As the waxing moon rose in the east, he secured a stack of blankets from the captain and carried them to the maids. He refused to look at her, but as he turned to go, he made certain to veer close enough to her to mutter audibly.

"Did not."

She wrapped herself in one of the blankets and took her place amongst the others curled up on the trunks for a bit of sleep. But as the other maids dozed and the men of their escort nodded off, she found herself strangely awake and aware of Sir Hugh's location. Propping herself up on her elbow, she located him and watched him pace the deck. He reacted with a start each time one of the ship's crew moved across the deck in the moonlight.

He was tense and unsettled inside, and she guessed that their confrontation was at least partly responsible. Good, she thought. As the abbess sometimes said after a confrontation with Father Phillipe, men needed to have their delusions challenged. Especially ones regarding themselves. It kept them honest and humble. And if there was anything *Sir Hubris* needed, it was a bit of humility.

He must have felt her gaze on him, for he turned slowly toward the stack of cargo, searching it visually and finally spotting her. He stilled and stared at her across that moonlit space.

They had a great deal in common, she thought. Upbringing. Education. Sense of duty. In another life, at another time, they might have been allies, comrades, fellow pilgrims, or even teacher and pupil. But here and now they were set irrevocably at odds by the fact that they had been born into separate divisions of humanity: male and female. And the desire that the Almighty intended to bring men and women together was, for them, the very obstacle that prevented all possibility of mutuality or understanding.

It was a sobering insight and produced a sense of limitation that would shape her world for some time to come. She was a woman, and because of that, some doors, some minds, and some hearts would be forever closed to her.

But the sense of loss that discovery produced in her was something he would never suffer. For him, the longings of the human heart were worldly dross that would only interfere with his scholarly and spiritual ambitions.

Wretched monk.

In the moonlight she soundlessly lashed him with one last accusation before settling back beneath her blanket.

"Did, too."

THE NEXT MORNING, AS THEY REACHED the English shore and started up the tidal waters of the Thames River, there was an air of expectation aboard the small barque. The men of the escort party lined the railings, pointing out various landmarks, quays, and villages, and a flotilla of barges which was said to be something of a town for sailors who superstitiously shunned dry land altogether. Here and there the vistas broadened to include views of fields being planted and flocks newly sheared and set out to pasture once more. It was a glimpse of home for the men and of the future for the maids, who watched anxiously from perches on the crates and barrels of their collective dowry.

As Chloe looked at the eager faces of her new sisters, the weight of her responsibility settled squarely on her shoulders. She had promised Sister Archibald that she would see the others properly mated and wedded. But after the rigors of the journey and seeing the attitude of some men regarding women's character and abilities, her confidence in her ability to keep that promise was beginning to waver.

Still, her heart beat faster at this glimpse of what might have once been and certainly would become her homeland. This place held the keys to both her past and her future. While she contemplated that, her gaze fell on Sir

Graham, who was strolling by and nodding to the maids perched on trunks and crates.

"Good morning," she called to him as he neared. He beamed good humor as he corrected his course to join her.

"It won't be long now." He leaned against the barrels and nodded toward the greening fields around them. "We'll reach London by noon and be under way to Windsor within an hour or two."

"We're not staying in London?"

"Just long enough to take on a pilot and unload some of the captain's cargo. This vessel has a shallow enough draft to carry us upriver to Windsor."

"Oh." Her spirits sank. "I thought we would see London first."

"Believe me"—he chuckled—"you won't be missing a great deal."

That hint that expectation and reality might have little to do with each other caused her to resettle herself uneasily on the barrel top.

"Tell me about the king, Sir Graham. What kind of man is he?"

He thought for a moment.

"Decisive. Determined. The kind of man others would follow regardless of rank. He knows what he wants and has the will and strength to take it."

"Like the Aquitaine," she observed. "And how does he treat women? His wife? The ladies of his household?"

"His wife, Queen Philippa, he treats quite well. She is often in his company and often with child. But his mother, Isabella, he exiled at the beginning of his reign."

Her dismay must have shown in her face, for he smiled.

"You needn't fear. He demands chivalrous behavior toward the women of his court, and feels a great responsibility to set a high standard for his knights and nobles. Chivalry demands that men of noble birth defend and provide for the weak and defenseless."

He spoke as if he assumed that the king would naturally include them among the "weak and defenseless."

"Does he listen to advice, or does he insist he already has the Almighty's word on every matter that comes before him?"

He looked at her with mild surprise and then canted his head, studying her in a new light. "You've a sharp wit, Chloe of Guibray. The king appreciates a keen mind. I think neither of you will be disappointed in the other."

She relaxed a bit, praying that he was right.

"And will you be going home after you've delivered us safely, Sir Graham?" she asked, searching for a less volatile topic.

"No, I won't see my home again for some time to come. It's quite a ways from London . . . west . . . on the coast of Devon."

"Perhaps you can tell me." She saw no harm in asking: "Are there any Gilberts in your Devonshire?"

"Gilberts." He scoured his memory. "I'm not certain I know of any . . . in Devon or elsewhere. But, then, I have no head for lineages and kinships. I have trouble recalling the begats and bequeaths of my own house. Why?"

"I have relations by that name," she said as casually as possible. "I was hoping I might be able to meet them . . . perhaps visit someday. Who would be the keeper of such information? Is there a record of noble houses somewhere?"

"Absolutely." Sir Graham laughed. "It's called *the rolls of taxation*. If there's a House of Gilbert anywhere, it will be on the Lord Treasurer's list."

"Ah, yes." She nodded, relieved to have a place to start. "The tax rolls."

His gaze fell to the hands she had tightly clasped in her lap, and she separated them and smoothed her gown over her knees.

"I confess I would be a bit anxious for connections, too, in your shoes," he said, lowering his voice. "Sent away from a safe and familiar home to a distant land to marry a perfect stranger."

"A stranger he will most certainly be. But I pray every

day that he will not prove *perfect*." Seeing that her candor surprised him, she blushed.

"You would not have a *perfect* husband?" He seemed truly puzzled.

"He will not be getting a perfect wife, after all. And we are more forgiving of others when aware of our own shortcomings."

He studied her for a moment, then chuckled. "You have no cause to worry. I have yet to meet an Englishman without at least a few flaws." He turned a warming gaze on the other maids, sitting nearby. "Unlike the maids who come from the Sisters of the Order of the Brides of Virtue." His attention was quickly intercepted by Lisette, who slid from her seat on a trunk and swayed sinuously toward them. He froze like a bird entranced by an approaching snake.

"Good morning, Sir Graham," she said with a smile so demure that it almost seemed a parody of that virtue.

"Good morning." He stiffened noticeably.

"Has Chloe been asking you about our new home?"

"She has." He gave them both a terse nod, pivoted, and strode away.

Lisette's eyes danced as she watched his retreating back. "Have you noticed the way his ears go flaming red when he's flummoxed?"

"Lisette"—Chloe frowned, studying the maid of Mornay's all too visible ambition—"How do you know he isn't already wedded?"

Lisette folded her arms and turned a knowing look on Chloe. "No man who is well wedded and bedded is adverse to a bit of feminine adoration. Only a man who is free and afraid of being caught would flee a mere maid's company."

Chloe thought on that as Lisette swayed back to the others. Then she slid from her seat, wondering if that knowledge came from Lisette's experiences before coming to the convent or if it was just passed along to Frenchwomen in their mother's milk. She started toward the railing and looked up just in time to see Sir Hugh halt in his tracks, reverse course, and stride vigorously back up the deck to avoid her.

She glanced over her shoulder at Lisette, who had seen his reaction and smiled as if her judgment had just been vindicated.

Alert now, she glanced back at Sir Hugh as he reached the bow of the ship and leaned on the railing. Free and afraid of being caught. It certainly seemed to fit. But who did the insufferable man think was likely to chase him? Her?

SHORTLY AFTER MIDDAY, AS THE BOAT nudged away from the stone quay in the heart of London's congested waterfront, Hugh joined Graham at the bow of the ship. Together they leaned on the railing and watched the sailors chanting as they pulled rhythmically together to raise the sail.

"It won't be long now," Graham said, looking toward the rear deck where a troublesome bouquet of femininity sat in full, enticing bloom. "They'll soon be the king's problem."

"A damned relief that will be," Hugh responded, refusing to look at them again. He'd *looked* all night. All bloody night. He'd scarcely had more than a wink of sleep. Every movement on deck, each snap of the sails, every sound of feet on the deck had brought him to his feet with his hand on the hilt of his blade. More than once his gaze had met old Mattias's, Withers's, or Fenster's across the deck, and he'd realized they were watching, too. Nobody, it seemed, got much rest. Except *them*.

Suddenly he couldn't resist looking at them. Searching them for that dark blue woolen cap . . . that shining fall of auburn hair . . .

"You know"—Graham folded his arms across his chest and rubbed his bristled chin—"my father has been asking when I might take another bride."

Hugh snapped upright.

"Ohhh, no."

"Why not?" Graham straightened, too, and looked down the deck to the maids. "I'll have to produce an heir soon, and I don't need a large dowry. That little Margarete . . . pretty as a spring robin . . . biddable and sweet-natured . . ."

"Have you lost your mind?" Hugh grabbed his friend's arm. "She was raised in a bloody *convent.*"

"Ohhh"—Graham's chest swelled with male pride—"I think I could coax her past that 'convent modesty.' "

"You don't have a clue, do you?" Hugh tightened his grip. "They've *taught* them things in that convent. All kinds of things. They can *read.*"

"The hell you say." Graham's smile vanished. "You're making that up."

"I am not. Chloe of Guibray said they all learned Church Latin . . . and some even read English and French and Greek."

Graham thought on that for a moment, then adamantly dismissed it. "Not Margarete. I'm sure of it. She hasn't the wits or the constitution for such stuff."

Hugh considered his friend's wishful thinking. "And what if the king decided to give you that dark-eyed one—Lisette—instead?"

Graham sobered instantly. "I'd flee to the nearest monastery and shave my head. She's trouble, that one. Those *come-ye-hither* looks of hers. Have you seen the way she walks? As if every step she takes gives her some wicked pleas—" Embarrassed by his own potent conjuring, he shook it off and glanced irritably at Hugh. "It will be interesting to see who Edward sentences to a life with Chloe of Guibray. Now, *there's* a handful."

Handful. The word triggered visions in Hugh's sleep-starved brain . . . the moisture on her bare skin shining like golden dew . . . her long, damp hair glinting as it clung to her bare shoulders . . . and generous *handfuls* of—

He rubbed his eyes to banish that image and left Graham puzzling over the words he ground out as he walked away.

"I did not."

Chapter Eight

THE GREAT ROUND TOWER OF WIND-
sor Castle came into view well before the boat arrived at the stone quay that served the castle and the
bustling town that huddled outside the stone curtain wall.
They were greeted first by guards posted at the dock who
recognized Sir Hugh and Sir Graham and quickly provided a cart to carry the maids, and wagons to carry their
chests and dower goods up the winding path to the castle
gate.

The air was festive with sound and delicious smells as
the cart bounced along the road that wound along between
merchant shops, craftsmen's stalls, and pushcarts laden
with everything from tinware to hot meat pies. At first
Chloe and the others were entranced by the bustle and the
novelty of it all. It was like a summer fair, with peddlers,
jugglers, hawkers, and a crush of common folk . . . tradesmen shouting out their wares . . . colorful banners snapping in the breeze . . . children scurrying . . . craftsmen's
hammers ringing out. By the time they reached the castle
grounds, the maids had realized how little of the world
they had glimpsed until now. Paling, they sought the comfort of each other's hands.

As the cart rumbled across the drawbridge, Chloe sat
stiff as a plank, praying in earnest, promising the saints
fervent devotion and the Almighty scrupulous obedience
in exchange for help. Buckets and barrels of help.

She looked around at the massive stone walls, the
fierce iron portcullis that hung over their heads as they
passed through the gate, and the great stone ramparts bris-
tling with scaffolding and covered with workmen who
looked no larger than ants. She wasn't sure what she had
expected, but this was far larger and more intimidating
than anything she might have imagined. This was the seat
of the power that had floated an army across the Channel
and taken vast territories in France by force of arms.

And she had supposed she could blithely walk into the
King of England's hall and demand that he permit her
some say in the marriages he intended to bind his nobles'
loyalty and reward their accomplishments? She had to be
mad.

At least Sister Archibald would have had a habit to
remind him of the weight and authority of the church
behind her. The realization left her reeling: *It should have
been Sister Archie who came to see to their welfare.* How
selfish of her to scheme and contrive to take the old
Sister's place when the abbess—in all her experience and
wisdom—had decreed that she should stay and serve their
beloved order!

Dearest Heaven and all the Saints Above, she pleaded,
HELP!

As they wound their way toward the great round tower
that commanded the hill, the town, and the surrounding
countryside, they spotted a cluster of people gathered at
the base of a smaller round tower under construction. A
maze of wooden beams extended up the exposed center
of the structure, some of which hung out over the rising
walls and were fitted with ropes and pulleys for hauling
stone to the top. Stone-cutters, hod-carriers, apron-
wrapped master masons, boys bearing armloads of scrolls,
and a variety of well-dressed men had collected, craning
their necks and offering opinions on the work.

Spotting the king at the center of the crowd, Hugh dismounted and shoved his way through the assembly to find Edward of England holding a freshly cut stone, examining the workmanship while listening to a debate between his architect and master mason on one side and his councillors and Lord Treasurer on the other. As Hugh parted the edge of the crowd, the stone chips all around crunched underfoot, and the king looked up. His face lit with a smile of relief.

"You're back!" he declared, dropping the stone and halting the debate over the cost of construction in the same instant. He acknowledged Hugh's bow with an extended arm, and Hugh rose and clasped it.

"I've brought the duke's daughters, Sire. Safe and sound." He held out the leather-bound sheaf of documents. "I hereby deliver them into your wise and merciful hands."

"Here and now? Excellent!" the king asked, deflecting the packet of documents to the hands of a portly fellow wearing a great gold chain of office, then craning his neck to look for the maidens. "I confess a strong curiosity about these long-lost offspring." Spotting the cart and escort party not far away, he pulled Hugh closer and began to move. "Ugly as sin, are they?"

"Not quite, Sire," Hugh said stiffly.

"Not quite ugly or not quite sin-worthy?" The king's desultory laugh caused a wave of knowing smiles in the courtiers clustered around him. "Let us see if these wenches are truly worth a duke's ransom."

Ten paces from the cart the King of England stopped dead, staring at a bevy of bright, sun-blushed faces with widened eyes, set in a torrent of shining tresses. The crowd around him grew quiet as he studied them and, one by one, they modestly lowered their gazes and heads.

"These are the maids?" His Highness seemed to choke on the notion. "These are Avalon's daughters?"

"They are," Sir Hugh declared. "As presented to me by the abbess of the Convent of the Brides of Virtue." He strode to the rear of the cart, motioned to them, and began to hand them down to the ground.

All watched the king take in their fresh countenances, appealing figures, and demure curtsies. His surprise and pleasure were both evident as he strolled closer and examined them.

"Take note, Bromley. We've uncovered Avalon's secret treasure!"

The stout, florid-faced fellow holding the adoption documents chuckled as he came forward to join the king. "One should never underestimate the Brides of Virtue. You recall, Sire, I told you about the Earl of Whitmore's dealings with them. They sent a 'husband judge' home with him . . . made him pass a 'husband test' before giving him a bride."

The king barked a laugh that registered royal recall. "So they did."

The husband test. Despite her anxiety, or perhaps because of it, Chloe was struck forcefully by that casual reminder. Sister Archie's wry references to the test required of the Earl of Whitmore had never failed to fill the abbess with a cryptic delight. Clearly they shared some secret, and Heaven knew, the abbess loved a bit of intrigue. . . .

"Lady Alaina de Cluny . . . Lady Helen of Ghent . . ." Sir Hugh was introducing them to the king, using their newly acquired status as a duke's daughters for the first time. Chloe felt her throat tightening and her tension rising. Everything was happening so quickly. But this could be her best chance to speak to the king, perhaps her only chance! "Lady Margarete of Cologne . . . Lady Lisette de Mornay . . . and Lady Chloe of Guibray."

Speak. Say something. Anything!

Chloe dropped on weakened knees into a deep curtsy before raising her face to him.

"I have been honored with the duty of conveying to Your Highness the greetings and good wishes of the abbess of the Convent of the Brides of Virtue."

"Indeed." The king's brows rose as he nodded, allowing her to rise.

"And if it please Your Highness, I also bear a more solemn charge from the abbess." When he continued to look at her with interest, she went on. "I am to see that the convent's obligations to Your Highness, to the good duke, and to my beloved sisters are properly discharged."

"And what obligations are these?" The king studied her while watching Sir Hugh's eyes narrow in censure.

"To be certain that the daughters of the Duke of Avalon are properly matched . . . to present the noblemen Your Highness has selected as our husbands with the best possible wives." She clasped her hands tightly. "May I inquire—"

"Apologies, Sire." Sir Hugh's nostrils flared briefly before he turned to the king. "It has been a long journey and the duke's daughters—"

"Have a question that I wish to hear," the king said, waving aside Sir Hugh's objections.

"Thank you, Your Highness." Chloe flashed a heartfelt smile. "Our abbess merely wished to inquire whether you have decided what method you will use to match us with the husbands you have chosen."

The king's pensive expression said she had just created a new wrinkle in the fabric of the royal mind.

"For if you have not yet decided how it will be done, may the good abbess of our convent be so bold as to suggest a way?"

"This is not something to tire the king with, Lady Chloe," Sir Hugh insisted. His frustration grew more visible when the king gave another, more emphatic wave that forbade efforts to silence her.

"I will hear the good abbess's suggestion," he declared with a twitch of amusement at one corner of his mouth.

"The abbess proposes that the convent's 'wife test' be applied. For surely it is Your Majesty's desire to see his nobles not only wedded, but happily paired with well-suited wives."

"Surely." The king shot a look at the one he called

Bromley, who came to attention. "The 'wife test.' And who does your abbess suggest to administer this ordeal?"

"Oh, it is no ordeal, Highness. It is merely a time of assessment and revelation, meant to benefit both the man and the maid."

"A courtship, then?"

"More a test of compatibility, Highness. The abbess suggests your humble servant"—she bowed her head modestly—"to carry out this task."

"Forgive Lady Chloe, Sire." Sir Hugh's face was crimson and his fists were clenched as he stepped partway between her and the king. "She has acted as the maidens' representative during the journey and—having been raised in a convent—is woefully unacquainted with royal protocol."

Chloe held her breath, staring first at Sir Hugh's broad back and then around him at the king's intent expression.

"How am I to know that you speak for the abbess?" the king demanded.

Chloe felt her tension begin to melt. *This* she was prepared for.

"I believe there is a letter to that effect in the documents. The abbess took pains to acquaint me with the writs of and the contents of the dower goods. She appointed me to speak for the five of us."

"Five?" The king looked from her to the others and, for the first time, seemed to realize that she was included in the tally. "There are *five* of you?"

"Yes, Highness." Her tension came flooding back. "With the stroke of a quill, the duke reclaimed *five* daughters." She held her breath.

"Five at one stroke. The duke wields a *mighty quill* indeed," the king quipped, sending a titter through the crowd. Then he settled his gaze on her in a way that reminded her of old Sister Abbingale, whose singular gift to the convent community had been the unerring detection of dirty ears.

"Very well. I shall consider this letter and the good abbess's suggestion." He looked squarely at Sir Hugh.

"With the queen indisposed, I have asked Lady Marcella of Hector to take charge of the maids. She will see them settled, and they will dine with us this evening in the great hall." He nodded to them as they sank into hasty curtsies, then turned and strode off with the crowd parting ahead of him like the biblical Red Sea.

The minute the king disappeared from sight, Sir Hugh whirled, clamped a hand on Chloe's arm, and pulled her forcefully toward the great round tower, leaving the others to stare at each other and then scurry after them.

"What a damned fool thing to do!" Sir Hugh ground out, just loud enough for her to hear. "Have you no sense of place or person?"

"I only did what the abbess would have expected of me," she said, struggling to keep up with his long strides.

"Then your abbess is a fool. No woman, not even an abbess, can issue commands to the King of England."

"The abbess merely offered the king assistance in deciding who marries whom."

"And *you*—a mere maid—to put yourself forward as some authority on the mating of men and women—"

"I have not claimed any sort of authority," she hissed back. "I have simply offered to administer the convent's test of compatibility. *The wife test*. If you were getting a wife, wouldn't you—"

"If *I* were getting a wife, I'd impale myself on the nearest blade!" he snarled, lengthening his stride.

She glared at the back of his rigidly held shoulders as he pulled her along.

"And probably not even leave room on it for your bride to join you!"

THE GREAT HALL PROVED TO BE LARGER than most churches and inspired the same sort of awe and reverence. The beams that supported the roof were handsomely carved, the windows were made of colored glass, and above the long tables hung great wrought-iron chandeliers. The floors were made of smooth slate and covered with rushes only under the massive U-shaped table.

The daughters of Avalon were escorted through the hall and handed over to an older lady with a pronounced squint and a rather distracted air . . . the aforementioned Lady Marcella of Hector. They followed her through a series of passages and up at least two sets of steps . . . which took a while, since her eyesight was quite poor and she had to move slowly.

At last they arrived in a sizable chamber furnished with four raised cots topped with straw-filled mattresses, an open hearth, and a great beaten-copper tub for bathing. Lady Marcella squinted good-naturedly up at each of them, trying to put faces to names. Chloe was last, and just as Lady Marcella took Chloe's hands, she dropped them.

"Virgo's Virtue," she declared, counting the maids again. "Five! There are more of you than there are beds. This will never do. How could we have made such a mistake?" She hurried out to call servants to correct the imbalance.

As soon as the old lady's footsteps faded, the others turned on Chloe with expressions ranging from outrage to panic.

"We're to be *tested*?" Alaina flushed with indignation.

"You knew about this, Chloe, and you didn't warn us?" Helen asked.

"*Sacre coeur!*" Lisette was taken aback for entirely different reasons. "How can you know how good a wife we will make—you are not even a man!"

Margarete looked devastated. "What if we don't pass this test? Will they send us back to the convent? Do we still get to be the duke's daughters?"

Their reaction to her hasty gambit hadn't occurred to Chloe. How was she going to reassure them, short of telling them there wasn't any "wife test"?

"No, no." She rushed to take Margarete's wringing hands and put an arm around Helen's stiff shoulders. "This isn't a test to see if we're worthy. We're already the duke's adopted daughters—nothing can change that.

This is a test that allows the abbess to match men and maids . . . by learning something of the man's true needs and nature and matching it to a maid's essence and abilities."

That seemed to mollify them a bit.

Alaina's nose unwrinkled. "Then we don't have to bake bread or stuff mattresses or mend garments?"

"Heavens, no." Chloe tried not to think about the fact that she hadn't a clue what she *would* have them do if the king agreed to the "abbess's" request.

"But what if the king does not accept the convent's wife test?" Lisette asked. "How will he decide who we wed?"

"Line us up and pair us off by height?" Alaina said with an edge that contained both anxiety and umbrage.

"Display us to his unwedded noblemen like a tray of plum tarts and tell them to take their pick?" Helen, too, was rigid with indignation.

"I don't know," Chloe admitted, trying not to show her uneasiness.

The chamber was west-facing and warmed by the late afternoon sun. One by one, they turned away to settle on the cots, not speaking, trying to digest all they had experienced in the last few hours and to comprehend the fact that in a few hours their fates would be sealed by a king who knew nothing about them but considered them his own personal assets, to be disposed of as he saw fit.

After a time Chloe surfaced from her thoughts to find all four of the others staring at her anxiously, expectantly.

"What will we do, Chloe?" Margarete said in a small voice.

She swallowed hard and drew herself up straight. They looked to her for direction and she owed it to them and to dear old Sister Archie to provide it. If the king rejected the "wife test," she would just have to think of something else.

"I'll tell you what we will do. We will don our best gowns and go down to the great hall to dine with the king and his nobles. They will stare at us and search us for flaws and find none. We will be the most modest and respectful and mannerly young women this court has ever seen." Her determination grew with each word. "The good Sisters have taught us every subject and skill we could need as chatelaines of noble households. We must demand respect for their labors by being so virtuous and capable that we make these Englishmen wish every wife in England came from—"

There was a thumping and voices outside the door, and she sprang to her feet as a brawny fist was laid to the iron-bound planks. She called permission to enter, and the door flew back to admit several servants overseen by none other than Mattias and Withers. The maids brightened at the sight of familiar faces and hurried to greet them.

"Had to make sure ye got yer chests." Mattias wrung the woolen hauberk in his hands and looked around the chamber. "F-fine billet ye got here."

"Thank you, Mattias," Chloe said, following his gaze around the chamber. "Will you and Withers be released soon, to go home?"

"Naw." Mattias wagged his head and Withers copied him. "We ain't got no fam'ly. Our old lord, he got killed at Crecy, an' Sir Hugh said we could go join his household, up north. Me and Withers here, Fenster an' Willum and some others . . . we said we would."

"So you'll be going to Sir Hugh's home?" She felt a sudden sinking in her stomach at the thought of them staying with Sir Hugh. She stood straighter to compensate. "It was good of him to offer you a place."

They nodded and smiled awkwardly. Mattias looked as if he had more to say, but they backed to the door before he stopped and spoke again.

"Me an' the men, we wish ye Godspeed. And if ye ever need anythin' . . . just send word and we'll come."

Chloe felt tears welling in her eyes and was on the verge of embarrassing herself when Margarete flew past her and flung her arms around the burly old soldier's neck.

One by one they hugged Mattias and Withers, and by the time they were finished there wasn't a dry eye in the chamber. The men ducked out the door, wiping their noses and grumbling about the way the dust in the castle made their eyes water. Chloe and the others watched them go, knowing that bittersweet farewell marked the true end of the journey and the beginning of their new and uncertain lives as English ladies.

THE TORCHES WERE LIT, A FIRE CRACKLED in the huge stone hearth, and the great hall was already full of people when they arrived. The serving was beginning, though there were a number of men still clustered around the hearth, drinking, and a number of finely dressed ladies were just arriving. The duke's daughters trailed Lady Marcella like a row of downy ducklings around the linen-draped table toward the king's chair at the center of the long, U-shaped board.

Silence followed in a wave as they passed the nobles, knights, and ladies of the court; talk ceased as they approached and started anew the instant they were past. Servers with trays and pitchers and pots on poles paused to watch as they swept by. Not a head in the room didn't turn to follow their progress and watch them approach the king.

In honor of the occasion the maids had dressed in their finest garments: gowns of soft, supple woolen adorned by intricate silk embroidery that curled and entwined over necks, sleeves, and hems. Loden green, sweet russet, marigold yellow, dusty claret, and hollyhock blue . . . the colors had been chosen to compliment their strikingly different coloring, and together they created the impression of a vibrant, living rainbow.

Until that moment, feeling scores of pairs of eyes focused in judgment on them, Chloe had never envied Helen, Alaina, and Margarete their skill with a needle. She glanced self-consciously at her own gown, with its lack of ornamentation, and told herself that her worth lay in other talents. Reading and writing and . . . just possibly . . . hoodwinking kings into listening to her.

Lady Marcella led them before the king himself, where she paused and executed a perfect curtsy that set the maids bobbing to copy her.

So this was how a king dined, Chloe thought as she took in the king's ermine-trimmed silk tunic, jeweled coronet, ornate gilded chair, and the heavy gold dishes and wine cup arrayed before him. To King Edward's left sat a lavishly dressed man wearing velvets and a lesser coronet. Lady Marcella squinted to be certain who it was, then greeted him as "Your Grace" and motioned to them behind her back, instructing them to imitate her display of respect. To the king's immediate right sat the same "Lord Bromley" who had accompanied the king earlier that day.

A motion of the king's head dismissed them to the care of a page who led them to a rank of prime seats above the common run of nobles and surprisingly near the king himself. As they were seated, old Lady Marcella informed them: "You have just made your curtsies to the King of England, the Duke of Bedford on his left, and the Earl of Bromley, the Lord Treasurer of England, on his right. Bedford is the one man in the kingdom who can best the king at chess and live."

"The Earl of Bromley is the Lord Treasurer?" Chloe looked back at the portly fellow with the great chain of office around his neck and the shrewd look in his eye. "Is he the one who keeps the tax rolls with the lists of noble houses?"

"He is indeed." The old lady chuckled. "The king declares he is the one man in the kingdom who knows the secret of getting blood from turnips."

She chuckled at Chloe's widened eyes and beckoned a servant over to fill their cups. Before long they were being waited upon by a steady stream of servants bearing platters, baskets, and pots. They were all so intent on remembering table customs and sneaking peeks at the elegant headdresses the ladies were wearing that it was some time before Chloe became aware of an odd prickle in her skin.

Across the hall, on the far wing of the banquet table,

a number of young men were gathered in a tight cluster, engaged in a heated exchange with someone in their midst. Several times they paused to stare over their shoulders at her and her sisters, then returned to their conversation with increased vigor. When they returned to their seats, farther down the great table, she discovered Sir Hugh had been at the center of that volatile clique and now was staring at her with a face like a thundercloud.

She refused to quail or cower, but the strength required to keep up that resolve left her little energy to enjoy her first banquet. So she sat like a bolt of unembellished woolen, scarcely able to taste her food, praying that the king would render his decision soon and end this wretched suspense.

Hugh had watched his former charges enter the hall and conquer it without so much as a sidelong glance. He studied the shining hair, sparkling eyes, and shy, maidenly smiles that were sending every unwedded man in the hall . . . and a goodly number of the married ones . . . into an acquisitive frenzy.

That was an ache for Edward's head, he told himself. None of his concern.

But moments later his thoughts circled stubbornly back to the problem of what would become of them. He had tried to speak to the king again as the day wore on, but Edward was closeted first with his treasurer and then with his pregnant wife for most of the time. He thought of the eager young nobles who had just quizzed him on the maids and gave Graham, seated nearby and mooning visibly over them, a dour look.

He had tried to talk to his friend, but, against all advice, the rut-maddened wretch had raced all over Windsor looking for the Earl of Norwich, hoping to get him to carry a matrimonial petition to the king. Upon learning that Norwich had already returned to his estates, Graham hotfooted it to Bromley to see if the Lord Treasurer might be willing to do him the same service. He was practically panting for a Bride of Virtue.

Hugh's nose curled.

Undignified.

Unmanly.

He glanced across the hall at Chloe of Guibray and thought again of her audacious conduct and of the king's reaction to it. Clearly, Edward was amused, which was not necessarily a good thing. The king was known to take—*and even make*—diversion from the predicaments of his courtiers and was not above using even his most devoted knights and nobles for a bit of sport. Imagine what he could do with a brash insolent young wench with enough beauty, wit, and innocence to be truly dangerous. If only there were some way to peel open her head and pour some caution and common sense into—

"Chloe of Guibray. Lady Chloe."

With a start, Hugh realized that it was the king who had spoken. Edward, too, had been staring intently at her.

"Yes, Your Highness?" Chloe of Guibray sprang up like an untied sapling, drawing old Lady Marcella up with her.

Chapter Nine

A HUSH FELL OVER THE ASSEMBLY as the king turned to Hugh and gave him a worrisome look of appraisal before swinging his gaze back to Chloe.

Hugh's stomach contracted into a knot.

"I believe your abbess has offered your services in assisting me with a weighty decision," the king continued.

"Yes, Your Highness." At the sound of her clear, lilting voice, all other conversation in the hall abruptly stopped.

"I have given the matter consideration," the king continued. "But before I render a decision, I must know more about this 'wife test.' How long will it take? You see, I would not keep my nobles from their lands any longer than necessary at this time of year."

The slight pause before she replied went unnoticed by everyone but Hugh.

"A week should be sufficient, Your Highness," she answered.

"And at the end of that week, what would happen?" His sly, conjecturing tone gave Hugh a very bad feeling.

"I would present to Your Highness the results of the

'wife test' . . . in the form of . . . suggested pairings of your nobles and the duke's daughters."

"And these standards you will use . . ." The king leaned forward with a hint of a smile. "How do I know they are fair and reasonable?"

"The test has been used and refined by our convent for over a hundred years. The reputation of the brides who have come from the Convent of the Brides of Virtue speaks strongly for the wisdom embodied in it."

"Just what are these wise and wonderful standards?" Edward's long face lit with a wry smile. "Saints! Should you not publish them far and wide?" He swept the hall and the lands beyond with a hand. "Would they not improve the state of wedded bliss in every corner of the earth?"

Laughter rolled through the hall, then was stifled in favor of her reply.

"We do not presume to know what is best for all of humankind, Your Highness . . . only for the maids raised in the convent's care and the noblemen who wed them. As to the exact details of our standards, they are never revealed. To publish them far and wide might lead unscrupulous persons to try to take advantage and pretend to be that which they are not."

Hugh could stand it no more.

"Surely, Sire, you cannot be serious about permitting a mere maid to sit in judgment on nobles of the realm"— he lurched to his feet—"to decide the course of their lives and the bearers of their heirs. She may be the abbess's appointed one, but for godssake, she is still little more than a girl!"

The mirth in the king's face faded as he turned to Hugh.

"I believe Lady Chloe has stated she will *recommend* pairings." Though his tone remained genial, there was an edge to his words. "It is I, Sir Hugh, who will decide the future of the nobles of England." When he turned to Chloe, his features warmed once more.

"Thus is the flaw in your abbess's plan revealed," he declared.

She paled visibly. "F-flaw, Highness?"

"If we are to rely on these closely guarded 'standards' and on your judgment regarding your sisters' mates . . . then whom do we rely on to judge you? As the holy church teaches, no man is a proper judge of himself. How, then, am I to decide on *your* future husband?"

A flaw indeed. From all over the torchlit hall, it was evident that she had been caught flat-footed by the king's question. She looked to her sister maidens, then back at the king with what could only be a hint of panic. Hugh felt a huge and utterly unexpected wave of anxiety. . . .

Then the king himself rescued her.

"The solution is clear to me, Lady Chloe. I must appoint someone from my own court to administer this 'test' to you."

Calls of "I'll test her for ye, Majesty" and "Give me an hour or two with her, an' I'll tell ye what kind o' man she needs" mingled with raucous laughter and proposals for methods of "testing" wives before marrying them.

"No, truly, Your Majesty, that won't be necessary," she called out.

But the king was now listening only to his own sardonic judgment.

"We would need someone extraordinarily cool-headed and rational," he said, searching his guests as if measuring all present for a possible appointment to that post. "Someone not easily swayed by a fetching smile or a flirtatious glance. Someone whose vast learning and uncompromising personal standards would allow him to weigh the very hearts and souls of the distaff side." He suddenly rose from his chair, drawing his subjects to their feet all over the hall, and raised his arms in grand oratorical style.

"I believe there may be just such a man amongst us. A man whose learning, logic, and inclinations make him uniquely suited for this task. A man whose reputation with and knowledge of women—I believe I can safely say— are quite unparalleled in English nobility." He turned his gaze on Hugh. "That man is Sir Hugh of Sennet."

There was an instant of shocked silence before laughter erupted through the hall. The king himself broke into a broad and exceedingly wicked grin.

"B-But, Sire—" Hugh stammered, reeling, blindsided by the king's double-edged praise.

"No, no, Sir Hugh. None of your wretched modesty. You are known throughout the court as a perceptive and dispassionate *critic* of women, are you not? And since you are already acquainted with these maids, who better to help administer this 'wife test'?"

The king watched Hugh's ill-disguised horror and gave a hugely satisfied sigh, indicating to all who knew him that his mind was made up.

"Yes, I believe that is quite the solution. It is my decree that, together, Sir Hugh and Lady Chloe will 'test' the maids and present their nuptial pairings to us in seven days. The vows will be spoken the following day in this very hall."

As the realization of what the king had just done to him settled in, blood began to roar in Hugh's head and his vision washed crimson. He all but missed the king's second major pronouncement of the evening: the identities of the grooms-to-be.

"The lucky husbands of these maids will be William, Baron of Chester . . . Sir Jaxton, heir to Louden-Day . . . Simon of Cornwall, newly created Earl of Candle . . . Sir Graham, heir to Ledding . . . and . . . Horace, Earl of Ketchum."

A great murmur went up. These were important marriages indeed.

When the king turned to him, it took every ounce of Hugh's battle-honed self-control to nod and accept the demeaning charge he had just been given. Afterward, he stood rooted to the spot while the king turned back to his meal and clapped his hands to call for music.

The guests quickly resumed eating and drinking, and the hall began to hum with music and speculation. Chloe of Guibray stood on the far side of the hall, staring at

him, her dismay every bit as obvious as his. When old
Lady Marcella moved down the table to whisper in her
ear, she sank abruptly onto the bench and lowered her
gaze with a small, forced smile. She neither ate nor drank,
while her fellow maidens finished their meal and spoke
quietly amongst themselves.

After what seemed an age, Lady Marcella gathered
them up in her motherly wings and ushered them from
the assembly. Chloe, last in line, paused at the door to
cast Sir Hugh's a turbulent look before following the other
maidens.

The rest of the evening Hugh spent trying to avoid the
drunken toasts raised to his appointment as the realm's
official "wife judge." All he wanted was to escape the
hall, the castle, and the dreadful specter that he felt rising
out of the darkest recesses of his mind and body. Something shapeless, encroaching, and alarming. Something he
had wrestled to a standstill in the dark on the deck of the
ship, and believed he had vanquished. The seductive and
utterly corrupting pleasure of having *looked*.

Since that quick and volatile glimpse in a cottage on
the French shore, the sight of her naked body had never
been more than a wink away from his thoughts. Only the
most constant and ruthless vigilance had kept it from rising and repossessing his senses, as it was doing even now.

She was formed of a tantalizing geometry of curves
and lines unlike any others found in nature. Breasts . . .
cool, tempting globes . . . like apples or those scriptural
"pomegranates" . . . crowned with velvety peaks that rose
and fell with every breath. When he could tear his attention from them, it focused on her throat. A slim, delicate
column hugged by moist tendrils of hair that flowed down
over her shoulders. And such shoulders . . . veiled coyly
by dark tresses . . . broad and smooth . . . like polished
ivory . . .

Saints beseiged. Under her garments she must always
look like that . . . soft, ripe, and voluptuously curved. A
very vision of Original Temptation. Woman at her most
elemental and alluring.

His mental gaze recoiled to her shocked face and caught on her eyes. Seductive blue pools . . . clear and unsullied . . . harboring a deep and subtle flow.

And like deep waters, treacherous as the Devil himself. Each time that shattering vision of her nakedness gripped him, he was rescued by the memory of one of old Brother Hericule's diatribes on the nature of women. Beware the woman of apparent virtue and quiet capability, the old monk had proclaimed. Females were at their most dangerous when calm and cooperative and seemingly well-contained. Better by far to have to bear with females of blatantly giddy, witless, and shallow natures . . . they quickly reminded men of their baser sides and caught no man unawares.

Canny. Capable. Self-possessed. Wrapped in a deceptive cloak of innocence. Not yet fully aware of her power, but wielding it, all the same. It was as if the old brother had foreseen Chloe of Guibray standing naked in the firelight.

He began to tremble.

She was right.

He had not only looked, he had *liked* it.

Fleeing the wine-heated revels of the great hall for the cool night air outside, he spotted a glow coming from the open chapel door and headed for it. By the flickering light of a single tallow lamp, he found the priest assigned to hear evening confessions, Father Ignatius, snoring loudly on a stool beside the screen that separated him from potential confessors.

He shook the portly priest awake and proceeded to pour into his ear a shockingly detailed list of transgressions. Thirty-two generalized damnings, seventeen eternal condemnations of specific persons and objects, nine irreverent and possibly profane exclamations of the sacred name . . .

"How penitent of you to keep such a scrupulous tally, my son."

. . . several incidents of anger to the point of physical violence, three major falsehoods, pervasive ill-temper, resentment of and the urge to defy their God-anointed sovereign . . .

"We all have moments of weakness and ingratitude, my son."

. . . then the juicier revelations that made the priest sit straighter and listen more eagerly . . . powerful carnal desires, incidents of nocturnal pollution, and a nearly continuous stream of prurient and lustful thoughts . . . including the sight of a woman's full, naked breasts . . . the slide of her soft, fire-kissed hair over his own naked skin . . . the erotic resilience of her smooth, well-rounded hips as he pressed his own engorged loins against them . . . the parting of her cool, sleek thighs and the tantalizing heat that lay at the dark, moist nexus of them . . . lips like juicy, just-ripened cherries that he wanted to bite . . . and teeth like pearls that he wanted to feel dragging across his skin . . . biting his shoulder, his belly, his . . .

The ample priest staggered from the confessional later, having doled out enough penance to keep the wretched confessor on his knees for most of the night, and discovered it was none other than Hugh of Sennet draped over the chancel railing and muttering in agonized tones the litany of penitence he had just assigned. Sir Hugh of Sennet. A man raised by a strict order of monks. A man of lofty spiritual aspirations and unassailable morality. Until now.

Father Ignatius shook his head to rid it of the images Sir Hugh's shockingly vivid iniquity had burned into it. Clearly, something had happened to the good knight . . . some major visitation of temptation . . . some devastating encounter that initiated his senses into the pleasures of the flesh. The priest's eyes widened and he clicked his parched tongue, thinking of the wine flowing freely in the king's hall. This could be worth something.

LITTLE DID CHLOE GUESS THAT THE king's appointment of her to administer the "wife test" would cause changes in the way her sisters behaved toward her.

"Do you have enough blankets, Chloe?" Alaina asked with unprecedented generosity.

"Oh, no, you wash first. I need only a little water," Margarete insisted.

"Would you like to try my lavender soap?" Helen offered.

"I have a bit of tatted lace that would be quite fetching on the neck of your gown, Chloe," Lisette said as Chloe brushed her plain gown and hung it on a peg between the others' highly decorative garments.

But even more pointed changes were revealed as they finished their evening ablutions, removed their outer garments, and knelt in their shifts by the cots for evening prayers.

"Holy Mother Mary, I entreat you to intercede for our sister Chloe . . . that she be given a wise and discerning heart," Alaina prayed. "And that her heart will show her it would be best for me to have a husband who appreciates great beauty and has a deep purse and a love of fine clothes and elegant linen."

"Guide our Chloe to make the right decisions for us," Helen said earnestly, her clasped fingers pale. "Help her to decide that I would best suit a man of wisdom and dignified bearing . . . a man who has the king's ear . . . a man who bears responsibility and needs a comforting hand on his care-worn brow."

"Let her recall how much I hate it when someone belches at the table or lets food collect in his beard when he eats," Margarete said bluntly. "Give her the wisdom to choose me a clean and orderly lord who bathes weekly and will not object to keeping several laundresses."

"Notre Belle Dame"—Lisette added fervent petitions with one eye trained her way—"help our Chloe to see that sometimes what is best for us is not the most obvious. Sometimes we of hot blood must be paired with a calmer, more temperate mate . . . one who can absorb our fiery

passions, and in so doing, cool and sanctify our tempes-
tuous spirits."

The prayers may have been addressed to Heaven,
Chloe realized, but they were aimed squarely at her. Her
sisters expected her to let their wishes influence her judgment. And she would have been more than pleased to
oblige *if it were up to her alone*. She smiled weakly at
them, climbed between her blankets, and as Helen blew
out the lamp and darkness settled over the chamber, sank
into a full-blown panic.

Things had gone rather well until Sir Hugh interrupted
and the king decided to subject her to *his* wretched judgment. Knowing the contempt in which he held women—
and especially her—she could only imagine what sort of
husband he would select for her. Then it occurred to her
that he wouldn't be able to select just anyone; her husband
had to come from a list of five unwedded noblemen. She
relaxed slightly. Perhaps it wouldn't be so bad. The king
seemed to think they would make desirable wives. He
surely wouldn't choose to give them to men who weren't
deserving in some way.

She was yanked back to the edge of her nerves when
she recalled that he was required to judge her based on
her own nonexistent "wife test."

Now she had to come up with one.

Out of the whole cloth of her own mind.

By morning.

"Holy Mother, Almighty Father, Beloved Son and all
the Blessed Saints"—she privately petitioned Heaven
through every possible avenue—"help me to think of
something with which to 'test' them. And if it wouldn't
be too much trouble, could you give Sir Hugh a few ugly
boils, a nonfatal fever, or a galloping case of the scours
to keep him out of the way?"

HEAVEN, IT SEEMED, WAS RATHER SELEC-
tive about the petitions it chose to grant the next morning.

After a long and fitful night Chloe awoke with a clear

head and a handful of inspired requirements for a "wife test." She was feeling quite hopeful about it, until she descended the stairs to the chapel for morning prayers with her sisters and came face-to-face with Sir Hugh's tired but nevertheless healthy scowl. Sir Hugh, after an equally tumultuous night, had finally purged his accumulated guilt and emerged from his penance determined to rid himself of the duke's offspring once and for all. He was feeling good about that resolve until he heard a murmur moving through his fellow attendants at morning mass and looked up to find Chloe of Guibray and her hoard of virgins invading the chapel where he had taken refuge against them.

Father Ignatius looked up from assisting his bishop in making preparations at the altar to behold Sir Hugh of Sennet staring irritably across the chapel at five of the freshest, comeliest young maids he had seen in years. Without a doubt, the Duke of Avalon's daughters. Castle gossip was raging about them. Four of the five took no special note of Sir Hugh's presence, but one of the maids bristled at his scrutiny and stared back at him. So hotly, in fact, that the air between them approached the flashpoint of combustion.

Years of experience with the vagaries of human desire led the priest to the unerring conclusion that *she* was the one who had awakened in Sir Hugh that most unwelcome strain of carnality. He smiled to himself.

As the echoes of the benediction and dismissal faded in the stone chamber and the participants filed out of the chapel, Father Ignatius scurried down from the altar to slip out the side door of the chancel. Down a little-used passage, he emerged directly into the main yard and watched the king's party emerge from the chapel and head for the great hall. He hurried across the courtyard, and once England's chief parishioner was seated at the high table, breaking his fast, the canny Father approached his chair from the side.

"I had a most interesting night at confession, Your

Majesty," he murmured as he bowed and kissed the king's hand.

"An interesting night for you makes for an interesting morning for me," the king said, smiling behind the cup of morning ale he held.

"I noticed Sir Hugh of Sennet seemed distracted during chapel," Father Ignatius continued. "I know he has been *greatly burdened* of late and so watched to see what or *who* might be responsible. There was a young maid in the chapel . . . one of the Duke of Avalon's daughters, I believe . . . who claimed the Almighty's share of Sir Hugh's attention during mass. It gave me cause to wonder, considering my busy time at confession last evening . . ."

The king sipped his ale and smiled.

"I share your concern, Father. I, too, will watch to see what might afflict our beloved knight." The priest withdrew, and the king mulled over the priest's words until he spotted Sir Hugh charging through the main doors and heading straight for the ale. Some moments later Avalon's daughters entered, and he visually searched them, one by one, wondering which had managed the prodigious task of making monkish Sir Hugh look with passion upon a woman. It could have been any one of them; there wasn't a toss-back in the bunch.

He chuckled privately. This daughters-for-ransom business just got better and better.

After a few moments he leaned toward the Lord Treasurer, Bromley, who now occupied the chair to his right.

"Of late, the Earl of Sennet has plagued me with petitions about his son. He wants the lad wedded and heired before another disaster befalls his line."

"Can't say I blame him." Bromley shook his head as he took another mouthful of cold pasty. "He's lost two fine sons before getting an heir out of them. The one he has left is downright monkish. I'd be beside myself, too."

The king rubbed his chin as he watched Hugh toss back his ale, square his shoulders, and stride across the hall to where the maids were breaking their fast. Every aspect of the strapping knight's demeanor declared hostility toward

the maids he was now required to attend. The king beckoned the head of his household guard, and as the soldier
bent to listen, he lowered his head to hide his words from
whomever might be watching.

"Summon the Earl of Sennet to court. Tell him I would
hear him present his frequent petition in person."

HUGH STOPPED BEHIND THE SEATED MAID-
ens with his arms crossed and his legs spread and braced.

"Can you not break fast a bit faster?" he asked.

"Beg pardon?" Chloe of Guibray turned on her seat to
look up at him.

"We must begin this 'test' of yours straightaway," he
declared. "The king has agreed that we may offer our slate
of pairings earlier, if we wish."

Chloe forced down the mouthful of bread she'd been
chewing and rose. Behind him a veritable sea of faces
was trained intently on them . . . including one at the head
table wearing an ornate gold coronet.

"I have said quite plainly that the test will take a
week."

"Nonsense." He jammed his thumbs into his belt and
stared disdainfully at her. "What is the first task?"

She could feel his impatience churning the air between
them, and for a moment it daunted her. But only for a
moment.

"Our first task, after taking nourishment, is to see that
my sisters and I meet the men King Edward has selected
for us."

"Easy enough." He turned and beckoned. Sir Graham
and three other freshly shaved young noblemen sprang up
from a bench against the far wall and adjusted tunics,
belts, and sleeves as they approached. Three of the four,
including Sir Graham, had hair cut in the bowl shape that
identified them as knights. The fourth, who was slightly
older than the others, had the build and carriage of a knight
but had neatly trimmed longer hair. As they arrayed themselves before Chloe, and the other maids abandoned their

food to rise and collect around her, the noise in the hall lowered noticeably.

"Graham of Ledding, you already know." Sir Hugh made a desultory motion in his friend's direction, then continued in a perfunctory tone. "Jax, heir to Louden-Day . . ." The tall, lean young lord with a superior air and eyes the color of winter frost made a quick, exquisitely controlled bow. "William, Baron Chester." The roan-haired fellow was of unremarkable stature, but had vivid, twinkling eyes and a handsome mouth that seemed to be tickled at the corners by impish impulses. "And Simon of Cornwall, Earl of Candle." The new earl was just passing thirty . . . robust of frame, refined in manner, and elegant of dress.

Then he pointed at each of the maids in turn.

"Alaina, Helen, Lisette, and Margarete." When she glared purposefully at him, he corrected his presentation. "Lady Alaina, Lady Helen, Lady Lisette, and Lady Margarete." When she crossed her arms and intensified her glare, he jerked a thumb at her. "And this one is Chloe. *Lady* Chloe. My lords, your ladies. My ladies, your lords." He turned to her. "What next?"

"There are so many people here." Chloe looked at the faces turned on them, then at their guide and chaperone, who had reluctantly abandoned her food. "Lady Marcella, is there not a place where we can be out of the common eye?"

The old lady thought for a moment, then nodded. "Perhaps the queen's courtyard. With her due to be taken to childbed any day, she prefers the comfort of her chambers. Her Majesty won't mind if you met there each morning."

"I know the place." Sir Hugh looked at the husbands. "East of the tower."

There was no need to suggest that the noblemen act as escorts. Each man eagerly offered one of the maids his arm. It was only then that Chloe realized they were one husband short.

"The Earl of Ketchum isn't here yet," Hugh said, seizing her elbow and dragging her along after the others. "The king had to send for him."

"Oh? Then, perhaps we should wait to begin—"

"Ohhh, no. We're going to get this 'test' done. I want you safely wedded and bedded and out of my—" He halted and started again. "*The lot of you* . . . safely wedded and out of my hair."

She looked up and found him reddening.

They emerged from the hall into a beautiful late spring morning. The air was fresh, and the sun was warm on their shoulders. The courtyard nestled between the great round tower and the curtain wall on two sides and was accessed through archways on the two others. It was paved in the center with large, flat stones and was planted around the edges with pear and plum trees trained against the walls. Around the trees were irregularly shaped beds planted with all manner of flowers. The crocuses and hyacinths were just fading, the honeysuckle, heart's ease, and blue iris were coming into full bloom, and everywhere there was the promise of a bountiful crop of roses, lilies, lavender, and hollyhocks.

Strolling around the lovely courtyard, ignoring Sir Hugh's impatient noises, Chloe was brought up short by a score of expectant faces peering at her through one of the arched entries. As she turned back, she spotted a number of heads sticking out the long, narrow windows above them. Women's heads. The queen's solar overlooked the courtyard, Lady Marcella informed her.

"So." Sir Hugh's forbearance seemed to be wearing thin. "What now?"

"Firstly, each of our husbands-to-be will recite for us their favorite poem, epic, or oration," Chloe declared and braced for their reaction.

"What?" Sir Hugh's incredulity was echoed by four other voices as the men crowded behind him. "You cannot be serious."

"I assure you, I am."

"I thought this was to be a *wife* test." Sir Graham spoke

for the male contingent, who nodded and muttered under their breaths.

"Oh, it is. I assure you." She had to work to maintain an authoritative air. "We must learn something about you in order to know how to best match you with a maid." She asked her sisters and Lady Marcella to seat themselves on the nearby benches, then turned back to the men. "Now, my good lords and gentle knights, who will be first to prove both his memory and his courage?"

It was a challenge they could not fail to meet . . . not with half of the court hanging out of windows and peering through the archways at them. The others shoved Sir Graham forward and quickly retreated to an opposing bench.

After an awkward moment he began to recount a rhyming story from his youth. Despite a number of lapses and restarts, he was able to convey a tale of two stalwart brothers, representing vaunted heroism and unsung service, who proved that both fates were noble, even indispensable in human society.

Then solid, dignified Simon, Earl of Candle, recited a short piece from Seneca on the qualities of a good ruler; the elegant Sir Jaxton rattled off a number of couplets in extravagant praise of Beauty; and William, Baron Chester, recited a rhyming verbal calendar of tasks for good stewardship on an estate . . . which included a number of lines about livestock and spring that made the men smirk and the maids glance at each other in puzzlement.

As they finished, a hum of opinion could be heard buzzing from the gallery of onlookers that had collected on the top of the wall and around every exposed bit of courtyard.

"That's done." Sir Hugh pushed to his feet. "What next?"

"A Bible passage," Chloe declared with less trepidation. "Some bit of scriptural wisdom they have learned and held in their hearts to guide them."

"What does the Bible have to do with taking a wife?" Sir Jaxton demanded.

Chloe turned to Sir Hugh with folded arms and a raised chin.

"Shall I tell him or shall you?" Her gaze tangled in his, conveying her expectation that he of all men should see the wisdom in such a requirement. "Being the religious scholar that you are, I would expect that you have committed any number of helpful passages to memory."

Heat flared in his eyes.

"How do you know that—you would have me recite for these fellows some of *my* learning and moral guidance?" He looked at the four men standing uneasily by. "Very well. Here is a passage that has never failed to guide me: 'Give not thy strength to women, nor thy ways to that which destroyeth kings.' "

Chloe drew her chin back and blinked. He took advantage of her shock.

"And here is another: 'To keep thee from . . . the flattery of the tongue of a strange woman . . . lust not after her beauty in thine heart. Neither let her take thee with her eyelids.' That is the sort of thing you were looking for, is it not? I have several mo—"

"That will be sufficient, thank you."

"But I have quite a number of instructive passages. Like: 'A woman is a deep ditch, and a strange woman is a narrow pit. She lieth in wait for a prey.' "

"That"—she shook a finger at him—"is despicable. Misquoting Scripture to suit your purpose."

The accusation clearly surprised him.

"I do *not* misquote Scripture. To do so is blasphemy."

"So it is."

"I have most certainly *not* committed blasphemy."

"It is not 'woman' condemned in that passage, it is 'whore,' " she declared, sending an audible gasp through the maids behind her. "It refers to an infamous and immoral woman."

"Whatever gave you such a ridiculous idea?" he demanded.

"My own two eyes. I have read that passage myself, numerous times."

"Read it where?"

"In the convent library."

"Pardon . . . Lady Chloe?" Sir Graham's voice intruded.

"Yes? What?" she snapped.

"We are prepared to recite a Bible passage now."

Chloe glanced at Sir Graham, who drew her gaze to the other men, who nodded.

It was only when she turned back to Sir Hugh that she realized her nose was scarcely an inch from his and that she was flushed and breathing hard. She lurched back a step. It was all she could do to nod to Sir Graham to begin and then stalk back to a seat on the bench among the others.

The men's recitations came largely from the customary catechism for lads of noble birth: the *Pater Noster*, the Ten Commandments, the Beatitudes, and sundry well-known Psalms. As they recited she forced her attention to their chosen passages and the way they presented themselves.

Feeling oddly removed from the possibilities they represented, she looked instead to the rapt faces of her sister maidens, on the bench beside her. Their demeanor was admirably modest and their cheeks were blushed with virtuous pleasure. But their eyes—bright with eagerness, anticipation, and a hint of determination—told their true state. They were already sorting out which man they liked best.

It struck her forcefully: what if she didn't agree with their choices? Worse still—what if two decided they liked the same man?

"That's done. Thank God." Sir Hugh strode into her line of sight and stopped with his arms crossed, the very picture of indignation. "What's next? Reciting the provisions of the Magna Carta? Recounting the lineages of every English king back to Alfred the Great? Or perhaps tracing the Biblical 'begats' back to Adam himself? All useful stuff." He leaned tauntingly closer. "A husband never knows when he might need to *recite* his wife into a deep sleep."

His sardonic tone sliced through the bonds that had confined her authoritative little abbess to the dark recesses of her heart. She rose, determined to retaliate by turning his scorn to her advantage.

"I appreciate your efforts, my lords. We all do. In all fairness, I had planned to have my sisters recite their favorites as well . . . as a demonstration of their mental ability and attention to religious duty. But I see now it would only bore you." She ignored the four shaking heads behind Sir Hugh and the accompanying protests of interest. "I have heard my sisters recite on numerous occasions and already know which passages they favor. Clearly, Sir Hugh feels no need to hear them." Her sisters sent her heartfelt smiles.

She struck a pose and clasped her hands together with a deliberateness copied from the earthly template of her inner abbess.

"As to what comes next . . . I can say without fear of error that all five of us share a common and regrettable deficit." Her sisters, no less than their intended husbands, stared at her in dismay. Even Sir Hugh was caught back by her declaration.

"But it is a deficit that with your help may be remedied. In providing assistance, you will test our willingness to learn, to apply ourselves, and to meet life's challenges with courage and resourcefulness."

"Just what is this *deficit*?" Alaina demanded, a heartbeat ahead of Sir Hugh's demand to know the same.

The husband candidates, the maids, Sir Hugh, the people crowding the archway and hanging from the windows above . . . all strained closer to learn the duke's daughters' singular flaw. It was as if the castle walls themselves inhaled in expectation.

"None of us knows how to ride a horse."

There was a collective murmur of surprise and, among the husband candidates, a covert exhalation of relief.

"That is hardly news," Sir Hugh declared testily. "We

had to cart you all the way from France like barrels of—"

"Rare and precious wine," she supplied. "What *is* news, my lords, is that you will be required to teach us how to ride. The quality of your instruction will prove an aspect of your character, and our willingness to learn will prove an aspect of ours."

This time not a single word of contention was raised.

It was brilliant, actually. A contrivance that would have done the abbess herself proud. Learning to ride was a time-consuming process that would require considerable interaction between maids and men, but would not focus so directly on the fact that they were both evaluating and being evaluated.

As they adjourned to the stables, she had a further brainstorm: each day each maid would be taught by a different man. That way she could observe all the possible pairings, and they would have the chance to get to know one another better. When they arrived at the stable doors and she announced that condition, the men were amenable, declaring it reasonable, and the maids acquiesced.

She was feeling almost smug as the lords arranged for and brought out saddled palfreys and the group sorted themselves rather naturally into pairs of teacher and pupil. As one by one the men helped the maids onto the side-facing saddles, Chloe found herself standing and watching. *Just* standing and watching. There were five maids and only four husband candidates.

Why was it that her brilliant plans always had one devastating flaw?

As the lords began to lead the horse-mounted maids down the hill to the grassy park that lay just beyond the inner curtain wall, Lisette saw Chloe standing alone by the stable doors and called out, "Oh, but, Chloe, you must come, too."

"No, no. You go on," she called with forced enthusiasm. "I will make up the lesson later, when the Earl of Ketchum arrives."

She watched them turn quickly back to the business of becoming acquainted. Their eagerness caused a physical tug at the center of her chest. A potent and totally unexpected longing swept over her, not unlike the ones she had experienced at the convent as she listened to the other girls speak of their families. She straightened, squared her shoulders, and reminded herself she was keeping her promise to Sister Archibald, seeing to her sisters' welfare. She was doing her duty.

She really should walk along after them . . . watch to see how they were getting along and who seemed to pair well with whom. But the prospect of watching their pleasure in discovering both the young lords and their own feelings filled her with a dread she hadn't anticipated. Raising her chin, she glanced distractedly around and slammed into Sir Hugh's formidable glare.

He was leaning back against the corral fence with his arms folded and his legs crossed at the ankles, staring at her as if he were trying to evaporate her with just the heat of his gaze. She froze, feeling oddly panicky and exposed. Then, just as her discomfort reached the do-something-do-anything stage, he dropped his fists to his sides, rolled off another word of the sort one had to report in the confessional, and strode furiously into the stable.

Chapter Ten

"DAMN, DAMN, DAMN, DAMN, DAMN!"

Hugh stalked down the stable alley, refusing to count those among his tally for the confessional. He damned well deserved a bit of leniency; his worst nightmare was coming true. He was saddled with Chloe of Guibray . . . having to talk to her, having to *look* at her, and, unless he could think of some way around it, probably having to *touch* her, too. If the road to perdition was paved with *looks*, that pavement was greased every step of the way with *touches*.

Selecting an older, gentle-looking mare, he led it out of the stall and sent one of the grooms for a lady saddle and a leading halter.

Infuriating female. He felt his heart beating faster. She had just stood there, watching the others ride off together with that look on her face. The memory of it clung to the walls of his mind like pitch . . . a trace of sadness in her eyes, a hint of wistfulness . . .

The groom returned and he grabbed the halter and bridle and fitted them over the horse's head. When he emerged from the stable, she was already through the gate in the curtain wall and halfway down the slope leading to the green.

"Stop right where you are!" He lengthened his stride to catch up with her.

She turned, looking startled, and continued backing several steps as he thudded down the slope toward her with the horse in tow.

"You didn't think you were going to be exempted from this, did you?"

"It's not necessary. I have plenty to do until—"

"Oh, but it is necessary. *I* have a test to give, too, remember?" He grabbed her by the waist and instinctively dragged her against him. *Not a good idea.* Thrusting her back to arm's length, he lifted her off the ground and shoved her up onto the saddle, where she teetered and flailed.

"You cannot mean to make me ride this beast in this fashion," she declared, struggling for both balance and dignity.

"Lady saddle or astride . . . it makes no difference to me." He gave an exaggerated wince as he seized one of her knees between a thumb and forefinger and directed it over the wooden bow of the saddle to stabilize her. "But you should know that if you choose 'astride,' you will scandalize other ladies of the court who consider this saddle a great improvement, and you probably won't be able to walk for a week." He watched her absorb that information and weigh the possible consequences. A lowering of her shoulders betrayed her decision.

"You grip the bow of the saddle with your legs. That's how you stay on." Then he gathered the reins and handed them to her. "These are what you use to direct the horse."

"I know that," she snapped. "I was raised in a convent, not a barrel."

"Your left foot goes in the stirrup." He placed it there.

"And my right?" She wagged the slipper-clad foot hooked around the bow of the saddle.

"Can do whatever it pleases, as long I don't have to watch."

Watch. The word stirred an unwelcome eddy of anticipation in him. Those legs . . . bared that first day in the cart . . . clad in a man's tights . . . standing naked in a dim cottage. Memory melted into possibility as his mind filled with an image of those cool, silky limbs wrapped around his—

A tug on his hands caused him to look down, and he realized with no little horror that he was still holding the foot resting in the stirrup. Dropping it as if it had just sprouted fangs and scales, he grabbed the guide rein and pulled the horse toward the grassy expanse of the castle green.

"How am I supposed to watch the others if I am busy trying to hold life and limb together on the back of this beast?" she demanded, gripping the edge of the saddle with both hands as she swayed back and forth.

"You don't have to watch them. I will."

"You haven't the faintest notion of what to watch them for."

"I don't?" He refused to look up. "Well, then . . . why don't I just watch to see which one of these poor wretches is most likely to put up with Alaina's preening and appetite for adoration . . . which will be able to live with Helen's royal airs and ambition . . . which one can suffer Margarete's inability to apply her wits for more than a heartbeat . . . and which is least likely to be reduced to a cinder by Lisette's all-too-visible heat?"

"Is that what you see when you look at my sisters? I'll have you know . . . Alaina is a good bit more than just a vain girl. She took it upon herself to gather the remnants of woven goods from all over the convent and used them to make garments for children whose mothers had died. And during an outbreak of illness last year, aloof, 'ambitious' Helen went without sleep for days in order to tend the sick. I'll have you know . . . Margarete is not so scatter-witted that she cannot make certain everyone around her has water to wash, fresh garments to wear, and a clean place to sleep. And our Lisette is as true-hearted and capable as she is passionate."

He paused to look up, considering her words as he studied her.

"And you? What have I missed about you . . . besides that you're querulous and stubborn and unholy full of yourself?" A vengeful glint appeared in his eye. "Oh, yes—you're scared to death of horses."

"I am not."

"Then I think it is time you demonstrate your ability to 'apply yourself ' and—how did you put it—your 'willingness to meet life's challenges.' " He smiled at the way her face paled, then continued on down the greensward with her, sending several goats, sundry domestic poultry, and a bedraggled pair of peafowl scurrying out of the way.

"Use your heel on the horse's side to get her to move, pull back on the reins to get her to stop. And keep your mind on what you're doing," he called back over his shoulder. "The moment a horse thinks you don't have the upper hand, you'll find yourself dumped flat on your arse."

"Sounds like the abbess's advice on husbands," Chloe muttered.

"What?" He glanced over his shoulder, and she gave him a determinedly blank look. "Another thing," he continued, looking forward again. "Every horse is different. Some are stubborn and some are eager to please. Some are wicked smart and others are dumb as dirt."

"Just like husbands," she murmured.

There was a hitch in his stride.

"Did you say something?"

"Not me."

"You have to treat each horse differently," he went on, glancing irritably over his shoulder. "Some need a firm hand, others a kind word. Some will kill themselves to please you—literally run their hearts out. Some would just as soon kick you through a wall. Establish your authority early on and you won't have any trouble."

"Easier said than done."

This time he heard her and turned with a testy look.

"Riding involves a good bit more than just climbing aboard a horse and roaring off."

"I can see that."

"Too many people believe that telling the front from the back end of a horse is all they need to know."

Her inner abbess seized control and sank her gaze straight into his.

"In that way, riding is a great deal like marriage," she said irritably. "Too many people think they know all about it, when, in fact, they don't know heads from tails."

He refused to look at her again until they reached the flattest part of the green, where he pointed to a low stone-and-rail fence that separated the greensward from the knights' practice field.

"Ride down to that fence, turn, and ride back."

Summoning all of her courage, she complied and soon found herself sitting on horseback, wedged headfirst against that barrier, unable to get the horse to move. No amount of pleading, banging her foot against the beast's side, or pulling on the reins seemed to make a difference. She was stuck.

Looking down the fence, she spotted three of her four sisters in a similar predicament and sagged with relief. It wasn't just her!

"Having difficulty?" When she turned around, Sir Hugh was striding toward her looking entirely too justified by her performance.

"It's this horse. I don't think he likes me."

"*She* doesn't have to like you. She just has to obey you."

"I believe I would do better with another mount," she said stubbornly.

"And just which horse do you think you would do better with?" He gestured toward the others as he took hold of the horse's halter and pulled the animal around to start them moving again.

He had a point. None of the palfreys looked a day under "ancient," and their temperaments seemed to range from indifferent to oblivious.

"Perhaps I would benefit from a change of teacher," she said shortly.

"Martyrs are in regrettably short supply." He swept a hand toward the others. "But if you think you'd do better with one of them, be my guest."

She rode across the green and then pulled back on the reins to halt and observe the husband candidates.

Sir Jaxton was clearly annoyed at the way Margarete refused to sit up in the saddle and threw herself around the horse's neck at the slightest bit of jostling. An irate Lord Simon was arguing with Alaina as he tried to adjust her posture and suggested she relax in the saddle so that she didn't bounce with every step her mount took. A grim Lord William kept having to rescue Helen from a horse that seemed determined to bite her and then rescue the horse from Helen's indignant swats of retaliation. Even more exasperated was Sir Graham, who was having to hold a strangely boneless Lisette by the waist continuously to keep her from sliding out of the saddle. If the rising volume of the instruction was any indication, her brilliant plan was turning into a colossal failure.

Sir Hugh arrived and rested a hand on the rump of her horse as he followed her gaze to the contentious pairs.

"Not a pretty sight, is it?" He didn't try to hide his pleasure in that fact.

"I believe it would be fair to say that these are not the pairings we will recommend. But I have confidence"—*more like a desperate hope, really*—"that we will find a satisfactory combination before the week is out."

"Assuming they don't strangle each other first."

"An excessively gloomy outlook. I would be more concerned if they were all perfectly patient and polite. With all of your experience of the world, Sir Hugh, I should think you would understand that there are many ways for men and women to come together. Sometimes it takes a while for them to come to appreciate each other's strengths and accept each other's weaknesses."

He slid his arm from the horse and his expression chilled.

"My *experience* has nothing to do with this. I was charged with helping to administer this test of yours, and I will do my part. But I don't have to like it."

Clearly she had struck a nerve.

"Why do you detest marriage so?" She came right out with it. "You've never been wedded yourself. Were you disappointed by someone? Was your parents' marriage a horror? Or were you poisoned by the opinions of others?"

"Marriage is a necessary evil. Required for the continuation of mankind." He tossed off the words so quickly and lifelessly that they sounded rote.

"Evil?" She was genuinely surprised. "It was instituted by the Almighty Himself. Did God not create us male and female so that we could come together in marriage?"

"It was and still is an accommodation for the lusts women cause in men. It was meant as a solution for the desires that distract us from spiritual pursuits."

"Ahhh." A twisted little nugget of theological wisdom . . . relic, no doubt, of his monastic upbringing. The abbess had railed about the way some men retreated into monasteries not so much to be close to God, as to escape women. "So you believe that those who marry are flawed and weak."

"Something like that." He glanced at her from the corner of his eye.

"And this includes *all* men who marry?" She tilted her head, studying him and his prickly attitude. "I was thinking of our good king. Do you consider *him* weak and flawed because he has married?"

"That is entirely different."

"How so? Is he not a man?"

"No. Not in the usual sense. He is the God-appointed sovereign of the kingdom. The lives of his subjects and the welfare of his lands are in his keeping. He is obligated to beget an heir to secure the succession and the peace and order of the realm."

"Obligated? Lady Marcella says the king visits the queen often and, by all accounts, enjoys her company.

Does he sin in taking pleasure in his 'obligation' to his wife and the begetting of his children?"

His nostrils flared with noble outrage.

"If you think to trick me into condemning the king—" He stepped back and gave her horse a sharp smack on the rump that sent it shooting forward.

She struggled to maintain her seat and regain control. The wretch. Let him think he might lose to a well-reasoned argument, and he resorted to unfair tactics. By the time her mount reached the far side of the green, she was able to turn it and urge it into a trot that carried her right back to him.

"You will not condemn the king . . . but you will blame my sisters, who are ordered into marriage to secure their father's freedom, and these good lords whom the king has seen fit to send into marriage with them. They are not to blame for these requirements in their lives. Do they have any less an *obligation* to fulfill their appointed duty than the king has?"

With his jaw clamped tight, he gave her horse another smack and sent it charging full tilt up the length of the green. Again she managed to rein the beast, turn, and ride back to him.

"You disappoint me, Sir Hugh." Her chest was heaving. "You freely allow for the variation in horses, but not in the hearts and minds of womankind. You declare animals must be handled according to their individual natures, but then treat all women with the same unearned contempt. Saints—do not women deserve at least the consideration you would show to beasts?"

The disturbance visible behind his rigid expression was some satisfaction.

"I confess, I expected greater fairness of mind in you," she said. "I am sorry to have been so wrong."

This time he didn't need to give the horse a smack. She reined sharply around and urged the beast to a run that carried her down the length of the field.

Hugh felt strangely both furious and powerless as he

watched her ride away. She believed him to be a woman-hating beast.

And why shouldn't she? The things he'd said—both in her hearing and outside of it—certainly constituted proof. He suddenly thought of his discussions with Graham. Did his closest friend also see him as narrow and rigid and even a little ridiculous because of the things he'd said about women and marriage?

Memories of a hundred different smirks and titters aimed his way by other courtiers came rushing in on him. The ladies' resentful looks and taunting winks ... the men's jests about his monkishness ... the king's tongue-in-cheek reference to his experience with women. For the first time, he truly glimpsed himself through the eyes of others: a superior, self-righteous aesthetic given to criticism of women, marriage, and all things pleasurable.

That assessment might be accurate, but it wasn't entirely fair. The monks who raised him preached fervently that emotion and pleasure were to be experienced and expressed solely in the service of God. He had tried to believe that, but in his heart he had held such dogma at arm's length, never embracing it fully. Something fundamental in him—fundamentally flawed, he had feared—refused to believe that there should be no love or pleasure or devotion in the world except that which was offered to God. Was that why he so often spouted that belief? Hoping to, trying to own it more fully?

Over the last several years at court and abroad with the king, he had come to see that many of the things he had been taught belonged within a set of cloister walls. There were other truths, different interpretations and expectations for life in the world outside of the monastic community. He had come to see the validity and even the necessity of both ways of living. The change in him had come gradually. He had been aware of and accepted the new developments in his thinking, but had not yet allowed them to transform his speech or his actions. Why was that?

Because it would seem to others that he was simply

giving in to the pressures and temptations of the world, he realized with no little shame. Others would say he was just succumbing to his own sinful nature . . . his flaws and weakness . . . and he couldn't bear to be thought of as flawed or weak. Chloe's troubled face appeared in his mind's eye. The irony was, she had uncovered in him a fault more insidious than any indulgence in a bit of pleasure: false pride.

Instead of living and upholding something he devoutly believed in, he found himself pretending to revere something he had long since left behind. That dissonance between his beliefs and actions shook him to the depths of his soul.

There was a word for men like him.

Hypocrite.

CHLOE PERSEVERED IN HER RIDING LESSON, in spite of the fact that her instructor had retired to the shade of a group of trees overhanging the rock wall and left her on her own. Gradually she made peace with her willful mount and learned to start and stop a horse and to turn in whatever direction she desired. The more proficient she became, the more the tension in her middle uncoiled; the less anxiety she showed, the better the aging mare responded.

Ironically her success came in part from her preoccupation with her volatile exchange with Sir Hugh. It had left her strangely disheartened. She had wanted him to prove to be more wise and fair-minded than he appeared. She had wanted to believe—hoped earnestly, in fact—that his glib disdain for women and marriage didn't extend all the way into his deepest thoughts and feelings. Just why she wanted to believe that was not something she was prepared to examine too closely, especially now that she'd been proven wrong.

The devil take him, she told herself. Let him stew in his arrogant delusions and grow old and curdled inside before his time. She had sisters to marry off and a family to find.

As they rode back to the stable a short while later, she watched the others plodding along ahead of her. They were not a pretty sight. The once elegant Sir Jaxton now looked sweaty and frazzled, and Margarete's chin was quivering. Lord William would not walk within six feet of a sullen, snappish Helen or her inexplicably carnivorous mount. Lord Simon trudged along behind Alaina's horse wearing a pained expression, watching her bounce determinedly all over the saddle. And Sir Graham . . . gentle, courteous, affable Sir Graham . . . looked as if he might be willing to *help* Lisette fall from her horse if she didn't quickly develop a functional spine.

When she glanced at Sir Hugh, he seemed to be studying them, too. But before she had a chance to learn what new complaint lay behind the grim expression he wore, they encountered a party of riders with falcons and hawks perched on their arms, returning from a hunt. As they poured into the stableyard together and the king's falconers scurried to remove their hooded charges to a nearby wagon filled with cages, the groups merged into one chaotic mass.

She lost sight of Sir Hugh, and when a pair of burly arms reached up to help her down, she accepted the assistance and soon found herself on the ground facing none other than the Lord Treasurer himself.

"Oh, thank you, my lord" she said breathlessly, clutching his sleeves as she struggled to stay upright on suddenly boneless legs. "Forgive my boldness—I seem to have difficulty standing."

"Pleased to be of service . . . Lady Chloe, is it?" Bromley said with a smile that did not entirely hide the keenness of his scrutiny.

"It is. And how kind of my lord to remember."

"It is no kindness, my girl, to recall the name of a beauty who happens to be clutching your sleeves." He chuckled at the way she blushed and lowered her lashes. "Your first time riding, I hear." When she looked up in

surprise, he informed her: "News travels quickly inside
Windsor. How did you fare?"

"Alas, none of us seems to be a born rider," she con-
fided. He had the sort of face that seemed to elicit confessions . . . a useful trait, no doubt, in a Lord High
Treasurer . . . the keeper of the tax rolls. She suddenly
brightened. Her distress at the discomfort in her lower half
was suddenly outstripped by her delight in having unexpected access to the source of information she so desperately wanted. "But neither did any of us fall off a horse
or get thrown."

The treasurer looked pleased. "Then you've done well
enough this day. Would you care for some assistance back
to the hall?"

"Yes, thank—"

"Part of learning to ride is learning to deal with the
consequences after," Sir Hugh's voice broke in on them.
Suddenly he was beside them, glowering, and Chloe felt
as if she'd been caught filching sweets from the convent's
pantry.

"Well, one of the consequences today is my sympathy." Bromley offered her his arm, and with a glance at
her sisters—finding them escorted—she accepted.

As they walked slowly up the slope with Sir Hugh in
tow, she seized the opportunity to ask the Lord Treasurer
the question burning in her heart.

"My lord, can you tell me if there is a house of
'Gilbert' ?"

"Gilbert?" He thought for a moment. "There are some
Gilberts to the south—Sussex, I believe. Small estate. A
barony, I believe. Why do you ask?"

"I was told I have relations—Gilberts—in England. I
hoped to one day meet them. Do you know if they ever
come to court?"

He scowled, thinking. "Can't say I've ever seen them.
I don't think they sent any men with us to France. I could
inquire—"

"My Lord Bromley!" A page came running up just

then with word that the king wished to see the treasurer immediately.

Bromley sighed and squeezed her hand as he returned it to her.

"Another time, perhaps, Lady Chloe. The king will not be denied."

She felt Sir Hugh's disapproval like a flame scorching her back. Lifting her skirt, she started again for her quarters, and he seized her elbow, propelling her along.

"They say 'a word to the wise is sufficient,' " he murmured just loud enough for her to hear. "Take care what favors you accept at court . . . especially from well-fed lords like Bromley. They always expect payment."

She halted and glared up at him.

"What payment could the Lord Treasurer of England hope to have from me? I'm virtually penniless—" She faltered, realizing that the "payment" he spoke of was made in an altogether more worldly sort of currency. The wretch.

"I, too, have a word to the wise." She raked him with an accusing look as she jerked her elbow from him to walk back to the hall on her own. " 'Beware of measuring other men in your own half bushel.' "

THE DUKE'S DAUGHTERS DINED IN THEIR chamber that evening. None of them was fit to descend the stairs and sit for hours on a hard wooden bench under the relentless scrutiny of king and court. They had bruises on their thighs, strains in their backs and limbs, and aches everywhere else.

Lady Marcella sent her serving women for some fresh willow twigs, mustard, and goose grease, and together she and Chloe brewed a tonic that eased the aches and made a rub that drew heat to the maids' abused nether regions. After that bitter brew, Lady Marcella insisted each drink a full cup of sweet, undiluted wine, which not only relaxed their aching muscles, it loosened their tongues.

"That Lord Simon"—Alaina needed no coaxing with

her complaint—"seemed so handsome and dignified at
first. But he treated me like the veriest simpleton. Said I
was bouncing about like a puppet. Can you *imagine*?"

"He couldn't have been any worse than that smirking
Lord William," Helen declared irritably, brushing her hair.
"I could swear I saw him pinch that awful beast to make
it bite at me."

"Really, Helen." Chloe tried to inject a bit of reason.
"I can't imagine he would intentionally—"

"I kept telling Sir Jaxton I felt about to swoon, but he
refused to let me down," Margarete said in a petulant tone.
"Then he complained that I wasn't sitting up straight
enough. How could I when I was hanging on for dear
life?"

"If only I'd had Sir Hugh to teach me," Helen said,
giving Chloe an envious glance. "Did you see how well
Chloe was doing?"

"And without him prattling constantly and harranging
her," Alaina added. "If only we had several Sir Hughs . . .
there would be no question of who should marry whom."

"And we could all have a perfect husband," Margarete
declared, nodding.

"Listening to you, I feel a bit guilty," Lisette confessed.
"I had a rather enjoyable ride. Sir Graham is so chivalrous. When I had difficulty staying in the saddle, he
kindly held me there until I got my balance." She looked
to Chloe. "I hope I get to stay with him for tomorrow's
lesson."

Chloe was so caught up in her own thoughts and emotions that she was scarcely aware that she nodded. Margarete's words were circling around and around in her
head like a devilish taunt—"*perfect husband . . . perfect
husband . . . perfect husband.*" She looked from one of her
surprised and annoyed sisters to another, thinking that
their reactions mirrored hers.

How could they possibly think Sir Hugh would make
any sort of husband, much less a *perfect* one?

*   *   *

THE NEXT MORNING THE HORSES WERE saddled and waiting when they reached the stable. The maids were helped aboard their mounts and taken down the slope to the green by different instructors . . . except for Lisette. Sir Graham was a bit bewildered by the other maids' seeming avoidance of him and grimly offered Lisette his arm and his knee for mounting. Soon the four pairs were on their way down to the green, and Chloe was once again watching her sisters strike off toward their futures without her.

"I thought you said they were to change partners each day." When she turned, Sir Hugh was standing behind her with his arms crossed, scowling. "Why is Graham saddled with Lisette again?"

"They were the only pair who weren't ready to draw and quarter each other after yesterday's lesson. Why upset the one bit of harmony that was achieved?" She picked up the reins and waited for him to offer her assistance.

"Lack of conflict does not mean harmony," he declared, making no such offer. "Did it never occur to you that Graham's silence might conceal a deep dislike or even contempt?"

"For Lisette? Don't be absurd." She glanced toward the gate where the pairs had just disappeared. She should have known better than to allow Lisette's headstrong desire for Graham to sway her judgment. Sir Hugh was looking for an excuse to call the wife test into question, and she'd just handed it to him. "Lisette is a beautiful, graceful young woman—"

"Who looks at men as if they've been dipped in honey and she is one exceedingly hungry bee."

She copied his stance, chin up and arms crossed, while scrambling for a response . . . a defense . . . a means to redirect his challenge. Miraculously, when she opened her mouth, one came out.

"There you go, measuring others in *your* half bushel again." When his arms dropped abruptly to his sides, she quickly thanked Heaven for that bit of assistance. "Just because *your* mind strays frequently into the fleshly realm doesn't mean others are so afflicted."

"I am *not* afflicted with immoral thoughts," he declared hotly.

"I'm not passing judgment," she said calmly. "I'm merely making an observation."

She watched him struggling for self-control. After a moment he lost.

"Keep your 'observations' to yourself, and get on the damned horse!" He bent one knee under the stirrup and, with his jaw muscles flexing visibly, extended a hand to help her.

"The worrisome thing isn't the lustful thoughts, you know," she said as she settled onto the saddle. "They're simply the result of the way men are fashioned . . . with a weakness for looking at women's bodies."

"I do *not* have a weakness for—" He turned away and pulled on the halter to set the horse in motion.

"The worrisome thing is the way you refuse to admit it," she said, enjoying having the upper hand and reluctant to relinquish it. "Lustful urges themselves are not necessarily sinful. It is the way you choose to act upon those urges that determines whether or not you sin."

"Did they teach you that in the convent," he snarled over his shoulder, "or is it just a little heresy of your own devising?"

"What have I said that is wrong?" she demanded.

He halted and turned to look up at her.

"Everything. Firstly, I am *not* plagued with lustful and immoral thoughts." He jerked a thumb at his chest. "Not all men desire to look upon a woman's nakedness. Furthermore, the church teaches that we're all sinful from the start . . . from the moment we're born into the world . . . every single day of our lives . . . for as long as we live. Our thoughts as well as our actions condemn us."

She could only stare at him, surprised by the intensity of his response and the depths of unrelieved guilt it revealed in him.

"So you and the holy church are in complete agreement, then?" she finally said. "Every single soul is steeped in sin and degradation from birth?"

"Absolutely."

"We sin ceaselessly . . . by every thought, word, and deed?"

"Yes."

"We cannot escape it?"

"That's right."

The game suddenly lost its savor. Something in the middle of her collapsed and sank, taking her spirits with it.

"Then what about forgiveness? Compassion? Love? Where do they exist in this hopelessly wicked world that you and the holy church inhabit?"

His gaze climbed slowly, irritably to hers. For a moment she glimpsed the confusion in him . . . the desire to be righteous and blameless . . . the turbulent passions that he struggled constantly to conquer. She watched the tumult rise to an alarming level before he slammed that portal closed.

He wheeled and gave the animal a stinging slap on the rump. "He-ya!" The horse shot forward like an arrow released from a longbow, and all she could do was grip the saddle frantically with her knees and one hand. Pulling back on the reins did no good; the animal was too excited or too frightened to respond. It raced pell-mell down the green with her, headed straight for the low stone wall.

"Nooo! Sto-o-o-p—"

When it was clear the horse wouldn't stop, she held on to the saddle with both hands and held her breath. Beneath her, the animal gathered itself and jumped.

Time seemed to slow, every instant seemed to last a lifetime. For a brief, soaring moment elation replaced pure mortal terror. Then the horse touched down, and she slammed back down on the saddle with a bone-jarring thud. Her heart lurched in her chest to beat wildly as the horse continued to run across the open field before them.

She was scarcely aware of the distant commotion . . . the screams of her sisters, the shouts of the husband candidates, and the alarm sounded among the knights at the far end of the tilting field she had just invaded. She had no way of knowing that Sir Hugh had cleared the wall himself on foot, and was racing after her and yelling frantically to the mounted knights to go after her. All she heard was the pounding of hooves, the rasp of the animal's breathing, and the roar of her blood in her ears.

The horse continued to run for a time, slowing gradually, giving way to the hindrances of age and inactivity, but not before she experienced the thrill of horse and rider settling into a rhythm and working together. It was marvelous. Her fears melted away as they reached another low wall and the horse responded to direction and turned to follow it to a broad, open gate and a well-used path leading off into the countryside. As they exited the opening, her winded mount slowed to a walk, and she leaned down to pat its neck before turning to head back to the castle.

She hadn't gone far when she spotted a horse and rider barreling toward her at a dead run. As he neared she recognized Sir Hugh, and as he reined up and maneuvered his horse beside hers, she realized he was red-faced and furious.

"Are you all right?" he bellowed, his chest heaving, his shoulders and arms swollen with tension as he grabbed her arm and visually scoured her for signs of damage.

"Yes," she said, "I'm fine. I was frightened at first, but—Sweet Heaven—what a ride! Did you see her?" She reached down to stroke the horse's neck. "She jumped the fence and then ran like the wind."

Hugh tightened his grip on her arm, searching her glowing face, her sparkling blue eyes and wind-whipped hair. She was not only unharmed, she seemed downright enlivened by her brush with catastrophe.

"You might have been killed!"

"Well, I didn't exactly have a choice," she said between breaths. "The horse bolted, and all I could do was hold on for dear life."

"You're sure you're all right?"

"A bit shaken, but otherwise, fine." She realized her cap was dangling down the back of her hair, and righted it with trembling hands. "Saints—I can see now why people love riding fast and furious." She took a deep breath, sighed with cleansing relief, and smiled. It was a glowing, pleasure-filled expression that dazzled him momentarily.

How could she have survived something that would have injured or at least terrified most women and then *smile* about it? Clearly, the shock of the near calamity had eclipsed her recollection of what had caused the horse to run away with her.

"We'd better get back to the others," he said gruffly. Forcing his gaze from her, he looked toward the great round tower visible in the distance and saw in the blue sky all around it the vibrant color of her eyes. Clear and unaccusing eyes. They rode in silence for a few moments before she spoke again.

"Thank you for coming after me," she said, and he felt a pang of guilt that clamored for expiation.

"It was the least I could do." He sat straighter in the saddle and made himself say it. "Considering that it was me who caused the horse to bolt in the first place."

He could feel her looking at him, searching his grim expression, no doubt remembering his dangerous burst of temper.

"I never meant to . . . I never intended . . ."

She had every reason to be furious with him. His knightly oath demanded that he protect and defend her and his personal code of conduct demanded even more: respect and Christian concern. In one overwrought moment he had violated both standards and put her in jeopardy.

Her silence quickly became unbearable. He glanced over at her and found her looking at him with a strangely intent expression. Then she broke into a small, speaking smile that caused everything to contract inside his chest, making it hard to draw air.

"I know you didn't mean any harm," she said. And clearly meant it.

In that moment Hugh of Sennet felt the foundations of his world being turned over like sod before the share of a plow. Suddenly everything he had been taught and had assumed to be true was being exposed to new air, new light, and new questions. The realization that it all began with and centered on Chloe of Guibray was nothing short of alarming.

She *forgave* him.

Dammit.

THEY WERE GREETED BY A CHORUS OF concern the instant they came into view of the greensward. Picking up the pace, they rode quickly through the main gate and paused to reassure Chloe's sisters that she was unharmed. To Hugh's relief, no one in the bridal party seemed to have noticed what caused her mount to bolt. Equally annoying was the fact that everyone had seen her heroic jump over the wall. It was all they could talk about as they started back to the stable.

Then, as they rode up the rise to the gate in the curtain wall and the maids continued to turn in their saddles to talk to her, one of their number suddenly cried out and fell from her horse.

Hugh paused long enough to lift Chloe down and set her on her feet before rushing to see who was hurt.

Lisette lay on the ground beside her saddle, her face pale and her eyes closed. Even in distress her limbs were gracefully arrayed and her dark tresses had spilled in a fetching tangle around her. Graham knelt beside her, warily shaking her shoulder and calling her name.

"Let me through!" Chloe fell onto her knees to check her sister's head and limbs. Everything seemed to be in order. She stroked and patted Lisette's cheek and called to her. Soon Lisette's eyes fluttered open and began to focus.

"W-what happened?" She moaned softly, holding her forehead.

"You fell from your horse," Chloe told her. "Can you

see? Are you in pain? Do you hurt anywhere?"

"Just my head." Lisette moved her other parts one at a time, testing them. "Ooooh, and my *derriere*."

Chloe looked up to reassure their worried sisters. "I think she will be all right." Then she turned naturally to Hugh. "We need to get her to our chamber, where she can be checked more thoroughly."

Hugh kicked the saddle out of the way and knelt by Lisette's feet. "Can you sit up?" As she did so, his gaze fled back to the saddle and narrowed. "No wonder you fell, your saddle came loose." He reached for the cinch strap and pulled it up, expecting to see ripped stitching dangling from one end. Instead, he pulled up half of a strap . . . straight and smooth across most of the end, as if cut more than half through, then torn the rest of the way.

When Lisette tried to stand she grew dizzy and her legs buckled. Hugh was drawn back to the problem at hand and declared that he and Graham would carry her to her chamber. They formed a makeshift chair by crossing their arms at the wrists and grasping each other's hands. Chloe and Lord Simon helped Lisette to a seat between them and placed her hands on their shoulders, telling her to hold on.

Hugh charged Lord Simon with seeing that the other maidens dismounted safely and were escorted to their quarters.

"And Simon," he added.

"Yes, Hugh?"

"Take that damnable saddle to the tack shed and find out who let a damaged saddle—a lady saddle at that— out of the king's stables."

As they carried Lisette toward the great hall and the maidens' chambers, she moaned softly and leaned against Sir Graham. Soon her arms were around his neck alone, and one of her breasts was pressed strategically against his chest. Graham's face heated a bit more with each increase in contact. Beads of sweat appeared on his forehead and upper lip.

The sight of a swooning maiden being borne through the great hall by two eligible nobles set the entire castle awag. By the time they reached the maidens' chamber, Lady Marcella arrived with cloths for bandages, medicinal herbs, and two stout serving women. She was relieved to find that they were not needed.

"Thank you, Sir Graham, for your kindness to me." Lisette's arms lingered for a moment around Sir Graham's neck as they lowered her onto her cot. Out of sight of the others, she gave him a brush on the cheek with her lips. "I promise I shall do better next time."

Graham sprang away from her like a startled buck, then, realizing that he had overreacted, reddened and backed stiffly to the door.

"Mend quickly, Lady Lisette."

WHEN THEY LEFT THE MAIDS' CHAMBER, Hugh and Graham headed for the stable to see what Lord Simon had discovered. They found the earl in the tack room, where he informed them that nearly all of the lady saddles had cinches that were cut . . . including all of the ones the duke's daughters had just used.

They sent for the saddlemaker, who declared in bewilderment that the cuts seemed fresh and did not seem the result of accidental damage or even misuse. Judging from the narrow strips of leather that held some of the cinches together, they were fortunate not to have had maidens hitting the ground all around them.

As the saddlemaker hurried off to get supplies to make repairs, Hugh stared at the damaged leather and chilled at the memory of the way Chloe's horse had plunged headlong over the fence with her.

Dear God. Such a jump . . . and with a bad cinch . . . she might have been . . .

His gut tightened.

"Why would anyone do such a thing?" Graham asked as they headed back to their own quarters.

"Most of the saddles maintained here are for the king's unmounted guests and functionaries of the castle," Hugh observed. "Knights keep their saddles in their quarters, and nobles visiting Windsor generally bring their own squires and grooms who see to their horses and equipage." Hugh turned it over and over in his mind. "Why would anyone tamper with lady saddles . . . saddles that no one of great importance would ride?"

"No great importance?" Graham halted, and when Hugh stopped to look back at him, he was highly indignant. "I'll have you know, one of those lovely maidens will someday be the Lady of Ledding."

"Ah, yes," Hugh said with a wicked look. "Lady Lisette of Ledding. It has quite a ring to it."

Graham's face lost all trace of humor.

"That's not funny."

LATE THAT NIGHT, IN THE TOWN OF Windsor, a stealthy figure slipped inside a sour-smelling tavern and made his way around the long tables of ale-soaked planking to the rear, where a pair of men wearing hooded tunics sat huddled over tankards of cheap ale.

"Oui?" one of the two, the French knight Valoir, asked the newcomer.

"The one who fell . . . she was not hurt badly."

"Are you sure?"

"I have bought the favors of a wench who works in the castle kitchens. Word travels quickly in that cursed pile."

"Sacrebleu!" Valoir responded. "What does it take to get rid of one of *les putaines*?"

"They are charmed cats," the other snarled, then turned to their informant. "Keep your ears and your eyes open, eh?"

With a nod, the informer drew his hood closer about his face and stole from the murky corner toward the door.

"They will surely ride again," Valoir said, rubbing his grizzled face. "Sooner or later they will have to go beyond the castle grounds."

"We will be ready, *Capitaine*," his companion declared. "I have learned of a gang of poachers who are said to be able to deliver any kind of wild game for a price."

Chapter Eleven

THE DUKE'S DAUGHTERS SPENT THE next morning in their chamber with Lady Marcella and her two perky little dogs. Since she could no longer see well enough to stitch, the old lady spent her time collecting bits of information and gossip gone astray, and proved to be a veritable fountain of knowledge. She took the maids' birthdates and promised to chart their stars, then launched into news of the queen's condition and the latest castle gossip.

"The Lord Treasurer—who keeps a huge kitchen and spends a fortune on foods from Italy and Spain—brings the queen those *or-anges* from Spain each time he comes to court," the old lady rattled on. "The queen loves them. Just like the king and his French wine." She leaned toward them and lowered her voice. "Troth—that Bromley is a master at currying favor with food."

Chloe sat with her needle poised over the lace Lisette had given her for the neck of her gown. The old lady's mention of the Lord Treasurer's political use of food suddenly gave her a much-needed idea.

"Speaking of eating . . ." Chloe looked brightly at the

others. "Are you ready to hear your next task in the wife test?"

Her sisters received her great inspiration with less enthusiasm.

"We have to go down to those hot, stinky kitchens?"

"We have to tend a hearth like common pot-minders and spit boys?"

"Among all that grease and ash? We'll ruin our clothes!"

"How do we know what our beloved lords will like?"

"That's the best part," Chloe declared, making rules up as she went. "You *don't* know. You'll simply make your favorite dish, and let 'taste' help decide who belongs together."

There was silence for a moment as they thought it over. It was Helen who signaled their acceptance of the challenge:

"How will we know what foods the cooks may have in their cellar?"

Lady Marcella sent for the king's chamberlain, who called for the head cook. Soon they were all huddled in the whitewashed kitchens, amidst worktables and piles of baskets filled with wrinkled wintered turnips, dried beans and peas, and pungent onions. After learning of the availability of foods and spices, the maids retreated to their chambers to decide on the dishes they would present to their prospective husbands.

By the time they delivered their lists of ingredients to the kitchen, the place was atizzy with talk of them and their culinary "test." The story worked its way through the various outbuildings, including the knights' quarters, then into the round tower, and finally into the great hall itself.

Hugh was there with Lord Simon, informing the king and the captain of the king's guards about the damaged saddles, when Graham, Sir Jaxton, and Lord William hurried in to demand if it were true that the maids were now required to cook for them as part of the wife test. With the king looking on, Hugh was forced to admit:

"I . . . haven't discussed it with Lady Chloe."

"I'm surprised at you, Hugh," the king said, with a glint of amusement. "I would have expected greater diligence in this duty. Perhaps you should go and *discuss* it with her now."

As he watched the blanched Hugh withdraw and charge out the door leading toward the maids' chamber, Edward smiled.

Hugh was met in the upstairs passage by a serving woman who directed him outside. He found Chloe and her sisters in the queen's courtyard, basking in the sun and enduring the avid curiosity of courtiers stationed at windows overlooking the court or lurking just outside the arched entry.

"I want a word with you, Lady Chloe," he declared, planting himself before her with his fists on his hips.

"Certainly, Sir Hugh." She set her little-used birch hoop with its hopeless tangle of colored yarns aside. "I meant to speak with you—"

"Come with me," he growled, taking her by the wrist and pulling her out of the courtyard and down the gravel path that wound between plots of herbs and sheltered niches stacked with weathered barrels and old poultry ricks.

At first a few intrepid hangers-on followed them, but as he darted with her down little-used paths, they eventually fell away, and Chloe found herself alone with him and being dragged to thither-and-gone.

"What is this about?" She pulled against his grip, trying to get him to stop, but he stalked grimly on. "Has something happened?"

He remained stubbornly silent until they reached an isolated stretch of wall that was sheltered by one of the round towers. There he wheeled, grabbed her by the shoulders, and thrust her back against the sun-warmed stones.

"I don't like being made a fool," he growled.

"No one does," she said, seizing his wrists and trying

in vain to remove his hands from her shoulders. "Do you mind?"

"This cooking nonsense—why didn't you tell me about it? Everyone from the pot boys in the kitchen to the king himself has heard of it. I was asked about it in front of the king, and I couldn't even hazard a guess!" He squeezed her shoulders. "I want to know the rest of this cursed wife test—every damned step of it—every task, every requirement. And I want to know it *now*!"

Again she tried to remove his hands from her shoulders, but he was too strong and too determined. She raised her chin to show she wasn't intimidated.

"Ladies . . . are required to oversee the kitchens in their households, and it is only sensible to see that the tastes of husband and wife are in harmony," she declared. He was scarcely inches away, filling her vision, invading her on the very air she breathed. "My sisters will prepare their favorite dishes and their husbands-to-be will choose their favorites."

"And?"

"It will demonstrate a likeness of taste and sense."

"And?"

"That is the sum of it." She avoided his eyes, only to have her attention fasten impulsively on his lips. "I-I will be able to match who made a dish with who preferred it."

"A simple matter of preference?"

"An *important* matter of preference," she insisted.

"And what if several men prefer the same dish?"

"In that event . . . I . . . shall . . . take note and it will still be useful."

He considered that for a moment. "What is next?"

"Another riding lesson," she managed. "We still have much to learn."

"You'll get no argument on that. Then what?"

She swallowed hard and looked past his shoulder, scrambling to decide which of the tasks she had considered would sound most plausible.

"Then there is the test of . . . *the gift*. Each of the

husbands-to-be will present the maids a gift that represents his home."

"What is the point of that?"

In the brief silence she felt her throat tightening and her skin heating beneath his hands. Having him so close and touching her was making it devilishly difficult to concentrate.

"My sisters will listen to each man tell the story of how it represents his home, and then they will choose which gift means the most to them."

"Preferences again. What if more than one maid chooses the same gift?"

"Again . . . it will be useful no matter who chooses which gift."

"It seems to me"—his voice was suddenly lower—"that this 'wife test' of yours depends a great deal on simple preference. But 'preference,' I have learned, is not always a simple matter. What happens if, in the end, all of the men prefer the same maid? What if there is one maid no one wants?"

"I doubt that will occur."

"But it is possible. And let's say that it happens. What then?"

"Then . . . they will have to trust in the wisdom of the test."

"In our judgment, you mean. For isn't that what your precious 'test' comes down to? Our judgment? Our *preferences?* Yours and mine?" Then he asked the question that had deviled her sleep for the last two nights. "What happens if *we* don't agree?"

She drew a shaky breath and forced herself to look up at him. His sable and russet eyes were glowing.

"Th-then we will discuss it and come to some sort of agreement."

"Negotiate, you mean."

"Discuss it," she insisted. "Exchange points. Engage in give-and-take."

"Meaning: you take and I give. For, without knowing the details of your precious 'test,' I will always be at a disadvantage. Then, in truth"—he paused to draw an alarming conclusion—"what this all comes down to is *your* preferences." As he thought on that, his gaze wandered over her face.

"Why don't we save ourselves a great deal of time and effort?" He leaned closer. "What *are* your preferences, Chloe of Guibray?"

Her skin flushed with heat. All of it. From her scalp to her toes.

"To make the best possible matches for my sisters—"

"I mean your *personal* preferences. You are to be wedded, too."

Rivulets of warmth began trickling down the walls of her body to pool below her waist, carrying her indignation, her determination, and most of her concentration with them. Even her voice seemed to have been affected; it was suddenly little more than a whisper.

"I don't have preferences . . . of that sort."

"Come, now." He pulled her toward him. "You've listened to them and watched them with your sisters. The handsome Jaxton. Simon the diplomat. That charming rascal William. Good-hearted and easily-led Graham. You can't say you haven't thought about it. This is your chance to declare your preference, *negotiate* for your choice." He pulled her still closer, as if that might somehow force it out of her. "Which one do you want?"

"I-I hardly think this is . . ." She tried to wrest free and might have succeeded if he hadn't slid his arms around her and hauled her fully against him.

"Tell me." They were so close she could feel his heart pounding through their clothes. "Who do you want?"

Everything happening inside her—thought, heartbeat, breath—halted as the answer sprang from her heart to her mind and then her lips, where she just managed to stop it from escaping.

You.

Her legs weakened as that truth crashed over her in a sudden, overpowering wave of longing. She jerked her head aside to keep him from seeing what was surely as plain in her eyes as it was in her heart. How could this be? How could she possibly want him, knowing what sort of man he was . . . how he despised women and marriage? He was everything she knew to spell disaster for a peaceful and harmonious married life.

He cupped her face with his hand and forced it up. The last thing she saw as she closed her eyes was his mouth lowering toward hers.

For that first, stunning moment all she could do was feel. The strength of his arms around her, the hardness of his body against hers, the paradoxical softness of his lips . . . she was engulfed by new and overwhelming sensations. This was a kiss. This was what those handsome lips felt like when they were pressed against her own. Sweet heaven—it was wonderful. How could she have imagined anything this intimate, this delicious, this enthralling?

Then his mouth canted and began to move over hers, caressing her lips, coaxing a response from deep inside her. She grabbed the sides of his tunic to steady herself as she grew warm and pliant, melting against him, tilting her head to better receive his kiss. It became a subtle dance of desire and fulfillment between them, of curiosity and discovery.

Her second recognizable thought was that the feel of his body pressed against her was somehow familiar. It felt strangely as if she knew his embrace, even though she had never experienced or even imagined anything like it. She ran her hands up his back, measuring with the span of her fingers those broad shoulders that were proving not to be quite so impervious after all. He responded by running his hands firmly, hungrily over her back and sides. Each stroke unleashed a wave of pleasure that made her want to experience more.

She slid her arms up his chest and around his corded neck. In her mind dozens of stored images appeared: the line of his cheekbones, the soft curl of his hair, the breadth of his shoulders, the sensual sway of his shoulders as he walked, the hint of beard that grayed his jaw . . .

Then something in the feel of his mouth against hers changed.

He opened his eyes and jerked his head up, breaking that heavenly contact. A moment later he ripped his over-heated body from hers and lurched back, looking at her as if she'd just sprouted horns and cloven hooves.

Abandoned abruptly, she staggered back a step, where she smacked the stone wall. As she shoved her hands out at her sides to support herself, every half-pleasured part of her was screaming in protest. But the look on his face silenced whatever voice she might have given to those complaints.

He turned on his heel and blindly strode off, banging his shoulder into the side of the tower as he fled.

The impact of what had just happened caused her knees to buckle, and she slid partway down the wall. Handsome, powerful, enigmatic Sir Hugh had *kissed* her. It was all she had dreamt of and more than she could have known to imagine. She touched her newly sensitive lips and tried to hold on to echoes of the pleasure he had stirred in her. But the sensations were fading quickly, growing elusive. Her awareness quickly broadened to admit a larger, more sobering reality. Arrogant, self-righteous, abstemious Sir Hugh of Sennet had *kissed* her.

Since that first night in the woods she had relived again and again those moments with him pressed against her, touching her face, and staring into her eyes. She had told herself she was merely studying the encounter, learning, anticipating the feel of being a wife in relation to a husband. But, in truth, what she had been anticipating were far more specific pleasures: the feel of *Sir Hugh's* arms around her ... *his* lips on hers ... the tingle of her skin at *his* touch.

The horror in his expression as he backed away washed over her anew. Where were her wits, her common sense ... her instinct for self-preservation? How could she have let herself stumble into such a disastrous attraction? He was her royally appointed overseer, her adversary, the lone threat to her "wife test" scheme. But, even worse, he was the one man in the kingdom who could calmly and with full theological justification pull a lovesick heart from a smitten breast and stomp on it.

What on earth was she going to do?

Looking around, she spotted the round tower at the top of the hill and headed for it. Frantic to escape the turmoil of her emotions, she ran head down, headfirst into a group of men coming down the main path.

"Lady Chloe!" The king himself grabbed her by the shoulders and set her back. "Are you all right?"

"Y-yes, Your Highness." She dropped into a deep curtsy, and her knees were so weak that she could scarcely rise again. When she looked up, the king was staring intently at her, and she quelled an urge to hide her lips behind a hand. "I was out for a walk and am on my way back to my sisters."

"Did Sir Hugh find you?" he asked casually. "I believe he had something to discuss with you." Behind him, Lord Bromley made a noise somewhere between a cough and a choking sound and two other nobly dressed fellows looked abruptly away.

"He did," she said, blushing in spite of herself.

"Good." He motioned to the others. "Come, my lords. The tilting matches. Our royal defenders await."

Chloe couldn't have known, as they left her and she gathered up her gown and raced first to her chambers and then to the chapel, that she was in fact following in footsteps Sir Hugh had laid down only a short while earlier. He, too, had seemed distracted when he ran into the king's party. His lips had also been swollen, and his eyes glistened with the same smoky allure.

She couldn't have known that the king responded to her hasty departure the same way he had to Hugh's: with a sardonic chuckle. Nor could she have guessed that the priest assigned to hear confessions that day, Father Ignatius, reacted with equal amusement to the sight of her heading for the confessional.

Impure and unworthy thoughts, she confessed.

"An unfortunate consequence of the human gift for

imagining," Father Ignatius declared philosophically.

Uncontrollable and misdirected desire.

"The inevitable result of the Almighty's insistence on giving mankind both free will and a bred-in-the-bone mandate to 'be fruitful and multiply.' "

Recklessly lustful and impassioned contact with a man.

"*Tsk.* Most unfortunate." The canny father templed his fingers and produced a secret smile. "Tell me more, my child. . . ."

THAT NIGHT AT DINNER IN THE GREAT hall, the men and maids were seated opposite each other. There was precious little conversation at their section of table or elsewhere in the hall. Everyone, even the king, was watching and listening for the slightest clue as to the state of relations between the intended couples. But the most telling detail seemed to be the fact that Sir Hugh was seated well down the table from the group, all but ignoring them.

When Edward called for a report on how the wife test was proceeding, Chloe rose at her seat and answered that it was going as expected. When the king called her forward and demanded details, she volunteered a description of the "cooking test" set for the next day.

"Sir Hugh," the king called out. "Am I to assume that you have discussed this with Lady Chloe and are in agreement?"

Hugh rose slowly, trying to swallow the gulp of wine he had taken just as his name rang out. He succeeded and obeyed the king's beckoning hand.

"Yes, Highness." He moved forward to stand by, but not beside, Chloe of Guibray. So much for his plan to keep at least a county's worth of distance between them.

"I confess, I am surprised, Sir Hugh, to see you wear your responsibilities as the realm's 'wife judge' so casually."

He felt his ears heating.

"If it appears that I do so, it is only because I have

such confidence in Lady Chloe's ability as the convent's 'wife judge.' "

"Confidence may sometimes be misplaced." The king's genial expression thinned enough to reveal the determination underneath it.

Edward of England would not be cheated out of his entertainment. He was serving notice that he would not tolerate Hugh distancing himself from the proceedings.

"Your opinion of Lady Chloe's abilities has risen considerably. Two days ago she was a 'mere girl' unfit to pass judgment on England's noblemen."

Hugh flushed crimson but held his ground. What had he ever done to deserve such punishment?

"Two days ago I had not learned the secret of the wife test."

"Aha!" Edward sat forward, his eyes alight. "And this 'secret' is?"

"Why, a *secret*, Highness," he said earnestly, serving notice that he would obey, but not without being allowed some dignity. The king eyed him for a moment, then sat back, yielding that point. Inspiration struck. "Lady Chloe and I have decided that, since the weather looks to be favorable, the cooking test will be held out in the countryside, away from the palace."

"Feasting outside," the king declared with such enthusiasm that one might have thought the notion originated with him. "Nothing like being out in the warm air and sunshine to stimulate the appetite."

There was a taint of wickedness in the laughter that rolled around the hall, and with a wave of hand the king dismissed them.

"Dining out in the countryside?" Chloe said in a fierce whisper as they returned to their seats. "What in heaven's name made you say such a thing?"

"Haven't you had enough of Windsor hanging over your shoulders and watching your every word and step?"

She had indeed, she thought, glancing around at the faces turned on her and her sisters in sly conjecture. It would be a great relief to be out of the common eye for a while. She glanced back at him, trying to imagine why he would try to arrange such a thing. Then a cooler, more rational impulse took over. What did it matter why he did it, as long as it helped?

She gripped the edge of the bench, forcing herself to set her own reeling emotions aside and think of what was best for her sisters. In the end, what did it matter that she wanted him desperately and that he couldn't bear even the thought of wanting her? They might have drastically different desires, beliefs, and destinies, but just now they had a common duty to complete the wife test. In her sisters' interest, she would have to lock away her troublesome desire for him. She would have to do that anyway in five more days, when she approached the altar with her royally appointed husband.

She looked down the table to where her sisters were stealing looks at their husbands-to-be, anticipating the future and imaging each of the four noblemen standing beside them as vows were read.

Four noblemen. Not five. Where was her future in all of this?

Secondary, she realized with a leaden feeling settling in her stomach. And she might as well begin to make peace with her lot. After all, she was the one who had chosen it.

GETTING AWAY FROM THE CROWDS AND constant scrutiny at Windsor was a laudable aim but, in point of fact, much easier said than done.

The kitchens were in a flurry and the cooks apoplectic the next morning, preparing the maids' dishes in a transportable form while going on with the task of feeding a small army of nobles, ladies, knights, clerics, retainers, and servants. Outside, the stables grew crowded with residents and visitors who decided at the last moment to go riding . . . including Lord Bromley, a pair of ambassadors from Italy, several minor nobles, and the Lord Bishop of London.

Hugh and Graham had selected a spot near a stream at the edge of a wood, a place where they had often paused while returning from a hunt. Hugh had to tell the cooks first thing that morning to allow them to prepare, and word of their destination had time to spread. By the time the cart bearing the food arrived at the designated place, there were a number of people on horseback milling around, churning the sod and leaving horse piles all over the area. The kitchen steward had a difficult time clearing a space for the equipment they had brought and marshaling his helpers to set up the table, lay the linen, and light the braziers.

When the nuptial party arrived on horseback, at midday, the once placid retreat looked like the first day of a long-awaited hot fair. All that were missing were jugglers and bull-baiting dogs. The maids looked to Chloe in dismay; Chloe looked at Hugh in annoyance; and Hugh looked to Heaven for understanding as he let fly a fiery one-word summary of the situation.

Irritably he took charge and ordered the husbands-to-be to help him clear a space around the tables and order everyone not in the bridal delegation to move back. The onlookers retreated. Then Lord Bromley and his party arrived and rode right through that established perimeter, and everyone else took advantage of it to invade them again.

"My Lord Treasurer." Hugh intercepted Bromley as the portly lord dismounted. "To what do we owe the honor of this visit?"

"Curiosity, Sir Hugh, curiosity. I am a great lover of food and was informed that you will be having some most excellent fare. I was hoping to sample a bit of it and perhaps coax the recipes from your charges."

Hugh dragged a hand down his face, searching for a diplomatic response.

"Perhaps, milord, you should wait until these dishes are tested by others."

"Oh?" Bromley chuckled and looked at Chloe, who stood nearby with her arms crossed and scowl prominent.

"You think there may be danger lurking in those crocks and cassoulets?"

Hugh was left standing in the middle of a milling crowd holding the treasurer's horse as the rest of Bromley's party dismounted.

The glen was suddenly inundated with idle nobles, knights, and ladies poking around in the outdoor kitchen and demanding to know what was on the menu. And if that weren't enough confusion . . . a number of monstrously large hounds appeared out of nowhere and began racing through the gathering, barking and yelping. Everyone talked over the din at first, then had to shout as the noise increased.

"Where did these damnable hounds come from?" Hugh caught sight of Chloe and Margarete being set upon by dogs who had deemed them potentially edible. He waded through the crowd to rescue them.

"Off, dammit! Get off—get out of here!" He shoved the animals from Chloe and steadied her on her feet.

"Coming out here was your idea," she declared irritably, resettling her cap and brushing paw prints from her gown. "For heaven's sake, *do* something."

The hounds had headed for the cooks and were climbing all over the cart, sniffing and pawing at the hampers to get at the food inside. Hugh set Graham and the others to keeping the beasts from wrecking the food, then turned to the crowd, planted his fists at his waist, and roared:

"Who brought these cursed hounds with them?"

"I did!" came a voice from a distance. "They're mine!"

The glen quieted as the bridal delegation and onlookers alike craned their necks to see who was so bold—or reckless—as to claim responsibility. The crowd parted to make way for an older man leading a horse. At first glance he appeared to be a nobleman or well-fixed knight. As he drew closer, they could see wisps of graying hair straggling out from under a drooping felt hat and legs that were slightly bowed inside a pair of ill-fitting hose. His long velvet tunic had probably been quite elegant . . . before it was covered by dog hair and dribbles from dinners past.

"Ketchum?" It was Lord Bromley who recognized him.

"Yes. Who is that?" The fellow squinted toward the Lord Treasurer. "Bromley? Is that you?"

"It is indeed." Bromley held a out a hand in greeting. "How good to see you! Come, let me introduce you to the Duke of Avalon's daughters." He seized Chloe by the hand and pulled her toward the old fellow. "Horace, Earl of Ketchum, may I present to you Lady Chloe . . . one of the tempting young beauties who may soon be your bride."

The color drained from Chloe's face as she extended her hand, and the old fellow took it in a pair of bony claws and gave her a yellow, gap-toothed smile. Her reaction was repeated as the other maids were presented and the old fellow shoved his face into theirs and squinted through the introductions.

The minute they were done, he gave a loud whistle and dogs came running from all over the field to jump on him and lick his face enthusiastically. One of the noble onlookers quipped that the old boy would likely never get that kind of enthusiasm from a wife. The raucous laughter that followed caused Chloe's cheeks to burn with embarrassment for the old fellow . . . who grinned as if he either hadn't heard or hadn't understood, and began to fish inside his tunic for bits of dried meat to reward his hounds.

When she looked away, she spotted Lord Bromley watching her, noting her discomfort. The Lord Treasurer then turned to the old earl.

"Troth, you've a fine kennel there, Ketchum." The treasurer studied the hound-loving earl, who beamed and fondled the ears of two dogs whose front paws now rested on his shoulders. "It's been a while since I had a good run with a pack. Mind if I borrow your beasts? My grooms can act as whippers-on."

"I-I'm not sure they'll run for anyone else." The earl seemed torn between pleasing Bromley and keeping his beloved hounds by his side.

Bromley invited a few of the other knights and nobles present to join him, and soon had gathered an impromptu hunting party.

Relieved to see some of their audience departing, Chloe called for the bridal party to join her at the table, which was being set with steaming crocks and platters. Hugh dragged the Earl of Ketchum over, explaining what was taking place . . . then explaining it all over again more loudly.

"I hope they got something wi'out pepper. Can't tolerate pepper." The earl clasped his melon-shaped belly with both hands and curled his nose. "Gives me a bout o' th' green an' gassy."

Just as the kitchen helpers set the last platter on the table and Chloe began to lift the covers on the food, there was a sudden resurgence of barking and baying in the near distance. The old earl jerked around and shoved past Sir Jaxton and Lord Simon to stare down the edge of the trees.

"They got somethin'! They got a scent!" he called and began to run after the hunting party.

But a moment later his hounds came rushing back . . . some streaking across the open field, others darting into the underbrush and following the line of the trees. All were focused on something that brought them to a fevered pitch.

As the thrashing and snapping of branches grew closer, Chloe and the others watched in rising alarm. The men urged the maids back as they heard the frantic yelp of a dog and a low ominous rumble that grew steadily louder. It took a moment for Chloe to place the sound: wild pigs. Hugh and Graham reached the same conclusion an instant before a huge black boar broke from the trees.

"Climb!" Hugh roared as he lurched into motion, pushing men and boosting maids out of the way. "The trees, the cart—anywhere higher up!"

Maids screamed, horses reared, and husbands-to-be raced to rescue both. Then, just as the boar might have veered and run off through the adjacent field, the earl's hounds caught up and turned it back to the very heart of the gathering.

More than half a dozen mangy hounds hurtled over and under the linen-draped planking . . . knocking the table over and sending food, crockery, and wooden platters flying. The smells of meat and pastry distracted some of them, and for a moment several slowed and ran back and forth over the ruined feast, sniffing and trampling it. Then one of the kitchen helpers screamed and overturned the braziers into the boar's path. The beast squealed as it encountered the burning grass and searing coals, and the dogs abandoned the wrecked table to search out the source of the smell of scorched boar.

Cornered now, between rocks and cart and dogs, the boar wheeled and charged blindly at the pack, slashing its tusks from side to side, sending dogs scrambling and yelping. Then it made a quick, canny swerve and headed for the cover of the brush on the far side of the wrecked table.

Standing directly in its path, frozen with horror, was Chloe.

"Out of the way!" Hugh shouted, giving the maid in his hands a toss up onto the cooks' cart, where others stood screaming. He rushed for Chloe and reached her just as the boar slashed at her legs with its tusks. Launching himself at her, he managed to knock her back and out of the beast's way.

She came down on her back in some scraggly bushes, covering her face and struggling to breathe against the weight pressing down on her. Through her fear and confusion she managed to realize that the weight on top of her wasn't thrashing dogs or an enraged boar. She opened her eyes. It was Sir Hugh, covering her head, pressing her face into his chest. He was shielding her with his body as they were swarmed by dogs charging after their quarry and then nearly trampled by the mounted hunting party pursuing boar and hounds.

Sir Hugh. All she could think was that with his strength and power around her, cradling her, she was safe. She lay motionless, scarcely able to breathe but unwilling to relinquish the slightest part of that trusted shelter. The baying and thrashing of undergrowth around them slowly ceased. When it seemed the worst was over, Sir Hugh thrust up on his arms above her.

"Are you all right?" When she nodded, he pushed up further and glanced around, taking stock of their situation. Deciding that they were clear of immediate danger, he pulled her up to a sitting position.

"Where are you hurt?" he demanded, helping her rid herself of twigs and leaves sticking through the weave of her woolen gown.

"Everywhere," she muttered, trying not to whine as she removed a sharp twig from her side. "I feel like a pincushion."

"Can you get up?"

"Only if I have to." She rubbed the backs of her scratched arms and the back of her neck. When she looked up, she found him sitting on his heels astride her knees, looking at her with what appeared to be genuine anxiety. Having just survived a charging boar, she ventured something even more dangerous . . . gazing directly into Hugh of Sennet's eyes. She knew the instant their gazes met that her bravado was ill-advised. The intensity of the anxiety and relief she glimpsed in those pools of liquid bronze melted holes in her recent resolve.

Then he reached for the cap dangling from her hair and, without taking his gaze from hers, pulled it free of its pins and handed it to her. One by one he pulled leaves and twigs from her hair and tossed them aside, his hands lingering to let her tousled tresses slide through his fingers. When the leaves were gone, he touched the side of her cheek, a place that was stinging, and ran his fingertips gently over the scraped skin. His touch was so tender that she felt its soothing effect all through her, all the way to her reeling heart.

It wasn't until voices approached that he pulled his gaze from hers, pushed to his feet, and pulled her up with him. When she swayed, he caught her by the arm and steadied her until she found her legs.

"Are you all right, Lady Chloe?" Sir Graham and Lord William rushed up.

"I am, thanks to Sir Hugh," she said, rubbing the backs of her arms and neck to relieve the small scrapes she'd suffered. Then she halted, alarmed. "Is anyone else—are my sisters all right?"

"Fine," Graham declared, jerking a nod to the cart across the way, where they had weathered the danger and confusion.

Suddenly the old Earl of Ketchum came panting up, pulling his wild-eyed mount behind him. "Got to go!" he shouted, clamoring up into the saddle and flapping his heels against the horse's sides. "Got to be there for th' kill!"

Hugh watched the old cod charge off to join his precious hounds, then turned to survey the damage.

Chapter Twelve

THE ONCE TRANQUIL GLADE WAS nothing short of a disaster. The entire area had been flattened . . . the bushes, the wrecked table, the stools and blankets . . . and covered with food, broken crockery, and scattered serving vessels and baskets. Nearer the stream, several of the kitchen helpers were frantically beating out the last of the flames caused by the overturned braziers, inadvertently fanning the smell of charred vegetation everywhere.

Onlookers, kitchen helpers, and the bridal delegation were coming down from their roosts looking a bit stunned. A number of horses were running nervously about the field while their riders—including Lord William and Sir Jaxton—gave chase. Averting his eyes with a groan, Hugh spotted someone lying a distance away under a tree with one of the maids by his side. He ran to see who was hurt, and Chloe and Graham quickly followed.

It was Lord Simon and Helen. She related that the earl had been moving their mounts out of harm's way when one reared and came down on his foot. She had seen it happen and, as soon as the boar and hounds disappeared, ran to help him. She was holding his hand, stroking it, looking at him with undisguised admiration. Despite his pain, Simon seemed to be returning that sentiment. Hugh looked away in annoyance.

"I think we're finished here," he declared. "Graham, get everyone mounted up."

The bridal delegation straggled back to Windsor behind their audience, who rushed back to the castle to spread the tale of what had happened. Hugh brought up the rear, watching Graham being cornered by Lisette, Simon being attended earnestly by Helen, and William and Jaxton riding protectively alongside Margarete and Alaina.

He felt strangely dislocated . . . removed from his usual reactions . . . as if his interior landmarks had somehow been uprooted. And he only had to glance a bit ahead and to his left, where Chloe rode, to understand why.

He had vowed to keep his distance, to remain detached and aloof from this wife test nonsense and especially from *her*, but each time he tried to remove himself, the king or fate or happenstance conspired to force him back into the thick of it. Back into contact with *her*.

Just now he had remained coolheaded and rational in the midst of the chaos, until he saw the boar headed for her. His entire world had narrowed abruptly to a curvy little body and a freckle-prone face that of late had become part of his mental landscape. Seeing her in danger, he had launched himself over a rampaging boar and risked life and limb—

He'd have done the same for any of the maids, he told himself. And that was probably even true. But he wouldn't have felt as if his own life depended on saving any of the others. And afterward he would never have touched their hair or face, or felt such consuming relief doing so. And he sure as hell wouldn't have come within a hair's breadth of kissing any of the others.

God and the Devil—what was happening to him?

He was being squeezed hard in the grip of Temptation, that was what. Yesterday he had given in to it briefly, telling himself that the taste of her lips would somehow dispel his growing preoccupation with her. He'd kissed her thoroughly, and she responded just as he had expected: she'd kissed him back.

That, according to his superior male logic, should have been that. Their kiss should have demystified her allure for him and proved to her that she harbored the same grievous stain-of-the-flesh as the rest of her sex . . . rampant sexual passion. But instead of dismissing his fascination with her, that kiss had somehow enshrined it in him. It was all he'd thought about since.

Now, instead of proving his courage and Christian concern for others, this rescue had just proved that one kiss was not enough to disillusion, disgust, or deter him from wanting her.

He felt a shiver of dread as he made himself face the truth.

He wanted her. Completely. Totally. The way he'd never wanted a woman before. In the bloody *biblical* sense. *Dammit.*

He was still brooding over that alarming thought when he entered the great hall and found the old Earl of Ketchum holding forth before the king and a number of nobles on the day's impromptu hunt.

"Fine boar—biggest I've seen in many a year," the old earl declared, his eyes bright and mood boyish. "Was surprised to see you havin' to import game t' your forest, though, m'lord."

"Import game?" The king frowned. "What do you mean?"

"Found a cage as we came back. Not far from th' ladies' dinner." The old boy stroked his chest, pleased to have news that drew the king's interest. "Game cage, it was. Boar shite inside. Your warden must've just set it loose."

The king looked to his chamberlain, then his secretary and his treasurer.

"I saw it myself, Sire," Bromley declared, lowering his cup of ale. "It struck me as odd until we discovered it was boar. There hasn't been boar in that part of the forest for some time, so I thought perhaps you ordered—"

"Why would I have given my wardens orders to secure boar? I don't even like boar hunting," Edward demanded, scowling. The king was well-known to be a devoted falconer who preferred to hunt with a bird on his arm. He turned to Hugh. "A fortuitous end, then. None of the duke's daughters were injured."

"Yes, Highness. Most fortunate." Hugh stilled, his whole body tensing.

"A pity to have such culinary delights ruined," Bromley put in. "From the smells, this 'cooking test' seemed most promising."

"Promising, eh?" The king brightened and looked at his portly treasurer. "Then why don't we re-create it here in the hall, where we can all sample their dishes?" He turned to his chamberlain. "Instruct the kitchen steward to make the same the dishes for us all . . . straightaway . . . we'll dine late this evening. . . ."

Hugh heard no more. He was in motion, heading out the doors of the hall, stopping servants and pages to demand Graham of Ledding's whereabouts. He found his friend on the practice field, wielding a sword vigorously against a well-hacked wooden post, and pulled him away from it to the side of the field.

"What the devil—" Graham panted, giving him an indignant look.

"You've had enough practice for the day," Hugh declared.

"The hell I have . . ." Graham dragged him to a halt.

"We have a problem." Hugh stepped closer and lowered his voice, though the men hacking at the posts behind them showed no interest in their exchange. "That boar. Bromley and old Ketchum found a cage. The beast was imported and released not far from the place everyone knew we would be eating."

"So?" Graham wiped his sweaty face on his tunic sleeve and sheathed his sword. "Nobles are always bringing in game to stock their lands for hunting."

"Edward knew nothing about it. He'd given his wardens no such order."

Graham shook his head, missing the implication.

"Don't you see? This is the second mishap that endangered the duke's daughters in as many days. First, damaged cinches and now a boar set loose." Graham frowned at him, and he straightened emphatically. "It's not *two* random mishaps, it's four attempts on the duke's daughters."

"Four?"

"They were attacked twice before we reached the Channel, remember?"

"I thought we agreed that was the work of renegade soldiers looking for whatever might bring them a bit of profit."

"But the orders came from a lord . . . probably one who lost lands or family during the fighting." Hugh paused, trying out the idea in his own head before voicing it. "What if he is more angry and more determined than we supposed? What if he followed us across the Channel?" It grew more plausible by the moment. "Once here, it wouldn't be difficult to learn where the duke's daughters are and what they are doing. Everyone in Windsor seems to know their daily schedule. Scores of people are in and out of the stable, and half the castle turned out to the damned cooking test."

Graham's eyes widened as it sank in. "Then the duke's daughters may still be in danger."

Hugh was relieved to have his suspicions given credence. Perhaps he wasn't losing his mind after all.

"What do we do?" Graham said anxiously. "Tell Lady Chloe and the others?"

"And have a clutch of hysterical females on our hands?" Hugh gave him a withering look. "Besides, we have no real proof." He glanced toward the great round tower that commanded all of England. "Dammit—if Edward had only taken a few moments to hear . . . I never got the chance to tell him about the attacks in France."

"You didn't?" Graham's shock was probably foreshadowing the king's.

"He was occupied and then closeted with the queen. Then he ordered me to help with this wife test nonsense,

and there didn't seem to be a good time to put it before
him." His shoulders sagged. "And, truth be told, it didn't
seem all that urgent, since the maids were safe at Windsor."

"Still"—Graham shook his head—"he should have
been told."

"I know. I'll request an audience tonight after—dammit!"

"What is it?"

"He's ordered feasting tonight. He decreed that the
whole court will partake of the maids' dishes, to make up
for the ruined cooking test." He winced. "God knows
what else will strike his fancy before the night is over . . .
dancing . . . balladeering . . . versifying . . . it could go on
forever."

Graham gave a sympathetic groan and fingered the hilt
of his blade.

"Should we tell Simon, William, and Jax?"

Hugh considered that for a moment. Edward wouldn't
countenance being the last to know of a possible threat.

"We'll tell them to stay close to the maids and keep
alert . . . that two accidents in two days is one too many.
God knows that's true." He clapped a hand on Graham's
shoulder as they headed back to the castle. "And we'll
make certain they wear their blades."

AS IF THE AUDIENCE THEY ENDURED DUR-
ing the cooking test weren't enough of a strain, the maids
were now informed that the entire court would partake of
their special dishes along with their prospective husbands.
They were under no illusion; the tasting was the lesser
part of the evening's agenda. Unspoken was the understanding that the entire court would now have a chance
to offer opinions on their merit. The others looked to Chloe
in dismay, Chloe looked to Lady Marcella, and Lady Marcella squinted at her star charts and decreed that the evening would be auspicious for gustatory indulgence . . . or
for fumigating one's linen storage. . . .

As they entered the great hall, it was clear that everyone who was anyone at court was present, robed in their finest garments. Voices were spirited and there was wine-warmed laughter from several quarters. The side tables had been lengthened to accommodate more people and the rushes underneath had been sweetened with dried flowers. The torches that hung on brackets along the side walls had been replaced with fresh bundles of dipped rushes, and the linen draping the head table was adorned with embroidered hangings.

The special trappings were intended to honor the queen, who arrived on the king's arm, looking burdened by her advanced pregnancy but regal nonetheless. As the first course was brought out, officially tasted, and set before the king, he called out to Hugh and Chloe, who sat opposite each other.

"Who is responsible for this dish?"

Since Sir Hugh didn't know and couldn't respond, Chloe rose and spoke for them both.

"Actually, Highness, that is meant to remain a secret."

"Why so?" Edward gestured to her sisters. "Should not the creator of the dish receive credit for her work?"

"Yes, Highness. But it is part of the test to have the husbands-to-be choose their favorite dish without knowing who sponsored it. In that way a true pairing of the senses may be achieved."

The king studied that, then nodded and turned his scrutiny to the bowl that had been set before him. "And what is this called?"

"Lasagne, Highness. The flat noodles are covered with a sauce of ground basil and pine nuts and the oil of olives. Then a special tart cheese from Parma is sprinkled between the layers."

"Lasagne." He gave his taster, standing nearby, a glance. The fellow seemed hale enough. He reached for his knife and cut a portion of the wide, flat noodles. The noise in the hall dipped noticeably as all watched the king partake.

"Good. Quite excellent, in fact!" Edward declared with

a smile, turning to the queen. "Here, my dear, you must try this."

Deprived of the identity of the author of the recipe, the king's guests quickly turned their energies to guessing which maid seemed likely to have produced it. In that, they followed the lead of the husbands-to-be, who rolled their eyes with pleasure at the piquant flavors and teased the maids about who was most likely to prefer such food.

Then the second dish came out: a Lorraine tart made of eggs and cream in pastry, and filled with bacon, leeks, and a pungent yellow cheese imported from the mountains between Italy and the German provinces. Chloe explained the list of ingredients, and again the king tasted it and shared it with the queen.

"Deceptively simple," Lord William declared to the maids and bachelors with a grin. "Must be Margarete."

"A refined taste for such simple ingredients," Lord Simon ventured with a smile at Helen, who glowed. "That can only be Lady Helen."

All around the hall, the dishes were drawing praise for being artfully seasoned and tempting to the eye as well as the palate. The meal validated the renown of the wives produced by the Brides of Virtue and heightened respect for the convent's standards. If the duke's lovely daughters were as knowledgeable in other household areas as they seemed to be in "cuisine," the courtiers agreed, then the men slated to become their husbands were fortunate indeed.

Next came a dish of grilled mackerel with a sweet, peppery cameline sauce . . . a spicy, cinnamon, raisin, almond milk, and white wine concoction with a tang of black pepper, which complimented the smoky flavor of the fish.

"Unexpectedly spicy," Lord Jaxton opined. "This is from Alaina."

"Too much pepper," the old Earl of Ketchum declared, dropping his knife and stubbornly folding his arms. "I'll not spend the night in the garderobe."

Then came a cherry duckling *ambrogino* . . . a cassoulet of duck that was fried and then steeped in a sauce of tart wine, mustard, spices, brown sugar, and dried cherries. Sweet and sour, filled with intricate layers of flavor . . . it elicited groans of pleasure from diners all over the hall.

"So complex . . . it must be from Alaina."

"Seduces the senses and the judgment. From Lisette's hand, surely."

"Don't care who made it. 'Tis a pure invitation to the gout."

It was the first dish that the husband candidates truly disagreed on. Chloe was heartened. Each man seemed to hold a different opinion on the taste and a different idea on which maid was responsible for it. The maids, to their credit, parried the men's inquiries and compliments with admirable grace, while keeping the identity of the dish's sponsor a secret.

Then came a fifth course . . . a *taillis*, a dried fruit pudding that had been chosen by all five of the maids together as a proper finish to the main meal . . . before the final *entrements* . . . almond-stuffed dates, apple jelly sweets, and honeyed walnuts.

Chloe watched the pudding being tasted and served to the king and turned to her sisters in alarm.

"But that was to come last. Where is the fifth dish . . . the quail pie?"

Catching one of the servers, she asked him to go for the kitchen steward. Some minutes later the harried fellow appeared, looking as if he expected to have his ears boxed. He bore news of culinary catastrophe, sputtered profuse apologies, and rushed back to the kitchens to try to make amends. Sir Hugh saw Chloe's distress and the steward's pleading manner and demanded to know what was wrong.

"One of the dishes is missing," Chloe revealed, raising her chin.

"How can that be? We have been served five courses."

"The last of which, the *taillis*, was agreed upon by all of us. One of our individual offerings is missing. The test won't be complete without it."

"Whose dish is it?"

"To say would defeat the purpose of the test, would it not?"

"I'm helping to *give* the damned test, remem—"

The king's voice issued suddenly through the hall.

"Lady Chloe!"

She paled and, after taking a moment to compose herself, rose.

"Let us proceed with this cooking test," the king commanded.

"I fear that will not be possible, Your Highness," she said, stepping out from the her seat to stand before the royal couple. "There was to be one more dish . . . and the kitchen steward informed me that there was a mishap. It cannot be served until tomorrow. Thus, the finish of the test must be postponed."

"Wait!" came a voice from the steps that led outside and to the kitchens. "Wait, milady—we've managed to rescue one of the pies!"

The red-faced kitchen steward bustled through the assembly, ushering ahead of him two kitchen lads carrying a wooden litter on which sat a large, flat-bottomed dish covered with pastry. It was clear as the dish arrived that the pastry had been charred along the edges and then trimmed to remove much of the damage. It was hardly the elegant presentation expected for such a dish. But when Chloe looked at the steward, his anxiety was perilously close to her own.

"There were to be several special quail pies," she said, turning apologetically to the king and queen.

"But since this one has come through, can we not make do with it?" the king asked in a way that made it less a question than a command.

She made a small curtsy. "We can, Your Highness." When she beckoned to the appointed husbands to come and sample the pie, Sir Hugh joined them and the maids scrambled up to collect nearby, holding hands, their eyes wide with expectation. Suddenly everyone in the hall was hurrying forward and crowding around to watch.

The steward dabbed sweat from his brow, then produced a sharp knife and made several long, shallow cuts across the broad pastry top. Nodding nervously to Chloe, he peeled back a small piece of the center crust.

Four white doves suddenly burst from the pastry and began to soar toward the rafters, drawing exclamations and squeals of delight from the courtiers and even the queen herself. Laughter erupted as the Earl of Ketchum was startled by one of the birds and snorted, flailed, and sputtered.

"Fine quail indeed," the king said laughing. "It's not the first time I've seen such pie . . . but it is certainly the most satisfying! I cannot help speculating as to which of you maidens might be responsible." He looked to the men he had chosen to honor with brides and took matters into his own hands. "So, let us get on with the choosing. As I understand it . . . the husbands are to state their preferences." He looked to Chloe, who seemed a bit flustered by his sudden exercise of authority, but nodded. "Good! Bring each of the dishes forward and place them before us."

There was a scramble to locate the remnants of the other four dishes and place them side by side on the table, in front the king and queen.

Chloe felt events spiraling out of her control as one by one the men stepped forward to declare their preference. Miraculously—or perhaps in an intentional effort to avoid conflict—each of the men chose a different dish; Lord Simon, the lasagne; Sir William, the Lorraine tart; Sir Jaxton, the grilled mackerel with cameline; and Sir Graham, who seemed to be holding his breath as the others chose before him, picked the cherry duckling. Then all looked to the old Earl of Ketchum, who scratched his head.

"Too much pepper all around." He snubbed the four main dishes. "So I'll take . . . that quail pie. Though," he added grudgingly, "th' meat could stand to be a site better cooked." There was considerable laughter, which the old boy joined when he realized he had just made a jest.

"Now, Lady Chloe, reveal to us the sponsors of the dishes," the king commanded, and was struck by another idea. "And we shall pair them up for the dancing!" The court cheered the notion.

Chloe found herself the object of a hundred stares, none of which were as intense or meaningful as those of her sisters. Their flushed faces were filled with covert pleas for her to consider their preferences and pair them with their favorites. She caught a glimpse of Sir Hugh watching her with his arms crossed and his expression suspicious. He was just waiting for her to hand Sir Graham over to Lisette again and Lord Simon over to Helen. She had to show him that the wife test didn't bow to her or anyone's preferences.

"The Lorraine tart was Lady Alaina's," she declared. Sir William held out a hand to that nettled-looking maid. "The lasagne was Lady Lisette's." Lord Simon, who was leaning on Helen's shoulder, peeled his hand from her to offer it to the maid of Mornay. "The mackerel with cameline was Lady Helen's." Sir Jaxton seemed a bit surprised, but moved quickly to offer her his arm. "And the cherry duckling was Lady Margarete's." Graham's eyes flew wide with delight, and he eagerly offered Margarete his hand.

"The quail pie . . . was . . ." She swallowed, unable to make herself say it.

"Lady Chloe's, of course." Sir Hugh's voice came from behind her and carried out over the gathering. "Who else would value cleverness over taste?"

He stepped forward, grabbed Chloe's arm, and hauled her over to place her hand on old Ketchum's crusty sleeve. When she looked up in ill-disguised dismay, he gave her a faintly vengeful smile.

"Music!" the king's voice rang out and he clapped. The reedy strains of lyre, pipes, and recorders quickly swelled and were joined by the infectious *tam* of a drum. "Clear the floor! Let us have some dancing!"

THE LONG SIDE TABLES WERE CLEARED and dismantled as the musicians began to play. The first dance was a simple ring dance, which allowed the maids to easily mind their feet as they discharged their duty. Afterward, they retired quickly to the benches at the side of the hall and settled alongside their appointed escorts . . . where they endured long silences as they watched the courtiers perform more complex steps.

The evening proceeded with music and ballads and the copious consumption of wine and ale. Toasts were made to the queen's health and the coming child, and then she retired. As the king escorted her out, more toasts were raised to the royal couple . . . all of which gave the husband candidates a chance to rise and drink and escape their partners for a while . . . except Sir Graham, who stayed close by Margarete's side. During one such interval, Chloe called the men together to announce the next day's task . . . the "gift test," and then Sir Hugh snagged the reluctant Sir Graham by the arm and dragged him out of the hall.

Ballads were sung in praise of courtly love, heroic battle, and the excitement of the hunt. As the wine and ale flowed, the songs grew more raucous . . . celebrating in vivid imagery the passions of red-haired women, the trials of growing old, and the tumult of married life. When a group of tipsy nobles pulled her sisters out into the center of the hall to teach them dance steps, Chloe declined the invitation and remained behind on the bench. After the lesson the maids retired quickly from the floor, settled in a silent row beside Chloe, and eyed her coolly.

She glanced at the Earl of Ketchum, dozing on the other side of her, and was thankful that he had finally succumbed to the wine and ceased his rambling on the pedigrees of long-dead hounds and the glories of hunts gone by. Her spirits wilted as she surveyed his shrunken, drooping jaw and stringy frame, and realized that of all the present pairings, this was probably the one that would prove a glimpse of things to come.

There were five future brides and only four manly and agreeable young bridegrooms. One of them had to marry the aged, hound-obsessed earl. And since she had vowed to see her sisters settled in good and proper marriages, that left only herself to pair with him. Was he to be her punishment for presuming to take her destiny into her own hands?

Sir Hugh's face flashed into her mind as she watched the old fellow's nose drip. Imagine kissing him like—

No, *don't* imagine.

"Chloe? That you?" When she looked up, Lady Marcella was leaning on a walking stick, squinting down at her in the uneven torchlight.

"Yes, Lady Marcella. It's me." She scooted to one side to make room for the old lady, and gave the wood beside her a pat.

"Off in Camelot, were you?" The old lady smiled as she settled her bones wearily on the bench. "Spinning dreams out of minstrels' songs?"

"Not exactly." She looked at old Ketchum, snoring on her other side, and felt her throat tighten as she spoke. "I don't have such dreams, milady. I know what my future holds, and a sow's ear is still a sow's ear even if you do manage to make it into a purse."

"A sow's ear?" The old lady gave Chloe's tightly clasped hands a pat. "I used to believe it was better not to listen to dreams . . . that they would lead you astray . . . make you long for things you shouldn't."

"Used to?" Chloe asked, studying the old lady with the bent shoulders and faded eyes. It was difficult to imagine she was ever a young girl with great, romantic dreams.

"I was always such a clever one." Marcella raised one knotty finger, then used it to tap her temple. "Too smart to get caught up in 'building castles in Spain.' I had a young cousin, you see . . . a dear, sweet thing who fostered with us. So lovely and fresh. Everyone's favorite. Her eyes were so big and blue. . . . She fell in love with a foreigner and ran off with him." Her face seemed to grow older and sadder with each word. "Died soon after, we heard. In a strange land, wi' no family to comfort her. I was bereft." She tapped her temple again. "But I learned. Married as my old father bid me and bore my husband five children. All dead now. Then, when my husband's nephew inherited all, he took pity on me and brought me

to Windsor to serve the queen. Bromley was always such
a good-hearted boy."

"Lord Bromley is your nephew?" Chloe sat straighter,
seeing in the old lady's lined face a lifetime of broken
connections, losses, and tragedies.

"My husband's." Lady Marcella looked to the floor,
where the dancing was spiced by bursts of laughter and
wine-warmed flirtation. "Look at them."

Chloe followed her gaze, expecting a diatribe on the
silliness of people under the influence of too much wine.

"I never danced, you know," the old lady said. "Never
imbibed too much. Never dallied with men who came to
see my husband, or stayed abed all day, or wore fancy
headdresses and lots of jewels. I kept to my place . . . never
went to bed without confession . . . tended the sick . . . kept
a worthy household . . . and bore my sorrows in seemly silence. Now I have to wonder why.

"No children survive me. I have no home, but that
which is allowed me out of charity. Worst of all, I have
no joyful memories to sustain me or even to pierce my
heart." She sighed and looked at Chloe sadly. "When my
sweet cousin and I meet in Heaven, I wonder who will
have had the better life? Her years were cut short, true,
but at least for a time she was *happy*."

She reached over and squeezed Chloe's hands.

"I am not so eager to denounce 'dreams' anymore, my
dear."

Chloe's throat was tight, but she managed a small smile.

"Oh, I almost forgot," the old lady said, brightening.
"I cast your stars, as I promised. You've quite a bit of
excitement ahead. Your Venus is rising and transecting
your Mars, who seems to have settled in your ninth
house." She frowned. "Or is that your Moon rising? No,
no . . . I don't think your Moon ever transects your Mars.
Mars is so touchy . . . and it's difficult to get things right
if you can't see all the angles. . . ."

Chapter Thirteen

HUGH HAD DRAGGED GRAHAM FROM the hall and up the tower stairs to appear before the king and his privy councilors on the rampart of the round tower, where a handful of soldiers were standing watch. He clasped his wrist, glanced anxiously at Graham, and waited for the king to respond to the news he had just delivered . . . the abduction attempts on the other side of the Channel.

"Details. I want every godforsaken detail," Edward demanded, leveling a your-head-is-hanging-by-a-thread glare on the pair. "And I want it now."

"There were less than a dozen the first time," Hugh began, "dressed in rags to pass themselves off as thieves. We took one prisoner and found they wore mail and armor beneath. The prisoner said they took their orders from a *seigneur*, but he swore he did not know the lord's name." He glanced at Graham, deciding how much to reveal. "We took pains to see that the maids were secure, thinking they might try again. They attacked the next morning, just after sunrise and carried off some of our men who were disguised as the maidens. We had hoped to learn the identity of the lord behind the attacks, but in defending themselves, my men had to kill their abductors. I decided it was best to get the maids to the ship and to England as quickly as possible."

"And you didn't see fit to inform me of these attacks until now?" the king demanded irritably. What had begun as a diversion, a pleasant interlude in an otherwise grim bit of ransoming, was turning into a serious political threat.

"The moment we arrived, I was assigned other—" Hugh quickly changed course. "We believed we had left any real danger on the other side of the Channel. But now . . . the cut cinches, the wild boar set loose near the spot where the duke's daughters were known to be . . . two such incidents in two days point to a continuing threat."

"What I don't understand is why," Graham spoke up. "Why try to harm a handful of maids fresh from a convent?"

"They are not just maidens, they are *ransom*," Bromley declared, meeting the king's gaze. "There are many in the king's newly claimed French provinces who would gladly spill blood to disrupt English rule."

"Prevent the marriages and the duke's ransom goes unpaid," Hugh said, reasoning it out. "And the longer you hold the duke—"

"The stronger the sentiment against me will grow in Normandy and the Aquitaine," Edward declared, sitting forward, staring intently at a treacherous political tableau only he could fully see. "The question is . . . how large is this plot? Who is involved? And why haven't I heard something about it from Essex and Northumberland? They occupy the largest cities and noble seats. . . ."

The king's gaze hardened as his thinking went one grim step further. All present could see suspicion flicker across his face. What if his trusted nobles had decided to betray their king and use their positions to further their own ambitions? In the game of thrones, all loyalties— even strong ties of blood and pride—were subject to ambition and often available to the highest bidder.

Edward rose and paced back and forth in the strained silence, thinking, pausing occasionally to study Hugh and Graham. After a time he halted and turned to Bromley.

"Send word to Norwich. I want Avalon brought here as quick as his arse can be hoisted into a saddle."

"You think Avalon could be party to such treachery?" Bromley interrupted. "He's given you his daughters and, despite his part in the fighting, he has always been a moderate with regard to English claims in the Aquitaine."

"Seeing my armies storm across his lands and take his villages may have hardened his attitude," Edward said archly. "When Norwich arrives, I will have to determine who had access to or may have communicated with Avalon since he has been in Norwich's keeping." He turned to Hugh and Graham.

"I want you to watch and guard the duke's daughters. Enlist Candle's help . . . and Chester's. Use them all. Keep the maids close to the castle and know where they are at all times. Bring me immediate reports of anything unusual. I don't want them to sneeze without me knowing it."

"Surely you don't suspect them of—" Graham blurted out.

"In perilous times a king is a fool not to suspect everyone," Edward declared, his features taut with resolve. "I accepted Avalon's daughters as part of his ransom because I desired a strong tie between his house and English fortunes in France." He paused a moment, speaking to himself as much as to them. "But anything that has the power to forge such ties also has the power to break them."

As they hurried down the tower steps, Hugh began to lay plans.

"I'll speak with Jax and old Ketchum, you tell William and Simon. They're not to let the maids out of their sight. Escort them to their chamber straightaway, and don't leave their door until guards are posted outside."

"It's bloody well not fair," Graham muttered. "The first time I have a chance to be with little Margarete, you and the king go and ruin it for me."

"It could be worse," Hugh said tersely. "You could be on your way to the dungeons, under suspicion of treason."

"You don't honestly think the king suspects *us*?"

"Someone is trying to prevent the duke's ransom from

being paid. Such opposition could come from any one of a hundred different quarters ... some of which are damned close to the king."

They were silent for a time as they hurried through the passage leading to the great hall.

"I used to envy him, you know. I used to wish I could be that rich and powerful," Graham said grimly. "Sometimes it's good *not* to be the king."

LATER THAT EVENING, INSIDE THE MAIDS' chamber, Chloe was so lost in her own thoughts that she didn't notice the deep silence that descended. Out of habit she removed her cap and hung it on a peg, then began to untie the cords at the sides of her overgown. After a few moments she looked up to find her sisters staring intently at her.

"You didn't have to give them the true order, you know," Alaina said, and the others nodded agreement.

"You could have let Sir Graham believe the cherry duckling was mine," Lisette added with crossed arms and a petulant look.

"The test is ... the test." Chloe faced them squarely, surprised by their prickly attitude, but somehow not surprised. "It was not up to me to change that. Tomorrow will be a different test—the 'gift test'—which will undoubtedly yield different pairings."

"Will it?" Helen said, studying her in a way that made her feel like bacon tossed onto a hot griddle.

"Most certainly." She forced a smile. "After all, I mustn't keep milord Ketchum all to myself, must I?"

A chorus of stifled groans was interrupted by a knock on the door. Outside stood a ragged servant boy with a covered earthen crock in a willow basket.

"What is this?" she asked, feeling heat radiating from the crock as he thrust it into her hands.

The boy shrugged and hurried back down the steps toward the kitchens, leaving Chloe staring after him, until her gaze fell on two pike-bearing guards not far away on the landing. Castle guards in the passage? Had they always been there at night, or was this something new?

"What is that?" Helen asked as Chloe stepped back inside and kicked the door shut behind her.

"I have no idea, but it's from the kitchens." She placed it on the table and, grabbing a length of toweling, lifted the hot lid. A billow of steam rose into the chamber, and the others crowded around to look at a gray, unappetizing mélange of lumps with pungent, pepper-laden fat pooled around the edges.

"It looks like Alaina's mackerel," Lisette said, giving it a sniff and then rubbing her tingling nose. "Only with lots more pepper."

"How dare they suggest my recipe needs improvement?" Alaina was outraged. "And look at it—it looks like they dumped the kitchen slops into it!"

"If it's a peace offering from the kitchens," Helen said testily, "they've sorely misjudged the depth of our ire."

"Not to mention our tolerance for garlic," Margarete added with a wince.

"Well, it's insulting. I'll have none of it and neither will you!" Alaina declared furiously, slamming the lid back on it. She carried the basket to the window and looked as if she meant to toss it out crock and all. But the window well was deep and sharply sloped, and after a moment she reconsidered and set it down on the floor in front of the window instead. It was soon forgotten as the maids removed their garments, brushed and braided their hair, and knelt for evening prayers.

And pointed prayers they were.

"Open our eyes to the consequences of our hurtful stubbornness."

"Help Chloe to see that bonds of the heart are already being forged between some of us."

"And help her remember that a *good* wife must first be a *willing* wife."

As the tallow lamps were blown out and they settled beneath their woolen blankets, Chloe longed to tell them the truth, to assure them she would do her best for them. But if they knew she had made up the wife test, they would feel entitled to demand their own preferences. And what if their preferences were a disaster in the making? Like Lisette, who had her heart set on Sir Graham, who went pale every time she looked at him. Whatever was she going to do about Lisette?

Then Margarete made one last comment that descended on Chloe in the darkness, delaying her sleep and then deviling it with disturbing dreams.

"I wonder which dish Sir Hugh would have chosen."

THE NEXT MORNING THE WIFE TEST BE-gan to unravel.

The maids and husbands met in the queen's courtyard midday for the conduct of the "gift test," which had been announced to them last evening. Each man brought a gift that represented his home in some way and laid it out anonymously on a bench in the courtyard. Then the maids were called upon to chose which gift meant the most to them. They all stubbornly selected the same one . . . a newly weaned puppy which had been brought by the old Earl of Ketchum. The husbands were outraged, Chloe was dumbfounded, and Sir Hugh nearly fell off a bench laughing.

Chloe hedged and stammered and pulled her sisters aside to try to get them to reconsider their choices. The maids closed ranks and crossed their arms, utterly unrepentant.

"A dead trout? What kind of gift is that for a wife?" Alaina hissed, eyeing the smoked fish lying on the bench nearby.

"And a hunk of wood. You'd think he'd at least have the decency to have it whittled into something useful first," Helen complained.

"A carding comb. Do they honestly think our hair looks like raw wool?" Lisette gave an indignant toss of her sleek raven locks.

"But these things were meant to represent their homes," Chloe pleaded. "Well-stocked streams . . . lovely walnut trees . . . lots of fine wool . . ."

"They were also meant to be gifts to us," Alaina declared.

"If they were thinking at all, it was certainly not about *us*," Helen added.

"If all of us chose him, which of us gets him?" Margarete asked, cradling old Ketchum's puppy against her and scratching its silky ears.

Lisette gave a throaty laugh. "Who? The puppy or the old earl?"

Clearly, her sisters' behavior was aimed at her as much as it was those admittedly unappealing gifts. Chloe had chosen the rules of her test over their wishes . . . now they would let their wishes try the limits of her precious test.

Desperate to get things back on course, Chloe declared it was time for another riding lesson and ordered them to adjourn to the stables. Her directive was instantly countermanded by Sir Hugh, who rose and declared that the stables were closed for the foreseeable future.

"Closed? How can that be?" She turned on him and was surprised by the depth of his determination. It almost equaled his arrogance.

"The saddles are all being examined and repaired . . . to avoid a repeat of what happened to Lady Lisette the other day."

As the others stared expectantly at her, Chloe scrambled to decide which of the other tasks she had planned might be able to bring the men and maids together again. What did men like to do that women could bear to learn?

"Wait here," she ordered her sisters, then turned to the husbands. "I shall return shortly." She didn't see Sir Hugh signal a smoldering Sir Graham to watch the other maids, and then strike off after her.

"Where do you think you're going?" His voice from close by startled her.

"To seek the king's permission for us to visit his mews for a lesson in falconry. Any objections?"

"It happened just as I said it might," he said, ignoring her question. "They all chose the same gift."

"And why wouldn't they?" she said shortly. "A cuddly, adorable puppy."

"So, what did you learn?" When she glanced over at him, there was a small, superior arch to his brows. "You said if they all chose the same dish or the same gift, it would still be useful. What did you learn from it?"

"That perhaps . . . all of the maids respond better to . . . a playful, sensitive, and sympathetic heart." When he hooted derision, she flushed so hot that even her hair seemed redder.

"I'll give you 'playful' . . . the old boy's hip deep in a second childhood," he declared. "But sensitive and sympathetic?" He began to laugh, and she found herself staring raptly at him, entranced by the sound. "Ye gods, woman—the old clout's just plain daft about his hounds!"

It took her a moment to recover, summon a suitable glare, and stalk on toward the great hall.

Half an hour later, as the group traipsed down the hill to the mews, there was none of the usual pairing. The maids walked together in a clump, chatting noisily, and the men trailed behind in sullen silence.

Her sisters' laughter caused Chloe to look back and give them a censuring look, which they ignored. When they arrived and spoke with the head falconer, Chloe suggested they sort themselves into pairs for instruction, and then had to finally assign them into pairs herself. Ignoring her own smarting pride, she paired Lisette with Graham and Helen with Simon. And in the interest of efficiency, she assigned Jaxton and Alaina, and Margarete and William to work together. To her chagrin, Lisette and Graham seemed to have nothing to say to each other and even the formerly cozy Simon and Helen seemed strained together.

What followed seemed to be the longest afternoon on record. The falconers were less than pleased at having to disrupt their training, the birds were fractious, the maids

were skittish, and the men were less than chivalrous in
their reaction to the maids' fears. For every abrupt movement there was a scream, and for every scream there was
an unsettled bird that had to be hooded, stroked, and put
away in the dark mews until it calmed.

Chloe was bitten on the finger as she tried to reward a
bird with a morsel of food, Margarete swooned when a
bird shrieked unexpectedly in her ear, and Helen got sick
as she watched a hawk eat a baby rabbit it caught.
Strangely, of all of the maids, it was Alaina who seemed
to take to the birds and handle them with interest and
confidence. The day's one consolation was the sight of
Sir Jaxton and Alaina walking side by side as they returned to the castle, exchanging smiles and speaking eagerly about the fine mews at his home in Somerset.

Chloe was tense to the point of numbness as she climbed
the steps to their chamber behind her sisters, late in the day.
She was doing her best to see that they would be well wedded and happy. Why couldn't they believe that?

As they reached their chamber, one of Lady Marcella's
serving women came running up the steps after them, calling to Chloe.

"What is it Moll?" Chloe caught the distraught woman
in the doorway.

"Milaidy's beasties . . . is one of 'em here? Milaidy had
me come to freshen yer linen an' the li'l minx followed
me. Must've stayed behind." Moll pushed past Chloe and
began calling, "Cherub, come'ere, ye little rag mop!"

They all began to peer under the cots and around the
chests, calling the little dog. Margarete screamed and
everyone froze for an instant before rushing to see what
caused it. There on the floor, beneath the window well,
lay the furry little dog with its legs rigid and eyes closed.
Moll rushed to pick it up, but all could see as she did so
that it was too late.

"Did you find her?" Lady Marcella's voice came from
the doorway. Then she spotted her dog in the servant's
arms. "There she is! Cherub, you naughty— What's
wrong? What's happened." She hurried across the room

to take the little body from Moll's arms. "Wake up, sweetness. Look at me . . . please . . ."

Chloe hurried to put her arms around Lady Marcella and lead her to a seat on one of the cots. The old lady clasped her little companion to her breast and rocked back and forth, muttering "no, no, no." Moments later she began to sob, and soon there wasn't a dry eye in the chamber.

"What could have happened to her?" Moll wiped her tears with her apron.

Chloe looked at the dog's face. The hair on its muzzle was matted with something gray and gooey . . . something it had eaten . . . probably just before . . .

She jumped up and ran to the window where the little dog was found. The lid on the pot that was delivered to them last night had been knocked aside, and some of the contents were missing.

"Cherub died right here. She must have eaten some of what is in this dish."

Moll wiped another tear and knelt to give the dish a sniff. "Can't be certain wot's in it, there's so much pepper an' garlic." She used the lid to disturb part of the sticky mass. "Could be bad meat . . . or bad mushrooms. . . ."

Chloe's throat tightened as she turned back to their distraught lady chaperone. The sight of those time-gnarled hands moving over the little dog again and again, smoothing its fur and trying to comfort it in death, was heartbreaking.

They wrapped the little body in linen toweling, and Chloe and her sisters sat with Lady Marcella while Moll and another serving woman carried it out.

"I'm so sorry," Chloe said, putting her arm around the old lady.

"They were all I had. My babies," Lady Marcella gasped between sobs. "Haven't I lost enough?" When she looked up with her faded, red-rimmed eyes, Chloe had no answer. "My sweet cousin . . . my children . . . my husband . . . my home . . . gone. And now my little—" She clasped her hand over her mouth, unable to even say the name.

"It's not fair," Lisette said with tears running down her cheeks.

"Why would anyone want to poison a sweet little dog?" Margarete demanded with a tearful sniff.

"It was an accident. I'm sure it was never meant to hurt . . ." Chloe's heart stopped for a harrowing moment, then gave a violent thump and began to race.

Whether stuffed with poison or just made with food gone bad, the dish could not have been intended for anything but ill. And it had been sent to *them*. She thought of the ragged boy who delivered it, of the way he thrust it into her hands and ran off. Not even the lowest and meanest of the castle servants was so dirty and poorly dressed . . . or so rude. Someone had sent that dish to them hoping they would eat it and sicken. Or worse.

She looked at each of her sisters, realizing that if it hadn't been for Alaina's fit of pique, they might have actually tasted it. It would be one or more of them lying cold and lifeless.

But why would anyone want to harm one of them? Then she recalled the attempted abductions on their way to England and remembered Lisette's fall from the horse and then the morning's narrow escape with the boar. She had dismissed them as accidents at the time. The possibility that they were more sinister finally sank in, sending a cold shiver through her.

Her first and most powerful impulse was to seek out Sir Hugh and tell him what had happened. Whatever his personal feelings about her as a person and about them all as women, he was still a knight and devoted to the protection of others. Surely, he would listen.

Excusing herself to seek out Sir Hugh, she hurried down the stairs and into the great hall. Tables were just being erected for the evening, and she approached the king's chamberlain to ask if he had seen Sir Hugh. She was directed to the knights' quarters and the chapel. Father Ignatius roused from his nap behind the confessional screen to inform her he hadn't seen Sir Hugh for two whole days. She stopped a familiar-looking knight outside the knights' quarters to ask if he'd seen Sir Hugh or Sir Graham, and was told that some of the knights were still on the practice field and others had gone into the town.

It was darkening quickly now. She paused at the juncture of two roads, one leading back across the summit of the hill toward the practice field and the other leading out the castle gate. Then, in the groups of workmen, merchants, tradesmen, and day women making their way through the gate back to the town, she spotted something—someone.

It took a moment for her to realize that it was a small, ragged boy.

"You there—boy! Stop! I want to talk to you!"

The boy saw her, wheeled, and ran as if the hounds of hell were upon him. She ran after him, following both his reckless course and pace, bumping and jostling people out of the way.

"Stop!" As she emerged from the gate, she called to the people along the road: "Stop that boy!"

But the boy squirmed from their hands and raced for the heart of the town, where the streets were now filled with people and carts and animals being driven to butcher or stable. With her lungs beginning to burn and her limbs aching, she ran on as well.

Off the main thoroughfare the streets narrowed. The houses nodded together over the streets so that the little remaining sunlight was blocked and the streets and footpaths below were cast into deep shadows. Twice she lost sight of the boy as he darted around a corner, but was able to spot him again when she made the same turn. Then he ducked through a bank of stalls outside some shops, grabbing at food and upsetting racks and carts filled with wares.

She followed the commotion in the boy's wake until it led her down another narrow side street. The noise and bustle of the market corner died, and she found herself on a darkened lane that wound down a slope toward the smells of stables, animal pens, and slaughtering yards. Her heart was pounding so that it felt as if it would leap out of her chest, and her legs were turning to mush. She slowed, trying to catch her breath.

Weathered barns and storehouses loomed on either side of her, and a taint of urine and lye from a nearby tannery made every act of inhalation unpleasant. The few people abroad in that rough quarter scurried along with their eyes on the path, seeming anxious to be off the street. When she asked if they had seen a boy run by, they shook their heads and quickly moved on. More wary now, she continued on down the path and around a bend, where she came across an open stable door, lighted from within by a tallow lamp that emitted a thin yellow glow.

The boy stood at the edge of the doorway, silhouetted, and she ran toward him, so intent on catching him that she didn't realize he was turning . . . pointing at her. By the time she realized the men who were glaring at her, they were already in motion and coming her way.

"No—oh, no!" She halted and then stumbled badly as she tried to turn and run. They reached her an instant later and grabbed her by her gown and her hair, yanking her off her feet. As they carried her into the stable, she drew breath and screamed with everything in her.

FATHER IGNATIUS WAS THE FIRST TO TELL Hugh that Chloe was looking for him. The king's chamberlain was the second, and when he arrived at the maids' chamber, Helen and her sisters also said Chloe had left saying she needed to speak with him.

"What did she want to speak with me about?" he asked.

"She didn't say," Helen answered for all of them. "But I would guess it was about Lady Marcella's dog."

"Her what?" He scowled irritably.

"Her pet dog. It was poisoned today. Right here, in our chamber."

A frisson of alarm ran up his spine. "Poisoned? How?"

They showed him the dish of food that was delivered to their chamber.

"It could have been any one of us," Lisette said anxiously. "Are we in some kind of danger?"

"Stay here. Do not set foot outside this chamber," Hugh ordered, already moving toward the passage. "Close the door behind me and bolt it. Don't let anyone but myself or Sir Graham in."

"What about Chloe?" Alaina asked, glancing at the darkened window.

"I'll find her," he said grimly.

He raced down the steps two at a time, his mind spinning, and was relieved to find Graham and the other husbands in the great hall. After a quick recounting of what the maids had just told him, Hugh sent Graham and Simon to the king with the news and took William and Jax with him to find Chloe.

There were a thousand places to disappear in a castle as large as Windsor, so they concentrated at first on places she might have gone to look for Hugh. The knot forming in the pit of his stomach tightened with each empty location and every person who claimed not to have seen her. Then the guards at the main gate reported seeing a young woman in blue . . . a pretty maid . . . running through the gate as if chasing someone . . . into the town.

He gained speed with every step he took, until he was running full tilt down the main street of the town. William and Jax veered off into the narrower lanes, and Hugh continued down the main thoroughfare toward the stables and the livestock yards. He could hear them calling her name and began to call for her, too.

Then, from somewhere in the distance, came a scream.

THEY WERE FRENCHMEN. FOUR OF THEM. Dirty and grizzled and pent-up from days of lurking around the stables and trying to escape notice as they went about the castle and town. The boy had led her straight to them, and they seized her and celebrated as if she were a battle prize.

They stopped her screams with a rag and carried her

out the rear door of the stables. There, they began to argue. Chloe was a bit dazed from a blow to her head, but managed to make out most of their guttural French. One wanted to kill her straightaway, but the others wanted to take time to enjoy her first. Two of them threw her onto a pile of straw, held her down, and began to paw at her while the third held their knife-wielding comrade at bay. The argument going on around them combined with her resistance to give her one brief opportunity to wrench an arm free and rip the rag from her mouth. Her scream earned her a blow across the mouth, but even dazed, she fought on, kicking and thrashing as they pushed up her gown up and pinned her legs with their knees.

Please God—help me—please—

It suddenly seemed as if time itself slowed. Their rough hands pawed clumsily at her . . . her nails took forever when raking across one of their faces . . . even her screams seemed to elongate . . . hanging harsh and potent on the air.

Then abruptly one of the men kneeling over her fell forward and lay motionless, all but smothering her. Through the blood roaring in her head, she heard shouts, scrapes, and grunts, and the clang of metal on metal. Their attention was suddenly elsewhere, and she had both arms free. Shoving at the man sprawled over her, she managed to roll him to one side and scramble from beneath him. There was fighting nearby; blades flashed and grunts and curses flew.

She scrambled back, trying to escape, but her way was blocked by the side of the stable and some wooden fencing. Frantically she began to feel her way along the stable wall toward the corner. Just as she reached it, everything in the deserted stableyard went silent. She hurled herself toward that corner and what would hopefully be the cloaking darkness of the interior of the stable.

But someone grabbed her arm and pulled her back, and she began to kick and flail with all her might.

"Lady Chloe! It's all right. You're safe! Chloe, listen to me—"

The voice slowly penetrated her panic. A familiar voice. A welcome voice. She stilled and held her breath. The bands of sinew wrapped around her relaxed. She pushed back and looked up to find the one person in the world who meant safety to her.

"Are you all right? Did they hurt you?" Sir Hugh's voice was raspy and his words came in bursts. As he brushed her hair back from her face, his hand trembled with the energy of unspent violence. "Tell me—are you hurt?"

She managed to tell him "no" before her knees buckled. He caught her, and at his urging, she clamped her arms around his neck, buried her face in his shoulder. William and Jax arrived just then with blades drawn, having tracked the sounds of the fighting. He assured them that she was all right and had them take the attackers' bodies to the castle and carry word to Chloe's sisters that she was safe.

"Are you well enough? Do you want to ride or can you walk?" he asked.

"Walk," she managed.

Looking at her dazed face, he propped her against the wall on a barrel top while he led one of the aged horses in the stable from its stall. There was no saddle readily visible, so he simply lifted her onto the animal's bare back and kept one hand at her waist to hold her there. They proceeded so slowly that Jax and William soon caught up with them on the way to the castle, and he waved them ahead.

"What were you doing, anyway, running into town by yourself and after dark?" he demanded, hoping an irritable tone would cloak the anxiety that still had not released its grip on his throat.

"I—I was looking for you." She sounded oddly far away. "To tell you about Lady Marcella's dog. It was poisoned. In our chamber. I saw that boy . . . the one who brought the food to us last night . . . and when he ran, I ran after him. He led me to the stables and those men. They were French. . . ." A fresh sense of urgency entered her voice and she sat straighter. "They argued and—my sisters—they're going to attack my sisters!"

"Your sisters are safe." He had to clamp both arms around her to hold her on the horse. "I sent Graham and Simon to guard them. They're safe!"

It took a moment for that to register. The last of her fear-generated strength suddenly drained, leaving her drooping . . . then sliding. He caught her as she fell and pulled her limp form against him to keep her from smacking the ground. He coaxed her arms around his neck, then was able to wrap his arms about her and hold her more effectively. The shock of the attack was wearing off, and she was literally melting in his arms.

"You'll be all right," he insisted, telling himself not to stare down into her upraised face, but unable to resist it. Her widened eyes glistened hauntingly in the moonlight. "You just need some wine and a good night's sleep."

Her chin began to quiver, tears rolled down her cheeks, and she buried her face in his chest and released the horror of her experience in sobs. He stroked her hair and made low, shushing noises he had never made before in his life. As he did so, it seemed that some of her tumult was migrating into his own chest, tightening around his lungs, clutching at his heart.

After a few moments, she wiped her face with her palms and pushed back in his arms with a deep breath that signaled the worst had passed.

"Better now?" he asked.

"I think so. I was just . . . so frightened." Her eyes again filled with tears. "And all I could think was that if they killed me, I wouldn't ever . . ."

"Wouldn't ever what?" he said, lifting her chin toward him.

He was so close and so gentle with her that she couldn't have held back the truth if it meant she would drown in it.

"See you again."

Chapter Fourteen

A THRONG OF PEOPLE BURST FROM the castle gate and came rushing down the road toward Chloe and Hugh. Jax and William led the group, which included Graham and Simon, who was still limping along with Helen's help, the rest of Chloe's sisters, Lady Marcella and Moll, Lord Bromley, and several knights and castle guardsmen. They called and waved, and shortly Hugh and Chloe were engulfed in a sea of bodies and a jumble of emotions.

When they reached the great hall, the king was standing outside in a circle of torchlight, surveying the bodies of the Frenchmen who had lain in wait on his very doorstep. He watched as they approached, then pulled Chloe up from her unsteady curtsy and looked her over with what appeared to be genuine concern.

"You aren't injured, Lady Chloe?" When she said that she was not, he seemed relieved. "Thank God for that. I am sure Sir Hugh will report to me on the particulars, I won't trouble you for those. What with cut cinches, wild boars, poisoned food, and now this . . ." He glanced at her sisters, then back at her. "The daughters of Avalon have had a harrowing introduction to life in England. I assure you, there will not be another opportunity for anyone to harm you while you are under my roof. I gave you a week for your abbess's wife test, Lady Chloe, but in the interest of your own safety, I must declare an early end to it.

"Sleep well. Refresh yourself," he ordered gently. "Tomorrow morning, just past *tierce,* you will present to me the results of your test. And with my blessing, the nuptials will be held shortly after. I want this business concluded before *none.*"

Chloe was so exhausted when she sank onto her cot, later, that she couldn't rise again. Her sisters quietly set about tending to her needs: helping to remove her gown, bathe her face and hands, and then plait her hair for the night. They tucked her beneath her blanket and gathered around her, stroking her hair and holding her hands as she released the last of her tension in tears and finally drifted off into a deep sleep.

"Poor Chloe," Margarete said, dabbing at her own eyes. "To have suffered such a terrible thing . . ."

"She is strong," Helen said, giving Chloe's hair a gentle stroke. "With rest and care she will recover quickly."

"I hope so," Alaina said quietly. "For this is her last night as an unmarried maid."

Lisette had some difficulty summoning her customary insouciance.

"Tomorrow night we will all lie in the arms of a husband," she said with a surprisingly tentative edge. "Let us hope Chloe didn't think we were serious when we all chose that puppy."

SOME DISTANCE AWAY, IN THE KING'S dimly lighted privy chamber, Bromley and the Duke of Bedford were closeted with the king.

"Damned close, this night," Bromley said tightly, then sipped from his wine cup.

"Too close. Four of them. Under our very noses." The king pounded a fist on his chair arm. "How could four strangers speaking French go undetected in a town no larger than Windsor? Where the hell were our informants, our spies?"

The duke scowled. "We generally depend on locals hereabouts—the bailiff, the reeve, the wardens—to spot strangers and report possible troubles. They were busy, distracted of late. They're not used to so many people here in early summer. Your Highness is usually on progress by now."

"And would be again if the queen weren't about to come to her term," the king said grimly. "They were French. No doubt about that. And well armed, with coin in their purses. Sir Hugh's reports were right on target. There must be a lord or lords behind them. The questions that remain are 'how many' and 'who.' I've got to have more information." He looked over at Bromley. "Any word on Avalon?"

"Norwich sent a rider ahead, Highness. They'll be here by midday tomorrow."

The king sighed. "Just in time to see his daughters wedded." His eyes narrowed as he contemplated the French duke's possible role in this deepening plot. "I want to see Avalon with my own eyes, talk with him. I have to know if he is the kind of man who would send his daughters—even bastard daughters—to their deaths in the service of French sovereignty."

"Greater treacheries than that have been carried out in the name of royal dominion," Bedford declared grimly.

The king nodded, recalling all too well his own battles, a few years past, to wrest control of his kingdom from his greedy and treacherous mother. The worst power struggles were often the ones that engaged the passions of those who were intimately related. Brother against brother. Nephew against uncle. Mother against son.

After a few moments he returned to the problem at hand.

"I need information. Bedford, Bromley, set your best 'secret hounds' loose on the trail of these conspirators. I have to know more about who is behind these attempts on the duke's daughters and what they will do when they learned that they've failed."

THE NEXT MORNING, WELL AFTER DAY-light, a small army of servants appeared at the maids' door carrying buckets of water, an armload of fresh lavender, and piles of clean linen toweling. The maids staggered from their beds, said their morning prayers, and fell upon the tray of fruits, soft rolls, and cheeses that the king's kitchens provided, along with a new feature . . . a taster.

Lady Marcella roused herself from mourning to attend and keep them company. While they bathed, she consulted the stars—declaring that they favored unions made that day—and surprised them all with marital advice that was a great deal more specific than that which the good Sisters had provided.

Chloe felt her sisters tiptoeing around her, avoiding the topic that saturated the chamber like the scent of fresh lavender . . . the matter of the pairings she would recommend to the king. To their credit, they neither importuned for nor demanded their choices; they knew Chloe well enough to know that she would hold firmly to what she believed to be the best decision. And at bottom they trusted both her and the wisdom of the convent's wife test. The thing that tempered their confidence in her was the fact that one of their number would have to marry the hound-obsessed Earl of Ketchum.

The hall was crowded with a motley assortment of Windsor's people when they arrived, mid-morning. As they threaded their way to the center of the hall and approached the king's chair, there was a collective sigh of approval.

The king was in his great chair, flanked by Lord Bromley and the other privy councillors, and the appointed husbands sat in a tense row on a bench at the king's right. A herald greeted the maids and ushered them to a bench by the first table on the king's left. Wary smiles and covert glances of anticipation flew both directions across the hall.

Chloe's nerves were pinging with both dread and anticipation. This was the moment she had dreamed of and prepared for since the day she learned of the duke's unique ransom payment, yet she felt so ill-prepared.

She had risen while it was still dark and gone to the chapel for first mass. Afterward, she spent an hour in earnest prayer, asking for wisdom, guidance, and blessings upon the outcome of her choices. As she meditated and mulled over various combinations of maids and men, it became clear that no set of pairings was without some difficulty. Sir Hugh was right. In the end it all came down to preferences. The only question was: whose?

As they took their seats, she looked around for Sir Hugh and didn't see him. Asking to postpone this audience so that she might confer with him was probably out of the question. As the king had said: they wouldn't be truly safe until they were wedded, bedded, and well away from Windsor, on their way to their new homes. Still, she couldn't help wishing she had had a chance to speak to him one last time. She needed to somehow rid herself of the ragged, exposed feeling created by the words she had uttered to him on the road last night. She closed her eyes, shrinking inside, wishing she could recall that naked admission—

"Well, Lady Chloe," the king called to her, "are you prepared to make your recommendations?" The noise in the hall died as all awaited her response.

Was she prepared? To lose the sisters she had only just gained? To sentence those same sisters to lives with men they had known only a few days? To never again see or touch the one man who could make her heart beat faster with a simple glance?

"I am, Your Highness."

"Proceed." He transferred power to her with the wave of a hand.

Her stomach was jittery and her head felt light and strange as she rose.

"If the bridegrooms will come and stand with me . . ."

Lord Simon led the way, though he had to do so while

leaning on a walking stick. Graham, Jax, William, and old Ketchum followed, and together they arrayed themselves in a semicircle before the king.

Chloe went to her sisters and extended her hand to Helen, who blushed with maidenly pleasure when Chloe led her to Lord Simon's side. Next she escorted Alaina to Sir Jaxton, and saw with relief that both looked rather pleased. Then it was Margarete's turn, and as she was placed beside Lord William, he beamed . . . until he encountered Sir Graham's disbelieving stare. That left only Lisette and Chloe herself. Sir Graham glanced between them and paled. Then Chloe looked at her sister and smiled, sending her to stand by him.

When he saw Lisette coming toward him with an elegant sway and eyes filled with earthy allure, Sir Graham looked as if he might run for his life.

Chloe could feel both her sisters' gratitude and their pity as she moved to stand beside old Ketchum . . . who was so busy picking bits of dried food off his tunic that he didn't notice her until she touched his sleeve. He cocked his head at her, looking a bit confused, then seemed to understand why she was there.

She turned at the earl's side to face the king and struggled desperately to keep tears from forming. Thank Heaven Sir Hugh wasn't there.

"These are your pairings, Lady Chloe?" the king said, studying the couples before him. "And what does Sir Hugh say to these matches?"

Hugh had watched the proceedings from the side of the hall with growing turbulence. Jax and Alaina, Simon and Helen, William and Margarete . . . the maids were smiling and the men seemed content enough. He couldn't argue with those pairings. And much as he regretted seeing affable, even-tempered Graham paired with a woman would could strip hide from bone with a single glance . . . it was Graham's own damnable fault for putting himself in harm's way.

No, the thing that had him churning inside was the sight of Chloe of Guibray—proud, fiery, infuriating

Chloe—seeing to her sisters' futures and then taking her place meekly beside old Ketchum. Anything that could reduce the vibrant and passionate Chloe of Guibray to such insipid virtue was nothing less than obscene. Stifling the protest of his inner monk, he pushed off from the wall and headed for the dais and the king's throne.

"I say, Highness," he called out, causing every eye in the hall to turn to him, "that the wisdom of the abbess of the convent of the Brides of Virtue should be celebrated. *And* . . . I say that the husbands of these fair maids should be congratulated on their good fortune." He paused between the king and the couples. "Lord Simon is wedding his match in both ability and ambition. Baron William has found someone who can bear his jests with good humor. And Sir Jaxton is marrying the one woman in the realm who is prettier than he is."

Laughter skittered through the onlookers, then was quickly snuffed in expectation. He did not disappoint.

"Then there is Sir Graham"—he crossed his arms and stroked his chin as he studied Graham's taut expression— "who will save a fortune on bed furs and firewood this winter." He glanced at the king and raised his eyebrows. The king's chuckle ignited a similar response in the crowd, and Graham looked as if he were a hair's breadth away from taking a swing at Hugh.

"But the one who truly deserves our praise is the Earl of Ketchum." He strolled toward Chloe and the old earl, giving them a visual inspection. He couldn't tell if the alarm in her huge blue eyes was caused by the prospect of marrying the juiceless old cod or by anxiety over what he might have to say.

"You have our admiration, milord. You exemplify courage and fortitude. A lesser man might have flinched at taking such a wife to his bosom . . . a woman so trying."

"T-trying?" Old Ketchum looked from Chloe to the king, confused by what he was hearing.

"Regrettably so." Hugh gestured to Chloe, inviting all present to judge for themselves the truth of his words. "A woman of great learning . . . educated beyond most men. A woman who reads and writes, can quote the Greek poets and philosophers, and ciphers like the wind. A truly prodigious intellect."

"S-she *reads*?" the old boy said, suddenly alert and absorbing every word.

"Several languages," Hugh answered, beaming. "But, being a man of letters yourself, you will no doubt be able to advise and correct her . . . save her from the vices that prey on those who stuff their heads with learning."

"Vices?" Ketchum's eyes darted anxiously over that disturbing tableau.

"Further, she is a woman of great thrift, practicality, and ingenuity. She will refurbish your household, and repair your barns, and even"—he looked at the old boy's besmirched garments—"re-upholster your hide. No doubt you will hand over your ledgers and accounts to her, and she will establish a program of frugalities to improve your income and cut your expenses. No more wagers on cock-fights and horse races for you, milord." He shook a finger of genial chastisement. "And no more 'out-hunting-with-the-hounds-until-the-crack-of-dawn,' either."

"N-no *hunting*?" Old Ketchum clutched his chest with a bony hand, breathing harder as he stared at her.

"You have heirs to make. And no more rich foods or two-day routs with a barrel of ale. She'll be certain you're around to see a whole raft of little Ketchums spring up. She's studied herbals in the convent, you know." When the old man shook his head, Hugh smiled benevolently. "Oh, yes. Always brewing up some smelly concoction or other and insisting everyone rub it on them or take it as a tonic. And did I mention how pious she is? Confesses constantly and hears mass twice daily. She will have you on your knees in no time. . . ."

The old boy was wild-eyed, teetering on the edge of either an explosion or a collapse. Hugh couldn't resist giving him one more little push.

"You may, however, have to dig a new well on your estate. She bathes frequently and insists on using plenty of water. And *soap*. Go on, give her a sniff."

The old fellow bit his lip, leaned warily toward her, and inhaled. The scent of lavender was apparently too much for him.

"Ohhh!" He clutched the front of his doublet with both hands and sank to his knees. "My heart . . . my spleen . . . my liver . . ."

Hugh and Graham rushed to his side, and he clutched their sleeves as they lowered him to the floor and called for the servants to bring a litter.

"Let me see him. I can help," Chloe said anxiously, trying to kneel beside them, but prevented by the old boy's outstretched arm fending her off.

"No, no—it's just one of my spells." On closer inspection his eyes seemed more widened with panic than pain. "Have awful fits an' spells . . . my liver goes cold and my spleen fluxes . . . nerves go all swarmy . . ." As a pair of servants scooped him onto a sling litter and carried him out, he halted them long enough to push up and address the king.

"Highness . . . I must beg that in my grievous infirmities I be excused from"—he glanced at Chloe with unmistakable dread—"the rigors of marriage."

The king rose and stared gravely at the old fellow.

"You are released, milord Ketchum. Retire to your home to recover your health . . . with our best wishes for God's restorative blessings."

Chloe burned with humiliation as she watched the earl being carried out. The horror of it—having the old man swoon publicly and plunge into a fit of illness rather than wed her!

She could feel the eyes of the crowd turning on her with reactions from amusement to confusion to outrage. Could they be persuaded so easily that she was a monster . . . a virago . . . a harridan with unnatural proclivities? She turned on Hugh with her eyes stinging with the threat of tears.

How could he do this to her? He knew her as no one else did, yet he described her in such a way that her virtues all sounded like hideous vices. He had cast her in such a vile light that she would probably be tainted and infamous—*unmarriageable*—forevermore!

"Well"—the king broke into her agonized thoughts—"that was certainly unexpected. It seems you no longer have a husband, Lady Chloe." He looked her up and down, clearly reconsidering her in the light of all he had just heard. "You *read*? Is this true?"

"It is," she said, her throat so constricted that it came out a whisper.

"And write in several languages and cipher and create herbal nostrums?"

She could only nod. He made such accomplishments sound freakish.

"What the devil am I to do with you, Lady Chloe?" The king sat down abruptly on his great chair and propped his chin on his fist. "I suppose I shall have to add you to my own household until I can find someone to take you off my hands. I doubt I will find another unmarried noble as rich and exalted as the Earl of Ketchum."

There were both mutters and laughter in the throng behind her, and she wished the earth would open and swallow her whole.

"Saints—who would take on such a woman?" He tilted his head from side to side, studying her with a dubious expression. "It would have to be a man of great wisdom and learning . . . and uncompromising standards and prodigious virtue . . . with the patience of Job, the inner strength of a saint, and the stamina of a warhorse . . . not to mention a curious indifference to hunting and wagering."

With each requirement, both his shoulders and her prospects for matrimony sank a bit lower.

"Wait!" He suddenly sat straighter and broke into a broadening smile. "Educated, uncompromising, virtuous, strong . . . I believe I have just described Sir Hugh of Sennet!"

More laughter rippled through the hall as the king looked to Hugh with thinly disguised determination.

"Sir Hugh, as it happens, is unmarried and in need of an heir." What came next caused the hall to erupt with excitement. "By all the saints—why not? It is my decree that Sir Hugh of Sennet shall marry Lady Chloe of Avalon. I know, Sir Hugh, that you have long aspired to the religious life. But Heaven seldom consults us in making its plans. It seems you've just been chosen for something far more difficult than a life of prayer and fasting . . . being a *husband*."

Edward turned immediately to his chamberlain and privy councillors.

"Send riders out to locate Norwich and Avalon and tell them to hurry. And rouse the bishop. Tell him I want these nuptials solemnized the moment the duke gets here." He rose and dusted his hands together with an air of finality. "Thank Heaven that's done. . . . I have a child being birthed upstairs."

CHLOE WATCHED IN DISBELIEF AS THE king strode for the steps that led to the queen's chambers and Sir Hugh strode for the doors that led to anywhere his future wife wasn't. Her emotions, her thoughts, her entire being were in turmoil. Sir High-and-Mighty had wrecked her marriage to the old earl only to be snared into marrying her himself. And while the thought of marrying old Ketchum had filled her with sadness and despair, the prospect of being forced to contend with an irate Hugh of Sennet for the rest of her days filled her with terror.

He was adamantly opposed to marriage and he openly disliked women. Including her. Especially her. And despite the fact that he had sealed his own fate with his outrageous descriptions of her, he would undoubtedly find a way to blame her for it. A husband could find a thousand ways to punish an unwanted wife for being unwanted.

Her sisters hugged her, and Lady Marcella, who was a bit bewildered by the drastic turn of events, embraced her and wished her the best. When they retreated to their chamber to prepare for the vows, her sisters came one by one to thank her for seeing into their hearts and making their wishes come true. She smiled and nodded numbly as Lisette added with an admiring wink:

"What a clever thing you are. However did you persuade Sir Hugh to talk you out of a marriage to the old earl and into a marriage with himself?"

AS SHOCKING AND TUMULTUOUS AS THE morning had been, the afternoon proved just as eventful. When the time arrived for the vows, the bishop sent for the maidens. Freshened and fortified, they descended to the great hall and were greeted there by a portly man in costly armor, with graying hair, lively eyes, and an air of authority that rivaled the king's.

"These are my daughters?" he said, his face lighting as his gaze flew from one comely face to another. "But of course they are. *Bon Dieu*—are they not a garden of earthly delights?"

As they were introduced, he embraced them with great dignity and a sense of ceremony, kissing them on both cheeks. He seemed generally pleased and parental until he came to the last maid.

"*Chloe*?" His face lost all trace of amusement, his hands tightened on hers, and he drew her closer to search her face with an unsettling intensity. "Where are you from, *fille*? How did you come to the convent?"

"I was brought as an infant, Your Grace. I have been there all my life."

"And your mother?" The pressure of his hands on hers grew alarming.

"I never knew her. I think she must have died."

"Her name?" The duke seemed quite affected by something about her.

"I do not know, Your Grace." Chloe felt something happening that she didn't understand. But something made her repeat what had become for her the new foundation of her identity. "All I was told was that there was a scrap of hide in my basket bearing the name Gilbert."

She sensed that there were many eyes watching their exchange and thought it best to add: "It was only of late that I learned you were my father."

He looked as if she had slapped him and abruptly released her hands. He stared at her with barely contained emotion for a moment longer, then turned and stalked away. She was too stunned and embarrassed to react at first. For the second time that day she'd been publicly rejected . . . first by a husband, then by a father.

Her sisters crowded around her, comforting her and speculating on what had caused the duke's reaction. It couldn't have been her claim of kinship, they reasoned, otherwise he would have responded that way to all of them.

They had no time to dwell on it. The bishop and the priests of the king's chapel quickly called for them to present themselves in chapel for the vows. Each of the maids was claimed by her intended husband . . . all but Lisette and Chloe. They looked around nervously for Sir Hugh and Sir Graham, but the pair were nowhere to be found. Then, just as they decided to go on to the chapel in hopes of locating their husbands, Sir Hugh and Sir Graham came striding up with wet hair and freshly battered faces. Grimly they seized their brides' arms and ushered them without ceremony into the rear of the crowded church.

The duke stood in the midst of the couples, his fists clenched and his face like a thundercloud. As the bishop began to ask the appointed questions and direct the exchange of vows and the placing of rings, the duke's gaze kept returning to Chloe. But each time it did so, it seemed that some of the heat and intensity left his stare. By the time the bishop came to Hugh and Chloe, she was so thoroughly rattled that she could scarcely mind her words or recall what she was supposed to do.

Sir Hugh took her left hand in his, looked down into her eyes, and in tones clipped with annoyance, promised to love, honor, and cherish her, to live peacefully with her all the days of his life, and to protect and provide for her. With some prompting, she promised to love, honor, and obey him, to live peacefully with him all the days of her life, and to bear his children as God saw fit to grant them. When it came time for the ring, he waved the bishop on, saying there had been no time for such things.

"I have a ring." The congregation parted reluctantly to allow the speaker to approach the couple. The well-dressed man was a bit shorter than Hugh and some years older, but aside from the graying temples and a bit of thickness around the middle, the two could have been twins. "It belonged to my sons' mother."

He held it out to Hugh on the palm of his hand, and after a long, tense moment, Hugh picked it up and slid it over the tip of the first and second fingers of Chloe's left hand before bringing it to rest at the base of her third finger. When instructed to give his wife a "kiss of peace," Sir Hugh glared at the bishop until the cleric simply cleared his throat and declared them husband and wife.

Chloe managed to stay upright through the mass that followed and to exit the chapel under her own power. She endured a seemingly endless round of blessings and good wishes, and managed to return similar sentiments to her newly wedded sisters. Then, when they reentered the hall and the duke gave each of his daughters a benedictive kiss on the forehead, he again gripped Chloe's shoulders tightly and stared into her eyes with a turbulent expression.

What had she done to deserve such wretched treatment from an adoptive father who only adopted her in order to use her to pay his ransom? How much of a disappointment could she possibly be?

Thoroughly dispirited, she sat at the king's linen-draped table, suffering endless toasts to the felicity and harmony of her marriage and feeling like an impostor at her own wedding feast. Sir Hugh had abandoned her the moment they were seated, and she was certain that everyone in the hall had taken notice. It was only when an uncannily familiar face and frame loomed up before her with an elegant bow that her reluctant husband reappeared at her side.

"What the devil are you doing here?" Hugh demanded in a combative tone.

"Good to see you, too," the Earl of Sennet said with defiant geniality. "And in better company than usual. Not a tonsure in sight."

"This"—Hugh gestured to Chloe and then the feast beginning around them—"changes nothing."

"This"—the earl extended his hand for Chloe's and, when she yielded it to him, brushed it with a gallant kiss—"changes everything."

"How did you know I was to wed?" Hugh demanded. "I was only commanded to do so this morning."

"The king sent for me three days ago." The earl gave him a superior sort of smile that taunted Hugh with the idea that certain things had been withheld from him. Hugh stiffened and shot a resentful look toward the king.

"Damn his devious hide."

"I fear I shall have to welcome you properly to the family at a later time, my lady," the Earl of Sennet said, giving her a dazzling smile that made her wonder if that was how Sir Hugh would look if he was ever moved to a true expression of joy or pleasure.

"Things are never so bad that they can't get a bit worse," Hugh muttered, unaware that he'd spoken aloud until he sat down again and found himself caught in a searching gaze.

"That is your father?" Chloe asked, looking between him and the earl.

"Only in the biblical sense."

"He certainly is . . . is . . ." She sorted through a barrage of impressions for a word to sum up the earl's powerful presence.

"Loud?" Hugh supplied several possibilities. "Arrogant? Overbearing? Infuriating?"

"Striking." She glanced at the earl, who was busy charming noble ladies and serving women with equal familiarity. "You look very much alike."

Hugh looked as if he'd just been doused with icy water.

"There is no need to be insulting." He rose, cup in hand, and abandoned her at the table until the food was served.

After the wedding dinner, the company adjourned to the knights' practice field to witness impromptu contests staged by a number of the younger knights and squires. Then as the sun lowered and the rest of the day went from tedious to terrible, tension over the coming night built steadily in all of the maids.

Despite the two full cups of unwatered wine, drunk in quick succession, Chloe's body ached with tension, her hands were cold, and her tongue felt thick and clumsy. Her condition was not improved by rowdy voices recounting increasingly explicit stories about wedding nights and couples who managed their first bit of "night work" with something less than success.

How bad could it be? Chloe asked herself as Lady Marcella herded her and her sisters up the stairs and deposited them each in a borrowed chamber with a giggling maidservant. In her mind's eye rose a vision of Sir Graham's pale face and drink-dulled eyes. Apparently bad enough that experienced knights could dread it. And she had a good bit more to dread than the average knight or bride.

It was some time later that Sir Hugh arrived at the borrowed chamber with a group of ale-soaked well-wishers at his back and propelling him through the door toward the final step in forging a marital bond. As the maidservant slipped out and the door slammed shut on them, he blinked and looked around the small chamber, taking his bearings.

The furnishings were simple but pleasant; a modest-sized bed; a tall, delicately carved wooden chest; a brazier that at this time of year was empty; a table with two simple straight chairs; and a gold damask bed curtain that hung from the ceiling and was pulled back and tied on each side of the bed. They had been supplied with fresh linen, a flagon of wine and cups, and a sizable pair of fragrant bee's wax candles that even now were supplying gentle golden light and sending their honeyed fragrance all through the chamber.

Chloe stood in the shadow of the bed curtain, wearing her spare shift and her hair down over her shoulders. She had given up trying to think of something clever or profound or even marginally charming to say. It was just as well; the sight of him standing there with his doublet loosened, his hair tousled, and his eyes dark and smoldering would have robbed her of speech in any case.

Her pulse began to skip and her lips felt bare and strangely warm. Every inch of her skin came alive beneath her shift, aching, yearning for contact of a sort that could only be satisfied in the depths of bone and sinew itself. Longing migrated inward along her limbs to pool in her middle. It felt strangely like physical hunger, and she suddenly understood why desire and appetite were often spoken of as one.

The way her body sprang to a life of its own, preparing, anticipating, shocked her. In a desperate bid to assert control over her own impulses, as well as the situation, she searched for a voice and found one. That of her inner abbess.

"This is all your fault, you know."

Chapter Fifteen

HUGH STOOD IN THE SMALL CHAM-
ber, inhaling the honey-sweetened air, looking at
the woman who had diverted his ambitions and by any
standard wrecked his life, and told himself he was in deep
trouble. He had already run the gamut of emotions from
outrage to self-loathing and had taken out his frustration
on his father, his friends, and even his confessor. Poor
Graham had the misfortune to confront him and demand
to know how he could have betrayed their friendship so
foully, and had ended up with a cut lip and an eye nearly
swollen shut. Not that Graham hadn't managed to land a
few well-placed blows, also; Hugh was sporting a
smashed mouth and few bruises himself.

It was just as well. They both worked their anger out
and afterward were able to think more clearly. And all of
his thoughts kept circling back to one thing: he had no
one to blame for his predicament but himself. He had
made the choice to intervene, and now had to live with
the consequences. Literally.

Why in Heaven's name had he inserted himself into a
situation that was well on its way to resolving the prime
conflict in his life without his help?

"You're right," he declared, folding his arms and widening his stance. "Foolish me. All I had to do was stand there and watch you sacrifice yourself to your sisters' happiness and marry decrepit old Ketchum, and I could have gotten on with my life."

"Why didn't you?" she said.

"Because . . ."

In order to do that he would have had to ignore the misery evident in her face and the overwhelming urges of protection and possession roiling inside him. He would have had to somehow forget the feel of her, the taste of her, and the longing in her eyes the previous night when she confessed that in her darkest moment her thought was of him. He would have had to somehow lock away the memory of her naked body, and the feelings she stirred in him every time those azure-sky eyes drifted over him.

Flawed and errant creature that he was, he didn't want to forget any of it. He wanted to rescue her from an intolerable fate and claim her for himself. The highest and noblest of his impulses had bonded inextricably with his lowest and basest ones. Together they overwhelmed his better judgment, and he found himself striding into the fray.

"Because . . . I was charged by the king to administer the wife test to you. And it was clear as rainwater that old Ketchum was not suitable for you."

"I would have married him," she protested.

"No doubt you would have."

"And I would have made him a proper wife."

"You wouldn't make anybody a *proper* wife," he countered. "Proper wives are biddable and demure and helpful and respectful and diligent."

"And I am not?" She stalked closer to him, unwittingly putting herself between him and the candles.

"Hell, no." He stalked closer to her, his blood heating at the way the light filtered through her shift, outlining her body. "You're overeducated and arrogant . . . outspoken to the point of brazenness . . . stubborn and willful . . . and without the slightest shred of modesty or deference for your betters."

Her nostrils flared.

"While you, on the other hand, are the very pinnacle of husbandly virtue," she charged. "Learned and wise beyond your years, uncompromising in both inner virtue and outward rectitude . . . patient as Job . . . enduring as the blessed saints . . . with the stamina of a warhorse, and no doubt the heart of a lion . . ."

"The king has declared that I am," he said archly. "It must be so."

Her mouth opened and closed without releasing a sound.

"You know, of all your shortcomings, my lady, the most unappealing is ingratitude. The least you could do is thank me."

"Thank you? For making me a laughingstock? For making me sound like an intolerable, unnatural shrew?"

"For rescuing you," he said, edging closer and breathing deeply, inhaling her lavender scent. "For sacrificing my future for yours."

Sacrifice, she thought. So that was what he called it. He rescued her out of the great "nobility" of his heart and now insisted she eternally laud and honor his selflessness. With no hint that he might have had other motives, like caring about her. Or less than altruistic aims, like taking pleasure in her. Even after going to astonishing lengths to keep her from marrying someone else, he still wouldn't admit that he wanted her.

"I am not ungrateful for your help," she said, reining her emotions, making herself think. "In truth, I am so mindful of it and so inspired by your example that I am now willing to make a sacrifice of my own. In honor of your selflessness, I intend to renounce my wifely rights to you."

"What?"

"Is that not clear? I intend to see that these vows go unconsummated. That will constitute grounds, in the clerical courts, for annulling the marriage."

"Don't tell me there is a lawyer inside that devious little head as well." He fell back a step, looking genuinely astonished. She could see him struggling to make the wheels turn in his mind. "Church law, important as it may be, is not the final authority here. The king himself has decreed we are to be wedded, and"—his eyes darted back and forth as if searching for a plausible objection—"refusing to comply, especially in nuptials related to a treaty, would be tantamount to treason. Kings take a rather dim view of treason."

"The king needn't know anything about it," she said, shrugging and sending her shift sliding off one shoulder. She saw light flare in his eyes as they fixed on her bared skin. "We can pledge ourselves to a 'spiritual marriage' . . . agree to live as brother and sister . . . and after a time you can petition to enter the monastery, as you've always wanted."

"There are more obstacles to my entering the monastery than just this marriage. My father and his accomplice, the king, will not be content until I produce an heir." He forced his gaze up to her face and dropped his arms to his sides. "Spiritual marriages do not produce heirs."

"True. But there are instances of married persons being admitted to monasteries once their duty to their line is done. It shouldn't take too—"

He seized her by the shoulders.

"Why this sudden desire to escape the vows you took today?"

"I don't want to escape them, *you* do." Her voice thickened as the heat and scent of him filled her head and began to curl through her veins. "I am merely accommodating you. Out of *gratitude*." She saw the conflict in his eyes and watched him realize that she had just met his stroke and effectively parried it. His hands tightened on her arms.

"I don't want your gratitude," he ground out, his breath coming faster, his eyes beginning to shimmer in a way that made her heart beat faster.

"Then what do you want, Hugh of Sennet?" Her body migrated a provocative fraction of an inch toward his. With her next question she drove her point straight to the center of his heart. "What are *your* preferences?"

She watched his eyes darkening, saw him lick his lower lip as he stared at hers, and sensed the primal pull her body exerted on his. She waited, praying that his desire for her could overcome the years of arid, loveless doctrine and give her a foothold in his heart.

"This. I want this."

He lowered his lips to hers and elation surged through her as he wrapped his arms around her and pulled her fully against him.

This was what she had desired, craved, and literally prayed for. His lips were warm and wine-sweet, and his body was hard and indelibly male against hers. She wrapped her arms around him and ran her hands up his broad back, finding an anchor for her new life in the thick columns of muscle running up the center of his back and the sinew fanning up and over his shoulders. More than once his powerful frame had been shelter and safety to her in perilous times. At that tactile reminder of what he already had been to her, she relaxed and entrusted herself to the hope of all he could someday be.

His hands slid down her back and along her sides, claiming every line and curve, every responsive shift and quiver of her body. She began to anticipate the flow of his hands and moved to meet his touch, then to coax and direct it with her responses. He slipped his hands beneath her shift to touch her skin directly, and the heat of his big, callused hands seemed to melt her very bones. She sagged against him, clinging to his broad shoulders for support, and suddenly he was lifting her, carrying her to the bed.

As he discarded his garments, she lay on the feather-filled ticking feeling warm and supple and lush with sensual possibility. Knowing that he watched her, she experienced a new and heady sense of power emanating from the deepest core of her woman's nature . . . the power to create desire, to evoke need and longing . . . and the power to fulfill that need and slake that desire.

He sank onto the bed beside her and lay propped on one elbow, running his fingers through her hair, tracing her profile with his fingertips, then dragging his knuckles down the smooth skin of her chest. When he untied her shift and opened it, she blushed and would have covered herself, but he held her hand away and smiled down into her eyes. To reassure her, he leaned over and kissed her forehead, the tip of her nose, her lips, her chin . . . and worked his way down the center of her body, kissing and nuzzling, adding licks and nibbles, pausing only to nudge away fabric and bare another small part of her to his adoration.

By the time he returned to her lips, she caught his heated face between her hands and held him there for a moment, searching him, searching herself.

"I don't want you to feel trapped," she said, her voice low and urgent.

"I am trapped," he responded with complete honesty.

"I don't want you to be angry and resentful."

"I've been angry and resentful. I'm . . . getting over it."

She swallowed hard, and he could see her bracing, deciding.

"I don't want you to hate me," she whispered.

There it was. The truth that, once released, could never be put back into the box. She cared how he felt about her. She cared about *him*.

"I could never hate you," he said, tracing her lips with his thumb. "Any more than I could stand by and watch you marry a man nearly three times your age. You deserve better, Chloe of Guibray." He grew more serious. "I'm just not sure you've gotten it."

She smiled. It was as close to an admission of caring as she was likely to get just now. And it was enough.

"Let me be the judge of that."

She laced her fingers around the back of his neck and pulled his mouth down to hers, offering him a chance to convince her in a more direct way. Their kisses deepened, growing steadily more intimate and venturesome. Soon she was kissing his ears and nipping his chin, and he was kissing the hollow at the base of her throat and trailing hot kisses down her breast to her burning nipples.

He stroked and caressed her and slowly slid his body over hers. Pleasure collected in her breasts and the hollow between her legs, making her burn for his touch on those sensation-rich parts of her. When he caressed and nuzzled her breasts, she felt her body drawing taut beneath him. As she parted her thighs and he settled between them, she felt herself being shaped, molded by his lavish heat to match his unique shape and weight, his distinctive frame. Then as they kissed and explored, he began to move, fitted intimately against her, initiating her into what would follow.

By the time he began the joining, she was fully naked and trembling with need. He tried to go slowly, to give her a chance to adjust, but she arched her body into his and wrapped her legs around him, urging him further, deeper inside her, and gasping when he breached her maiden barrier. And when at last he lay imbedded fully within her, he paused to look at her and found her face glowing with pleasure.

Then he began to move within her, over her, around her, filling her senses as he filled her body. The pleasure seemed to lift her on an ever-tightening spiral while paradoxically expanding the borders of her being. The distinction between her and him began to blur; her flesh seemed to merge with his, their heartbeats settled into a synchronous rhythm, and the breath that bathed their hot faces mingled as if coming from the same breast. They were joined and with each motion creating something entirely new, a new flesh, a new spirit, a new bond of heart and mind. When he finally took his release, she was so attuned to his response that she seemed to feel its tumult in her own tautly stretched nerves.

Somewhere in the wee hours of the morning, well before dawn began to gray the sky, she awakened to find him propped up on a cushion beside her, watching her sleep. She felt a growing coolness and realized she was lying naked . . . the bed linen pushed aside . . . bared to his gaze.

"What are you doing?" she whispered.

"Looking," he said softly, feathering a touch up the center of her body and smiling at the way she held her breath and closed her eyes to savor it. "You are so beautiful. I never . . ."

When she opened her eyes, he looked away as if embarrassed to have her see her effect on him.

"You never what?" She smiled and turned his hot face back to her.

"Never imagined it would be so . . ." He halted and avoided her eyes, searching for the right word. "So easy to look at you."

"It's not like you haven't seen my body before," she said, puzzled.

"I may have seen, but I didn't *look*. There is a difference."

The wonder evident in his reaction to their pleasure was too close to hers for her not to recognize what it meant.

"But you were a soldier. On campaign. Somewhere along the way you must have looked at a woman and . . ." She suddenly knew, without being told, that she was wrong.

"I was promised to God." She could see emotion rising in him. "I saw, all right. Too much. But I never *looked*. Until now."

An aching tenderness spread through her, unveiling a part of her she hadn't known was there, a place of gentleness and caring, a well of compassion from which all other good flowed. Suddenly she yearned to take him inside her, to surround him with warmth and protect the fragile, emerging spirit in him. She wanted to give him joy and pleasure and all of the other wonderful things his narrow and restricted upbringing had denied him.

She sat up and rolled up onto her knees before him. When he looked up with a guarded expression, she poured all of the love and compassion she possessed into one potent and adoring smile.

"I'm yours, Hugh of Sennet. Body and soul. I am here to partner your life . . . to share your pleasure and to comfort your pain. I was made 'woman' for you, just as you were made 'man' for me. This is the way Heaven intended it. And I think it's time you 'looked' your fill."

He squinted and blinked, as if stepping out of a darkened room into the midday sun. She took his hand and
pulled him up to face her. As he watched, hesitant but
hungry for sensation, she straightened his fingers and
dragged them across her face, down her throat, and
cupped them with hers over her breast.

He roared to life, wrapping her in his arms and lowering
her to the bed with him, kissing her, holding her, touching
her as if he could never get his fill. She giggled as he nuzzled her neck and squealed as he nibbled her ear.

"Oooh, stop! That tickles!" She was suddenly all
gooseflesh and shivers.

He pushed up on his elbows above her and her heart
stopped. His handsome face was lighted with the most
beautiful smile she had ever seen. She was so entranced
that it took her a moment to translate what he'd said before continuing to ravish her with sultry, wet kisses and
bone-melting caresses.

"Get used to it."

"I'll try," she breathed out on a sigh, giving herself up to
the tantalizing sensations he was stirring within her. "But I
should warn you . . . it will probably take some time. . . ."

WHEN CHLOE ROUSED AGAIN FROM SLEEP,
the sun was well up and Hugh was standing on the far
side of the chamber. She slipped from the bed to tiptoe
up behind him and slide her arms about his waist. He
growled with surprise and turned with a razor in his hand
and soap on his partly shaved face.

"Don't ever sneak up on a man with a shaving blade
in his hand. Think how it would look if I appeared in the
hall with blood pouring down my face."

She laughed and commandeered the razor, pushing him
to a seat in the sunlight and tilting his head to achieve the
proper angle for applying the blade.

"After your delightful description of me yesterday,"
she declared, "people will be so astonished to see you

emerge from this chamber at all that they probably won't even notice a little blood."

His chuckle drew a thump from her on his shoulder. "Hold still."

The sounds of their stirring drew the little maidservant who had attended Chloe the previous night, and Hugh reluctantly turned over the task of assisting Chloe's dressing to her. She brushed and braided Chloe's hair, and put it up in a style befitting a married woman. As she worked, she gossiped about the wedding feast and about how quiet everything had been outside the five nuptial chambers. Apparently there had been a number of people with their ears pressed to the portals . . . all of whom finally fell asleep or went away disappointed.

Hugh sat with his booted feet propped on the table, saying little as he listened and watched her dress and prepare for the day. He was quieter still as they descended the steps together, and by the time they entered the great hall and were greeted by a rousing "halloo," his features had settled into a light scowl she recognized all too well.

She tried to be gracious about the admiration and teasing aimed her way, but even simple curiosity seemed a vile intrusion on the closeness they had found in the night. The arrival of her sisters and their new husbands was a welcome diversion. She was relieved to see that they, too, had survived the night and looked, on the whole, quite content. Then on closer look she saw that Lisette's eyes were slightly swollen, as if she had spent some time crying. She resolved to talk to Lisette later.

Hugh relaxed a bit as Jax, William, Simon, and Graham joined him on the griddle of public scrutiny. He especially enjoyed Graham's uncharacteristic outburst of temper over the tales of howls and pleas for mercy supposedly heard coming from his chamber. But just as Hugh was warming again, a familiar voice rang out from the main doors of the hall, and he froze entirely.

"Where's my son?" the Earl of Sennet roared, snatching a flagon of ale out of a young knight's hand and downing it as he strode down the hall. "There he is, with his lovely bride! Ye gods, look at them—there's no doubt he got the wife-making done, eh?"

The laughter that generated grated visibly on every nerve in Hugh's body. He looked at Chloe's crimson face, rose, and offered her his hand to usher her from his father's presence. They hadn't reached the door when the king arrived with news of the birth of another son, and congratulations erupted in the hall, overshadowing even the tantalizing curiosity about the wedding nights of the Brides of Virtue.

It was later, just past midday, that the king summoned the newly wedded couples to his privy chamber and with a notable absence of fanfare, ordered them to return to their homes forthwith and begin their lives together. There was no discussion, and no reason was given for so abrupt a dismissal. But as they filed out, it was clear in their minds that such an order was meant to disperse the duke's daughters throughout the countryside and diffuse whatever danger they might still face.

Arrangements had to be made quickly; dowry divided, mounts and wagons secured, escorts arranged. The husbands saw to the preparations for the next morning's departure, leaving their wives to collect with Lady Marcella one last time in the room they had shared as maids. It was hard to believe, after all they had been through together, that this might be the last time they would see each other. They chatted about their new homes and shared secrets about their new husbands, and played with Lady Marcella's new puppy. The gift from the old Earl of Ketchum *to* the maids had become a gift *from* the maids to their dear guide and chaperone, to ease the heartache of her earlier loss. It was reassuring to see the old lady's careworn face brighten as she watched the little beast gambol and yip and try to chew everyone's slippers.

When night fell and the time came for them to return to their separate beds, they grew quiet and tearful, and hugged Chloe one by one before they slipped out. When only Lisette and Lady Marcella remained, Lisette seemed reluctant to leave and clung to Chloe's hand.

"Is something wrong?" Chloe asked, rubbing the back of Lisette's hand reassuringly.

"*No*. I mean, not really. It's nothing I cannot deal with." Lisette was choosing her words carefully, leaving things unsaid. Anxiety bloomed in her face, causing Chloe's heart to sink. There must be a terrible problem indeed to make determined and optimistic Lisette so gloomy and uncertain. "It's just that Graham . . . he seems to be so . . . uncomfortable with me and . . ." Tears rolled. "I think he would have preferred to marry someone else."

"Oh, tell him to quit whinin' and act like a man," Lady Marcella spoke up, surprising them both. "So he didn't get his pick. How many of us do in life? You're a handsome woman, Lissie . . . made for howlin' three times a night." The old lady narrowed her eyes. "Tell 'im to eat hearty an' count his blessings."

Chloe and Lisette both smiled at the old lady's mutinous expression.

"She's right," Chloe said thickly, squeezing Lisette's hands. "He is lucky to have you. Just give it some time."

Lisette nodded and gave both Chloe and Lady Marcella a huge hug. "Thank you for reminding me." She swiped at her tears and straightened. "We wouldn't have passed the wife test if we didn't belong together."

Chloe stood biting her lip, staring at the door after Lisette left, and Lady Marcella came to put an arm around her, saying, "She'll be fine, that one."

"I hope so."

FIVE SMALL TRAVELING PARTIES LEFT Windsor the next morning, the first just at daybreak and others over the course of the next several hours. Chloe had hoped to see her sisters one more time, but as they departed at different hours, from different locations, she counted herself lucky even to catch a glimpse of Helen and Lord Simon departing for his home to the south.

As she stood on the steps of the great hall, pulling her cloak tighter against the breeze, she felt a terrible sense

of loneliness and loss. This was inevitable, this parting of
their ways, but it hurt all the same. To lose her sisters just
as she had begun to feel they were family . . .

It would be so much easier if she had any idea where she
was headed and what Sir Hugh's home was like. But she
had had no chance to speak with him about it. He had been
late returning to their chamber last night, and she was so
exhausted that she fell asleep while waiting for him. He
hadn't disturbed her when he came to bed, and he had already risen and dressed that morning when she awoke.

Midmorning he escorted her into the great hall, where
they bade the king farewell and he wished them safe
travel. The Duke of Avalon, still under the constant escort
of the Earl of Norwich, was present in the hall and heard
the exchange of farewells. He seemed agitated by the
news that they were departing and intercepted them as
they neared the main doors. As Hugh responded to his
inquiries about the location of the Sennets' estates, it was
clear that the duke was more interested in Chloe; his eyes
never left her. Then, in wishing them well, he gave Chloe a
kiss on the forehead that was filled with unsettling emotion.

The strange encounter with the duke had weighted
Chloe's already drooping spirits as they emerged into the
gray weather. Now as she stood waiting for the horses
and wagons, her throat tightened and tears formed in her
eyes. When Hugh arrived with a gentle-looking young
mare and helped her mount, she tried not to let him see
how much leaving affected her.

Glancing away, her gaze fell on one of the wagons . . .
the driver, to be exact. The fellow looked up and caught
her staring at him. A grin spread over his face. It was
Mattias. Tears of pure relief rolled down her cheeks at the
sight of his grizzled face, and she sent him a heartfelt
smile. He pointed behind him, and shortly she was waving
at Withers and Willum and Fenster, mounted on horses
behind the wagons. Suddenly she didn't feel half so alone.

They were well down the winding road that led north,
when several mounted men-at-arms came charging
straight into the middle of their party. Immediately Hugh

went for his blade and wheeled to put his horse between them and Chloe.

"What the devil do you think you're doing?" he snarled, glaring at the leader of the intruders.

"Going to my home. With my son," the Earl of Sennet declared with a defiant smile that developed an admiring glint as it turned on Chloe. "And my new daughter-in-law."

Hugh had only one word for that.

"Damnation."

THAT EVENING THE GREAT HALL OF WIND-sor seemed strangely drab and empty. The excitement of the maids' presence and the intrigues of the wife test had been a welcome diversion for king and courtiers alike. Even as the last of the couples was leaving Windsor, the stories of their time there were being told and retold. No one loved the recounting more than Lord Bromley. And there was no audience more attentive than the Duke of Avalon. Since he was no longer an official prisoner of war, diplomatic courtesy demanded that Edward show the French duke full hospitality until he could provide an escort to the coast. Avalon was invited into the great hall, where he listened intently to every detail of Bromley's account of the maids' arrival and adventures, which was embroidered and amended by the comments of others, including the aged Lady Marcella.

The old lady was eager to tell her version of events . . . until she spotted the Duke of Avalon, and her nephew made a formal introduction. Something rumbled up out of memory, and she stuck her face into the duke's and glared at him from close up, searching his fleshy face and fine clothes.

"Manfred? A *French* Manfred?" she said with a sudden display of contempt that astonished her nephew. She rose and spat. "Go home."

Manfred, Duke of Avalon watched the old lady hobble away and avoided Bromley's unsettled look to glance at the English king.

"Not yet, old woman," he murmured. "Not yet."

*   *   *

MILES AWAY, IN LONDON, A SHIP THAT
had just crossed the Channel and followed the tides up
the Thames was unloading passengers onto a London
quay. Most of the travelers thudded down the gangplank
and trudged off on their own solitary way. But there was
one passenger, a thickset man dressed in simple woolens
and incongruously elegant boots, who was met by a small
cadre of what appeared to be sailors and waterfront toughs.

Without a word exchanged, he recognized and fell in
amongst them. They led him through several narrow, dank
alleyways to a small tavern with sleeping rooms above. It
was only when they were inside the low, cramped chamber and the door was safely bolted that he removed his
cloak and turned on the leader.

"Well?" the *compte* demanded in French. He knew
from Captain Valoir's grim expression that the news
would not be good.

"The wedding . . . it was a day ago."

"*Sacrebleu!*" The *compte* caught himself. "How many
of them did you manage to kill?"

Valoir looked down in silence and braced for the coming storm.

"Not one? You did not manage to rid the world of even
one of those dirty little tarts?" The lord kicked over a
nearby stool before hauling his temper under control.
"Tell me you at least managed to *ruin* some of them."

The captain blanched. "They were always under escort,
seigneur. Guarded at all times. We managed to injure one
and abduct another . . . briefly. I lost four men in the attempt."

"Idiots!" the *compte* flung his arms out and roared, as
if asking the cosmos to witness the depth of his trials. "I
am surrounded by idiots!" He grabbed Valoir by the tunic.
"You allowed all five of these bastard females to wed!"
Again he asserted control over his rising fury, as an even
more pressing problem presented itself. "Was the duke
there? Did he see them?"

"I—I believe he was present, *seigneur*."

The *compte* thought on that for a moment. "If he didn't say anything, he must not have . . . Where are these cursed females now?"

"They have left Windsor, *seigneur*." Valoir took an anxious breath.

"Where did they go?"

Valoir shrugged, watching his lord carefully. "To their new husbands' homes . . . all over England."

"And Avalon"—he turned to Valoir with his eyes flitting back and forth—"has he been released?"

"*Non, seigneur*. He was taken to the castle called Windsor and is now a guest of the English king."

"Edward probably hopes to turn his sympathies and send him home an ally. We must find a way to poison the well."

"The castle water, *seigneur*?" Valoir looked confused.

The count closed his eyes for a moment. "A figure of speech, you arse-head. Poison relations between them . . . find a way to discredit the duke and anger Edward." His voice developed a conjuring tone. "Perhaps even wedded, the females can be useful. Surely there is someone hereabouts who can be persuaded to reveal the truth about the devious and duplicitous duke."

Valoir looked surprised. "Reveal how much of his wealth was hidden and withheld from the ransom?"

"There is no need to be *that* truthful," the mercurial *compte* said with a nasty laugh. "Especially when the duke's own manipulations are quite damning on their own."

Chapter Sixteen

THE JOURNEY TO SIR HUGH'S ANCES-
tral home took the better part of three days. Despite the earl's insistence that there was no hurry, Hugh
seemed determined to spend as little time as possible on
the road. It took a while for Chloe to realize that his sense
of urgency had to do with their safety, and she ceased
objecting to the pace. By the end of the second day, however, her bottom was sore, every muscle in her body
ached, and she was heartily sick of Hugh's attitude toward
his father.

Each time the earl drew his mount alongside hers,
Hugh appeared on her other side to pull her away on some
pretext or other. In the evening, when they stopped at an
inn in a small village, Hugh installed her in a chamber
straightaway and sent food and drink to her, ostensibly so
that she could avoid "the smells and rough company of
the tavern." When the earl did manage to speak with her
for a few moments, to describe some of his home to her,
she kept looking over her shoulder and expecting Hugh
to come roaring down on them at any moment.

"What is it about your father that you dislike so?" she

demanded the second evening as they camped by the side of the road.

"Other than his prodigal and profligate ways?" he said irritably, poking at the campfire's reddened embers with a stick.

"You make him sound like a monster. Just because you don't approve of someone, doesn't mean he's depraved and unredeemable." She recklessly met his gaze. "You've held the same unreasonable—and, I might add, *erroneous*—attitude about the entire female sex."

"Erroneous? Ask anyone at court or in the shire. They will confirm my assessment of his nature." He leaned toward her. "But if you really want to know the truth, just ask the defenseless women who've had to bear his bastards."

There was no brisk, dismissive retort for so devastating a charge. Illegitimate children made upon defenseless women. No matter what grievances Hugh bore against his father, he would never make such an accusation unless it were based in fact. She thought of the glint in the Earl of Sennet's worldly eyes, his contagious high spirits, and the prowling heat that, even in so short a visit, had caused the ladies of the court to stare avidly at him from all over the hall. Everything about him declared that he was a man who indulged in pleasure whenever, however he could. It was little wonder that he and Hugh were at such odds; the lusty and recklessly charming earl was everything that pious and abstemious Hugh of Sennet would abhor. Despite their striking physical similarities, it was difficult to believe they were father and son.

The understanding that flooded into her face and softened her posture seemed to annoy him even more than her challenge.

"Just watch out for him," he ordered, rising to check with Mattias about the night watch.

THE FIELDS THEY PASSED AS THEY TRAVeled north were a lush June green and the orchards had

set blossoms enough for bountiful crops. The gently rolling hills were dotted with herds in which spring lambs
frolicked. Increasingly, the fields were divided by hedge-
rows and small stands of trees where birds nested undis-
turbed. It was beautiful countryside.

She postponed all worries about Hugh's growing silence and what would happen when they reached the hall
of Sennet, in favor of simply enjoying the bright sun on
her face and the sweet air in her lungs. Unfortunately, that
pleasure was not to last for long. The moment they
reached a small stream and forded it, the earl and his men
snapped to attention and began to ride more purposefully.
When she asked Hugh what was happening, he shook his
head and reluctantly relayed the question to his father. The
Earl of Sennet smiled broadly.

"We're home."

Soon a cluster of buildings became visible in the distance. As they approached, they spotted workers in the
fields along the road, tending crops and flocks. As they
passed, the people paused to stare at the travelers and,
upon recognizing their lord, began to wave and call out a
welcome. Some left their hoeing and stone-picking to
come and stand by the road, leaning on their tools and
craning their necks to see who the earl had brought home
with him. Hugh's father returned their greetings without
pretense, remembering many of them by name and in-
quiring about their families, their animals, or their crops.
Chloe watched his expressive face . . . surprised by the
concern he showed for his people and studying the respectful familiarity his people showed toward him.

The house and hall of Sennet stood on a slight rise,
surrounded by a modest stone wall and the beginnings of
a small village. The house was all of stone and timber,
but with its several parts constructed in different styles,
suggesting that it had been enlarged and improved over
the years. Still, since the additions were made with similar
materials, the overall effect was cohesive and pleasant.
And as they neared, it was clear that the wall was kept in
good repair, the slate roofs of the house and hall were

sound, and even the cottages and shops and byres just outside the wall seemed orderly and well maintained.

Inside the wall there were a small pond, several barns and a stable, a modest courtyard, and several plots of ground tilled and planted for kitchen gardens. As they approached the double doors of the main hall, a number of servants came pouring out and stood in a line to greet the earl. A groom ran up to take his horse as he dismounted, and a thin, graying fellow in slightly better dress than the others gave the earl a brief bow and a genial reassurance that all was well before turning to openly inspect Hugh.

"So, 'e's come home a last." The steward came over to give Hugh a nod of respect as he dismounted. "Sir Hugh. Good to have ye home again after all these years." Then he looked to Chloe. "And bringing a milady with ye." He gave her a courtly bow. "Welcome, milady, to Sennet Hall."

Before she could do more than acknowledge the greeting with a nod, a jumble of female voices burst from the open doors, quickly followed by a jumble of the females themselves.

". . . and you're always late!" a buxom young maid with dark hair and vivid brown eyes snapped at the girls trailing her.

"It's not my fault Corrine's always locking all the doors and putting things away where you can't find—" A willowy carrot-top with an abundance of freckles ran into the first girl, who had stopped abruptly at the sight of them.

"You blame *me* for everything!" a third maid, a small curvy little thing with untamed chestnut hair and enormous eyes, protested as she narrowly missed barreling into them on the step.

"*A-hem!*" the earl said, crossing his arms and looking stern. "We have guests, you little heathens. Your brother has come home to stay, and I'll have you show a bit of breeding around him and his lady wife."

"We don't have any breeding," the buxom one said

tartly. "Or so you tell us, at every opportunity."

"We're untamable vixens who ought to be caged," the redhead added.

"And fed only bread and water until we repent and begin to behave like proper human lasses. Whatever those are." The curvy little spitfire copied his pose, crossing her arm and raising her chin to a defiant angle.

The earl glowered at them. "Don't think I won't do it! Insolent pups. Get down here. And mind your manners as you meet your brother. Remember, you'll be living on his charity and goodwill for the rest of your natural days." He turned to Hugh, who stood by Chloe's horse, glaring at the living proof of his father's debauchery.

"Meet your sisters, boy. Ellen . . ." The buxom, dark-haired beauty gave a sinuous curtsy. "Lizabeth . . ." The fiery carrot-top with the upturned nose bobbed a greeting. "And Corinne." The curvy little one with the pale, memorable eyes looked straight up at him, grinned, and only remembered to curtsy when the redhead elbowed her in the side.

Hugh's mouth was drawn in a tight line as he looked between the three and his father. "You took them into your house, under your own roof?"

"I did," the earl admitted grimly. "Must have been drunk as a skunk." Then he remembered Chloe and shouldered Hugh aside to lift her down from her mount. "And this," he declared ominously to his three daughters, "is Lady Chloe, the new mistress of Sennet. Do as she says or rue the day." He narrowed his eyes and delivered in a threatening tone: "She was raised in a *convent*." While that registered in their widened eyes and uncertain expressions, the earl leaned toward Chloe and muttered for her ears alone: "God help you." Then he turned on his heel and strode for his hall, calling for ale . . . and plenty of it.

The hall was a spacious, arched and timbered expanse with whitewashed walls that were hung with a number of banners. There was a great hearth at the far end, a single long table down the center of the hall, and a goodly number of heavy, well-made chairs to go around the common board. On one side of the hall, in a large alcove, was a set of chairs filled with brightly colored pillows, tapestry-covered stools, and a large brass-bound chest.

There, Chloe met Mrs. Trueblood, the housekeeper, a severe-looking woman who welcomed her with a crisp, functional air and showed her immediately up the main steps to the chamber set aside for her. Trueblood, as she insisted she be called, gave Chloe a general overview of the house, the grounds, the responsibilities of the main servants and retainers. And as Chloe stood in her dusty clothes struggling to keep her head above that deluge of information, three heads appeared in the doorway behind the housekeeper, then quickly disappeared. As the house-keeper droned on, a hand appeared, making snippy talking motions. Then another hand joined it. Then another.

The drift and widening of Chloe's eyes betrayed the girls' game, and the housekeeper turned abruptly and flew to the door, causing the maids to scatter frantically. Through the passage the sound of giggles wafted back, and the housekeeper turned to Chloe with a taut expression.

"I done my best, milaidy. They ain't bad girls. But a servant, even a *housekeeper*, is no proper guide for a headstrong young girl. An' their father . . ." She frowned and glanced at the pitcher and basin on the chest near the window. "I'll send up water. And I'll have 'em bring up your things straightaway."

When she left, Chloe stood staring at the door, too travel-fatigued and overwhelmed to make sense of her introduction to her new home and this first, startling glimpse of her duties as the new Lady of Sennet. She settled for exploring her chamber and found it to be a good-sized room dominated by a large, well-draped bed set between two glazed windows.

The water arrived and her chest was delivered soon after. She removed her cap and her overgown, beating the dust from the latter and hanging it on a wooden dowel near the window to air. When Hugh arrived, she was try-

ing out the bed and quickly skittered off it to stand near
the window.

He looked around the chamber as if seeing it for the
first time.

"Is everything satisfactory?"

"Very much so." She glanced at the bed. "The mattress
is quite comfortable and the linen is soft and clean. There
is good light." She gestured toward the sides of the bed.
"And glazing in the windows." She studied his face and
found it unreadable. "Is it the way you remembered? Your
home?"

"I don't have any memories of it," he said shortly. "I
was barely five when my mother died and I was sent to
Saint Barnard's."

"But surely you visited . . ."

"I have not been here in almost twenty years." A muscle in his jaw flexed and his hands curled into fists at his
sides. "And to return and have his bastards flung in my
face. And yours. It's unconscionable."

"They're very . . . *spirited*," she managed.

"They're exactly what he called them: *vixens*. How
could they be anything else, sired by a reprobate and a har-
lot?"

"It's a bit early to condemn them as fallen women, isn't
it? They can't be a day over fifteen. If they're too full of
themselves, it's probably because they've been allowed to
run free."

"Or because venery, licentiousness, and disregard for
godly behavior runs in their blood," he said fiercely.
"Blood always tells. They're bastards and the sin of their
begetting taints their natures."

Those words sliced to the very core of her. And she
could never let him know it.

"You share that blood," she said through a tightened
throat.

"*His* blood. But my mother was a true-born and God-
fearing lady. And I have worked all my life to see to it
that *his* blood doesn't overtake me."

She suffered a chill and tucked her arms around her

waist. There in a nutshell was the rest of the explanation for his rejection of all things pleasurable.

"Well, your work hasn't gone for naught. You are nothing like him." She turned away, opened the lid of her chest, and began to unpack.

She could hear that he stood for a moment without moving, then turned and stalked out. When she heard the door shut, she gripped the edge of the trunk and felt the blood drain abruptly from her head. The righteous, arrogant Sir Hugh she thought was defeated had only been in temporary retreat. He was back now, in full strength, and ready as ever to condemn and pass judgment.

Especially on bastards.

THEIR EVENING MEAL WAS A PREDICTABLY noisy and highly charged affair. The service was diligent, and the food was tasty and varied. It was the mix of the company that created tension and sparked occasional conflict. Chloe felt caught in the middle and tried with modest success to negotiate the extremes of all parties present and contribute a dignified and calming presence. It wasn't easy, given that everyone in the household and the earl's small garrison scrutinized her every move and evaluated her every expression and gesture . . . most in a critical light.

More than once she found her inner abbess taking control to issue a chilling look in the direction of the earl's unruly offspring. To their credit—or perhaps because of the earl's threats involving her formidable background—the girls amended their behavior and led Chloe to hope that they were not only redeemable, but that they might become delightful young women someday.

If, she reminded herself grimly, one could overlook the shameful circumstances of their births.

It was under that cloud that Chloe retired to her chamber and, with the help of a perky little chambermaid, bathed, brushed out her hair, and settled into the linen-decked bed to wait for Hugh. But as she waited, listening to the night sounds of her new home, her hope that he would come to her began to fade. By the time the door opened and he crept inside, she had given up and fallen asleep.

Hugh stood for a while in the darkened chamber, looking down at her, feeling an alarming fullness in his chest and a tightness in his throat. He wanted to awaken her, pull her into his arms, and lose himself in her lush body and deliciously direct passions. He wanted to hold her and, more shockingly, to have her hold him . . . the way she had that first night . . . the night that was forever inscribed on his bone and sinew.

But he didn't disturb her. Instead, he sat for a while in a chair near the window, being careful to stay out of the moonlight streaming in. He didn't need that unsettling influence aggravating his already volatile impulses. Only when exhaustion began to claim him did he creep to the bed, fully dressed, and lie quietly down beside her.

The next day as they were breaking fast in the hall, the earl appeared, fresh from a crack-of-dawn ride, and volunteered to show them around their new home. His daughters objected, insisting that they be allowed to show Chloe around the house and hall and grounds. The ensuing argument was resolved only by Chloe declaring that she would be pleased to accompany the earl first—as was only fitting—and that she would spend the balance of the day with them and Trueblood, learning the workings of the household.

Their first stop was the stables, where the earl proudly displayed several fine animals and a number of palfreys kept for his daughters' use. Then they visited the dairy, the ovens, the granary and several barns, and the weavers' house. By the time they reached the kitchens, the sun was not the only thing rising. Chloe's estimate of both the earl and his management of his holdings increased with each well-tended aspect of the estate they covered. She watched Hugh's grudging revision of his expectations of home, and hoped that it would penetrate the shell he seemed to have grown on the journey north. He took an interest in the estate, and his hardened attitude seemed to be softening . . . until they returned to the hall for dinner and he encountered the earl's daughters engaged in a pitched battle over who was in charge of giving dinner orders.

The earl turned on his heel and abandoned the hall, and Hugh declared he would be inspecting the cellars until the meal was ready. Chloe watched father and son escaping the quarrelsome trio—abandoning her to them—and realized that the pair had more in common than either would like to admit. When she turned to the girls, they were glaring at one another and quickly turned those challenging glares on her.

Out of nowhere the abbess roared to life in her, and she struck a familiar pose . . . hands at her waist, leaning slightly forward, her eyes narrowed in potent censure.

"We need to have a little talk, you and I. Come with me." She started for the alcove, but soon realized they weren't following. Looking back, she spotted three jutting chins and three sets of stubbornly folded arms. With ferocious determination, she strode back and grabbed two of them by the ears and began to pull. Shocked and suddenly teetering on tiptoes, they scrambled along beside her, protesting. When they reached the alcove, she released them, and ordered them to "sit." All three fell onto chair bottoms with widened eyes.

"I've just treated you like the fractious, disobedient children you appear to be. If you wish more respectful treatment, you will have to earn it with more ladylike behavior." She laid it out for them. "I can be the ally and advocate of three lovely young maids, or I can be warden to a trio of vixens. The choice is up to you."

They exchanged sulky looks and sat back in their chairs, unwilling to test her authority further. At least for now. Making do with that grudging cooperation, which so resembled Hugh's, Chloe sat down in the fourth chair in the alcove and began her campaign for their rehabilitation, if not their allegiance.

"Now tell me," she said, hoping to begin with learning

their strong points. "Is one of you the seamstress who stitched the lovely cushions we're seated on?"

IT TOOK TWO DAYS FOR CHLOE TO BEGIN to penetrate the willful resistance the earl's brash three-some maintained to her. They were still loud and argu-mentative with one another, but increasingly they reined their behavior in the hall and showed symptoms of ra-tional thought and civilized behavior. She began to be-lieve they would eventually come around. She only wished the same could be said for their older brother.

In their first three days at Sennet Hall, she had scarcely had a moment alone with him. He spent all of his time out riding the estate, examining and evaluating every building and bit of equipment, training with the earl's knights and men, and getting to know the steward, bailiff, wardens, and craftsmen who made Sennet work. Each night she went to bed determined to stay awake and see him when he arrived in their chamber. Each night it seemed he arrived later, and each morning it seemed he rose earlier.

On the evening of their third full day at Sennet, she determined to do something about what could only be his intentional avoidance of her. She set aside her inventory of the household linen and sent the earl's daughters to the kitchens with Trueblood to oversee the production of a light evening meal. Then she headed for the stables, where she was informed by her testy father-in-law that his ar-rogant and self-righteous son was last seen.

She found Hugh recently returned from another day in the saddle and giving his horse a thorough brushing.

"There are grooms for that," she said, after watching him in silence for a time. He seemed to be enjoying the work, and she hesitated to interrupt anything that gave him satisfaction.

He started and turned, took a deep breath at the sight of her, and returned to the work. "It's my horse, my part-ner, my responsibility. It's the first thing a knight learns . . .

to take care of his mount diligently and personally. Besides—"

"You enjoy it," she finished for him.

"What if I do?" he said with an edge.

"What else do you enjoy, Hugh of Sennet?" she asked as she lifted her skirts and moved around him to the front of the stall. As the animal sniffed and investigated her, she stood still, waiting, patient as the horse decided about her.

"Why?" He paused in the midst of a long stroke down the horse's back.

"Because I don't think you've had enough enjoyment in your life of late. Answer me . . . or I'll have to pull your ear the way I did Lizabeth's and Ellen's."

He gave a start and looked at her. "Is that what you did to them? I wondered."

"It was just a tweak . . . like the abbess did to us when we were small and were being silly. It's usually quite effective."

Their eyes met and she swayed toward him and reached up to take hold of one of his ears . . . holding it, rubbing it gently, coaxing a response from him. He shivered visibly and lurched backward, breaking that contact.

The fact that he didn't want her to touch him made her all the more determined to do so. As he emptied his hands of brushes and spread a blanket over the horse's back, she summoned all her courage and slipped her arm through his, trapping it against her.

"Come, walk with me," she said, pulling him toward the stable door. "I have something to show you."

"I have things to do," he declared, trying to extricate his arm.

"All of which will wait until you've seen the garden niche the earl's daughters helped to build this spring."

The small garden was tucked away in a corner of the main wall, out of sight of the house and overlooking part of the pond. Some parts were overgrown, the remnant of an earlier construction, but some parts were clearly new work. The flat stones in the circular path seemed new, and there was what appeared to be a new wooden arbor at one end of the garden. It was wrapped and shaded by winding roses, and there were several bunches of what appeared to be lilies nearby, preparing to bloom.

"They did this on their own," she said, gesturing to the developing garden. "They're very fond of it."

"It's a good start," he said, trying for a sneer and falling short. He tried to dislodge a stone that seemed to be a bit too high in the path and found it to be larger and heavier than he supposed. Annoyed, he moved on, looking at the bushes and the somewhat weedy beds of old violets, Sweet William, and heliotrope. He paused at the arbor and ran a hand over it, judging the quality of the workmanship.

"It's not quite what you expected, is it?" she said, surprising him as she came up behind him.

"It's not bad work. Could be a bit more square . . ."

"I mean all of it. Sennet. Your home."

He turned to her with a protest on his lips, but somehow was unable to utter it. After a moment he answered her question.

"No, it is not. It's more orderly and productive. Not quite . . ."

"The holding of a foul and wretched degenerate."

He expelled a tension-laden breath. "If you're about to deliver another of your wretched lectures on 'forgiveness,' spare me."

"I don't think 'forgiveness' is what your father needs or wants from you."

"Oh? And what is it you think he wants?"

"What only you can give him. A son and heir that he can be proud of." She edged closer. "And perhaps a chance to get to know you. He's not really so bad. He's loud and sometimes outlandish, but he seldom gets angry, and he is always fair with his servants and tenants. He works hard to see Sennet run properly. And whatever you may think, he did a good and honorable thing in taking in his daughters when their mothers died. After all, he had no lady wife to consider."

"Only the sacred memory of one," he said with a tinge of bitterness.

"Your mother died a very long time ago, Hugh."

"He makes the name of Sennet a laughingstock . . . a byword for godless and immoral living."

She felt the hollow ache in her chest deepening, spreading.

"Be careful that in trying to undo that, you don't make it a byword for harsh judgment and pitiless rectitude."

"This is not your concern," Hugh said, stepping back and finding himself trapped against the corner of the arbor. His chest felt tight and his throat was suddenly constricted. She was so close . . . her voice so soft . . . her expression so gentle. The truth of her heart, of her desire for him, was so visible in her eyes.

"Isn't it?" she asked on a whisper that skittered down the inner walls of his body.

A volcanic surge of longing erupted in his chest and flowed hot and molten down the walls of his body. He wanted her. He wanted to touch her, to love her, to be with her. He wanted it with everything in him, and that was the part that terrified him so.

"God, Chloe." His voice sounded choked, his words half intelligible, as if spoken to himself. "Why do you have to make this so hard?"

She stepped closer, and of their own will, his lips descended on hers. Suddenly it wasn't hard anymore. Suddenly drawing her into his embrace was the easiest thing in the world. Suddenly, plunging into her kiss, drinking her in, and feeling her desire rising to welcome his were as natural as breathing. Successive waves of pleasure washed through him and were absorbed into every muscle and sinew of his body, like life-giving rain on parched ground.

Inside, he could feel some unwatered part of himself coming to life. Something that had lain dormant within him was moistening, greening, and beginning to open. It was a part of himself as yet unrealized . . . a depth of feeling, a widening awareness of self, a new way of being in the world.

He was Adam in the Garden. With his eyes suddenly opened. And there she stood with the ultimate apple.

He was in love with Chloe of Guibray.

In her lovely face he saw the reminders of a thousand sensations that together had formed the seeds of that desire in him. His heart began to thud in his chest as it did when the horns sounded on a battlefield. And though he knew it was too little, too late, he set her back from him and strode out of his sisters' half-finished garden.

Chloe watched him go through a steamy haze of frustration. He still wanted her; she could feel it in the tremble of his body against hers and in the hunger of his kiss. It was the only thing that provided her a life-giving trickle of hope that she might someday reach his heart. With a deep breath she headed back to the hall.

In the tradition of noble houses, she took up both her role as lady and the wine pitcher at supper that evening, pouring drink for the earl and Hugh and the earl's knights. As she filled Hugh's cup, she leaned close, pressed her breast into his arm, and threw down the gauntlet.

"Tonight," she whispered.

He stiffened, wondering if he could have heard her correctly, and then tried to resist the frisson of excitement that raced up his spine. As he watched her go from man to man, pouring the watered wine, he found himself holding his breath, watching her for something more.

Then she came back to the table and, with a beaming smile as she settled beside him, gave him more.

"I'll wait."

Between the poached fish with the garlic sauce and the civet of venison, she leaned closer and murmured for his ears alone: "In our bed."

Rattled by both the proposition and its public nature—made in front of his libidinous old father and his father's unruly and morally suspect offspring—he responded in kind.

"No," he whispered back . . . too loudly.

She smiled and ladled out more of the venison onto his bread trencher.

"Oh, but you must have a second helping. There's plenty to go around."

He glanced around and saw several faces turned their way, including his father's. Reddening in spite of himself, he buried his attention in his food. When he looked up, she sent him a secretive little smile. He rolled his shoulders and told himself that she could wait all she wanted . . . he wouldn't be there.

When the meal ended and the tables were cleared, he tried to escape, but she blocked his way and insisted he stay to hear Lizabeth play the lute . . . music being such a high-minded and improving experience for the maids, according to her. One instrument led to several being brought out, the music they produced led to singing, the singing led to dry throats, and the dry throats led to more wine. Then the earl's daughters pulled the earl out onto the cleared floor and made him dance with them. He pretended to know not one step of a dance, and they laughed and insisted he submit to their instruction. It was an altogether different side of the worldly earl . . . jesting . . . playing the fool for his daughters' amusement.

Hugh, however, was not amused. In fact, he was appalled at having to witness such a spectacle. The earl had little enough dignity, and to watch him gamboling and playing the fool with his daughters . . . Then in the midst of his judging and distancing himself from his father's ignominy, Chloe seized his hand and pulled him out onto the floor to dance, and he found himself suffering an all too similar fate, though with a good bit less enjoyment.

His mouth felt like it was coated with goose down as he followed her through turns, steps, and supposedly innocent touches of various body parts. She managed to make even the most casual of contact seem provocative and indecent; her hands roved further and lingered longer than was strictly required by any set of dance movements.

"I won't be there," he said under his breath as they came together and turned, clasping each other's waists.

She behaved as if she hadn't heard, until they were required to repeat that motion on the other side.

"Yes, you will."

Another series of steps, a hop, and a turn and they were back together.

"You want to." She caught his gaze in hers. "I can see it in your tights."

He stumbled and missed two steps while fighting an overwhelming urge to look down at himself.

Horror descended on him.

Suddenly the entire wretched cosmos was centered in that one notoriously unreliable part of his anatomy. He felt it riding full and snug against his damnable tights, chafing and heating against the wool and—*oh, God*—growing! It was a self-fulfilling prophecy; the more he worried about it the more prominent it became. It was like having a demon planted between his legs . . . one that was susceptible to women's wiliest craft . . . one they could raise at will.

And Chloe of Guibray knew just how to raise that decadent spirit in him.

He gritted his teeth and tried to pretend his body wasn't in a full-scale revolt against his higher nature. But by the time the song finished and he ushered Chloe straight to the steps that led up to their chamber, everyone in the hall had witnessed his battle—if not its primary manifestation—and guessed that it had to do with his fetching and attentive wife.

He dragged her into their darkened chamber, slammed the door, and turned on her.

"Don't ever do that to me again."

Chapter Seventeen

"DO WHAT TO YOU?" SHE SAID, BACK-ing up a step.

"You know very well what. Don't talk to me like that in public again."

"You would rather I say such things in private?"

"I'd rather you didn't say such things at all," he snarled. "It's indecent."

"But they're true. And I only say them to you. How can that be indecent?"

"Dammit, Chloe!" He stalked forward to tower over her. "Stop this."

She looked up at him without the slightest quailing.

"Stop what? Telling you the truth as I see it? Will not saying it make the skin of your belly quit warming when you're near me? Will not speaking help you to finally sleep when you finally come to our bed at night? Will it help me to look at you without this fierce longing to feel your body against mine?"

"Chloe . . ."

"Perhaps you want me to stop reminding you of what it was like when you bedded me on our first night . . . of how you kissed me all over and suckled my earlobes and nibbled my fingers . . ."

"I never suckled your . . . I *know* I never nibbled your fingers!" His voice was choked with horror.

"You did, too. And you whispered my name again and again, you kissed my breasts, and you tickled me with your tongue and made me squirm." With one step she closed the distance between them, pressing her body against his, adding a potent physical dimension to this tantalizing verbal seduction. Her voice lowered to a sultry rasp.

"Make me squirm again."

Her heart stopped as she waited for his response. She could feel his decision working its way up through him and prayed it came from something more pliant and susceptible than his spine.

Suddenly his arms clamped around her and his lips descended on hers. With a whimper of joy, she stretched onto her toes to meet his kiss and threw her arms around his neck. She met his kisses hungrily . . . exploring his mouth in every way she had imagined in these last six days. He groaned approval and began to walk her backward to the bed while being careful not to break that ravishing contact. They pulled garments from each other and sank onto the bed together.

Trembling with both joy and eagerness, she welcomed him in the cradle of her body and gave herself over to the driving heat that engulfed them. He soon joined their bodies and with fierce concentration rode the brink of his own completion to take her to new heights of sensation and pleasure. When he took his release, she felt a curious surge of "almost" that left her nerves tingling and, for all the pleasure she felt, strangely unsatisfied.

When she called his name softly and ran her fingers through his hair, all she got was a heavy, nasal sigh that sounded like a snore. She realized he'd fallen asleep, and warmth bloomed in her chest. He was exhausted. She smiled and gently stroked his hair. There was always next time.

Somewhere in the middle of the night, "next time" became "now."

She had fallen asleep beside him, with his head on her shoulder, and awakened in the moonlit chamber to the feel of him nuzzling her shoulder and running his hand over her naked hip.

"You see? Marriage does have its compensations," she said, stretching languidly.

"You won't be content until you've reformed all of my opinions, will you?" he said, dragging his palm in circular motions over the tip of her breast.

"Oh, I think I could be content with less. Especially if it was more of that. Or this." She reached up to give him a long, succulent kiss. "Or more of this." She feathered a hand down his front where it splayed across his pelvis and then curled around his hardening flesh.

"More. Oh, yesss," he groaned.

In a heartbeat he caught her hands in his and was stretching her arms above her head as he slid his body over hers. His kisses provoked a response more quickly this time, as if her desires had not entirely cooled from their previous loving. Arching above her, he teased her body with the purposeful movement of his own against it. Soon she writhed beneath him, both groaning and laughing at her own impatience, insisting that he end this wicked torture.

As he entered her, she almost heard the steam shooting through her veins, then quickly starting to build again. He concentrated his weight between her thighs and soon found the center of her pleasure. Quivering, she met his thrusts and began to direct them, reveling in the now-familiar tension they built in her loins. As the intensity of their loving deepened, she felt herself beginning to rise on a narrowing spiral of pleasure.

Each breath, each kiss, each stroke propelled her higher, further . . . and finally sent her hurtling through a bright, brittle barrier that shattered in each of her five senses. It was as if she had broken through the limits of her own body, expanded it, transcended it. And suddenly

he was there with her, floating free, suffused with pleasure, and intermingled in both body and soul.

For a few moments she wondered if her head or heart
had burst . . . if she were still alive. Slowly her senses
cleared, and she was aware of him all around her and of
a delicious heaviness in her body. It was like floating in
a sea of rich wine. Just as she was succumbing to that
marvelous exhaustion, he shifted to the bed beside her and
she looked up at him. He was smiling. His eyes were
dark-centered rings of golden bronze, glowing with satisfaction, his mouth was curved into a soft smile, and his
handsome features were relaxed. It was the most beautiful
face she had ever seen.

"Promise me," she said, snuggling against his chest,
"that you'll let me see that smile someday outside our
bed."

"If you could try to make me this happy *outside* our
bed, you would most certainly see it. Now, it's your turn
to promise . . . that you'll never tease me like that in public again."

She gave a laugh that he felt like a hum through the
wall of his chest.

"If you continue to make me this happy *inside* our bed,
I'll have no need to resort to such measures."

His mesmerizing smile broadened.

"Then I promise I shall devote my whole life to it."

As Chloe drifted into a deep, restorative sleep, Hugh
watched her, feeling oddly wakeful despite the fact that
his body was replete and utterly at peace. He wanted to
absorb her, to savor the wonder of every moment he spent
with her. In all his life he couldn't remember having anything that meant as much to him as she did. She was his
wife, his woman, his love . . . his life. She seemed to understand him better than he understood himself, and—
God knew—she was more forgiving of his flaws than he
was himself. He thought of the way she arrived at Sennet
and didn't murmur when she was burdened with responsibilities that would have given even the sternest of chatelaines pause. His wretched father had accorded her a

respect that was probably unique in his dealings with females. And if loutish Randall of Sennet so honored her,
it could only be because the depths of her intellect, character, and spirit were too obvious to miss.

He combed his fingers through her hair and stroked her
cheek with the back of his hand, thinking how blind he
had been at first, how unwilling to see. In his heart he
renewed in earnest that casual vow to devote his life to
her happiness. His whole life, all of his earthly days . . .
it was a small price to pay for all she was bringing to his
life, to their life together.

His whole life, all of his earthly days.

A cooling draft of remembrance washed over him with
that phrase, and behind it came a gripping chill of reality.
He had just promised her his heart, his devotion, his life.
That rash and ill-considered vow suddenly pierced him to
the soul. His heart was already promised. His faithfulness,
his constancy, and his love had been dedicated long ago . . .
to a very different kind of life . . . to a life of piety and
scholarship and contemplation. . . .

Daybreak found Hugh standing over Chloe's sleeping
form, trembling as he pulled on his garments. His eyes
burned for the comfort of tears and his heart pounded as
if he were in a race for his life. And according to the
things he had been taught for most of his life, he was.

The whole canon of his long-held beliefs had been
turned upside down and inside out in just over a fortnight.
A lifetime of study and prayer and certainty had been
eclipsed by a few short weeks in the company of one
tempting and beguiling female.

How could such a thing have happened? How could
he have proved to be so weak and vulnerable against the
onslaught of doubt and temptation? In his arrogance and
pride he had once declared that greatest of biblical patri-
archs, Adam, a fool for placing momentary pleasures and
passing desires above his duty to God. Now he saw with
frightening clarity how such a thing might have happened.
He, himself, had just taken a bite from that same apple.

He backed away from the bed, his hands shaking badly

and his blood draining from his head to leave him feeling a little sick. He had to get away . . . had to find a way to make it right . . . had to recant his abandonment of his sacred obligations. And there was only one place where he could find refuge from the demands of the world and chart a course that would lead him back to the arms of true faith and duty.

THAT SAME NIGHT, BROMLEY ENTERED the king's lamp-lit privy chamber with the captain of the king's castle guard. His grave expression befitted the news he brought to the king and his closest advisors.

"Our spies, Highness . . . they found a Frenchman in London . . . a man with information to sell."

"What sort of information?" Edward braced as he watched his loyal treasurer grapple with what could only be bad news.

"The sort that says the Duke of Avalon's daughters . . . are not his daughters."

The words caused a pall of silence to fall over the chamber. Edward leaned forward in his chair. "Is there proof of this?"

"Our informer has with him a man who claims to be one of the maids' uncles." Bromley scowled. "He charges that the maids are impostors . . . orphans and excess females sent to the convent out of penury. Some may have been bastards . . . but they were certainly not the good duke's."

There was a long, anxious moment before the king responded.

"I want to see this man with my own two eyes," Edward declared.

Bromley nodded. "I thought you might."

Moments later the king and his councillors were shown down the stairs of the round tower and through a heavily guarded doorway, to a sizable underground chamber lined with shelves, crates, and barrels. The two men waiting inside were forced by guardsmen down onto their knees before the king. In the flickering lamplight Edward approached and stood evaluating the pair. One was an aging knight with battle scars on both his outdated armor and his pain-lined face. The other was a younger, more vigorous man with an erect bearing and a solid, muscular build. Bromley indicated that he was Henri Valoir, the informer. Though he wore no armor, Valoir's hands bore calluses that spoke of a familiarity with blade weapons.

Their story, as told by Valoir, was just as Bromley had related it: the Duke of Avalon had concocted a plan to hold back much of his fortune from the ransom and strike a blow at the English king in one fell swoop. He ordered the abbess of the renowned convent to provide him with maids to adopt and send to Edward in place of coin and goods. He planned to return to France, secure his hidden fortune, and then rally what was left of the local barons to resist Edward's occupation of his province.

"He will say that the fool king of the English . . . has wedded his favorites to French *putaines*." He scowled, searching for an English equivalent. "How you say . . . draggle-tails . . . trollops." He averted his eyes from Edward's fury. "He wants the English to be . . . the cause of laughter through all of France."

Pounding his fist into his hand, Edward paced away and struggled visibly with the betrayal of a man he had just spent the better part of a week entertaining as his guest. Had the canny duke been congratulating himself all the while on the success of a scheme to humiliate his one-time captor throughout France? He strode back to the pair and grabbed Valoir by the tunic.

"Who are you? Why should I believe a word of this?" he demanded.

"I was once a knight in the duke's garrison. I helped guard his castle and defend his borders. Quiz me on his household and I will prove truthful." Valoir crossed himself and kissed a small wooden cross hanging around his neck. "He proved as treacherous a lord to me as he was a hostage to you. I was falsely accused of disloyalty and dismissed from his service. There are those in your French lands who do not wish to suffer more than they already have. Fearing what will be done when the duke's treachery is uncovered, they send me"—he gestured to his companion—"with Jean de Mornay as proof."

"Who are you?" Edward demanded of the older man.

"A knight, once in the service of the House of Burgundy," the old soldier declared through the translation of the Duke of Bedford. "Brother to a landed vassal of that province, Charles de Mornay by name. My brother died and his family fell on hard times. His wife, she sent her youngest daughter, Lisette, to the Convent of the Brides of Virtue, hoping they could find a future for her. She is no longer at the convent. I believe Lisette was one of the maids you married to your nobles."

Edward studied the man's careworn face and—grimly recalling that one of the maids was indeed named Lisette—made his decision. Turning to Bromley, he ordered, "Send for a clerk and set down in writing all the details this man can recall about the Mornay family and lineage." Then he looked back to the Duke of Bedford. "Where is Avalon now?"

"Probably just making London, Highness," Bedford said. "He can't have had time to reach the coast."

"I want him stopped and brought back to Windsor immediately. He must not be allowed to leave English soil."

"Depend on it, Highness. I shall see to it myself." Bedford bowed and withdrew while Edward then turned to the captain of the castle guard.

"Send detachments of men to Ledding, Chester, Louden-Day, Candle, and Sennet. Use Bromley's and Norwich's men if you must. The maids who were presented and wedded as the Duke of Avalon's daughters are to be placed under guard and brought to court as quickly as possible."

CHLOE AWAKENED AND STRETCHED LUXU-
riously and gazed at the light coming overhead. Smiling at the sight of the rumpled bed linen and the thought of

how it came to be so, she rose and washed and dressed. Forgoing her morning prayers this once, she hurried out of the chamber to find Hugh.

He wasn't in the hall and his observant little sisters declared that he had not yet appeared to break his fast. Perhaps he took a morning ride, she said, heading out to the stable to find him. Moments later she stood looking at his horse's empty stall and frowned. An aged stableman, shuffling by, was pressed to reveal that Hugh had come to the stable early, saddled his horse himself, and ridden off at a fast clip.

"Where was he bound?" she asked. "Did he say?"

"Somethin' about some saint . . . Bernard, I think," the fellow muttered, moving on.

Disappointed and feeling uneasy at the way Hugh had disappeared without a word to her after the events of the night just past, she returned to the hall and asked the earl if he knew where Hugh might have gone.

"One of the stablemen said he mentioned a saint of some kind. Is there a church of some kind nearby?" She tried not to let her sigh be too obvious. "He is very faithful about making confession."

The earl went perfectly still and looked at her with unsettling intensity.

"What saint?" the earl demanded.

"I'm not sure. Saint Bertram . . . or Bernard . . ."

The earl blanched.

"Saint Barnard's." He lowered his tankard, glowering, and uttered words that struck terror into Chloe's heart. "It's not a church, it's a *monastery*."

Hugh didn't return that evening. Or the next morning. Or next day. By evening everyone in the household was treading quietly around Chloe, even the termagant trio. They stared at her and whispered to each other, as if trying to figure out why anyone would be upset over the absence of their prickly and judgmental older brother. As Chloe's suffering grew more visible, they abandoned their search for reasons and simply accepted that she had an inexplicable desire for his companionship and was suffering in his absence. Their sympathetic looks only heaped coals of blame on her head.

She knew, in her heart of hearts, that his flight was her fault. If she hadn't pushed, if she hadn't demanded, if she hadn't forced his hand that night, he might still be at Sennet.

But as she stood in their darkened chamber, staring through prisms of tears at the bed where she had made him promise to bed and pleasure her, she realized that he had been withdrawing from a life with her well before her reckless bid for his passions. She had deluded herself into thinking that she had a chance at his heart, that he had grown and broadened his thinking, that the bonds of passion and tenderness developing between them proved that his desire to escape into the religious life had changed. But at best, as he lay in her arms promising her he would devote himself to her, his heart had been divided.

A short while later, he had risen from their bed feeling sullied and unclean, and fled straight to the purifying arms of the righteous and abstemious brothers. No doubt he was lying facedown on the floor of some chapel at that very moment, confessing to the saints and hosts of Heaven the depths of his "sin" with her.

A noise behind her caused her to turn, and she saw the earl standing in the doorway. He looked so much like Hugh that for a moment her heart leapt in her chest. Immediately she chided herself for her stubborn hope.

"He isn't coming back, is he?" she asked.

The earl wagged his head sadly.

"Who can say what he'll do? I knew he was stubborn. And I knew he hated both me and the notion that he would have to take up the reins of Sennet someday. But until now I never thought he was a damned fool."

Chloe cried herself to sleep that night and rose the next morning to go about her duties in something of a haze. She walked into a servant carrying wooden trenchers up to the hall and caused him to drop them. She realized she had forgotten a tally strip on which to do a cellar inventory, and when she retrieved one from the steward's

chamber, she couldn't recall what she had intended to do
with it. She had to ask the cooks three times what they
were making for dinner, even though she had planned the
menu herself two days before.

Thus it wasn't surprising that it took a few moments
for the words to penetrate, midday, when Lizabeth came
running to the newly finished laundry to tell her that
someone had arrived and she was needed.

"Hugh? Is he home?" She picked up her skirts and ran
before hearing the answer. Her hopes, with their treacherous tenacity, were quickly dashed.

There were a dozen armed soldiers on horseback arrayed before the doors to the hall, facing the earl, who
stood on the steps rod-straight with his fists on his waist
and wearing a combative expression.

"What is it? What's happened?" she asked, trying to
catch her breath while praying it wasn't news that something had happened to Hugh.

"Lady Chloe of Sennet?" the leader of the soldiers demanded, scowling down at her.

"Yes."

"You're to come with us." He produced a rolled parchment and extended it toward her. Seeing the earl's barely
contained anger and sensing the need to proceed slowly,
she made no move to accept it.

"Come with you? Where?"

"To Windsor Castle, milady. You are under arrest."

THE THICK STONE WALLS OF THE MONAS-
tery of Saint Barnard kept out blustery cold in winter and
searing sun in summer. But as they did so they also
banned bright light and fresh breezes and all sense that
there was a world outside that formidable bulwark.

Inside the enclosure it was chilled and damp . . . musty
with the scents of moisture-laden books, woolen robes,
and unvented male humors. The cheap tallow lamps that
hung in the dark chambers and corridors gave off light
and soot equally, and added another familiar but not al-

together agreeable smell to the mélange. Everything seemed colorless, austere, and self-abnegating . . . which was as it should be in an atmosphere meant to focus the mind and spirit on contact with and the revelation of God.

The solemn demeanor of the place matched Hugh's mood perfectly; he had no desire for either comfort or companionship. The call of the bells every three hours was familiar enough to be welcoming and indisposing enough to seem penitential, and the absence of personal interaction relieved him of the humiliation of having to admit to the brothers his lapse of religious devotion.

On the morning after Hugh arrived, the abbot called him into his personal solar and demanded to know the latest news from court before finally getting around to the topic of why he had come.

"Wedded?" The abbot seemed more puzzled than outraged by the news.

"The day after the vows, the king dismissed me from Windsor to return to my father's house at Sennet," Hugh revealed.

"Sent away from court?" That brought the lean, dessicated-looking abbot bolt upright in his chair. "How dare he do that to my—" Halting, he pushed to his feet and paced in an agitated but arthritic manner. "Wretched kings. Never do what they say. Always scheming." Then he paused to look at Hugh. "When will you be allowed back?"

"Back?"

"At court." The abbot came to seize his shoulder in a fierce grip. "How long before you return to Windsor?"

"He didn't say anything about my returning." Hugh was confused by the abbot's attitude. "I assumed he meant that I would stay at Sennet."

"Don't be an ass-head—of course he'll want you back." The abbot's eyes darted over some unseen mental tableau. "You must go as quickly as possible . . . remind him of his obligation to continue the work begun here in his name."

"The work?" Hugh shook his head.

"He has commissioned several books, including the Scriptures, to be copied for his use. And he has made generous donations each year since you—since he discovered what a vital and worthy task we perform." The abbot loosened his grip and gave Hugh's shoulder a benevolent pat before releasing him. "We must give it a while . . . allow him to miss you. Then I will send you to him with one of the books we are copying for him. He will welcome you back to his bosom, and all will be well again. You'll see."

Hugh watched his one-time mentor sway back to his chair and drop heavily into it. A moment later the abbot looked up and seemed surprised that he was still there.

"About my duties, Reverend Father . . ."

The abbot looked a bit nettled and waved him out the door. "You will likely find some way to make yourself useful until you can return to court."

Hugh exited with a deeply unsettled feeling. Not a word had been spoken about his marriage or the fact that his wedding vows might hinder him from taking religious ones. The abbot hadn't been at all concerned with the fleshly obligations his marriage placed him under or the spiritual conflict he faced. He had only seemed to care that Hugh was no longer at court to act as his agent and an advocate for the monastery.

Through the rest of the daylight hours, he mulled over the abbot's behavior. Years ago he had been puzzled and disappointed when the abbot sent him away for training as a knight instead of allowing him to take vows. He had always assumed that after a suitable length of time, he would be welcomed back to the monastery and taken fully into the order. But after four long years of devotedly serving the monastery's interests with the king, he found himself considered a disappointment . . . not because of his entanglement with the world, but because of his sudden lack of it.

He slept poorly that night, what with bells and prayers at odd hours, and rose in a testy humor. After a spartan meal of porridge and boiled barley water, Hugh wandered out to the stables and saw to the care of the monastery's horses and cows and other hoof stock, then spent some time in the copying room.

There, a score of tonsured heads were bent over tall, ink-stained tables, wielding quills and tiny horsehair brushes with alacrity and precision. This was the place he had loved as a boy . . . the place where the brothers created the elegant and intriguing illuminations that adorned the texts. He recognized most of the brother copyists and waited respectfully until they raised their heads and redipped their quills to greet them. Strangely, two of the older monks squinted fiercely at him and behaved as if they were meeting him for the first time. They looked gray and drawn, and their shoulders had taken on the hump so characteristic of those who sat stooped over parchment and quills, day after wearying day.

Feeling suddenly too confined, Hugh went straight to the chapel and spent the rest of the day there in prayer. What was he doing here? Did he honestly hope to stay and take up life as a monk? He thought of Chloe and of the vows he had made to her. He was caught between two worlds . . . trying to find his place, to find his way back to . . . something he feared he had lost.

After *none* prayers the next day, as he exited the chapel and began to walk slowly and meditatively around the inner colonnade of the cloister, he heard a rusty, strident voice and discovered old Brother Hericule settling into a corner of the colonnade with a number of novitiates, beginning a lecture on theology and doctrine. He approached the group and leaned against one of the thick stone columns, listening.

Hericule was even more ancient than Hugh remembered, and as he railed on about the temptations of the flesh and the corruption that contact with the world brought, Hugh realized that the words sounded very familiar. It was the same lecture, word for word, that he had heard more than a decade ago. But the venom the old brother reserved for the fallen was still every bit as potent as it had been in those days.

When the old monk paused for a breath, he followed his pupils' errant gaze to Hugh.

"Aha. Hugh of Sennet. Once one of our best and brightest." Hericule began with an uncharacteristic bit of flattery, but continued in a very different vein. "You abandoned us for the world and the lure of riches and easy living at court. What are you doing back? Did you wear out your welcome in the halls of the mighty?"

Chapter Eighteen

HUGH WAS TAKEN ABACK BY THE OLD man's harsh words and felt suddenly as if he were fourteen again and being stripped of pride and dignity by the old brother's fierce remonstrance. Shaken by the depth of his embarrassment, he had difficulty summoning a response.

"I was just . . . wedded and . . . I came to . . ." He was still at a loss to explain just what he had expected in coming to Saint Barnard's.

"To escape the befouling influence of the kept fools and devil's lackeys who serve the princes of this world." The old brother shook his finger at Hugh, then turned on the green youths whose heads were not yet stuffed with enough of his wisdom to merit full tonsure. "This is what happens when you embrace the world. They bewitch and befoul you . . . yoke you to things of the flesh . . . to women who infect you with their malignant ways until you are sick unto eternal death and damnation.

" 'To keep thee from the evil woman . . . lust not after her beauty in thine heart; neither let her take thee with her eyelids,' " Hericule quoted furiously. "Proverbs 6:25. 'For a woman is a deep ditch, and a strange woman is a narrow pit. She also lieth in wait for a prey.' Proverbs 23:27. Women are one with the beasts of earth . . . rutting and breeding . . . unclean . . . with minds so steeped in stinking female humors that they are not capable of higher things. They know nothing of prayer and communion with God. They must depend on men to intercede for them . . . to correct them and chastise them.

"Scripture says: If your hand offends you, cut if off. I say, if your body betrays you into the hands of women, cut the offending member out of your flesh. Better to go into the kingdom of Heaven maimed—a eunuch by your own hand—than to be cast down into the Pit!"

Hugh backed away, feeling choked, unable to breathe properly for all of the fury old Hericule had unleashed on the air. He could see in the eyes of the novitiates the same fear and desperation for salvation he had felt upon hearing such fiery condemnations of women and the flesh. The look on those callow, impressionable faces appalled him.

For the first time he heard those words as a mature man able to judge them against his own knowledge of a real flesh-and-blood woman. Chloe. And every damned one of the old man's poisonous charges failed the test. Chloe was nothing like old Hericule's demonic "woman" . . . stupid, deceitful, immoral, filthy, predatory, and godless. His Chloe was quick and clever, even-tempered and astoundingly forgiving, educated beyond most men, and wise beyond her years. She was considerate of others . . . generous, self-sacrificing. The very opposite, in fact, of all Brother Hericule declared women to be.

So, he realized with no little surprise, were her sisters.

He halted in the middle of the damp cloister walk.

So was Lady Marcella. And the queen. And his late mother.

None of them was like the temptresses of Hericule's diatribes. None were carriers of corruption and contagion, none were "deep ditches" or evil predators seeking to feast on juicy male souls.

Not even his own brazen little sisters . . . bastards though they were . . . exhibited the degradation he'd been taught to expect in females. He looked back over his shoulder and for the first time saw Hericule for the withered and pathetic old iconoclast he was. For years he had been spouting his views about women and the flesh, quoting Saint Augustine and John of Chrysostom . . . even the Scriptures themselves. How long had it been since he had even seen a woman? Did he know any, personally? Had he ever? How had he become the monastery's authority on the subject?

Striking off for the library, he walked fast and then faster. With his heart pounding, he insisted on having access to the great altar copy of the Scriptures. The old brother guarding the manuscripts was flustered by such a demand and scurried off to consult the abbot for permission. Hugh headed for the massive leather-bound copy of Scriptures that stood chained to a heavy stand at the center of the musty chamber. After turning the heavy pages for a time, he came to the book of Proverbs . . . reverently located the twenty-third chapter . . . and ran his fingers gingerly down the page to the twenty-seventh verse.

There it was. The copyists were truer to the Word than Hericule had been. "For a *whore* is a deep ditch, and a strange woman is a narrow pit." Chloe had been right. It wasn't a condemnation of women. Read with the true wording, it was a warning against venery and dangerous association. He straightened, feeling both vindicated and convicted. She'd been right all along. And he had learned that flawed version from—

How had old Hericule gotten away with such a bastardization of Scripture? Why would the abbot allow such poisonous falsehoods to be taught as truth, here, within these hallowed walls?

Reeling from his discovery, he backed away from the great Bible and stood staring at it. How many more errors had been drummed into his impressionable head under the guise of "truth"?

He began to pull volumes from the shelves, opening and reading from them, then stacking them, still opened, on the long table near the Bible stand. That was where the abbot and the librarian found him, surrounded by open books, feverishly searching them for things recalled or half remembered.

"What are you doing, my son?" the Reverend Father demanded with controlled alarm.

"Trying to decide if anything I learned during my days here is true," Hugh said, pain and fury warring for control in his countenance.

"Everything we teach is right and proper." The abbot seemed shocked, then indignant. "We are keepers of the truth and the glory of the church. Defenders of the faith."

"Which faith?" Hugh snarled, releasing the contempt that had been building in him. "Hericule's? According to him every married man in Christendom is irretrievably bound for the flames of hell."

The abbot finally perceived the depth of Hugh's turmoil. "Our good brother has strong feelings about the value of our celibacy. His teaching is sometimes forceful . . ." He seemed to suddenly recall Hugh's announcement that he'd been required to marry. "Is that what troubles you, my son? This marriage the king has forced upon you? You must know that God will not hold you responsible for so onerous a condition. It was surely not of your doing. Who is this wretched female he's shackled you to?"

Hugh lunged forward, but caught himself as the abbot lurched back with a gasp.

Wretched female. His Chloe?

Shackled. To Chloe's loving presence?

Hugh stood there in the library he had once loved with all his heart and felt the cosmos as he had known it grinding to a halt. The teachings, the certainty, the feeling of connection to the holy church—to God Himself—hung in the balance. But if the teachings were suspect or even wrong . . . and the certainty was lost . . . how much of a true connection to the holy church and to God could there be?

That, he realized, was what he had come here to do: retrieve that sense of connection to the holy and the sa-

cred, that feeling of inclusion and belonging to God. From
that anchor he had expected to chart his course with regard to the rest of his life.

He looked from the abbot's shrewd face to the librarian's simple one . . . and glanced around him at the dim
and dusty library full of books that few were permitted to
glimpse, much less study. And he strode out.

On the cloister walk he stopped and stared at the darkened columns that stood in near constant shadow, covered
in places with moss and lichen that gave them a moldy
appearance. The roof of the colonnade dripped water here
and there, and the ill-drained cloister green was a quag-
mire. Had it always looked so small and unkempt? Had
it always been so ingrown and adamantly exclusive?

In closing themselves off from the world to devote
themselves to God, the brothers had not only rejected un-
healthy influences, they had turned their backs on the
good the world had to offer as well . . . the generosity,
beauty, compassion, and nobility of the human spirit.

What was it Chloe had asked him? Where was the love
or joy or forgiveness in the sin-filled world that he and
the church inhabited? He looked around at the cold, iso-
lating walls. There didn't seem to be any room for it here.

With a rush of tumult, anguish, and triumph rushing
headlong together, he had the curious sensation of time
restarting around and within him. The earth stirred once
again. The heavens rolled. And he knew beyond the
shadow of a doubt that he would not find what he was
looking for in this place.

Gripped by a sudden urgency to see Chloe and talk
with her, to hear her eminently sensible thoughts and feel
her lush, loving presence, he headed for the stables. Behind him the brothers collecting for vespers were learning
of his bizarre behavior and being thrown into turmoil at
the idea that their beloved order was rejected and de-
famed.

"Hear me, my son!" the abbot called from the inner
gate as Hugh rode past him toward the main entrance.
"You mustn't go before you've had a chance to think on

this and repent your harsh words. You must stay and confess . . . purge your sins." Hugh kept riding. "What if you
should die on the road in such a state of anger and disobedience? Where would your soul be then?"

Night was coming on as Hugh turned his back on the
abbot's warnings and rode through the gate. But there
would be moonlight enough to ride by, and he would be
home by tomorrow midday. As he used his heels and set
his horse to a gentle gallop, he realized that in his thoughts
he had identified Sennet as "home." And for the first time
in days, he smiled.

IT WAS A LONG NIGHT. THE SILENCE OF
the moon-silvered countryside gave him a chance to think
of a way to make amends for leaving her bed to run off
to the monastery. Chloe being *Chloe*, she might feel hurt
and be irritable and difficult at first. But she had forgiven
him before, and he was confident enough of her good
heart that he believed he could talk his way into her good
graces again. Or *not* talk. Whatever the circumstances
might dictate.

He stopped only to give his mount water and a rest,
and again to break his fast at a small village along the
way. As he neared Sennet, well after sunrise, he rode faster and scanned the horizon for the outline of the estate
he now called home. By the time the village, walls, and
house came into view, he was eager enough to visually
search the outlying cottages and treeless castle approach
for signs of her . . . even knowing there was little chance
of seeing her there.

Things seemed oddly quiet as he rode through the main
gate and up the winding path to the front doors of the
hall. He dismounted and asked the boy who ran up to take
his horse where everyone was. The boy shrugged and
Hugh bounded into the hall, where he was greeted by a
chorus of "Hugh!" and "He's back!"

His sisters descended on him and all talked at once

before Trueblood arrived to silence them and help him make some sense of their chaotic story.

"Riders, soldiers, came from the king yesterday morn," Ellen declared anxiously. "They arrested Chloe and hauled her back to Windsor Castle."

"Arrested?" Hugh was stunned. "On what charge?"

"Father threatened to draw and quarter the lot of them, but Chloe . . . she insisted on going with them, to prevent blood from being spilled," Lizabeth continued breathlessly.

"Father declared that he would accompany her and keep her safe"—Corinne gave him a furious look—"since *you* weren't here to do it. He took Sir Magnus and old Sir Hereford with him, and several of those men you brought back with you from France."

"If he runs somebody through and we all get disoppressed—" Ellen began.

"Dispossessed," Lizabeth corrected her.

"Did I ask you?" Ellen glared at Lizabeth, before turning again to Hugh. "If we have to leave our home because you weren't here and Father did something gallant and stupid, and the king declares us all outlaws . . . we'll never forgive you!"

"What kind of brother are you, anyway?" Corinne said, looking him over.

"What kind of *husband* are you?" Ellen demanded with a critical sniff.

"Why, you little—" He was on the verge of exploding when Trueblood stepped between them.

"You'll be wantin' a bite to eat an' a fresh horse, I reckon."

Hugh somehow managed to swallow back his anger and belay an urge to brotherly mayhem. Flailing the three of them might be satisfying but wouldn't get him any closer to Windsor and helping Chloe. What the devil could the king have arrested Chloe for? He turned from his infuriating little sisters to the housekeeper with a look of unspoken gratitude.

"You reckon right." He caught the housekeeper back

by the sleeve. "What were the charges? Surely they said."

Her answer caused Hugh's universe to grind to a halt for the second time in two days.

"Treason."

FOR TWO DAYS THE DUKE OF AVALON had languished in the dungeon of Windsor Castle, given water and simple fare, a lamp for a few hours each day, and blankets to ward off the damp and chill of the stone walls. He had roared and threatened, paced and stomped, and demanded to be heard . . . to speak with the king, the Earl of Norwich, or even the Lord Treasurer. In frustration, he grabbed and rattled the heavy iron bars of the thick cell door, but to no avail. He saw no one but the warden of Edward's dungeon, and he was fairly certain that the fellow was either deaf and mute, or forbidden to listen or speak to him under penalty of death.

An uprising against the English oppressors wasn't likely; losses from the last round of fighting were too recent and too severe. That meant there were other troubles with keeping the peace in France, or something had gone wrong with the ransom. The ransom. His "daughters" were well-wedded and sent off into their new lives. His estates had been stripped, his coffers emptied, his brother and other supporters drained of assets on his behalf. What more could Edward want from him?

Just as he was sinking toward despair, the jingle of keys and the thud of footsteps brought him to attention. Shortly the Earl of Norwich, his host during captivity, appeared at his cell door with a dark and guarded expression.

"*Bon Dieu!*" the duke rushed to the barred door. "What is this about, Norwich? Why was I hauled back? I fulfill the damnable ransom to the letter, only to be held in a dungeon like a common thief?"

"I am not here as your advocate, Avalon." Norwich's lean face was grim. "Your guile has placed me and my house under a cloud as it is. I am here to let you know that your supposed 'daughters' have been recalled to Windsor and will soon arrive. The king has learned the truth about them . . . that they are not your by-blows, but base-born pawns in some treacherous game. Edward does not take kindly to those who repay his hospitality with cunning and his largess with political plots."

"I don't know what you're talking about," Avalon snapped. But when Norwich turned on his heel to leave, he recanted. "It's true—they're not my blood. But they are my adopted daughters. Legally and morally. And they're not base-born. They're true daughters of the nobility. Write to the convent—send for the abbess—she'll confirm it."

Norwich studied the duke's fleshy face and dark-circled eyes.

"Hone your arguments while you wait, Your Grace," he said darkly. "For when your daughters arrive, your impassioned pleas may be all that save them and you from a traitor's fate."

CHLOE RODE IN THE MIDDLE OF THE large, armed party, with her father-in-law on one side and an officer of the king's guard on the other. Beside every guardsman who rode ahead and behind them rode one of the earl's and Hugh's men. It was something of a comfort to have Mattias, Withers, Fenster, and Willum around her. But their presence also reminded her of the security she had felt in knowing Hugh was watching over her on her first journey to Windsor. And of the fact that he wasn't with her now.

The earl had argued with her over sending word to Hugh of her arrest. He insisted on sending a message to Hugh at the monastery; she was adamant that Hugh not be informed, lest he feel obligated to come to her aid. The earl tried to point out that he was her husband and that *was* his obligation . . . he damned well ought to feel it. Acquiescing to her wishes in public, the earl covertly sent a messenger to the monastery as they were leaving.

Now, after two days of hard riding, they approached Windsor on the same road by which they had left barely more than a week ago. The great round tower loomed larger on the horizon, dominating the view the same way it now dominated Chloe's life. This time as they wound through the crowded streets of the town of Windsor and approached the great gate with its huge iron portcullis, she felt a gathering of shadows dimming those brighter memories.

Immediately she was separated from the earl and taken to an upstairs chamber . . . the same one where she and her sisters had stayed as they awaited marriage. This time there were heavily armed guards outside the door.

Inside, she was startled to find three of her four sisters waiting. They cried out, rushed to embrace her, and soon they were all in tears. When the first wave of emotion passed, she sat back to look at them. Alaina, Helen, and Margarete looked fit and well-treated, except for the reddened eyes and puffy noses.

"I never imagined seeing you again so soon," Chloe told them, gripping Alaina's hand and stroking Margarete's cheek. "Especially under such horrible circumstances."

"I don't understand," Margarete said miserably. "We were adopted by the duke and wedded as his daughters. What have we done wrong?"

"I don't know any more than you do. Except that . . . the guards who came to fetch me said something about treason," Chloe informed them, and they watched as that lightning bolt of a word worked its way through their already unsettled emotions.

"Whose trust could we have betrayed?" Alaina said with tears rolling down her cheeks. "All we did was marry as we were required to do."

"Simon said something must have happened in France." Helen provided a broader perspective for them. "Perhaps the duke did something to displease the king . . . perhaps there's been an uprising of French nobles that has set everything on its ear. Such a development could make everything and everyone suspect."

"What I don't understand is how *we* could be under suspicion," Chloe finally spoke her own thoughts. "We were the ones so endangered that the king sent us away from court. Somehow, in less than a fortnight, we've gone from being victims to being traitors."

"It's something about the duke's ransom and our marriages," Alaina said dolefully. "It has to be. Why else would they bring us here like this?" She hid her face in her handkerchief, and her shoulders began to shake. "If anything should tear me away from Jax, I wouldn't want to go on living."

Chloe moved to sit beside her and wrap her arms around her.

"You won't lose him." Her reassurance sounded hollow in her own ears. "We'll find out what's happened and set it all straight. I know we will."

"What about Sir Hugh?" Alaina turned a tearful face to her. "Surely he's gone to see the king, to learn what all of this is about. What does he say?"

Her throat tightened and she fought back tears as she was forced to confess: "He isn't here. He doesn't even know I've been arrested."

Later that night, as they said earnest prayers and settled miserably onto their old cots, the sound of voices and the scrape of the key in the lock brought them bolt upright. The door swung open, and in lurched a dark figure swathed in a long cloak. The door slammed shut again, and through the intense silence came the sound of a choked whisper. The fifth member of the family had just arrived.

"Lisette?" Chloe bounded up out of her cot.

The cloaked figure wheeled on her.

"Chloe? Alaina? Helen? Oh, thank God!" Her knees gave way and Chloe rushed to help her to a seat on her old cot. The others lighted a pair of candles and gathered around to greet Lisette. There was a collective pause when the light revealed her face to be pale and drawn.

"Are you all right?" Chloe sat down by Lisette and hugged her. For a moment Lisette wavered, then her battered pride collapsed into their care.

"No, nothing is all right." She burst into sobs. "And I'm afraid it never will be all right again." After a few wrenching moments she looked up at Chloe. "I tried so hard to be just what he wanted . . . meek and modest and virtuous and obedient. And finally I was so desperate that I planted myself in his bed . . . and he . . . he . . . still . . . didn't."

"Didn't?" Chloe looked around at the others, wondering if they were hearing what she heard. They seemed equally shocked. "You mean *that* 'didn't'? He still hasn't bedded you?"

Lisette covered her face with her hands and shook her head. "I've tried to be what he wants. He wants someone small and quiet and pleasant and obedient. Someone who will never make demands on him." Her eyes shimmered with misery. "I think he wanted to marry someone else."

Chloe's heart sank. She'd made a grave mistake in pairing Lisette with the object of her heart. The knowledge only deepened the despair Chloe felt over the dismal state of her own marriage. Not even the three seemingly happy marriages could balance the calamity of the hurt and suffering her decision had caused. And how long would even the happy marriages survive if the king decided they had somehow participated in a great wrong against his throne?

Everything was falling apart.

The stricken look on her face caused the others to gather around her, and together they comforted her and each other. Their only solace through the long night was the fact that they had been reunited, if only for a brief time.

Lady Marcella arrived early the next morning with Moll and her other serving women. She bullied her way past the guards with food and fresh water and linen for the recent brides. She didn't seem to know anything about why they'd been ordered back to the castle, but she had learned from her nephew that they would be taken before the king later that day.

With that confrontation awaiting them, they bathed and dressed and prayed and waited. It was just past midday that the summons came. Lady Marcella insisted on escorting them down to the great hall, and, shortly, they were following her in a single, solemn line, as they had their first night at Windsor. The ducklings had become graceful, self-assured swans. But this time, instead of curiosity, they were met with dark looks and indignant stares from the crowd gathered in the hall. On the far side their husbands stood together . . . restrained physically by a number of burly guardsmen. As a wave of commotion swept the mostly noble spectators allowed inside to witness the proceedings, Simon, Jaxton, and William called out to their wives and encouraged them with determined smiles, then turned to trade snarls and threats with the testy crowd around them. Sir Graham stood with the other three, his face dark and turbulent, and stayed silent as the others defended their brides.

Chloe caught his eye and shot him a fierce, accusing look as she seized Lisette's hand and moved up to walk beside her. Lisette gave her a tentative smile of thanks, and Chloe realized that, unlike their sisters, there was no one to intercede for Lisette or her. They were unwanted wives. The sinking feeling in her middle deepened. She could scarcely make her legs bring her upright again when she curtsied before the king.

"Where is Avalon?" Edward demanded as he ignored the brides' dips of respect. The Earl of Norwich answered from a little-used doorway at the side of the hall, and the king looked up to find the hot-eyed duke being brought forward in iron shackles. Shock raced through the noble audience at the sight of a duke in such straits. Norwich was as blanched as the duke was crimson when he escorted the duke to a place in front of the king's chair. Edward held up a hand to prevent the duke from speaking and then turned to the Duke of Bedford.

"Read the charges."

Bedford gravely unrolled a sizable parchment and began to read.

"... did conspire to defraud the King of England and undermine the peace and tranquility of his domain ... by the fraudulent marriage of common females, not of his own blood or kin, as a payment of his duly owed ransom. And by conspiring to use such fraudulent marriages to rally opposition to England's dominion in the conquered territories of France."

As those terrifying words hung on the air, not a breath was taken or released in the hall. The duke's jaw dropped, the brides looked at one another in horror, and turmoil erupted among the husbands and nobles allowed into the hall to witness the proceedings.

"Lies!" The duke lunged against the hands restraining him and was narrowly caught by the men guarding him. "These charges are lies! It's a plot—"

"There, my good duke, we agree," Edward called out over the clamor in the hall. "It *is* a plot. Dangerous and wicked and damaging. But you should have thought of that before deciding to perpetrate such a vile and pernicious fraud upon myself and my subjects."

"What fraud am I charged with?" the duke demanded, looking astounded.

"Do you deny that these 'daughters' you supplied for marriage with my nobles are not of your blood?"

The duke looked to Chloe and her sisters, scowled, and then turned back to Edward. "I cannot deny it. They are not of my blood."

Turmoil erupted again. Chloe looked to her sisters in shock; the king had honestly thought that all five of them were the duke's natural daughters?

"You dare admit such to my face?" The king shoved to his feet on the dais and stood looking down on the French prisoner. "You wretched, deceitful son of perdition! You thought to pass off common dross as noble metal ... to mock my generosity and sneer at the sanctity of the English nobility ... to sow enmity toward me in the provinces of France!"

"I thought to pay your usurous ransom and secure my freedom!" the duke shouted back.

"Well, your scheming has earned you neither freedom nor the allegiance of your fellow conspirators."

"Conspirators?" The duke was taken aback. "I have no fellow conspirators."

"And I suppose you have no coin, no plate held back from the ransom?"

"You must know I do not!"

"I know nothing of the sort," Edward declared hotly.

"In my absence, your own men emptied my coffers, stripped my lands, despoiled my house. I have nothing left of worth except the loyalty of a few to whom I myself had showed loyalty at one time. I sent to the abbess of the convent and asked her to supply me with worthy maids, young women of noble birth and outstanding character to adopt. And adopt them I did. The writs of legitimization are as binding as baptism . . . executed under the seal of the Bishop of Rheims. They are my daughters in truth, if not in blood."

He shook off the grip of his guards and took another step forward.

"And as to them being 'common dross' . . . you yourself watched them, admired them, gladly wedded them to your advantage, never thinking that they could be other than noble of birth and fine character and disposition. How inferior can they be, my lord, if you yourself cannot tell their blood from mine?"

No natural father could have argued more ardently or persuasively on behalf of his offspring. After a tense moment, Edward turned to Chloe and her sisters.

"Is what he says true? Are you of noble birth?"

There were four nods and the king glanced at the frantic young nobles being held in check by his guardsmen. His only options were to allow himself to be persuaded of their lineage and worthiness, or to insist the bishop petition Rome and nullify the marriages straightaway. Judging from the outrage in the faces of four smitten young nobles, Edward decided patience and persuasion were the better choice.

"If you are nobly born, then you will know the detail of your lineage," he said to the brides. It was true. Regardless of king or country, one of the first things a noble child was taught was to recite his or her lineage . . . that which identified and secured his place in the world. Edward called for the clerks who recorded the details of all of his legal proceedings to come forward. "Each of you will, here and now, recite the details of your lineage. It will be written down and then verified by church records . . . if such exist. If your claims of noble birth prove true and your husbands have no objection, then your marriages will be allowed to stand."

And if not?

A palpable wave of relief went through the duke's daughters, and each turned to glance anxiously over her shoulder at her husband.

All but Chloe.

Chapter Nineteen

"WE WILL BEGIN WITH YOU." EDWARD pointed to Alaina, who stepped forward trembling visibly and began to recite a list of begets that went back seven generations. Her voice quivered at times, and she wrung her hands as she was forced to stop once and start again from the beginning. Heads nodded all over the hall as she fell into a singsong cadence. Lineages were usually learned and recalled by rhythmic rote. Having to go back to the start only lent credence to the fact that she had learned it in the usual manner and probably a long while ago.

When she finished she looked as if she might collapse, and Jax broke free of the guards' restraint to rush to her side and gather her into his arms. Edward watched the knight pull her against his side and turn a determined face to his king. After a long moment he nodded permission for Jax to stand with her.

Helen was called on next, and her voice rang out clear and true. Two French *comptes* and an English baron were sprinkled through her pedigree, creating a wave of murmuring around the hall. She finished proudly and stood with her head raised and her face composed. Lord Simon strode to her side and showed his support by pulling her arm through his and standing shoulder to shoulder with her. The king nodded thoughtfully, though his eyes were still narrowed with suspicion when they turned on Margarete.

Little Margarete's voice was constricted and high as she began to relate a rambling and ill-remembered family tree. She had to make five tries, each carrying her a bit further in the list, to get it all out in the proper order. William strode forward to embrace her with exuberance and quipped that he was relieved to learn—considering the nature of her wits—that her pedigree didn't include a number of cats. Edward looked briefly as if he might be fighting an urge to smile behind his hand.

Then it was Lisette's turn to recite. Chloe squeezed Lisette's hand before releasing her to step forward, then she turned to glare at red-faced Sir Graham. How could he be so unfeeling and judgmental toward his obviously devoted bride? His gaze guiltily fled hers and fastened on Lisette.

Several officials and council members collected around the throne as Lisette curtsied and launched into a recounting of her ancestry. The king received a scroll from Lord Bromley, opened it, and perused it as she spoke, nodding intently now and then. When she finished, he sat forward and looked between her and the scroll in his hand.

"Well done. You did not miss a single name."

She glanced at Chloe in confusion, then turned back to the king. "I learned my lineage when quite young, Your Highness, but have had little cause to recount it in recent years."

"Not since you were sent to the convent by your widowed mother, I would suppose," the king mused aloud. "I have in my hand another accounting of your lineage . . . which, fortunately, matches your own."

"B-but wh-where did you—" She turned to Graham, who seemed immobilized by some inner turmoil, then looked to Chloe, who rushed to her side and wrapped a protective arm around her.

"You were testing her?" Graham finally demanded, stalking forward.

"Indeed I was," the king said, meeting his resentment

with frankness. "She passed. And in passing, she has helped to authenticate the claim of nobility for them all."

"How d-did you . . ." Lisette stammered again.

"Your lineage was provided by a member of your family, who helped to uncover the duke's scheme for us. Your uncle, I believe. Sir Jean de Mornay."

"Uncle Jean?" She came to life. "We believed he was dead. Wherever did you find him?" She looked frantically around the hall. "Where is he?"

"He is here, at Windsor," the king said, looking out over the onlookers without finding him. Edward then turned to Bromley, and after a brief exchange, Bromley ordered a pair of guardsmen to summon Lisette's uncle.

"I'll go," Graham declared, stepping forward to take charge of the guards. He paused just long enough to give Lisette a turbulent look, then stalked out to retrieve the living proof of her identity.

While they awaited Lisette's reunion with her uncle, the king declared they would hear Lady Chloe's pedigree.

When Chloe looked up from her own feet, her sisters were staring at her with both compassion and dismay. The whole convent had known about her lack of credentials, though no one ever spoke of it. They had believed it was one of the reasons she was given to the duke as a daughter, to provide her with a family and a future. Now to be called to such a cruel accounting . . .

As silence stretched out to blanket the hall, there was a faint rustle of movement among the onlookers near the door. But Chloe and, in fact, everyone else was so intent on what she would say that the arrival went unnoticed.

"Any time now, Lady Chloe," the king commanded. "Begin."

She looked up, her eyes burning dryly, and glanced to the side of the hall, where the Earl of Sennet sat gripping his knees and nodding in support of her. Seeing the trust in his face—which looked so much like Hugh's—turn to disgust would be the most devastating thing of all. She braced inside, while knowing she could never truly be prepared for what was to come.

"It will not take long, Highness," she finally said, her voice small but steady. "I have no lineage to recount. I know nothing of my parentage."

Commotion broke out in the hall as the impact of that admission registered. The maid who had wedded the self-righteous Sir Hugh of Sennet did not even know who her family was?

"What the devil do you mean, woman," the king said tautly. "Speak plainly. You must know where you came from."

"I do know that, Highness. I came from a basket left at the gate of the Convent of the Brides of Virtue. I was . . . a foundling."

In a world where the circumstance of one's birth and the connections of generations of family determined the scope and substance of one's life, those words struck terror into hearts. Foundling. It meant she was unconnected by ties of kinship, ungrounded as to rank and place in the world. It was as if she had confessed to being a drop of rain . . . blown on the wind, fallen randomly to earth, and absorbed into humanity without anyone taking notice.

With the shame of her foundling status came the realization that in all likelihood, she was a bastard. Children born into even the lowest and meanest of circumstances had the comfort of knowing where they came from and who to blame. Those who left infants at the gates of convents did so because they had sins to hide. Worse still, those sins left indelible marks on the people those unfortunate babes became.

Foundling. Bastard. She might as well have thrown herself off the ramparts of the round tower. Her life, as she had known it, was over.

As if her sisters' pitying looks, her father-in-law's alarm, and the outrage stirred in king and council weren't enough, she heard footsteps behind her and turned to see Hugh standing some distance away. He was mud-spattered and windblown and his face was drawn with fatigue, as if he'd been riding day and night. His dark-circled eyes were filled with so many emotions that no one feeling seemed to claim the power of expression.

Her knees weakened at the sight of him, and tears began to fill and sting her eyes.

He had heard. Knowing how much he despised his father's bastards, she could guess what his reaction must be to finding himself wedded to one such as them. Still, hoping against hope, she sought his gaze with hers and, through a blur of tears, sent him a visual plea of apology.

Before he could respond, a rumble of protest came from the Duke of Avalon.

"Just because she has no known pedigree does not mean she was base born. It may yet be found that she has a true and noble father."

"And where do you propose we begin to look for this 'father'?" the king demanded. The duke straightened and turned his gaze on Chloe.

"Here."

It took a moment for the duke's point to register.

"You?" Edward gave a snort of derision. "You offer yourself as her father? Good God, but you French have ballocks! How many times will you try to make soup out of that old bone?"

"It is no ruse, Highness." The duke stepped forward, and his chains made a dull clanking sound. "I have reason to believe that this young woman may indeed be my natural-born daughter."

"Natural-born? Now you would have me believe you misplaced one of your offspring?" Edward bolted to his feet. "Take him away!"

"No!" Hugh's voice rang out as he rushed forward to prevent the duke from being dragged away. "Please, Highness, hear him out. It is my name and family at stake. Do I not have the right—as should Lady Chloe—to hear what he has to say?"

Edward studied Hugh's anxiety and then looked to Bromley and Bedford, neither of whom protested. With a growl of irritation, he sat back down in his great chair and leaned on one of the arms.

"Very well. Speak your piece, Avalon. And it had better be good."

"It is not generally known, but . . . I was wedded once before my current marriage," the duke began. "I was young. I had been sent to England to learn the language and help establish ties for the wool trade, and I lost my heart to the daughter of an English baron. Her family had little to offer, and, in any case, my father would never have countenanced my taking an English wife. But I was a fool in the hot grip of love and could see none of that. I carried her off with me to Calais and wedded her there.

"My father refused to recognize the marriage or allow me to bring her into his house, so we were forced to stay in Calais. She was soon with child and died in childbirth. I never saw the child . . . was told that it was stillborn and never drew breath." He turned to stare at Chloe as if seeing in her another's visage. "But I have reason to believe that this young woman may be that child."

"What reason?" Edward demanded.

"She is the very image of the wife I lost." The duke's voice thickened with emotion as he searched Chloe's face. "Looking at her is like rolling back the years. Eighteen years. How old are you, Lady Chloe?"

"Eighteen years," she managed to say.

"And what was it you told me on the day you were wedded . . . the name that accompanied you into the convent?"

"Gilbert." She swallowed hard, unable to fathom what the duke hoped to gain from this dangerous gambit. "The abbess said that in the basket that bore me into their care was a bit of hide with my name and the word 'Gilbert.' " She lowered her voice. "Please, Your Grace, you only make things worse for me."

The duke ignored her to turn back to the king.

"The maid I married was Clarice of Gilbert." A wave of murmuring raced through the hall. "In the short time we had together, Clarice spoke of naming our child 'Chloe,' if it was a girl."

Chloe heard what he said, but it seemed so outlandish,

so unbelievable, that the words just echoed meaninglessly in her mind. If the king would only stop him and allow her to escape this horror! But Edward showed no sign of halting the duke's ranting. The name Gilbert circled in her head. *Gilbert.* Somewhere in her the possibility finally lodged . . . Clarice of Gilbert. Was it a coincidence? She recalled the duke's strange reaction to her when they met: the way he stared into her face, the way he had gripped her shoulders. In all innocence she had spoken the name "Gilbert" to him on her wedding day. Now he used it as a wedge to give him room to escape his desperate situation.

"Why are you doing this?" she said in agonized tones that were swallowed up in the king's demand.

"What proof have you of this marriage? This birth?" the king demanded.

"You have in this castle, somewhere, an old woman," the duke continued, "who may be able to verify some of what I have said. A lady who, upon meeting me, called me Manfred. That is my given name, used by few in my lifetime. She must have known me when I visited England. She may know of my marriage."

"You mean my aunt? Lady Marcella?" Bromley recalled the incident, stepping forward.

Edward called for the old lady, who rose from a bench at the side of the hall, then swayed and staggered back onto her seat. Bromley rushed from the dais to her side, and after a worrisome moment, she seemed to recover and insisted on rising to answer the king's call. With Bromley's help, she presented herself and stood trembling with her nephew's arm around her. Her age-lined face was splotched with emotion.

"Lady Marcella"—the king gestured to the duke—"do you recognize this man?"

She squinted and wrung her hands in distress. "I—I cannot see so clearly anymore. And so many years have passed . . ."

The duke dragged both chains and guards along as he approached her, presenting himself for inspection.

"When we met, you called me Manfred," he said. "Who was Manfred?"

"The wretch who stole my little cousin . . . spirited her away. He wedded her and she died . . . in a strange place, without family or friends."

"Who was this cousin? Her name, my lady?" the king prodded gently.

Lady Marcella looked over at Chloe and tilted her head, squinting. Then she pushed Bromley's assistance away and tottered over to Chloe, remembering. But was she remembering the story or the fact that she had told it to Chloe not long ago, or simply Chloe herself? "My little cousin. My little Clarice. We were like sisters." The old lady's eyes filled with tears as she reached out to touch Chloe's cheek. "This cannot be her. She is dead."

Chloe clutched her chest as her heart stopped for an instant, then began to beat wildly. Lady Marcella's little cousin was Clarice? She looked to the duke in dismay. Could the duke be the foreigner who stole her away from Marcella?

"This is an outrage, Highness!" Bromley rushed to reclaim his aunt. "Trading on an old woman's sadness . . . claiming to have married and fathered a child . . . all without a shred of proof!"

"But there is proof! Send for my brother, the Compte de Sabban. He was there—he can attest to the vows and the child. You must—" The duke suddenly tried to reach Edward's chair and was rushed and thrown to the floor by his guards. Edward leapt up and shouted an order for the duke to be taken back to the dungeons.

"I am a duke—a prince of France. I have the right to hear the evidence against me!" the duke shouted as he was being hauled away. "Where is this 'informer' who told you of my treachery? Send for my brother—"

The courtiers witnessing the proceedings broke from the restraint of the guards and surged forward. As chaos threatened, Edward ordered Chloe held under guard and order restored, then exited with Bedford in a cordon of castle guards.

Chloe turned to Hugh as she was being led away. His gaze was narrowed and fierce, his face ruddy with anger and humiliation. She was desperate to touch him, to plead with him, to beg him not to hate her for bringing such shame down upon him. But he gave no sign that he would even listen, much less accept such a plea.

As the king's guards pulled her toward the small door where the duke had just disappeared, she brought with her the image of Hugh standing like an embattled colossus, with his pride and his disgust for the venality of her birth both evident in his countenance.

"No! Where are you taking her?" Lisette rushed to put a protective arm around her, dragging them to a halt. "She's no prisoner—you cannot take her to the dungeon. She is a lady and innocent of any wrongdoing!" She appealed to Lord Bromley and Lady Marcella. "Please, my lord, my lady . . . you cannot let them treat her like a common prisoner!"

The Lord Treasurer melted under the entreaty of his aunt's bewildered face and caught the notice of the captain of the guard.

"I believe confinement to her chambers would satisfy the king."

AS THE DUKE AND THE GIRL CHLOE WERE being led away, *Capitaine* Henri Valoir had pulled the hood of his tunic closer about his face and slipped out the main doors of the great hall. Rounding his shoulders, he measured his pace to blend in with a number of people headed down the path that led into the town of Windsor. He had much to report . . . some success, some failure. Dreading his capricious lord's reaction to the mixed news he bore, he threaded his way through the people and past the carts that clogged the main street. Soon he was again at the little-used stable where the *compte* and his men waited.

"Well?" His *seigneur* now pounced on him the moment he entered and dragged him toward the light coming through the rear door. "What news? What's happened?"

"The duke was brought before the king and council, along with his false daughters. The English king is furious . . . feels betrayed . . . smells deceit everywhere . . ."

The Compte de Sabban rubbed his hands together with delight.

"*Dieu!* If I could only have been there to see it with my own eyes. What next? *Les putaines*, what does he do to them?"

"The English king . . . he has allowed them to recite their lineages. If the church records can be found . . . he says . . . the marriages may stand."

"What?" The news went through the *compte* like a lightning bolt. "How can he do this?" He pivoted away and smacked a post with his fist. The pain that shot up his arm was small compared to that of watching his plot against the Duke of Avalon unravel. "It is an insult to the families of—has he no sense of obligation to his nobles?"

"The husbands did not seem willing to part with the women, *seigneur.*"

"If he places their rut-maddened mewling above his own royal honor, then he is a bigger fool than I thought," the *compte* spat. "And the one they call Chloe? What of her?"

"She did not have a lineage to recite. The king . . . he ordered her to be held under guard."

"What excuse did she give?"

"None, *seigneur.*"

Sabban took a long breath and seemed more in control. "What did the English fool say to that? More important, what did Avalon say?" Valoir shrank back a bit, causing Sabban to grab his arm. "What?"

"*Le duc* said . . . he may be her father."

The *compte* looked as if he'd been impaled. "*Merde!*" He whirled away, holding his middle, then gradually straightened and began to pace the straw-littered floor. "How could he think such a thing? He believed the child!"

"He said that she is the image of her mother . . . he recognized her. And she seems to have mentioned something to him. The name of Gilbert."

"Sacrebleu!" A frisson of bitter recognition went through him as he recalled those events of years ago. "I left the whore's name with the child so that she might be identified if *I* ever needed her. *Idiot!*" He smacked his forehead with his open palm. "I feared something like this from the moment I learned she was among the ones the convent sent to ransom my pig of a brother." He ground his teeth. "I should have smothered the little bastard when I had the chance."

Then suddenly, in the midst of pacing and muttering, he stopped. His shoulders squared and he looked to the door, thinking of the castle beyond and the two confined within its walls.

"Perhaps it's not too late to rectify that mistake." He spoke to himself more than Valoir. "The duke is accused of treason, of seeking to foment an uprising against English rule. If he were to escape . . . along with his bastard daughter . . . and both were to die on their way back to France . . . there would be no one to disprove the charges against him. They would be deemed true." He smiled with cool malevolence, feeling once more in control, once more driving events. "The duke's estates would fall to his young son . . . who would, of course, need the guardianship of a dear and attentive uncle." His chuckle was humorless. "And boys of twelve are so very prone to accidents."

He turned to Valoir with a new glint in his eyes.

"We will need garments and armor . . . like that worn by the castle guards."

HUGH STOOD SPEECHLESS WITH DISBELIEF as Chloe was ushered off under armed guard. The shame and confusion he had felt when he heard her confess that she had no parents and no lineage was even now being dispelled by the sight of her anguished face and the realization that whatever his embarrassment, hers must be many times worse.

And Edward—how dare the king order his Chloe dragged away and held under guard like a criminal? What did it matter that she had no knowledge of her forebears?

She certainly *had* forebears or she wouldn't even be here. What did it matter that she couldn't rattle off a list of names? How could a streak of ink on dusty parchment in moldy parish books improve her—or the lack of them diminish her?

She was perfect just as she was . . . his bright, headstrong, impossibly forthright and loving wife. Chloe, who never ceased to think the best of everyone, even *him*, and to put a good construction on even the worst of situations. Who thought of others first, especially *him*, and never lost faith in the possibility that someday he might lay down his saintly burden of guilt and superiority to become just a man. A good man. A whole man. A *loving* man.

How could the king think her guilty of anything more than being a pawn in a game of power and dominion? How could the king do this to her? Or to *him*? This was *his* marriage, *his* heart, *his* love the king was interfering with!

He looked up to find his father bearing down on him with a fury in his eyes that seemed like a reflection of that which was rising in Hugh. Before he could speak, the earl drew back a thick, leathery fist and laid him out on the floor. By the time the hall stopped spinning and his eyes focused once more, Hugh's father was standing astride him with that same fist cocked, ready to administer more of the same.

"Where the hell have you been?" the earl demanded.

Hugh sat up slowly, holding his head, trying to make "down" stay down and "up" stay up. "On my way here, dammit." He looked up, examining his throbbing jaw, and managed to focus both his vision and his will. "You'd better never try that again, old man."

"I'll do it a thousand times over if that's what it takes to knock some sense into that thick head of yours." The earl grudgingly stepped back to allow Hugh to rise. "I've seen some horse's arses in my day—why the hell didn't you speak up—say something—defend her? You've got to get her back for us. My girls need her. Hell, even *you* need her. Though, God knows, you don't *deserve* her."

"I figured that out for myself, thank you," Hugh snapped, testing his face and rolling his shoulders. He eyed both the door where she had exited and that ominous door on the far side of the hall through which the duke had disappeared.

"What are you going to do?" the earl demanded.

"How can we help?" Jax approached with Simon and William.

Hugh scrambled to decide the best course—whether to gather evidence first or approach the king first to request time and resources to sort it all out.

"I have to see Lady Marcella and then the duke. We need to find out who was behind informing the king about the maids' parentage. Whoever was behind those earlier attempts to keep us from fulfilling the duke's ransom hasn't stopped trying to cause damage." Jax nodded and Hugh gave him a thump on the arm. "Find Graham and this 'uncle' of Lisette's, then talk to Bedford and Norfolk. See what you can learn."

CHLOE SAT IN HER ONCE AND CURRENT chamber, staring at the empty cots around her. She had never felt so alone or so hopeless in her life. She kept seeing in her mind Hugh's face as she was being taken from the great hall. The horror, the revulsion in his expression settled on her heart like a stone. She could scarcely draw breath around it.

She had finagled her way into a duke's family, hoping to cloak the shame of her origins with his name and rank, and now her straw house of small deceits and sins of omission had come crashing down around her. The white lies she had employed, thinking they could do no harm, had come back tenfold to ruin her. How could such a small amount of bad so overwhelm all the good she had done and tried to do? Was she to blame or was she simply caught up in and overwhelmed by someone else's wrongdoing?

What did it matter who was at fault? she thought dismally. Hugh probably hated her. He would undoubtedly repudiate her and annul her and charge right back to his precious monastery to rid himself of the taint of her flesh and infamy. And where would she go? The convent would never have her back after the way she tricked them. She would be homeless and friendless—

Voices sounded just outside the door, and she had to listen for a moment to be certain she'd heard something. A voice . . . She rushed to the door and pressed her ear to the heavy iron-bound planks. A woman's voice. A moment later the door opened slightly. Lisette whirled through the opening, and as the door closed behind her, she flashed a smile at the guard, who admitted her to the chamber.

"Lis-ette?" The name caught on the lump in Chloe's throat.

Lisette opened her arms, and Chloe burst into tears and fell into them. Together they made their way to the nearest cot and sat down. Lisette hugged her and stroked her hair as her sobs gradually subsided.

"I've disgraced him, Lisette, in front of king and court. He'll never forgive me." Chloe sat back with a shuddering breath, swiping at a last trickle of tears on her cheek. "He could barely stand to be with me when he believed I was a duke's daughter."

"But there is hope," Lisette said reaching for her hands. "Perhaps they will discover that you truly are the duke's daughter and all will be well."

"The duke's daughter?" Chloe sniffed and gave her a pained and rueful smile. "Not even I, as desperate as I am, would aspire to such a thing."

"But, if it isn't true, why would the duke try to claim it so?"

"To pacify the king. He is under a charge of treason. His very life is at stake."

"Then, how did he know of that name . . . what was it? *Gilbert?*"

"I told him myself, on our wedding day." She scowled, recalling the duke's unsettled response. Could that have been caused by true recognition?

"Then, how did he know of Lady Marcella's cousin . . . her name and the fact that she eloped?" Lisette continued. "And how did she know to call him by his baptismal name?"

That was not so easily explained. Chloe was silent. The turbulence of emotion was beginning to subside, and her mind began to work. She examined each piece of evidence, turning it over and over in the cooler light of reason.

"Lady Marcella told me about her cousin. She might have told others."

"Would she not have mentioned that she told the duke? And she looked at you and said you were the image of—what was her name?"

"Clarice." Chloe's heart began to pound. "But that was many years ago, and as she said, her eyesight is poor and her mind sometimes plays tricks on her. She may have forgotten what her young cousin looked like."

"They were raised together, like sisters," Lisette countered. "If you had a beloved sister taken away, could you forget her?"

"No," Chloe whispered. "I could never forget someone I loved." She thought of her four adopted sisters, of Sister Archie, and of Hugh. She would carry their faces in her heart until the day she died.

But what of Hugh? Could he just renounce and forget her? Her thoughts took another turn. He had known and loved the monastery where he spent his earliest and most impressionable years. And he had obviously never forgotten or abandoned the love of his teachers and brothers.

An emptiness opened inside her, deepening with each remembered bit of evidence that his heart had been claimed long before she entered his life. The look on his face when she admitted she knew nothing of her parentage made that emptiness feel suddenly cavernous. He had fled her to return to his first love, the monastery . . . only to be called out of it to face the disgrace of being married to a foundling.

She felt herself sinking deeper and deeper into despair.

Then, in an impulsive burst of sympathy Lisette hugged her, and within that spontaneous burst of affection Chloe felt the bloom of unexpected grace. The downward spiral of her spirits was halted by a simple touch that said she wasn't alone in the world, that someone truly cared for her. In a moment where all connections and attachments seemed broken, that gesture was nothing short of lifesaving. Inside that yawning emptiness appeared a spark of hope.

"I have to know if it's true." She drew back, her face set with determination. "I have to find out for myself if the duke is telling the truth. Will you help me?"

"Me? Help? Of course, though I cannot imagine what I might do."

Chloe pushed to her feet and began to pace, rubbing her palms together.

"I have to see him, talk to him face to face."

"How? The king has ordered you held here. There are guards outside."

"How many?" Chloe demanded, grabbing Lisette's hands.

"Two. But it may as well be a full garrison. They almost didn't let me in to see you."

"But they did let you in." Chloe's eyes narrowed. "And if they let you in, they have to let you out, right?

"I suppose, but—"

"And while they're letting you out, you can talk to them"—she felt her spirits rising back and dragging with them a plan—"distract them."

"Me?" Lisette drew back as if afraid of catching whatever had suddenly infected Chloe. "Not me."

"Yes, *you*." Chloe pulled Lisette to her feet and set about tidying her hair. "There isn't a woman alive who can distract men better than you."

"Me? I-I cannot— I—"

"A smile, a toss of your head and they won't be able to see anything else." She paused, searching Lisette and seeing how deeply Sir Graham's rejection had wounded her. "Think about it, Lisette. How can Sir Graham be the only man in the world immune to your charms?" Lisette looked as if she might protest. "Remember the way you got old Mattias to talk to us? And Hugh would talk to you when he wouldn't even look at the rest of us . . . especially me.

You have a knack with men, Lisette. So there is only one reasonable answer to the question of how Sir Graham can resist you. He can't. He just wishes he could." She glanced away, seeing in Graham's behavior a clearer explanation of Hugh's. "Saints—are all men such cowards?"

Lisette bit her lip and shook her head with a wistful expression. Chloe seized her shoulders.

"Don't you see? Sir Graham doesn't despise you, he is simply afraid. He wants you, and he can't control that wanting. Control is something men believe they're supposed to have . . . they seem to think it's the very measure of their manhood. If he can't control himself, he'll have to control you instead . . . insist you be silent and undemanding and ignorable."

Lisette was perfectly still, absorbing every word into her battered heart, but then slid again toward despair.

"No, I think it is more than that. I think he wanted someone else." She paused to gather strength to speak the truth. "He wanted to wed Margarete."

"Margarete? Don't be ridiculous."

"Truly." Lisette nodded. "I learned that he has been wedded before . . . to a pure sweet girl who was very young and died before he had a chance to take her to his bed. Margarete seems just like her. I've tried being obedient and sweet and demure and helpful and quiet and modest . . . like Margarete and his precious little Lady Jane."

"Ah, but have you tried being *Lisette*? Lush, lovely, compelling Lisette? Lisette, who collects men's stares and makes their blood heat with only a smile? Lisette, who knows just what to say to get men to trip over themselves to grant her slightest wish? Lisette, who understands that Sir Graham needs someone to release his passions and teach him what a full-grown woman is?" She gave Lisette a challenging scowl. "Are you going to give him up to the memory of a girl who never had the chance to love or disappoint or even *pleasure* him?"

Color flooded into Lisette's face, and she began to straighten. In what should have been a fleeting moment of uncertainty on their wedding night, she realized she had absorbed his anxiety and allowed it to undermine her determination and confidence. From that moment on, she had questioned her every word and action, damped her enthusiasm, muffled her wit, and abandoned her will in favor of what she thought he wanted. Hurt and bewilderment accumulated with each failure to secure his approval, and in the course of days, she had retreated further and further from her true self. The woman he had rejected in so many ways wasn't even her!

Look at her . . . lamenting losing the battle for her husband's love and affection when she had yet to raise a single one of her weapons!

"You can do this," Chloe said, watching Lisette's eyes begin to glow with a familiar and reassuring light. "You have to do this, Lisette. To prove it to yourself as much as to help me. Now, go out there and work your womanly magic on those guards!"

AVALON WAS IN A BAD WAY; RAGING with fury one moment and sunk into a pit of despair the next. He had not one ally in the place, no one to listen to him or believe him. And now he had dragged the girl into it. He should have saved his revelations for a far less public forum. But she had stood there, looking so miserable and devastated, looking so much like his Clarice, that his heart had damned near broken. If he hadn't tried to defend her, his very blood would have boiled in his veins!

A rustling sound in the passage outside his cell caused him to still and then lurch up from his straw-littered pallet. He braced in the middle of the cell, staring at the door. The face that appeared in the narrow opening was none of the ones he might have expected. It was Chloe and the sight of her—so like the woman he had loved—sent a pang of longing through him.

"Your Grace?" Her face was pale and her voice was small as she peered through the thick iron bars stretched across the opening in the wooden planks.

"Child." The duke stalked on wooden legs over to the

door and stood staring at her in the dim light.

"I must know. Do you truly believe I am your daughter?" She paused and swallowed with difficulty, hesitant to speak the rest. "Or was that just a ploy to secure your freedom or further some political scheme?"

"There is no 'scheme,' I swear," he declared thickly. "I do not know what roused Edward's ire against me, but I have authored no designs or intrigues." He reached toward the slender fingers that were wrapped around the iron bars. When she didn't pull away, he settled his hands gently over hers. "You are my daughter. As God Almighty is my witness, I believe that to be true. The uncanny resemblance, the fact that you are called Chloe, the way the name 'Gilbert' accompanied you into the convent . . . I do not know how I may prove it, to you or to anyone else. But somehow, when I look into your face, I know."

Chloe searched his anguished eyes and the tenderness with which he touched her. He genuinely believed he was her father. Could it possibly be true? The hope was too sharp, too painful for her heart to hold. Her limbs weakened, and she sagged against the door, unable to summon a single word.

"I thought perhaps the old woman . . ." The duke's voice was hoarse with emotion as he caressed her hands. "I believe she knows, but her memory and her sight grow dim. The only true evidence of the marriage is in the church records in Calais. The marriage is surely recorded there, but I cannot say about the birth. I doubt you were baptized . . . being supposedly stillborn."

"But if I am your daughter, how were we separated?" she finally managed to utter. "How could I have come to the convent with two names, neither of which was yours?"

The duke's face aged years in that brief moment.

"I have thought of little else since the day I first saw you. My half brother was with me in Calais when Clarice was brought to childbed. He had just brought word that the duke threatened to disinherit me. When he said that you both had died, I was so distraught that I couldn't bring myself even to look at you." His voice thickened with tears as he saw those tumultuous events through a very different set of eyes. "He said he would take care of the arrangements. All of these years I have felt such gratitude to him for what he did." His hands tightened on hers as his face reddened.

"It had to have been him. My *helpful* brother. Alfonse, now the Compte de Sabban." Disbelief and pain mingled in his expression. "He took me from Calais to Paris and left me there while he went home to intercede with my father. Later, when I arrived at my home, my father behaved as if nothing had happened and started immediately to search for a bride for me." He paused and clamped his jaw for a moment against a tide of emotion. "I bent to my father's will and was wedded a year later. We never spoke of what had happened.

"*Bon Dieu.*" He roused as if coming out of a fog. "I cannot be certain he even knew of my marriage to Clarice." He suddenly saw his whole life in a very different light. "Alfonse told me that he was furious and refused to suffer my English bride under his roof. How much of my life was shaped and altered by my brother's—" He looked at her with fresh horror. "*He* was in charge of collecting my ransom. *He* swore that there was nothing left to send, that my lands and house were picked clean. And I sent him word that my 'new daughters' were being taken from the convent to England."

"Could it have been his men who attacked us on the road?" she said, feeling her wits reassembling, making connections between events. "Could he have tried to prevent us from marrying and fulfilling your ransom?"

"Who else?" the duke said furiously, seeing now the full extent of his brother's treachery. "Damn his lying eyes. If I ever see him again, I will—"

"There she is," a graveled voice declared, startling them both.

Chloe released the bars and whirled to see several castle guardsmen approaching stealthily from the nearby shadows. The one who had spoken remained some feet away, at the edge of the lantern light, while the others continued to advance with an air of coiled readiness.

"I-I wasn't trying to escape. I only came to speak with His Grace, and I've learned some things that must be put before the king." She backed down the passage that led toward the great hall. "You must escort me to him right away."

"Of course, my *ladee*," the leader of the guards declared with a strange lilt. Just as she realized it sounded French, he nodded to his men and they lunged after her.

Confused and jolted by their aggression, she whirled and tried to run for the passage to the great hall—but too late.

"What are you doing?" the duke demanded, jamming against the bars and watching helplessly as they seized Chloe. "Release her this instant!"

"Non, non, mon duc." With her in hand, the leader strolled forward and planted himself directly in the duke's line of sight, blocking his view of them subduing her and stifling her screams. "I fear that will not be possible."

The duke recoiled from the opening, shocked to recognize his face.

"Valoir."

"Oui. Valoir. Whom you discarded like so much refuse." He ordered the cell door unlocked, and when it was opened, he stepped inside. He stood for a moment, studying the duke with satisfaction. "It seems all of your sins are coming back to haunt you, *non*?"

Beyond Valoir, the duke could see Chloe struggling futilely against her captors. They had bound her hands and stuffed a cloth in her mouth, which they tied in place with a length of rope.

"Let her go!" The duke lunged for the door opening, but the *capitaine* lurched between him and the opening, savagely bringing down the hilt of a sword on the side of his head. Avalon's head snapped back and he slammed to the floor on his hands and knees, dazed and fighting to stay conscious.

"Two birds with one stone," Valoir sneered as he motioned his men into the cell to seize the reeling duke. "Even easier than I expected."

Chapter Twenty

IT WAS SOME TIME LATER THAT Hugh arrived at the king's privy chamber with Lord Bromley and Lady Marcella in tow. It was clear that if it hadn't been for Bromley's standing with the king, Edward would have refused to see them or to reconsider his decisions regarding the duke and Chloe. Through the partly open door, Hugh could hear Bromley reasoning with Edward, persuading him, drawing on their long-standing association to get him to see Hugh and listen to Lady Marcella again.

When at last they were ushered into the privy chamber, the king waved the old lady to a seat beside him on a bench beneath an open window. Before accepting, the old lady drew herself up before him and, with her nephew's assistance, executed a deep curtsy. When she was seated, the king bade her speak and tell what she knew of the duke's story.

Lady Marcella's voice trembled as she began her story of young love and tragedy. The king listened with forced patience to the story of a young nobleman who arrived on her father's estate with a trade delegation when she was a young woman. The young nobleman was bold and quick-witted and enthralling to all of the maids in the household. But his eye fell and lingered on her cousin, Clarice of Gilbert, and the girl soon succumbed to his charm and promises.

"A sad tale to be sure," the king declared, frowning. "But there is no proof that the duke is the Frenchman of your story."

"But his name was Manfred and so is the duke's," Bromley countered. "I heard my aunt call him that with my own two ears."

"Do you remember anything else?" the king asked the old lady. "Anything about his family or companions?"

She shook her head regretfully. "He was introduced simply as a wealthy Frenchman. There were whispers that he was heir to a title, but it was never confirmed lest local resentment fall on him. After he stole Clarice away, my father blamed himself for having dealings with the treacherous French, and we were forbidden to speak of it. Now it has been so many years . . ."

"But, Chloe," Hugh prompted. "She resembles your cousin Clarice a great deal." He dropped to one knee before her and took her hands in his. "You must think, my lady. Her future, her life may depend upon it!"

"She does. Quite so." The old lady began to weep. "I didn't know if it was real or just in my mind. My eyes grow dimmer . . ." She dabbed at her tears with a handkerchief Bromley offered. "And my mind sometimes wanders. I never know . . . so . . . I said nothing about it."

The king himself reached over to pat the hands wringing in her lap.

"Please, Highness, you must see that something else is at work here," Hugh pleaded, frustrated to have no clear and unequivocal evidence. "Someone wanted the duke's ransom to fail. Someone who attacked us on the road and then sent assassins to finish the task after we arrived safely. Why take such a roundabout route to stir up resentment and outrage at English rule—especially while the duke is still in English hands? Surely they would know he could be blamed." He paused absorbing the impact of that conclusion himself. "It seems to me that these events must be directed more at the duke than at England, Highness. And I would bet my life that if properly questioned, the duke may be able to shed some light on who is responsible."

The king searched Hugh, then turned to Bromley and Bedford, who gave him grave nods. "I believe Sir Hugh has the right of it, Sire," Bedford murmured.

"Very well. Escort your aunt back to her chambers," he told Bromley. Then he looked up at Hugh. "I have already dispatched Norwich to Calais to recover any records that may exist of a 'first marriage.' " He gave a weary sigh. "I believe I am ready to hear what your bride and troublesome father-in-law have to say."

AS HUGH STRODE BACK THROUGH THE hall, headed for the chamber where Chloe was being held, a commotion occurred at the side door of the hall. Hugh broke stride and stared as Jax, William, Simon, and Graham staggered into the hall carrying between them a crumpled figure draped over a makeshift stretcher.

"What's happened?" Hugh rushed to help, and they laid the injured man out on one of the long tables. He was older and obviously of the knightly class, though his armor was of an outdated style and sadly ill-tended. Along the man's side, coming from under his mail, was an alarming broad smear of crimson.

"Where is the king?" Graham demanded, looking around wildly.

"He has withdrawn." Hugh declared, realizing that Graham had missed what had happened with Chloe and the duke while he was out of the hall. He looked at the aged knight lying white and silent on the tabletop and sensed who he was even as Graham spoke.

"Sir Jean de Mornay, Lisette's uncle. He's been attacked—run clean through. Where is she? Lisette?"

"I'm not sure. With the other brides, perhaps." Hugh declared, struggling to make sense of the attack on Lisette's uncle. If he truly was Lisette's uncle, why would anyone bring him here to bear witness to the brides' parentage and then stab him afterward? Except . . . he realized with growing dread . . . to keep him from bearing witness to anything else . . .

"We have to inform Bromley and the king. Jax, fetch a physician—quickly! William, find Bromley . . . he's probably still with Lady Marcella. Graham—"

But Graham was already in motion, headed for the doorway leading out to the queen's courtyard. He bounded up the uneven steps two at a time, his heart pounding, his fists clenched to keep them from shaking. But in the courtyard he found only three of the new wives. They told him that Lisette had been worried about Chloe and had insisted on trying to see her. He retraced his steps to the great hall and headed for the stairs that led to the brides' former chamber.

As he approached the landing, he was halted by two burly guardsmen who refused to allow him to pass. He reasoned and bullied and finally got one of them to admit they had allowed Lisette to enter the chamber. It was a short step from there to convincing them to knock on the door and tell Lady Lisette her uncle had been found and needed her. After an agonizingly tense pause, one of the guards backed up the two steps to the landing and set his fist to the door.

Lisette appeared, her voice pouring through the otherwise silent passage like warm honey. "Lady Chloe is resting—"

"Nay, milady, a fellow asks to speak to *you*," one of the pike-bearing guards declared with an eager smile and entirely too much warmth in his tone.

Graham jolted back and came down unexpectedly hard on the step below.

"Not 'a fellow,' you dolt . . . the lady's husband," he barked, reversing course and stalking up the remaining steps. "Lisette!" The door opened wider and Lisette stepped into the doorway. "Your uncle is in the hall, gravely injured. You must come."

Closing the door behind her, she brushed past the guards and flew down the steps just ahead of Graham. He caught up with her, seized her elbow, and ushered her down the steps into the hall, where a knot of men was gathered around one of the long tables.

"Let her through," he said, making way for her.

She stopped abruptly and gasped.

"Uncle Jean!" She rushed to his side, her gaze flying from the old man's pale face to the crimson slash running down his side to the priest arriving to administer prayers and perhaps rites. He raised his hand and she seized it and pressed on it a desperate kiss.

"Lis-ette . . ." The old man had barely enough breath to form words. "*Ma petite* . . ." He had difficulty swallowing, and she leaned closer to hear him. "They said you were . . . taken . . ." His breathing filled with ominous bubbling sounds and he coughed. Blood appeared at the corners of his mouth.

"They lied, *mon cher oncle*. I was not forced to do anything. I am safe and lawfully wedded," she said, the words catching in her throat.

"You are wedded, *petite*? You are hap-py?" The old man's chest rattled worse with each inhalation. He managed to turn his head enough to look at her. When she nodded through her tears, the anxiety the old man felt for her began to ebb along with his life. "*C'est bon . . . ma . . . petite . . . heureux. . . .*" His grip on her hand loosened. "*Le . . . bonheur . . .*" His eyes closed.

"Please, Sir Jean, tell us . . ." Hugh tried one last time to elicit information from the dying man. "Who did this to you? What did they look like?"

"Val—Valoir." The answer was even more faint. They bent closer and the priest halted to allow them to hear. "He found me . . . said Lisette . . . *le compte . . . non . . . non . . .*"

Then his pale lips stilled.

"*Oncle* Jean!" Lisette touched his face, calling to him again and again, but his chest no longer stirred. He was gone. Her tears fell onto his pale, still cheek, and she wrapped him in her arms and began to sob. The drone of Latin began again.

After a respectful moment Graham said her name and gently pulled her away from the old knight's lifeless form. She swayed and he caught her to him to steady her. She looked up with all the misery of her heart visible in her luminous eyes. He sank visibly into those fathomless pools now filled with grief. He pulled her tightly against him and cradled her head against him.

All looking on crossed themselves.

"I am sorry for your loss, my lady," Hugh said after a moment's silence. Then he turned to his father, Jax, and William. "Valoir. And something about a count. I must speak with Chloe, then we have to see what the duke has to say."

They had started for the doorway leading to Chloe's prison, when Lisette's tearful voice halted him. "She isn't there." When Hugh halted and turned, she clarified it. "She went to see the duke, to speak with him and learn if he truly believes she is his daughter."

"But she was being held under guard. How could she have—"

"I distracted the guards and she slipped out," Lisette said, her tear-splotched cheeks crimsoning. "She believes she must discover her parentage and prove herself if— You must look for her in the dungeons."

Alarm shot through Hugh. "Just like her to try some—" He caught himself before he uttered *damned fool nonsense*. Chloe of Sennet didn't have a foolish or nonsensical bone in her body. If he had learned anything these past few weeks, it was that everything about her was good and earnest and imminently sensible. Except, perhaps, her love for him. Which didn't make a bit of sense. And when he caught up with her, he was going to make certain she knew just how grateful he was for that merciful lapse in judgment.

Hugh motioned to his father, Jax, and William and headed for the door leading to the dungeons.

As they approached the chamber where the Duke was being

held, they could see that the door was already open and the guards usually stationed at the end of the passage were missing. Hugh rushed into the chamber and stood looking at the empty cot with disbelief. The duke couldn't have gotten out without help.

"Did Chloe let him out?" He wheeled on the others. "How would she have gotten the key? Surely she knows better than to—"

He looked up at the others, then at his father, and a new fear gripped him. He ran out into the passage and down a nearby set of steps that led to the warder's chamber. The guards usually posted there were missing as well. In searching the area, the earl spotted a heap of bodies stripped of clothes and armor lying in one of the empty cells.

They had both been taken. Chloe and her father.

"He's got them—the bastard's got them," Hugh muttered in disbelief. "He reached into the king's own dungeons and snatched them out."

"Who?" his father demanded.

"Our mystery lord. The one who tried again and again to prevent the duke's ransom." The certainty of it settled over him; this was all about the duke. "The one who hates the Duke of Avalon enough to destroy many innocent lives in order to see him disgraced."

Something inside Hugh erupted with a white-hot fury he had only felt once before—on a battlefield. This time it was preparing him to fight, too—only this time he would fight to save and protect his wife, his love. He rushed back through the dungeons and up to the great hall, headed for the king's chambers.

Graham was still in the hall with Lisette, whose sisters had just arrived to comfort her. At the sight of Hugh's fierce manner, he demanded to know what was happening. When told that Chloe and the duke had been taken out of the dungeon, he looked grimly down at Lisette, clearly torn between staying with her and helping Hugh. It was all Lisette needed.

"Go," she said, giving him a gentle push. "Help him find our Chloe."

He fell back a step, then halted and grabbed Lisette, kissing her ardently on the mouth. A moment later he was rushing after Hugh and the earl as they headed toward the king's chambers.

A short while later they emerged from the privy chamber bearing with them the potent force of the king's full authority.

"They'll be headed back to France . . . down the Thames . . . to London . . . from there back to France," Hugh said, his mind racing but not missing a step. "Boats or horses?"

"Horses to London," the earl declared. "The river is too slow this time of year and too obvious." The others murmured agreement.

"Horses it is. They'll move fast . . . keep away from the main roads . . . at least until they've . . ." He swallowed the new fear rising up the back of his throat. "Assuming they've taken Chloe and the duke with them." He rejected the desperate thought that they might have disposed of them straightaway. "Simon, Graham, go to the barracks. Recruit every man not on duty. Have them mounted and out on the green in a quarter of an hour."

IN EXACTLY A QUARTER OF AN HOUR three search parties left Windsor at a gallop, one crossing the river, one riding the near side, and one fanning out to scour the countryside for evidence of several riders moving fast. Hugh rode the river route at the head of a party composed mostly of men who had returned with him from France . . . including Mattias, Withers, Fenster, and Willum.

He bent to his horse's neck, scouring the moonlit countryside, hearing only the frantic drumming of hoofbeats in his head and feeling only the searing heat of urgency in his blood. A curious distortion of time overtook him. Each moment elongated and every sensation slowed for examination. It felt like he had all the time in the world . . . he would find her . . . hold her in his arms . . . finally tell her that he loved her . . . and prove to her that his heart was no longer divided.

Chloe. Dear God. If only he hadn't been such a stiff-necked ass about everything. If only he hadn't insisted he had all of the answers.

If only—his regrets quickly became prayers—if only God would allow him to find her and save her and love her all the days of his life. . . . Could I love You any less? he asked God. Could I not love You more for all the joy and pleasure and faith she gives me? Would I not be a better man for thinking of another above myself?

In the distance, heading over a low hill, he spotted something that caught his attention then vanished from sight. Motioning to Mattias and Withers and the others, he pointed to the ridge, and they raced along after him, scouring the night-silvered fields of grain that moved like sea waves in response to their passing.

As they spurred their horses and raced faster, they spotted what appeared to be a group of riders disappearing into a small wood off to the left, a path that, if continued, would lead them down to the river's bank. Both they and their mounts labored for breath, but they pushed on, fixed on that dark line of trees.

They had to slow to negotiate the treacherous path as they entered the darkened woods, and their only consolation was that the count's men must have had to do the same. They picked their way along the narrow, branch-cluttered path, and used the slower pace to catch their breath. Then ahead of them they could see that the trees ended, and the moonlight once again seemed as bright as day. Something about that meeting of darkness and light spoke caution to Hugh, and he drew his blade as they rode a bit faster. The others, copying his example, drew their swords and tightened the grip of their knees on their horses.

Just as they emerged into the moonlight, they were attacked from both sides. Horses reared, blades clanged, and several of the men rolled off their mounts to take on the enemy hand to hand.

"We've got them!" Mattias bellowed at Hugh, who was still mounted. "Go on!"

With only a moment to decide, Hugh accepted the old campaigner's assessment, shouted for the still-mounted Fenster and Willum the Axeman to follow him, and spurred his mount across the field that led down to the river.

Cresting a rise, they caught sight of a horse and rider disappearing into a shallow swayle, but not reappearing on the other side. Alarm shot thought Hugh. They were taking to the river! By the time they reached that same spot, it was clear, the count's men had charged down a shallow ravine that led down to the river's edge. There, they could see a sizable boat with a sail anchored not far off the bank.

They charged down the ravine, toward the boat, counting perhaps a dozen men visible . . . some on the boat deck, others struggling through the water with what appeared to be trussed figures, and still others stationed on the bank with blades drawn and glinting in the moonlight. The rear guard spotted them and, with blows and shouts, drove some of the horses back up the ravine to block their way. Hugh tried to squeeze his mount through the horses scrambling up the narrow chute for open ground.

It seemed to take forever to get past the horses. All the while Hugh's eyes never left the deck of the boat where Chloe and the duke had been dropped in a heap atop a coil of rope. There was activity everywhere: boatsmen hauling anchor and rushing to the ropes to unfurl the sail. They were leaving—he had to get aboard that boat!

Still on horseback, Hugh charged straight into the water. His startled mount hesitated just long enough for the count's men to close in on him. He parried blade blows and slashed at them, but they came at him on all sides. Suddenly one lunged at him from an unguarded angle, and he went toppling out of the saddle. His padded leather tunic and mail were enough to sink him, and he had to struggle to find his feet and break the surface to draw breath. They charged him again and he had to wield his blade desperately while clearing water from his eyes and scrambling for footing in the mud.

Fenster and Willum reached him moments later and with the odds suddenly changed, he was able to dispatch one of the count's men and turn on another. A high-pitched scream from the deck penetrated the roar in his head, and when he looked up, he spotted the boat edging away from the shore. By the time he heard Chloe's second scream, he had dealt his second opponent a bloodletting blow and was thrashing desperately through the water . . . desperate to reach the receding hull.

There were shouts in mingled English and French and frantic movement on the deck above him. Fighting the weight of his armor to keep his head above water, he began to plow the surface with his arms and after what seemed an eternity, reached the weathered wood of the boat's hull. He clamped his blade between his teeth and kicked desperately, straining upward for a handhold in the planking.

"Weigh anchor! Leave them!" he heard an authoritative voice shout. "We have what we came for."

He finally found purchase on the slippery wood and was drawn along with the boat, toward the main channel. Hand over hand, he pulled himself around the boat to a place where iron rungs formed a ladder on the side. Gritting his teeth and feeling the bite of the blade at the corners of his mouth, he hauled himself up as quietly as possible. He glanced back over his shoulder at the men he'd left behind on the bank. His only ally now was surprise.

Peering through the battered railing, he counted six armored men, one of whom stood with a shorter, stouter man over Chloe and the duke. They spoke in French, a bit too quickly for him to catch what they said at first. But the taller one's laugh had a wicked sound, and the shorter one reached down to turn Chloe's face to the moonlight.

"So it is you who has caused me such trouble, eh?" the Compte de Sabban declared in English as he studied her.

"You won't get away with this," Chloe said, her voice dry and strained.

"Oh, but I will. In fact"—the *compte* raised his hands, palms up—"I believe I already have."

"Bastard!" the duke spat, struggling to roll enough to face his brother.

"So I am," the *compte* said with a sudden murderous edge. "A fact that you and my accursed old father never let me forget. He took me into his household after my mother died and taunted me with the disgrace of my birth while heaping praise and favor on my younger but *legitimate* brother."

Hugh saw that most of the men were focused on the drama unfolding at center deck and seized the opportunity to haul himself over the railing undetected. Sheathing his sword, he drew his dagger and crept toward the nearest soldier.

"The coronet that went to you should have been *mine*. I was first. And you"—he swept Chloe with a contemptuous hand—"with your wilting lily of a bride and your defiance of our father's wishes—you appreciated nothing except your own desires. And still he insisted you inherit." He dealt the duke a savage kick that forced a groan from him.

Hugh's dagger stuck home beneath a set of ribs in the same moment. He lowered the body to the deck and crept around the cargo on deck toward another.

"My blood was tainted, impure because my mother was not pure. I swore you would pay." The *compte* seemed to be enjoying his moment of power. "And pay you did. *Bon Dieu* how you sobbed." His voice shifted into falsetto. "My love, my sweet Clarice . . . my poor dead babe . . . I don't want to go on living." His voice shifted back. "It was all I could do not to oblige you."

There was a slash of motion on the coil of rope, and the count's henchman staggered back with a yelp. Chloe had kicked out with her bound legs and caught him off guard. With no one to stop him, he lunged forward and brought a fist crashing down against the side of her head.

The sickening sound of her stifled cry cloaked the noise of the second soldier falling.

"Valoir!" the duke snarled, clearly trying to deflect the *capitaine*'s anger and turn it toward himself. "How like you to beat a defenseless woman. You always were a brute. And a dumb one at that. The fact that my brother pulled you into his sick schemes is proof."

"That, brother, is all your doing," the *compte* said, restraining Valoir. "If you hadn't been so stupid as to banish him from your lands, he wouldn't have found his way to mine. And I would not have had a strong right arm to accomplish my revenge."

"Enough, Alfonse." The duke's anger made him reckless. "If you intend to kill me, do it now, and spare me more of your braying."

"Don't you want to hear the rest of my plans?" The count grabbed the duke by the hair and hauled him up by it so he could watch the duke's face. "Don't you want to hear how you will have died escaping the English king and heading back to France to gather a rebellion against English rule? Don't you want to hear how I, a loving uncle to your son and heir, will be appointed his guardian? How, after a year or two, he will meet with one of those unfortunate accidents that plague ungainly young boys learning knightly skills?"

"You wouldn't . . ."

He released the duke's head, laughing at the horror in his brother's eyes.

"Oh, but I will. And then I shall have murdered *both* of your children." He pointed to Chloe and ordered Valoir, "Get her onto her feet."

Valoir and another soldier hauled Chloe to her feet and dragged her toward the side of the boat. Hugh froze, then allowed his third victim to slide to the deck. He was suddenly out of time.

As he drew his sword the metal sang. Valoir, a battle-seasoned soldier, recognized the sound and came to attention, tensing, his hand hovering at the hilt of his blade as he scoured the deck for the source of it. Hugh lunged from behind a pair of barrels with a roar and managed to drive his steel deep into the soldier on the near side of Chloe. But before he could grab Chloe and pull her away from the edge, Valoir had drawn his blade and was bearing down on him with a murderous cry.

As Valoir slashed and hacked at him, he retreated, his attention divided between the fight and the fact that the count had grabbed Chloe and was wrestling her toward the edge. He saw her go down onto her knees and roll over onto the deck, trying to maneuver enough to kick at him. Then Valoir's blade bit into his chest and the pain jerked his full attention back to his own peril.

The jolting clang and the flash of light from the blades narrowed Hugh's concentration and pared away all but the most essential perceptions. All he saw were lines and angles, arcs and trajectories, and the subtle shifts of Valoir's head that indicated where his blade might strike next.

"Hugh!" Chloe's voice just penetrated the adamant cloak battle had drawn around his senses. Again he was out of time. He had to strike now. He watched for an opening, praying without words, and suddenly it was there. A hitch, a lapse of concentration on Valoir's part . . . and Hugh lunged in with a roar and sank his blade between Valoir's ribs and mail. He staggered slightly as he pulled his blade free of Valoir's fallen body, and then he whirled and found himself facing the count holding Chloe against him . . . at the edge of the deck.

"Well, well. Quite a performance," the count said icily. "Now the real decision comes." Hugh glanced from him to the duke, who was struggling against his bonds, trying to free himself. Then he looked back at Chloe, bound hand and foot. Her eyes were huge with fear . . . that transformed suddenly into one last, unmistakable look of love.

"Which do you want more?" The count blithely demanded he choose. "To kill me or to save your precious little wife?"

He pushed Chloe over the edge.

Her scream touched off an explosion in Hugh. With intent of its own, his body lunged at the duke, gave the ropes binding him one savage slash of his blade, and then propelled him across the deck. He drew one last frantic breath and dived over the edge after her.

Chloe screamed until she smacked the water, and suddenly her mouth was full of water. She kicked her feet wildly, hoping to free them or to thrust herself to the surface so she could breathe. Panic gripped her as the darkness closed in and made it impossible to tell up from down. Still, she kicked . . . until it occurred to her that things often floated to the top of water and she stopped thrashing. Just as she felt herself beginning to rise, something bumped into her, and she panicked and began to kick again.

Desperate for air but unable to find the surface, she sucked in water and then convulsed and struggled, trying to force it back out. Then mercifully everything began to fade . . . the cold of the water, the pressure in her lungs . . . the darkness all around her. It grew darker still and quiet. Her last, strangely peaceful thought was of Hugh's face.

By the sheer grace of God, he located her in the water. As he touched bottom and then pushed off to shoot back to the surface, he bumped into her near the surface. Grabbing her, he pulled her up with him. But he had to let her go while he clawed at the ties of his doublet and ripped it from his chest. Lighter now, without the sodden padding, he reclaimed her now limp form and began the slow, arduous fight to drag her with him toward the bank. Every stroke of his arms was a blow dealt against death in a contest that was far from decided.

Again time stretched out, but this time distance was distorted with it. It seemed to take forever for the bank to get closer. He was not a good swimmer; it was only by sheer force of will and desperate effort that he managed to keep them both afloat and moving toward safety.

Noise, voices came from the near bank, and he looked up to see riders on horseback at the edge of the water. He shouted and tried to wave. His arm felt like lead and barely broke the water. His voice sounded as sodden and heavy as his garments.

It was his father's graveled voice that responded, shouting orders, but to him it had the sweetness of Gabriel's trumpet. Suddenly there were horses in the water and all around them, and they were being ferried to the shore.

He collapsed on the bank for a moment, gasping for air, but his main concern was Chloe. He dragged himself to her inert form, rolled her over and listened. She wasn't breathing. Frantically he rolled her onto her side and gave her back a heavy thump, then another. He had seen that work once in France, where English armies had forged several rivers. Then his father shoved him aside and rolled her onto her stomach. He pushed on her back and lifted her arms several times.

Hugh put his face close to hers and called desperately to her.

"Chloe! Can you hear me? Breathe! Come on, Chloe, breathe!"

After some effort the earl sat back on his heels, looking at Chloe, and then lifted a look of pain and disbelief to Hugh.

"No!" Hugh grabbed her up into his arms and pushed the grass and leaves from her face. "No—don't you do this! Don't you dare die and leave me, Chloe of Guibray! Don't you dare make me love you . . . turn my whole world upside down . . . then die on a riverbank before I even get the chance to tell you. . . ."

He shook her.

"Chloe! Please, God—don't let her—"

Something . . . the shaking, the pleading, the loving . . . penetrated the darkness in Chloe's senses, and the pall of death began to lift. Her lungs went into a spasm, her chest contracted around them, and suddenly she was choking and coughing up water. She gasped and coughed, fighting to draw breath against whatever was wrapped so tightly around her. It took a few moments for the fog in her head to clear and for her to realize there were voices all around her, bright happy voices. The tightness around her was arms; someone was holding her.

When she heard her name and felt something touch her face, she opened her eyes and there was Hugh, nose to nose with her, and shortly, lips to lips with her. She wasn't sure how she'd gotten here, but she wrapped her arms around him and refused to let go.

"Thank God. You're alive," he murmured into her ear as he held her tightly against him. "Don't even *think* about leaving me again." He set her back for a moment. "Ever!"

She looked around and realized she was lying on a riverbank dripping wet . . . she remembered more . . . being taken . . . brought to a boat . . . the count and Hugh . . . a fight . . .

"I don't think leaving you was exactly my idea," she said hoarsely. "Hugh, you're hurt." She touched the cut that had gone though his tunic and narrowly missed ripping into his throat.

"It's not so bad. I think most of the bleeding's already stopped."

He laughed and helped her to sit up. Suddenly there were a number of faces peering down at her. Hugh's father. Mattias. Withers. Fenster.

"Ye give us a right good scare, milady," Withers said with a big smile.

"I told ye, if ye needed rescuin', we'd be there," Mattias said, jerking a thumb at the group behind him, who all nodded and agreed.

"The duke!" She struggled to rise. "Hugh, we have to do something—he's my father, and the count is his brother and—"

"I know, I know," Hugh declared, refusing to release her. "I heard. As soon as we get you to safety, I'll—"

"*You'll* do nothing," the earl insisted, taking charge. "You two are going back to Windsor, and you're going to warm yourselves and get some rest." He extended a hand to Hugh . . . who looked at it, smiled, and then accepted both the help and the promise of reconciliation it offered.

Hugh insisted on carrying Chloe to a horse himself and was reluctant to part with her even long enough to mount and make a place for her on the saddle in front of him. Mattias and Withers wrapped her in a blanket and boosted her up to Hugh's arms. Moments later they were on their way back to Windsor, with Mattias and Withers as escort, while the earl and the rest of the men headed downstream to help Graham, Simon, and Jax intercept the boat.

Feeling Hugh's arms and warmth around her, Chloe sighed and felt her shivering subside. "You saved me," she said, looking up at him in wonder.

"You say that as if you weren't certain I would. Shows a dismal lack of faith in your husband, milady."

"But the last time I saw you—"

"I had just learned how great an ass I've been for most of my life, and that kind of revelation takes a bit of getting used to. Then, when I reached the hall and saw you standing there before the king and court, looking as if your heart was breaking . . . God, I could have strangled Edward with my bare hands!"

"Shhh." She put her fingertips to his lips. "Don't say that too loudly. I hear there's a foul plot afoot, and the king sees traitors under every rock."

"I'd shout it from the housetops, if need be," he said, his arms relaxing around her. He nuzzled her cheek. "But I'd much rather shout that I love my wife Chloe with all my heart."

"You would? You do?" Chloe sat straighter and wiggled a hand out of the blanket to touch his face. "Are you certain? I mean, I know you never wanted to—"

"With all my heart," he repeated. "And with all my mind, and—given the chance—with all my body, too."

"Oooh." She grabbed the front of his waterlogged tunic. "This is new. The last time this subject came up, you fled to the monastery."

"No, the last time this subject came up, I fled *from* a monastery." He caught her gaze in his. "I came back to you. Only you weren't there."

"You really came back to me?" She seized his face between her hands. "You decided not to renounce me and become a monk?"

"Not that it was ever really much of a contest. You had already ruined me for hair shirts and cold porridge and getting up three times a night to pray . . . but, yes, I came back. I've done a lot of thinking, Chloe. When I got to Saint Barnard's, it wasn't the same. At least, that's what I thought at first. Then I realized: *it* was the same. *I* was the one who had changed. For the better. And I knew exactly who and what was responsible. I couldn't bear even the thought of living in that suffocating stone pile for the rest of my days. Without *you*." His eyes began to glisten in the moonlight.

"I thought I'd die when I arrived at Sennet and learned you'd been arrested. What the hell could Edward have been thinking—sending an armed escort to *arrest* you? I'm going to have a talk with our exalted and august sovereign—"

"No, you're not," she said, grabbing the tops of his shoulders, grinning at him through the moisture rising in her eyes.

"Oh, yes, I am." He said stubbornly.

"Oh, no, you're not. We're going to explain everything that's happened and throw ourselves on his mercy and accept our royal pats on the head and tiptoe home like good little subjects to make babies and grow old together."

"Are not. I intend to have my say about a few things."

"Okay, then, I agree. Are not."

Confused, he tried counting backward with a finger on the air, trying to decide just where that put the argument. "I . . . I . . ."

"You love me." She provided the perfect conclusion. "And I love you."

He surrendered to that logic and pulled her closer. "You'll get no argument from me on that."

IT WAS NEARLY DAWN WHEN THE SEARCH parties returned to Windsor with an injured duke and a defeated and bound Compte de Sabban. Hugh and Chloe, who had arrived some time earlier and had a chance to put on dry garments and warm themselves with wine and a fire in the hearth of the great hall, rushed outside to meet them. The king joined them on the steps and ordered the *compte* taken straight to the dungeon. Having heard Hugh and Chloe's brief summary, he personally conducted the duke into the hall, where he called for a physician to tend the duke's injured arm, and provided them with blankets and mulled wine. Afterward, the king listened intently to the duke's explanations . . . a sordid tale of young love and great loss, of family rivalry and bitter vengeance.

Avalon looked pained and weary indeed as he spoke of his brother's abduction of Chloe as an infant, of the jealousy and scheming that ended in death, betrayal, and the peril of a dozen young and promising lives. But whenever he spoke of Chloe's mother, his voice and countenance softened. There was no doubt of his regard and affection for Chloe's mother. And all present—from the king to Chloe to the most skeptical courtier—sensed that the proof of the duke's claim of marriage would soon be returned from Calais.

"So the count acted alone," the king said thoughtfully.

"I believe so," the duke answered sadly. "He sent Valoir to tell you of a grand plot, so you would look for betrayals at every corner and ignore the earnest help and advice of those loyal to you."

"A strategy that very nearly worked." Edward looked toward Hugh and Graham. "And a valuable lesson."

"He is my brother," the duke said, wagging his head. "I trusted him with my life, with my home, and with my family's well being. And he would have killed my daughter and then me . . . then my son and heir . . ." It was a moment before he could go on.

"But even in the darkest of events there are seeds of promise, if we are willing to look for them." He looked up at Chloe, smiled, and extended a hand to her. "In losing a brother I have gained a daughter and reclaimed a part of my heart that I had thought lost forever."

Chloe left the security of Hugh's arms to come and kneel beside him.

"And I have gained a father . . . a husband . . . a home . . . and four wonderful sisters." She looked up at her sisters, gathered nearby with their husbands. All were present except Graham and Lisette, who seemed to have disappeared.

There was hardly a dry eye in the hall as Chloe hugged her father, her sisters, and then went back to Hugh and nestled once again in his loving embrace.

Hugh cleared his throat and leveled a serious look on the king.

"There is one more matter, Highness, that begs attention."

"Oh?" Edward turned a wary look on him.

"The little matter of my marriage to Lady Chloe."

"Ummm." Edward sat forward on his chair and stroked his chin. "Well, I'm afraid there is nothing I can do about it."

"What?" Hugh's expression turned stormy.

"It seems Lady Chloe is probably the duke's natural daughter as well as his legal one. I agreed to accept this marriage as a part of the duke's ransom and the marriage has been duly contracted and—I assume—fully consummated." He gave a regal sigh. "I'm afraid you're just stuck with her."

Hugh began to grin with relief, and the hall rang with laughter.

Epilogue

"THEY'RE HERE!" A SERVING BOY called as he hurried by the cozy alcove at the side of the great hall of Sennet, on his way to inform the housekeeper and the kitchens. Inside sat Chloe and her three little sisters-in-law, engaged in a daily stitchery lesson Chloe had insisted take place as usual, despite the impending arrival of long-awaited guests.

Before she could forbid it, the three girls jumped up, dropped their embroidery hoops onto their seats, and rushed for the main doors.

"Slow down!" Chloe called emphatically after them. "Ladies do not *run!*"

The eldest, Ellen, reined her gait to a more dignified trot, but the other two continued on as if they hadn't heard. Chloe narrowed her eyes and looked down at her greatly expanded middle. As soon as the babe was born and she was back to her old form, she'd have to take those three in hand . . . again.

She pushed to her feet with a groan and set her hands to the small of her back, arching against them. Trueblood met her at the entrance of the alcove.

"Ye needn't stir yerself—I'll see 'em in to you, straightaway."

"I have to get up and move about, Trueblood. I get cramps just sitting. Besides, it's been over a year, and I can't wait another minute to see them."

The housekeeper put an arm around her and helped her navigate the furnishings in the hall. As they emerged into the sunshine of a beautiful September afternoon, Chloe's face lighted and she began to wave excitedly.

"There they are! Lisette! Graham!"

The trim, dark figure being lifted down from her horse waved in return and soon was hurrying up the steps to throw arms around her.

"Chloe, my Chloe!" Lisette cried, hugging her as tightly as her condition would allow. "I told Graham that if he didn't get me here in time to see this babe born, he would have to make his bed in the hall for months!" She drew back to look at Chloe's belly, then her glowing face. "Look at you—you're beautiful!"

"I'm a walking barn!" Chloe said with a groan. "But I generally feel good and the babe certainly seems vigorous." She took Lisette's hand and pressed it palm first against her belly.

"I can feel it move!" Lisette giggled, moving her hand over Chloe's middle.

"*Ahem*," came a reminder from a young female throat.

Chloe looked up to find three pairs of eyes trained on them. Smiling, she introduced them: "May I present Ellen, Lizabeth, and Corinne . . . Hugh's sisters." Somewhere in the last year they had ceased putting the qualification *half* before the word *sister*. To her genuine surprise, they each executed a passable curtsy and uttered a pleasant and ladylike greeting. She saw their eyes dart toward the far side of the party of riders and wondered what it was that caused them to suddenly be on their best behavior.

"There she is!" Hugh's voice boomed as he rounded the horses with Graham in tow. "My beautiful wife." He leaned closer to Graham and muttered loud enough for everyone to hear, "Humor her—she swears she's giving birth to a whole regiment."

"Chloe! You're as lovely as ever." Graham kissed her hands. With a wicked laugh, she offered him first one cheek and then the other for the same treatment, declaring that she could use all of the attention she could get.

Just then the grooms started to lead the horses away, and on the far side of them stood several well-dressed young men. Graham waved them over.

"May I present my youngest brother, Damon, and our cousin Michael of Trent." The young men each stood straighter and nodded respectfully. "These others are John of Ellington, Harold of Gaunt, and Marcus of Avingale. They come from estates near ours and have just finished their studies at Saint Barnard's, also. They are traveling home with us."

"Welcome." Chloe beamed. "It will be good to have more young people at Sennet." As Hugh came to put an arm around her, she had an idea. "I know—we'll have dancing tonight in the hall."

"Dancing?" came the earl's voice from nearby. They turned to find him astride a horse, returning from checking on some far-flung tenants. His eyes went immediately to the exotic Lisette and he grinned. "A wonderful idea!"

But at dinner the earl watched his daughters watching the young men who accompanied Sir Graham and Lady Lisette, and began to reconsider his enthusiasm for the pleasures of the dance. In even the most staid of settings, eye met eye, hand met hand, and body sometimes brushed body in the course of a dance. The glint of excitement in his daughters' eyes suddenly alarmed him.

After the meal was over and the tables were removed from the center of the hall, Lisette volunteered to serve as dancing master. The earl insisted on partnering one of his daughters and coerced Hugh and Graham into part-nering the others . . . annoying the girls and disappointing the young men. Abandoned, Chloe rose and waddled into the midst of the dancers to seize Lisette's hand. Laughing, Lisette began to dance the man's part and Chloe maneuvered her way through skips and steps clearly meant for more maidenly figures.

At the end of the music Chloe paused, laughing, and then suddenly grabbed her side. Her eyes widened. Hugh saw her face and rushed to her.

"Chloe? What's wrong?"

She looked down at her feet and lifted her hem. She was standing in a puddle of water.

The sun was rising the next morning when the newest heir to the Sennet title and fortune drew first breath and wailed at being forced out into a cool, bright, and abominably noisy world. Hugh and his father were both present at the birth, Hugh having threatened to coldcock anyone who tried to remove him from the chamber, and the earl threatening to coldcock Hugh if he wasn't allowed to stay. They jointly drew a line, however, at permitting Hugh's little sisters to stay. They sent the girls to their shared chamber with orders to stay there until they were sent for.

Trueblood and Lisette assisted the midwife, and after hours of steadily building intensity in labor, a fine, healthy baby boy was brought forth to volleys of cheers and a flood of heartfelt tears. Chloe and baby had both come through it unscathed.

When the women had finished their work and Chloe was allowed to rest, Hugh sank gingerly onto the bed beside her and watched her nuzzle the baby's downy head. His heart was so full of love, it was overflowing his eyes and rolling down his cheeks.

"He's so beautiful." He stroked his new son's cheek and then Chloe's with the same finger, feeling the same tender amazement at having them in his life. "Just like his mother."

She looked up through eyes filled with love and touched his damp face.

"And strong . . . just like his father."

The earl, who was watching, cleared his throat as if something were lodged in it. "Ale! I say we adjourn to the hall and wet our throats. Damn long night." He glanced at Trueblood with a wicked smile. "Damned hard work, becoming a grandfather!"

Just as he reached the doorway, he was blown back into the room by a gale of daughters rushing in to greet their new nephew.

"Oh, look at him!" Ellen gasped with delight as they descended on the bed. "He's so little!"

"His hands—look at his hands—how tiny and perfect!" Lizabeth crooned.

"And look at that little rosebud of a mouth!" Corinne purred.

They pressed close to Chloe to ask how she was and to touch the baby. They each asked to hold him and, in fairness, Hugh agreed to allow each of them to hold him for a moment.

Ellen looked up from the bundle in her arms with her eyes alight.

"I want one," she declared.

"Me, too!" Lizabeth said, shaking her hands in impatience.

"Me, too. I want one, too!" Corinne declared shortly.

"Me first," Ellen insisted. "I'm oldest."

"Oh, no! Just because you're older doesn't mean you get to have a baby first!" Lizabeth complained hotly. "You're always hogging things—"

"I'm always last—I should get to have a baby *first*!" Corinne whined.

"Oh, no, you don't!" The earl strode into their midst and motioned Hugh to take the baby back immediately. "None of you is having a baby! Ever! You're never getting married. You're going to stay right here, all three of you, and take care of me in my old age." There was a storm of protest as he herded them out the door.

"We don't have to get *married* to have babies!" Ellen glared defiantly.

"*You* didn't," Corinne charged.

The earl bellowed as if he had just been gored.

Hugh quickly closed the door on that escalating turmoil and then strode to the bed to place his infant son back into Chloe's arms. When he stretched out on the bed be-side them and pulled them into his arms, he was chuck-ling.

"Serves him right," he murmured.

She smiled mischievously and snuggled her face a bit closer to his.

"You realize, of course, that you'll have to do some-thing. You can't let your son-and-heir's aunts go gallop-ing around the countryside having babies thither and yon."

She could feel the impact of her remark registering as he stilled and his arms began to tense.

"Damnation."

"There is, however, a solution."

"Which is?" She felt his breath stop as he waited.

"Find them husbands."

Hugh rolled over onto his back, his eyes closed, his face turning gray.

"God help us."